How did her life get this insane? Now her soft heart had doomed her...

Hajar tossed a few clothes into her bag and slung it over her shoulder. Trying not to wake Megan, she eased open the bedroom door and slipped out. To her surprise, at the end of the hall stood Mrs. Kerr, holding a garment bag.

"This is for you, Hajar."

"Thanks, Mrs. Kerr. What is it?"

"A way to help coax the code from Dr. Kano."

Hajar opened the bag and gasped at the shockingly scanty black dress. "This is little bigger than a bathing suit. Mrs. Kerr. I thought I had made myself clear about boundaries."

"Why yes you did, my dear, however, it seems that there has been a shift in the balance of power."

"I don't understand."

"You're a brave woman and I have no illusions that pushed too far you would die before violating your misguided moral code. What was it again? No murder, no sex, no corruption of faith."

"Where are you going with this?" Hajar asked as a cold knot formed in the pit of her stomach.

"You care for sweet Megan. I've watched as your relationship has blossomed over the past few months. It's almost like watching a mother-daughter relationship. That was a mistake. You cannot even entertain the thought of killing me now, because of what that poor child would suffer. She has just cost you what little control you thought you had. Checkmate, Hajar."

"Oh, no, Mrs. Kerr. Please, no."

"For daring to think you could dictate terms to me, I'm going to break you, once and for all. You will seduce the good doctor to get his code on *The Book of Xanadutha*. Then you will take your gun and kill him. I expect photos and a severed finger as proof of his execution. After your cold-blooded murder, I'll find some appropriately humiliating way for you to renounce your faith. Do you have any objections, Hajar?"

The powerful champion of a fallen angel she loves as a father, Maggie Black relishes her heroic life of danger and intrigue—until the day the angel betrays her and sends a witch to kill her. However, the assassin, Mrs. Kerr, is so impressed by Maggie's unearthly abilities, she kidnaps her, making her a slave. The woman fakes Maggie's death and changes her name to Hajar, which means forsaken. Once a hero, Hajar now serves the capricious whims of her new master, committing audacious crimes to support her lifestyle. When all seems lost, hope arrives in the form of a world-weary adventurer, Gideon Kane. Touched by Hajar's plight, he bargains for her freedom, offering Mrs. Kerr a prize the power hungry woman cannot resist—the legendary Tree of Life, whose fruit can turn mortals into Gods.

As Gideon and Hajar track down Eden, they face both old enemies and new, while fighting their growing desire for each other, unaware they are pawns in a deadly game that could decide the fate of life on earth.

KUDOS for *Forsaken*

In *Forsaken* by Ken Newman, Maggie Black is a Paladin, a warrior for good. Tall, beautiful, and fierce, she serves a fallen angel, Larry, whom she loves like a father, fighting evil with her magic sword Kali, in hopes of helping the fallen angel redeem himself and get back into Heaven. But Larry betrays her and Maggie becomes Hajar (the forsaken), a slave for an evil witch, forced to commit crimes to support her new mistress's lifestyle. Enter Gideon Kane, mercenary and champion for good. He was once a powerful warrior, but now he's a shriveled old man, at the end of his life. Maggie's witch mistress sends her after Kane, hoping he can decipher a mystic book for her. When Maggie shows up and reveals her painful story, Gideon takes it as a sign that he has one last mission before he dies and he decides to rescue Maggie and her fellow slaves from their evil mistress. Newman has crafted an adventure/romance/thriller with a little something for everyone. The plot is strong with plenty of surprises. It will catch and hold your interest from beginning to end. ~ *Taylor Jones, Reviewer*

Forsaken by Ken Newman doesn't really fit into any one genre. It's part romance, part mystery, part thriller, and part adventure. Our protagonist, Gideon Kane was once the kind of hero fiction novels were written about. But that was a long time ago, and now he's tired, old, lonely since his beloved wife died, and disillusioned. Still, when a young woman in trouble shows up on his doorstep, Gideon decides he's up for one last mission. Maggie, the young woman, was a warrior for good, the champion of a fallen angel. Then the angel betrays her and she ends up as a slave to the evil Mrs. Kerr. Controlled by a hair-thin collar around her neck, capable of inflicting unimaginable agony, Maggie is forced into a life a crime to supply her new mistress with the finer things in life, betraying her Christian values. Together, she and Gideon go on a quest to find the Tree of Life for Mrs. Kerr in exchange for Maggie's freedom. It's an adventure that will change both of their lives forever. *Forsaken* is a unique reading experience, reminiscent of *Indi-*

ana Jones and *The Shadow*. Although the story is set in present day, it has a bit of an old-time feeling to it which is very appealing. This one is a page turner, with enough twists and turns to keep you guessing until the end. *~ Regan Murphy, Reviewer*

FORSAKEN

Ken Newman

A Black Opal Books Publication

GENRE: PARANORMAL THRILLER/PARANORMAL ROMANCE

FORSAKEN
Copyright © 2015 by Ken Newman
Cover Design by Jackson Cover Designs
All cover art copyright © 2015
All Rights Reserved
Print ISBN: 978-1-626943-87-2

First Publication: DECEMBER 2015

Published by Black Opal Books http://www.blackopalbooks.com

To my wife, Christian

CHAPTER 1

The opulent hall was a sumptuous feast for the senses. Decorated with one-of-a-kind, priceless masterpieces from dozens of far-flung worlds and cultures, the hall reverberated with the music of a genius who lived and died on a world whose sun burned out before the earth was formed.

In different circumstances, Larry would have been delighted and savored the sights, smells, and sounds of his former life, but now he had more serious matters on his mind. Bound and guarded by two unearthly bounty hunters, he trudged along, his Chuck Taylors making an odd scuffing sound on the thick, rich carpet.

Larry sighed.

So, after ten thousand, seven hundred years and some odd days, this is the end of the line? Not with a roar of sweet victory, but with a whimper of bitter defeat. Well, perhaps a little torture and a lot of screaming, then the whimper of defeat. This really sucks.

The two guards were identical in every way, from their blond, flawlessly quaffed hair and perfect features, to their tailored, blue pinstriped double-breasted suits. Their chocolate-brown fedoras, cocked at the same precise angle, completed the ensemble, making them look like racketeers from the 1930s.

Their unwilling guest, however, was a different story.

Larry, although of the same celestial house and rank as his guards, clung to the appearance of a man of Chinese descent, sporting a wild Hawaiian shirt, faded jeans, and bright red tennis shoes. At chest level, pinning his arms to his torso, was an A'rtict Band.

The slim, golden ring, which glowed and pulsated in response to the prisoner's exertion, siphoned away his arcane energy, keeping him locked into his human form and powerless—or so his guards thought.

"So, fellahs, can we talk about this, before things get out of hand and I get my feelings hurt?"

"More than your feeling will be hurt when the Boss gets through with you, smart mouth. Now, move."

"So, this is how it ends? I always thought the entrance to Hell would be more gothic—more *Dantesque*. What do you say, Twiddledum?"

The guard on the left gritted his teeth while his burly brother snorted.

"Do you ever shut up? Since we got the drop on you, Larry, you have been determined to drive us crazy! I would love to shut that mouth once and for all."

"Now, now, let's not let tempers flare, boys. I know for a fact your Boss would pull out the rolled up paper if his yard dogs chewed on his favorite toy without his permission."

"Yard dogs!"

"He likes the sound of his own voice," said the guard whom Larry had dubbed Twiddledum. "I hope he likes the sound of his own screams as much."

"So, what would it take for you two fine gentlemen to look the other way? Cash, coupons, free car washes, trading stamps? How about a swimming pool of flea dip? Trust me, the sky is the limit."

"That's it," Twiddledee said. The angel grabbed the front of Larry's shirt and lifted him off the ground.

"Weeee," Larry said. "Can you spin me around, too?"

"Put him down," Twiddledum said. "The Boss will have your hide if the merchandise is damaged."

With a deep, inhuman growl, Twiddledee set Larry on his feet.

"That was fun, Daddy, do it again!"

"Move," Twiddledum said, as he shoved a chuckling Larry forward.

"All joking aside, fellows, can you at least turn down the power setting on this dohicky? The thing stings like I am making out with a bee hive."

"Oh we can't have that, now, can we?" Twiddledee said with a wicked smile. With a flick of his wrist, he turned the power drain to maximum. He laughed as Larry gasped.

"Guys," Larry said, "look, a three headed dog!"

As his guards turned to look at the impossible animal, the prisoner lashed out at Twiddledum, smashing him into Twiddledee. Using only his legs and a few well-aimed head-butts, he toppled his captors and ran with all his might down the hallway.

"Come on, you jerks, you are not going to let an asshole like me get away, are you?" Larry mumbled.

A few yards ahead of him both beings suddenly appeared, blocking his escape.

"Think you are clever, don't you? You need a lesson in manners, smart mouth," Twiddledee said as he produced a strange looking weapon.

The device, which looked as if it were made of solid gold, appeared as the bladeless haft of a sword. A bolt of dazzling blue fire lashed out, catching Larry square in the chest. To Twiddledee's surprise, the hallway exploded in light and holy fire.

The stunning force of the explosion knocked the two warrior angels off their feet, sending them sliding several yards down the room.

Twiddledee and Twiddledum groaned and struggled to their feet.

"What did you do, Brother? This is bad. This is *real* bad."

When the spiritual fire and smoke dispersed, the hall was completely destroyed and blocked with ruble. Larry was gone and all that was left was the scorched spiritual restraint lying in the middle of the smoldering carpet.

"You idiot! You vaporized him!"

"Oops," said the grinning Larry who stood behind the duo,

his own glowing weapon in his hand. "Talk about your classic goofs. Don't you know that firing a weapon at an active prisoner restraint can cause a bitch of a feedback, especially if it is set to maximum and the prisoner is throwing all his power into it? Give my regrets to Lucifer, boys. Tell Old Scratch I have to cancel our play date."

With a bright flash of blue tinted light, Larry stunned the angelic beings and turned to flee.

"Who are you calling Old Scratch, smart guy?" asked the smooth baritone.

"Aw crap," Larry said as his weapon drooped in his hand. "These guys were *your* muscle? Things must have gone to pot since I left."

Larry quickly knelt before the Archangel Michael. Michael stood dressed in an immaculate white dinner jacket that showcased his powerful form.

"Walk with me, Larry."

Larry obediently fell in step behind the Commander of the God's Army.

Michael paused before his groaning soldiers. "When I am finished with Larry, we will have a long, one-way conversation that you two dimwits will *not* like."

"But, Boss—"

"Don't 'but Boss me,' you imbecile! You blew up my house! Now beat it."

Wearing identical expressions of terror, Twiddledee and Twiddledum promptly disappeared.

Michael snapped his fingers and the ruined passageway returned to its original form, with the exception that the wallpaper and artworks were of a different style.

"Sorry about the mess, sir. I didn't know this was your place."

"Forget about it. I was getting tired of the motif anyway."

"So, are you going to toss me in the pit, sir?"

Michael opened a door. "After you," he said.

Larry gasped at the utter richness of the suite, so rich the human mind could not comprehend.

"You are just in time for dinner, only please change first."

Larry's clothes instantly transformed into a classic black, perfectly fitted tuxedo.

Michael looked down at Larry's bright red high-tops and wrinkled his nose.

"What's the matter," Larry said. "Got something against style?"

"You wouldn't know style if it bit you on the bum," Michael said. "The saying about making a silk purse from a sow's ear comes to mind."

"I don't understand, sir. First, I am on my way to the Big Barbeque and now I am invited to dine with royalty? What gives?"

"We had a little misunderstanding. I sent those two low-level rejects to track you down because I wanted to have a word with you without drawing any undue attention. They apparently assumed that I was going to bring your antics to a permanent end."

"Funny, I thought the same thing," said Larry.

"Because of your help with the Noah situation, I gave you my word that you were to be confined to the earth and not Tartarus, until Judgment Day, as long as you behaved. I never break my word."

"I have done my best to uphold the law."

"That is a bit of an exaggeration, don't you think? While you have bent and stretched the rules to the breaking point at times, I have always been impressed by your clever plots and schemes. Not to mention that you have been a thorn in the side of Satan. When he finally gets his hands on you, and he will, it won't be pretty, but until then, it is priceless to see him get a taste of his own medicine."

"I am glad someone is entertained. I will do anything to get my old job back, sir."

"That is quite impossible. Rebellion is death. You rebelled. You will die, case closed."

"I am not a rebel. I am a fool who was tricked."

"We have been over this before."

"Then why am I here?"

A smile split the handsome features of the Archangel.

"Something has come up and I need some...*advice*."

"Advice? From me?"

A thick manila folder appeared in Michael's hand. He tossed it to Larry.

Larry read the one-thousand-page report— twice—in one third of a second.

"This is bad," Larry said. "He has lost his mind."

"It is actually worse than that document alludes. What do you think of my proposed solution on page 989?"

"An epic disaster waiting to happen, sir. Honestly, you are a bit too straightforward for your own good. If you go through with this, although justified, this is murder. You will be stripped of everything and be in a worse position than me."

"A small price to pay."

"It will wreck everything and you know it. Not to mention that your big throw down with Goat-boy won't happen, and I already put down a non-returnable deposit on a ringside seat."

Michael smiled. "Do you have a better idea?"

Larry walked the room, his inhuman mind running countless scenarios and possible outcomes, before a smile spread across his face.

"I take that as a yes?" Michael asked.

Pulling a sheaf of paper out of thin air, Larry diagrammed an intricate plan. Michael smiled and nodded as he examined the plan. "What do you think, sir?" Larry asked.

"I think that I am glad you are on our side instead of Goat-boy. Your plan is splendid. I knew that the assistance of a wily fellow, outside of the normal network, who is well known for his creativity and fast thinking, would be just what I need. Not to mention, one who can keep his mouth shut."

"In other words, if this plan goes south, I will be the one who gets the blame while you and your network of choirboys can stand back in innocent, shocked dismay. I will be the one who gets the bum's rush to a permanent room without a view in the Big Barbeque."

"Honestly, Larry, your room is already reserved. If this 'goes south' as you say, you will merely check in a bit earlier than expected."

"I feel better already."

"When can we get started?"

"With all due respect, if I am to risk so much, what is in it for me?"

Michael smiled and took a goblet of wine. "Success will mean that I will pull a very large string."

"Excuse me?"

"I will personally vouch for you and your exile will be over. In fact, pull this off and you will join my personal staff as my chief strategist."

Larry looked at the powerful being in stunned silence.

"Well, well, I finally found something that would shut you up," Michael said.

Elated that at last his personal hell was over, Larry fell to his knees before Michael. "Thank you, sir."

"There is one, *small* stipulation."

"Stipulation?"

"Yes. It concerns your Paladin."

"Maggie?"

"The very one," Michael said. "End her, please."

"Excuse me, sir?"

"Kill her."

"I do not understand. Maggie is the best friend I have ever had. She has done enormous good. Why she is even a Christian! I can't kill her!"

"That Maggie Black is a good girl is completely irrelevant. It is her bloodline that worries me. She must die."

"And if I refuse?"

"The deal is off the table. Your ten-thousand-year struggle for redemption is for naught. Wave goodbye to Heaven and say hello to the Big Barbeque, all for the sake of a tenuous, emotional relationship with a being whose lifespan is as brief as a wave tossed on the ocean.

"But, sir."

"Look, Larry. Maggie Black will go to a much better place, just a bit sooner than she expected."

Larry looked at Michael for a long moment. Taking a deep breath, he scooped a goblet filled with Ambrosia from a small table and raised the frosted glass high. "Here is to burning bridges, sir," Larry said without the slightest hint of a smile.

"Excellent. I look forward to working with you. Now, let's eat. The Ra'Kash is getting cold. I am told it is your favorite dish."

"Yes, I have dreamed of it for ten thousand years."

"You will dream of it no more, my friend."

CHAPTER 2

Placing the food on the fine bone china plate with the precision of a Swiss watchmaker, the large, broad-shouldered man smiled and wiped his tattooed hands upon a dishtowel.

"Freaking perfect," he said.

Glancing at the whimsical Kit Kat Clock on the wall, he saw that he had finished with thirty seconds to spare. Looking down, his face wrinkled in horror at the single drop of grease staining his crisp, white apron. Swearing blackly, he dabbed at the stubborn stain.

"Is there a problem with dinner, Mr. Garret?" asked the voice of his master. "That would be very...*disappointing*."

"No, Mrs. Kerr. No trouble at all, in fact, your dinner's ready," he said softly as he gently lifted the plate, his volcanic temper held in check by his fear. Moving to a small, old-fashioned steel kitchen table situated in the center of the room, he placed the plate of Coq Au Vin within the perfect place setting.

"Ah, Mr. Garret, you have out done yourself," said Salome Kerr as she entered the kitchen. Thin and of medium height, with a wisp of a nose and large blue eyes, Mrs. Kerr was seventy years old, yet looked like a woman in her mid-fifties. Her hair was silver and hung down her back in a long, tight braid. Mrs. Kerr closed her eyes and inhaled the savory aroma.

"It smells simply wonderful. It should more than make up for the tepid soup you served me for lunch."

"Thank you, Mrs. Kerr." The chef gave Mrs. Kerr a small bow, stealing glance at the knife block sitting on the gleaming counter. For the briefest moment, he fantasized about plunging the eight-inch butcher knife several times into Mrs. Kerr's face. The result of such a foolish act sent a chill of terror through his soul.

"I hope you like dinner, Boss," said the well-built, bull-necked man who looked as if he would be more at home in a cage fight than a kitchen.

"I see that you have ruined your apron, Mr. Garret," said Mrs. Kerr as she opened her eyes. "How could you have been so careless?"

"N—no, not ruined just a little spot of grease—I'll have it out in a jiffy. I swear to God!"

"Very well," Mrs. Kerr said with a smug smile, relishing the power she held over the brutal killer. "I will inspect your apron before I retire. It will be clean or you will endure—*fifteen seconds*."

"It will be the cleanest apron you have ever seen," Mr. Garret said as his hands began to shake with fear.

"Go."

Mr. Garret beat a hasty retreat from the kitchen as Mrs. Kerr softly chuckled, taking her seat.

Music, please, she thought.

Sitting in the small, brightly lit kitchen, she savored the streaming dish before her. In the background, an ancient phonograph began playing a rare recording of Beethoven's "Concerto Number 4" in G major.

Without warning, AC/DC's "Highway to Hell" blared at an ear-shattering volume, seemingly from the very walls themselves.

"What the bloody hell!" Mrs. Kerr screamed. "Someone will pay for this!"

"Why, as I live and breathe, it's Mrs. Salome Kerr," Larry said as he appeared in the chair across from the irate woman.

Mrs. Kerr dropped her fork and looked at the angel in sheer terror. "What do you want?" she shouted over the din. "For the love of your God, turn off that bloody awful screeching."

Larry smiled as the staple of classic rock radio ceased.

Mrs. Kerr's entire "family," consisting of five men and two women, piled into the room and shoved automatic weapons into Larry's face.

"Can't two old friends share a meal together and reminisce about the good old days without someone getting testy?"

"Thank you, children, but I have this under control. Resume your duties."

As quickly as they came, the group left without as much as a word spoken.

"Nice family. Reminds me of the Waltons. Or was it the Mansons? I sometimes get the two confused."

"They serve me well enough."

"Your hellish 'bling' helps to ensure loyalty."

"It can be very motivational," Mrs. Kerr said.

"Motivational? Slavery by any other name."

"They are gutter trash. I give them a more noble purpose."

"Serving you hand and foot is a noble purpose?"

"What better calling could anyone possibly have?"

Larry snorted. "I hear the Black Circle is still royally pissed over the theft of their new obedience collars. Those guys tend to hold a grudge. I would watch my back if I were you."

"Nothing I can't handle," Mrs. Kerr said. "Witches love to wheel and deal. I suppose that is why Wall Street is swarming with them. I have a few valuable items that should more than make up for my slight indiscretion with their property."

"What a lovely— rather isolated home," Larry said. "Where are the owners?"

"Taking an extended holiday in the afterlife, I am afraid," said Mrs. Kerr. "Are you here to bully me into releasing my servants? I must warn you that the task will be harder than even you can imagine."

"Honestly, it makes your little band of psycho slaves all the more desirable."

Not the answer she expected, Mrs. Kerr knitted her thin brows in puzzlement. "Will you please get to the point?"

"A little bird told me that you were in the market for rare books. Or should I say, one book in particular?"

"I don't know what you are talking about."

"You have been desperately trying to find *The Book of Xanadutha.*"

"Xana...what?"

Suddenly, the table slid across the room. With impossible speed, Larry had Mrs. Kerr by the throat. Caught in the iron grip, Mrs. Kerr gurgled and gasped as she was lifted off the ground and slowly throttled.

"Let's try this again," Larry whispered.

"I don't—have the damn book—I swear to God!"

Larry grinned. "I know, because I have it." Larry dropped Mrs. Kerr who fell back gasping for breath. "I am offering it to you."

"What is the catch?"

"I asked you a question. Do—You—Want—It?"

"I have searched for over half a century, on three continents. Of course, I want it. What is your price?"

"The book, in return for a certain, highly illegal service. Are you game?"

"The actual book, no tricks?"

"I am offering you, Salome Kerr, the genuine, one-hundred-and-ten-percent authentic copy of *The Book of Xanadutha.*"

In a small flash of light, a large, bronze bound book appeared between them.

Mrs. Kerr unconsciously licked her lips with desire. "May I examine it, please?"

"Of course. Wouldn't want you to think you were buying a pig in a poke."

With trembling hands, Mrs. Kerr grasped the floating mystic book, which had been penned long before the Great Flood. Popping open the thick, bronze clasp, she gazed upon weird, blood-red text written on delicate ivory tinged, foil pages, Tears welled in her eyes as she lovingly stroked the tome. "What do you want me to do, Larry?"

In a flash, the book was gone.

"I need you to kill someone for me," Larry said as the smile fell from his face.

"Very well," Mrs. Kerr said. "Give me the details."

"The North Swallen Valley Library, of Swallen Idaho, will conduct its annual book sale in exactly fifteen hours. *The Book of Xanadutha* is very cleverly hidden somewhere within said Library. I have it on good authority that an hour after the sale begins, a young woman, going by the name of Maggie Black, will be there looking for the book as well."

"How do you know?" Mrs. Kerr asked.

"Because I have already given her marching orders and, as we speak, she is on her way. She handles messy jobs for me that, because of Heaven's restrictions, I can't touch. I have convinced her that this is merely a simple switch job, so Maggie won't expect trouble. If you and your boys are careful, she won't know what hit her. Here is her picture."

Larry gave Mrs. Kerr a photo of Maggie Black.

"Very pretty girl. This should be a snap."

"Don't let her beauty fool you. She is the most formidable warrior you have ever faced."

"I find that hard to believe," said Mrs. Kerr as she absent-mindedly rubbed the hard mass of scar tissue that covered her left shoulder.

"If you don't kill her instantly, she will ruin your entire day. I trained her myself and her martial skills are off the chart."

"Okay. How do I find the book, once I kill your stupid bitch?"

"Never let me hear you call Maggie that!" Larry screamed. "You are not fit to shine her shoes, or even breathe the same air!"

"My apologies," Mrs. Kerr said. "Once I kill the saintly, *Miss* Black, how do I locate my payment?"

"Inside one of the books for sale is a slip of paper with the exact location. Piece of cake."

"Why kill this woman? You obviously have strong feelings for her."

"Maggie must die," he said softly. "Everything I hold dear is riding upon her death."

"Why not kill her yourself?"

"I could sooner rip out my own heart."

"Yeah, about that, Larry. Again, why did you pick me? Why involve me in this weird murder-for-hire plot? What happened to the goody-two shoes fallen angel who went around doing good so that God would feel sorry for him and let him back into Heaven. You used to kick the crap out of people like me and now you want to use me to your dirty work?"

"I made a deal with Heaven and, after ten thousand years, we have come to an understanding. Don't ask me why, but part of that deal is for Maggie to die within a twenty-four-hour period. You and your slaves are the only force close enough who could possibly take her down."

"I am impressed. Murdering your right hand man to get what you want? And all this time, I thought you were one of those insipid, uninspired good guys. Bravo on revealing the darkness of your true nature."

Larry glared at the smug Mrs. Kerr. "Watch it."

She smiled. "Is this all?"

"One, last thing."

"What's that?"

"Kill her as quickly and as painlessly as possible. She does not deserve this and I don't want her to suffer."

"What kind of weapons does she carry?"

"A .45 and a knife."

"That won't be a problem."

"Did I mention, Kali?"

"Kali? Who is this *Kali*?"

"A living, supernatural weapon with no equal. She occupies the form of a kukri, however she is far more deadly. Anything living that touches her, whether it be natural or supernatural will die. Only Maggie can control her."

"Now that could be a problem."

Larry shoved a folded slip of paper at Mrs. Kerr. "This is a spell that will render Kali inert. She will be an ordinary kukri in the hands of a master fighter."

"That is still bad, but manageable," said Mrs. Kerr.

"You can use the spell only once and its effects last around thirty minutes. Do we have a deal?"

"Yes, Larry, we do indeed. It is customary to provide proof of death. A bit of jewelry, or perhaps a finger?"

"Absolutely not," Larry said. "This is our first and last meeting. I will see your evidence on the tube, just like everyone else. Be warned, Mrs. Kerr, fail me, and I will make you my special project."

Larry disappeared.

"While I finish my dinner," Mrs. Kerr said softly. "Everyone will pack their things. We have a long trip ahead of us."

CHAPTER 3

This looks like the place," Maggie Black said as she eased her rental car into the last parking space.

Before her was a smattering of cars and one large van that, according to the lettering on the side, belonged to the Friendlyview Baptist Church, of Ketchum, Idaho.

A paper banner, drooping across the brick façade of the three-story, Georgian styled building, proclaimed that the Fourteenth Annual North Swallen Valley Library Book Sale was in progress.

The tall, beautiful woman set the parking brake and switched off the engine. Opening her oversized, leather messenger bag, she produced a thick, dog-eared paperback titled *THE MANY LOVERS OF THE PREACHER'S DAUGHTER*. She smiled at the lurid cover art that sported an abundance of pouty lips, ripped abs, and windblown hair. "Oh, great Book of Spooky Stuff, what am I here for again?"

"*The Book of Xanadutha*, Maggie," said the low, feminine voice that emanated from the mystic book.

"Sounds very melodramatic and creepy, Spooky."

"It's a one-of-a-kind, mystic book written in a dead, undecipherable language, said to have been stolen from Heaven's archives. The tongue is so old and esoteric that even I can't translate it. Rumors abound about its content. Some say it is the history of the Antediluvian world before Adam and Eve. Some say it is a spell-book of cosmic power, even a few think it contains the name of God."

"In other words, nobody knows for sure. It could be a dessert cookbook as far as anyone knows."

"Right. However, Heaven has issued an astronomical bounty for its return. If it is a cookbook, its recipes are for trouble."

"If no one can understand it, how can it cause any trouble? It's like a gun without bullets, which makes it nothing more than a cool looking paperweight."

"The Boss wants it, and from his tone, he wants it real bad. He probably wants to swap it for some favor."

"I get that, but why did I have to cut short my long overdue vacation to come get this silly thing? Surely it could have waited another week."

"Not our job to figure out the Boss, Maggie. We just come running when he yells."

"You ask me, Spooky, Larry is the one who is undecipherable. I mean, don't get me wrong, I love the guy like my own dad, but he can be downright unpredictable at times."

"That is an understatement. So, Maggie dear, did we find any suitable companionship in Barbados?"

"Whatever do you mean?"

"Did you get laid?"

"What kind of question is that?" Maggie asked as she blushed furiously.

"In other words, no. You need to get over Ghost Boy. That ship has sailed—or sunk, depending on your point of view."

"None of this is your business, Spooky."

"I care about you, so I will make it my business. Your brief fling with a dead guy possessing his great-grandson is beyond weird. You need a normal guy to settle down with."

"A talking book discussing my love life is weird. What do you know about normal?"

"I know what I know. Maggie, you need a red-hot relationship that keeps you screaming all night and makes your teeth sweat when you think of him."

"Do you have his number?"

"555—"

"I was kidding."

"I am only looking out for you. I don't know if you realize it or not, but sad as it is, I am your only friend."

"You forget sweet Kali."

"You forget that sweet Kali would gladly eat you if she could."

"All friendships have little quirks."

"You need a man."

"It will happen. One day, I will find someone who fits me, don't ask me how, I just know it."

"I hope you are right," Spooky said. "Are you still going through with Larry's birthday surprise?"

"Shhhh. Keep it down, you never know when he might be eavesdropping."

"You do know that he doesn't have a birthday."

"Yes, he does. It is next Saturday. I am going to have cake and ice cream and a nice dinner."

"What, no pony?"

"Get serious. I got him a nice shirt and a decent pair of slacks. The man definitely needs a new look."

"I am sure he will appreciate the gesture. I have never seen him care about anyone like he does you, Maggie."

"Enough chit-chat, Spooky, I have a job to do. Now where do I find this mysterious book? How does a heavenly book written in an undecipherable language go unnoticed in a library?"

"It has a fake cover that reads: *THE RELATIONSHIP BETWEEN THE MODERN AMERICAN OVIS ARIS WOOL PRODUCTION AND ITS ASIAN COUNTERPART IN THE CURRENT WORLD ECONOMIC MODEL.*"

"Oh, Lord, I almost went to sleep from just hearing the title."

"You have to admit it's an effective cover."

Maggie opened her bag, reaching in up to her shoulder and rummaged around until her fingers found the book.

"This thing is monstrous," Maggie said as she pulled out a massive book. "Luckily, I have a bottomless purse."

"When you retrieve *The Book of Xanadutha*, replace it with this fake one. No one will ever be the wiser. You will find it located on the third floor, section ten, row eight, shelf three."

"Gotcha."

Maggie slipped on a black baseball cap that declared that *Zombies were once people, too.* Donning a pair of large, black-rimmed glasses that had a bit of white tape wrapped around the bridge, she checked her look in the rearview mirror.

"How do I look?"

"You look like you have a terminal case of the nerds."

"Thanks," Maggie said as she closed the book and slipped it into her cornucopia bag. "Canvas book bag," she said. "I like big books and I cannot lie. Blue font, please." Her bag transformed into a simple, empty cloth sack with the play on words spelled out in faded blue block print. "Excellent."

Popping open the car door, the tall woman walked across the lot and into the door marked, *Book Sale.*

ৎঠৎঠ

Salome Kerr and four of her people systematically searched the tables stacked high with thousands of books, looking for the elusive clue that would lead her to the hiding place of *The Book of Xanadutha.*

"Mrs. Kerr, she is here," whispered Megan.

"Maintain the plan and ignore her," Mrs. Kerr whispered, not looking up from her search. "If Miss Black gets spooked and bolts, all of you will pay. Now look for that blasted clue."

ৎঠৎঠ

Maggie smiled at the thin, elderly woman staffing the cash register. A white sticker pasted to her blouse said: *Friends of the Library Volunteer.*

"Can I help you find something, dear?"

"Do you have any action adventure novels?" Maggie asked. "I need some reading material for the beach."

"Oh, I wish I was going on vacation," said the woman. "Nothing is sorted, but we got a donation yesterday that might just fit the bill. Follow me."

Maggie fell in behind the little woman as she crossed the large room, weaving through the maze of tables filled with obsolete textbooks, magazines, and assorted dog-eared paperbacks. They stopped at a table loaded with three cardboard boxes filled with hardcover books.

"I could not believe it when these came in," said the volunteer as she picked up a thick book and handed it to Maggie.

Maggie smiled as she gazed upon the lurid artwork on the creased dust jacket. It depicted a ruggedly handsome man protecting a scantily clad, well-endowed woman from a creature that looked like a cross between a giant snake and a demon.

Blood Moon, Maggie read. *The dashing Kamikaze Kane and his stalwart companions, the Choirboys, fly into the green hell of the uncharted Amazon to save his beloved Ginny from a terror beyond human comprehension.*

"I know that it must sound kind of silly now, but when I was a girl, back in the fifties, I thought those were the greatest stories ever written," the volunteer said. "They were popular for a while then just disappeared. I guess supernatural adventure went out of style and was replaced with the giant bugs and creepy shit of the atomic age."

Maggie laughed.

"Anywho, I love adventure stories and none were ever better than the adventures of Kamikaze Kane."

"I never heard of Kane, but you have sold me," Maggie said. "I'm Maggie, by the way.

"You're in luck, Maggie," the woman said. "The entire collection of fifteen books is here. I'm Carol."

"I'll take them all, Carol."

"For a dollar a piece, I would say you got a bargain. That's at least a million dollars' worth of entertainment. I'll help you carry them to your car."

"That's all right, sweetie. I want to look around a bit first."

Maggie paid Carol and waited for her to move back to her post at the cash register. With no one looking, Maggie slipped all fifteen books into her bottomless bag. The mystic pouch neither looked nor weighed any more than before. If Maggie had wanted to, she could have loaded the entire library into the bag and its weight would not have varied a fraction of a gram.

"Enough dawdling, girl," she muttered to herself. "Let's get this over so I can get back to the beach."

Maggie made a beeline for the library elevator.

⁗⁗⁗

"Where have you been all my life, beautiful?"

Maggie looked up from the shelf at the leering man before her. In her hands, she held the disguised *Book of Xanadutha*.

"Why don't you just hand over the book, beautiful, then we can blow this joint and get a drink."

Maggie stood and nonchalantly dropped the book into her bag.

"In the first place I don't drink, but even if I did, I wouldn't drink with a douche like you."

"Why are all women so damn stupid?" Tim Garret asked as he opened his sport coat and flashed his holstered gun. "Have it your way but, in any case, you are going to give me the damn book."

"Okay, okay, please don't hurt me." Maggie pulled the fake book from her bag and tossed it at his feet. "You got the book, now please, leave me alone."

"'Fraid it don't work that way." Taking a step toward her, Garret pulled a wicked knife from his coat pocket. "Hold still. I promise this won't hurt."

"I am afraid it will," she said.

Maggie caught his wrist and broke it. Before the knife hit the floor, she grabbed his head and snapped his neck. As she eased his body to the floor, her photograph fell out of his coat.

"Oh, no," she whispered as she gazed upon her smiling visage. "I've been set up."

Looking up, she watched a wild-eyed woman brandish a sawed off shotgun.

Maggie dove for cover as twelve-gauge buckshot peppered the books around her. Producing her Sig Sauer, Maggie shot the woman twice in the chest.

A single, soft chime announced the arrival of the elevator.

The door opened on two of Mrs. Kerr's men, wielding AK-47s. They didn't have time for anything beyond surprise as Maggie shot them both in the head.

Pulling a fire alarm, Maggie spun around like an Olympic hammer thrower and slung her bag through the wide double pane glass window overlooking the rear parking lot. Without hesitation, she followed the bag out. Shrugging off the three-story fall as if had been from a stepstool, she scooped up her bag and dashed toward her car.

"Help me!"

Maggie turned to find a young girl with flaming red hair running toward her.

"He's trying to kill me! Help me!"

Two men armed with pistols burst from the door of the Library. One was large and beefy like a wrestler, while the other was short and thin, sporting a pair of wraparound sunglasses.

"I am going to kill that redheaded, pimpled-faced bitch!" cried the big man at the top of his lungs.

"Sunglasses" fired wildly, shattering the windshields of two cars flanking Maggie.

"Get behind me, girl," Maggie said as she stepped in front of the girl and took aim at the two thugs.

Before she could squeeze the trigger, Maggie grunted in pain as hundreds of thousands of volts coursed through her body. As she fell stunned to the asphalt, her last sight before blacking out was the redheaded girl standing over her with a stun gun.

❧❧❧

Larry sat on a barstool in Mike's Bar and Grill, nursing his third Shirley Temple. Except for the bartender, the bar was empty.

"Hey, fellah," said the petit, dishwater blonde bartender, sporting a nametag, *Corrine*. "You look like a guy with female troubles. How about something a bit stronger to ease the pain?"

"You must be psychic."

"Nah, broken-hearted guys like you are our bread and butter."

Larry smiled. "I will indulge in a shot of Glenlivet 21, but only if you will join me."

"Now you're talking," she said as her eyes lit up. Producing the bottle and two shot glasses, she doled out a generous amount. "For a guy with a fondness for girly drinks, you got great taste in scotch."

"Can I ask you a question, Corrine?"

"Shoot."

"Let's suppose for a moment that the one thing you wanted the most, the one thing you have worked your whole life for, sweated for, gave your absolute all for, was suddenly within your grasp?"

"Sounds like a great big 'but' is about to pop up like a stop sign."

"I still think you're psychic," he said. "Anyway, what if you had to kill the most precious thing in your life, to obtain your prize?"

"Toughie. Now when you say 'kill,' you are talking metaphorically right?"

"No. I really mean kill. In order to get what I want, I have to kill the woman I consider to be my best friend."

"I think you would be a sorry son of a bitch," she said as her hand hovered near the shotgun hidden under the bar. "And I think you need to leave."

"Yeah, I came to the same conclusion. I will go in a minute or two. I just want to watch the news first. By the way, your scattergun isn't there, so don't bother."

A quick glance confirmed his statement. The smile left her face as a glint of fear flashed in her eyes. Suddenly, the television over the bar came to life, making her jump.

A handsome, stern-looking, man sat behind a news desk.

"In Idaho today, tragedy struck the small town of North Swallen, when during a library book sale, gun violence erupted. While details are still coming in, we do know that five are known to be dead, including two women. According to our sources, one of the dead, a young woman, was found in the parking lot, the victim of an apparent cold-blooded execution. An hour ago, a North Swallen Police spokesman stated in a news conference that they can neither confirm nor deny any aspects while the investigation is underway."

Larry took a deep breath and raised his glass. With a shaky hand, Corrine followed suit.

"Here's to Maggie Black. You were the best, truest friend I ever had. I am sorry." Larry tossed back the scotch then laid a one hundred dollar bill on the bar. "Keep the change, Corrine. Thanks for listening."

"Where are you going?" she asked.

"I start a new job today and I can't be late."

CHAPTER 4

"Wake up sleeping beauty," said the motherly voice in her ear. "It's time to learn the facts of life."

Drenched in sweat and barely able to move, Maggie slowly opened her eyes and licked her parched lips.

While her vision was still fuzzy, a small hand slipped beneath her shoulders and lifted her slightly. A bottle of gloriously cold water was held to her lips and she drank greedily.

"Take it easy, Maggie. The worst is over, I promise."

Maggie blinked her eyes several times before her vision came into focus. "You were the girl—you shocked me."

"I am sorry about that, I really am. It was Mrs. Kerr's idea. I am Megan. Megan Franks." Megan wore Maggie's zombie hat. "I hope you don't mind," she said. "It's funny."

"It's all yours, Shortstack. Sorry about your friends. They didn't give me a choice."

Megan gave her a broad smile. "They got what was coming to them. Garrett kept trying to get me in the sack. Jean and Frank would have helped him if it wasn't for Mrs. Kerr. The Boss has some issues, but she kept those assholes from raping me."

"Who is this Mrs. Kerr, Megan?"

"She's our boss. She is your boss, too, so you better get used to the idea."

Maggie looked around the sparsely furnished bedroom. On the corner of the opposite bed sat her unopened bag. She and Megan were alone.

Play nice, Maggie, and learn as much as we can until we find out what's going on, she thought. *Then we can bust some heads.*

"How many is we, Megan?"

"Yumi, Roland, me, and now, you."

"I feel so weak. I can barely move a muscle."

"Like I said, in a few hours you'll be back to normal."

"That was one hell of a stunner to do this to me."

"It wasn't the stunner, Maggie. That was days ago. Mrs. Kerr put you under a sleeping spell until she could prepare you. This is what happens when you become *hers*."

"I don't understand. Who is she?"

"You will know soon enough," Megan said.

A large bowl of water rose from the ground and flew to Megan. Megan soaked a washcloth and slowly washed Maggie's face and neck.

"Are you a witch?"

"No." Megan chuckled. "Mrs. Kerr is the witch. I have what they call telekinesis. I can move things with my mind."

"Neat trick."

"Not really. It was the reason Mrs. Kerr took me away from my family. She uses me mainly for opening locked doors and bypassing alarms. I wanted to be a lawyer. She has turned me into a thief."

"Are the others...*special*?"

"Oh, yeah, but not like me. Roland is the muscle of the group. He's a were-beast. He can turn into a tiger, but most of the time he's a pig. Yumi is cool, though. He wears sunglasses all the time, even at night, and he likes to tell jokes. Weapons are his thing and, let me tell you, he can't miss, period. He can do things with a gun that you would have to see to believe."

"They were the two guys shooting at us."

"Yeah, that was just playacting or Yumi would have killed you. They were a distraction so I could get behind you. Sorry."

Maggie closed her eyes and gasped. "So weak. I feel like I am running a high fever."

"You are, but it is coming down fast. I love your accent. Where you from, Maggie?"

"Alabama, but I haven't lived there in a while. What about you?"

"Minnesota."

"I heard—someone told me to wake up."

"That was Mrs. Kerr. From now on, you will hear her voice—a lot. You want a cigarette?" Megan asked producing a crumpled pack and lighter from her jeans.

"I don't smoke and neither should you."

"I thought the same thing when I was first taken. In fact, I thought that people who used them were stupid, but now I am up to a pack-a-day. It is one of the few pleasures Mrs. Kerr allows us."

"What does Mrs. Kerr allow?"

"Not much. No drugs stronger than aspirin. No alcohol other than a single beer a week. We are allowed one hour of TV a day, we take turns picking the program, however news broadcasts are strictly forbidden. We cannot, under any circumstances, leave the house, unless we are on yard duty or we have an assignment. Lights are out at 9:00 p.m. and wake up is 5:00 a.m. House duties are assigned by Yumi and rotate weekly."

"House duties?"

"You know, cleaning, cooking, that sort of thing. Mrs. Kerr expects a spotlessly clean house."

"Screw that. I'm not a maid."

"Don't say that! She can hear you! Thanks to you, there are fewer of us now and we each have more work than before. I'm afraid that as the newbie you'll get the worst jobs—you know like toilets and scrubbing floors and windows."

"Sorry, Shortstack. Not my thing. How long have you been here?"

"Two years next April.

A small knock and the bedroom door opened.

Mrs. Kerr stood in the doorway wearing a blue silk blouse and slacks.

"And how is the newest member of our family?"

"She is doing great, Mrs. Kerr."

Maggie watched the friendly girl pale slightly. From her

body language, it was obvious to Maggie that Megan was terrified of Mrs. Kerr.

"Megan, why don't you go prepare some lunch for Maggie while I explain the household rules?"

"Yes, Mrs. Kerr," Megan said as she quickly left the room.

Maggie struggled and finally succeeded in sitting up as Mrs. Kerr took a seat on the opposite bed.

"Miss Black, my name is Salome Kerr. It is great honor to meet you."

"Why did you kidnap me?"

"You call it a kidnapping. I call it saving your life."

"Where are we?"

"We are in your new home, of course."

"You're confusing the hell out of me," Maggie said as she rubbed her face. "Give me the *Reader's Digest* version of what's going on."

"Very well," Mrs. Kerr said leaning back. "I was hired to kill you. Once I saw how incredibly formidable you are, I just had to have you for my own. You are my newest acquisition and latest member of my family."

"You do not own me and, when I am able, I am going to mop the floor with you."

"I beg to differ. As soon as you are able, you will eagerly do my bidding just as you did for your former boss, Larry. I hate to break it to you, my dear, but the days of being an insipid good guy are over."

"Look here, Kerr—"

"That's *Mrs.* Kerr. Nothing else will do, my dear."

"Look here, *asshole*—"

Maggie's world exploded into the kind of agony she never knew existed. It was if the very atoms that constructed her radiated sheer pain. As quickly as it came, it vanished, leaving her shaking uncontrollably.

"What—did you do to me?" she whispered.

"While you slumbered, I placed an obedience collar around your lovely throat. It is an ingenious device that, at my command, merges your soul with the fires of Hell itself. While you suffer unimaginable soulish torment, there isn't any actual physical damage." Maggie's hands went to her throat, but her searching fingers failed to find anything. "Oh, don't worry it's there," Mrs. Kerr said. "However, it is impossible to remove by any other being in Heaven or Hell. I am the only one who can remove it."

"Take it off, or so help me, God, I'll kill you."

"That would be a very bad idea. You see, my death would only result in the collar's activation. A sort of 'dead man's switch' if you will excuse the terrible pun. The pain will never stop and you would most likely go mad within a few hours, which means that my health is the most important thing in your universe."

"Larry will find me and he will shove this collar up your wrinkled, old ass."

Maggie received another, longer dose of the unbearable pain.

"I have some bad news for you, my dear," Mrs. Kerr said with a sadistic grin. "The last thing you want is for Larry to find you. You see, it was Larry who wanted you dead."

"Liar!"

"It's time to face the truth. How is it that we knew the exact time you were coming to the library and that you were to take *The Book of Xanadutha*?"

The color drained from Maggie's face. "No. You're lying."

"Larry came to me and offered me *The Book of Xanadutha* as payment for killing you. He told me the exact time to ambush you. He even gave me a photo so I could recognize you."

Maggie put her hand to her mouth in horror as she thought of the photo that fell from the thug's coat pocket. "It can't be," she said. "He's like my own father."

"Apparently, he does not share the same feelings. He told me about you, about the formidable weapon you have, I think the name he used was...*Kali*."

"No one knows about her."

"He gave me a special spell to neutralize her," Mrs. Kerr said. "He wanted to take away every advantage you had and make you as helpless as a lamb to the slaughter."

"But why, for God's sake?"

"He told me that Heaven made him a deal. In exchange for your death, he would be pardoned. He didn't tell me why Heaven is out to get you, but he was more than happy to kill you for his freedom."

"It can't be. It just can't be!"

"It is, so get used to it, Maggie. I own you lock, stock, and barrel, and there isn't a thing you can do about that. I have no reason to lie. What I have told you is brutal but, nonetheless, true."

Maggie swallowed hard.

"Everything I have done for him, suffered for him, and he betrays me? Oh God, I am a fool! He used me!" Maggie clenched her fists in rage as hot tears flowed down her face. "Do you know how many times I skirted death for him? How many ridiculous death traps I escaped trying to help him? I was locked in a safe and tossed into a lake—unarmed, trapped in a pitch-black maze with a whole herd of demons, and even stuck in the trunk of a burning car while it was in a car crusher—and that was only the first year!

"Did Larry thank me, or show any gratitude? No. I have fought supernatural creatures, from witches to demigods, even a few that were never classified, all to help Larry get back into Heaven. After all I have done for him, he tosses me under the bus without a thought."

"I am sorry, Miss Black."

"Sorry? You have taken advantage of this situation and made me your slave! I wished you had killed me!"

"Now, now," Mrs. Kerr said. "While it is true that I have taken advantage of the situation, I am prepared to give you an out."

"An out?"

"Yes. I have had a particular project in mind for years, but it required *The Book of Xanadutha* to make it a reality. Unfortunately, trying to subdue you, I never got my hands on the book. Serve me loyally, help achieve my goal, and I will release you."

"And just what is your goal?"

"Ah, that is for me to know," Mrs. Kerr said. "You know,

'loose lips sinks ships' and all that. However, if I am success-ful, not only will I free you, I will give you a golden oppor-tunity for revenge against your angelic Judas."

"What will Larry do when he finds out I am not dead?"

"Probably something appropriately horrifying to the both of us. Thus, I have taken precautions. After Larry extolled your many virtues, I toyed with the idea of a switch and we came prepared."

"How?"

"While it was rather short notice, I created a non-living doppelganger from your photo. While not exact, she would definitely fool any witnesses or medical examiner. As far as the world is concerned, you, Miss Black, are quite dead."

Mrs. Kerr sickened Maggie. She was an amoral monster through and through and Maggie was completely at her mercy. Nevertheless, she was alive and alive meant hope.

Maggie sat back and stared at the grinning Mrs. Kerr. Her emotions were in complete upheaval as her world lay shattered around her. "I want something made clear," Maggie said.

"Excuse me?"

"I will not murder anyone, period. Self-defense is one thing, but not cold-blooded murder. I'm not your whore or prostitute and I will not violate my Christian faith. Do you un-derstand me?"

"Miss Black, as long as you wear my collar, you will do whatever I say, period. Do you understand *me*?"

"The pain is bad. Hands down the worst thing I have ever felt. However, thanks to you and Larry, my life and everything I hold dear has been dropped into wood chipper. You're very fortunate that I'm not the suicidal type. Right now, your word to release me is the only hope I have left, and I repeat, the only hope. I'm holding onto the edge by my fingertips, so don't step on me just to show me who is boss. I will obey you and do your bidding, but cross the line, Mrs. Kerr, and I'll gut you, then kill myself."

"You know, Miss Black, I believe you would. Very well, I agree to your terms."

"You have a deal, *Mrs.* Kerr."

"I hope you like soup and sandwiches," Megan said as she entered the room, bearing a platter.

"In a second, Shortstack." Maggie struggled from the bed. Stumbling to her case, she threw open the flap and reached inside. Moments later, she produced *The Book of Xanadutha.*

Mrs. Kerr gasped.

"I believe this belongs to you, Mrs. Kerr."

"The book. It was under my nose the entire time"

"Now, Mrs. Kerr, hand over your credit card."

"What?"

"I need a makeover and it won't be cheap."

"Out of the question," Mrs. Kerr snapped. "I am sure you have money."

"Oh, I have a ton, spread over several banks," Maggie said. "However, if I move so much as a nickel, Larry will know that I'm not dead. Looks like you have another mouth to feed."

"This is outrageous!"

"If Larry or the bully boys up in Heaven get a look at my pretty face, guess who is the first bitch they are going to visit?"

Mrs. Kerr thought a moment before she fished out her wallet and handed Maggie plastic.

"Come on, Shortstack," Maggie said, "We're going to find us a salon and have makeovers."

"Mrs. Kerr, is this okay with you?" asked Megan.

"Umm…yes, Megan. Before you go, Miss Black, we have one last duty to perform. Now that you are mine, your old life is dead. You are no longer Maggie Black. You will now be known as Hajar, which means *forsaken.* Appropriate, don't you think? Now say it."

Maggie gave her a cold look while emotions raged within her. "Maggie Black is dead. I am Hajar."

"Excellent." Mrs. Kerr chuckled. "Now run along. I expect you to come back a different person."

CHAPTER 5

L ord God, please help me in my hour of need," Hajar
prayed. "Please don't let anyone get hurt. In Jesus's
name, Amen."

"Very touching, Hajar," Mrs. Kerr said. "But you are wasting my time. Move your ass."

"Yes, Mrs. Kerr."

The tall blonde slipped a mystic elephant-hair necklace
around her neck and waited for the slight wave of nausea to
pass. She then checked her weapon and slipped on a pair of
black-rimmed Wayfarers.

"Ready, Shortstack?"

"The security company isn't going to hear a peep out of
that place," Megan said.

"Don't forget cell calls to 911 either."

"I got it all covered. Even the guy's cable will be down,"
Megan said as she closed her eyes and concentrated with all
her might. "Hurry, before I get a migraine—again."

Kissing Megan on the head, Hajar exited her stolen Cadil-
lac and strode boldly to the door of Bosh and Sons Fine Jewelry.

Entering the small, brightly lit store, Hajar took stock of her
surroundings. She faced a long, glass display case. Its three
shelves were covered with, shiny, pricy bling from necklaces
and rings to watches. Behind the case leaned Jim Bosh, son of
the storeowner, Ralph Bosh. Bosh was a tall, thin man with
large, heavy lidded eyes, dressed in a shiny gray suit and

matching tie. He pulled a protruding toothpick from his thick lips and tossed it into a hidden trashcan. Bosh offered no greeting to his potential customer, other than a bored expression. He crossed his arms and leaned back against the wall.

Bosh did not see a tall, incredibly beautiful woman enter his shop, but instead, thanks to the mystic necklace around her neck, he saw a man with wild, bright red hair and a hockey player nose.

Hajar pulled a gun and shoved it into Bosh's face. A slight creak of a loose floorboard altered her to an ambush.

"That was a mistake, you greasy punk," Bosh said with a grin.

"Drop it, you dumb asshole," came the deep voice behind Hajar.

Part time street thug and full time security, Peabo "Big Boy" Nutt aimed a shotgun at Hajar's back. Shoving Bosh hard against the far wall, she turned and, with unbelievable speed, swatted the weapon from the hands of three-hundred-and-fifty-pound man.

"What the hell?" Big Boy cried as he found himself unarmed. Balling his ham-sized fist, he swung a wild haymaker. Hajar sidestepped the powerful, although clumsy, punch and laid him out cold with a single, crushing blow to the jaw.

"Oh shit," exclaimed the stunned Bosh as his security crashed to the floor like a felled tree.

"Hands in the air or your ass is next."

"Okay, okay, just don't shoot me."

Taking a hand full of plastic handcuffs, she managed to secure the big man's hands, who from this day forward would be known as Peabo "Glass Jaw" Nutt, behind his back.

"Good thing I buy these things by the gross," she muttered.

"Let's not allow this thing to get out of hand," cried the well-dressed Bosh.

Without prompting, Bosh quickly filled a plastic bag with the flashiest items in the main display case.

Shoving the sack at her, he snapped, "You got what you came for, now get out."

The bag full, Hajar waved Bosh into the backroom and the

massive store safe, where she tossed the bag into a metal trash container.

"I want the real diamonds," she hissed. "The ones you've been fencing."

"Go to hell, punk!" he snapped. "I hit the silent alarm. Cops will be here any minute."

"The cops are the last people you want snooping around," she whispered. "You called your private-thug security, consisting of Anthony, Billy Ray, and Jerome. I paid them a visit first. They are a bit tied up right now."

"Shit."

Taking a pair of flexy cuffs, she secured the man's wrists and ankles, slipped a black sack over his head, and eased him gently down to the floor.

Pulling up her left sleeve revealed a series of numbers written in black marker.

Thank you, Spooky.

Hajar quickly dialed the combination of the safe and swung open the thick steel barrier. Five black velvet lined trays held a fortune in stolen diamonds. Below that was a king's ransom in exotic jewelry piled in a yellow plastic bin the size of a five-gallon bucket.

"My kind of 'carat patch,'" she said. She quickly scooped the glittery fortune into a small sack. Leaving the stolen jewelry behind, she sprinted from the shop.

"You will pay for this! I will find your punk ass and you will pray to God for mercy!"

Not to worry. I'm paying now, she thought

c∕ɔc∕ɔ

Hajar slid behind the wheel of the car and after a quick "high-five," she and Megan drove home.

"Hit it, Shortstack."

Megan dialed 911 on her burner phone.

"Nine-one-one what is your emergency?" said the clinical, unemotional voice of the 911 operator.

"There is a robbery going on right now at Bosh and Sons

Fine Jewelry. Oh God, I just heard shots fired! He's killing those poor people!"

After giving a bloodcurdling scream, Megan ended the call and popped out the battery.

"That should put a stop to the rash of burglaries that have been all over the papers," Hajar said.

"Good to rip off someone who deserves it for a change."

"Yeah. How about some ice cream, Shortstack, to celebrate?"

"You don't have time for ice cream," Mrs. Kerr said. "Get home as fast as you can."

Hajar and Megan, in unison, gave their collars the finger.

Hajar tossed Megan a small black jewelry box.

Megan whooped and danced around the front seat as she pulled free the gold earrings.

"Happy birthday," Hajar said. "Don't worry, I bought them with my own money. I hope you like them."

"Like them? I love them!"

"Happy blah, blah, blah," Mrs. Kerr said. "If you are through having a female bonding moment, get your asses home, now. The laundry won't do itself."

☙❧☙

Hajar, along with her other mundane household duties, had become Mrs. Kerr's sole source of income. Since her arrival, Mrs. Kerr's coffers had grown into the millions. To date, Hajar had robbed three banks, two armored cars, a savings and loan, a drug dealer, and now a jewelry fence. She was moving up the FBI's most wanted list with the speed of a rocket-powered express elevator.

Taking advantage of her six-foot-six height, and dressing in men's clothing, she had the authorities convinced that they were hunting a man. With a bit of Mrs. Kerr's hoodoo, in the form of a distortion field created by a mystic necklace, the state-of-the-art security cameras never picked up anything but a blurry image. The eyewitness accounts were even less help to authorities, as descriptions ranged from Lemmy Kilmister to

Alfred E. Neuman. Hajar had the dubious nom de plume, the *Blur Bandit.*

It made Hajar sick to commit the crimes and to terrorize innocent people, but as long as she wore that damn collar, Mrs. Kerr was in charge.

The hurt and pain Larry caused her congealed into a white-hot rage—the like of which she had never known was possible. Larry tried to have her killed. He was responsible for her enslavement to a witch. He would die and it would be by her own hand. Unlike Larry, Hajar would not take the coward's way and hire someone else to do her dirty work.

Hajar swore that he would pay, even if she had to make a deal with the devil to give her the power to do it.

CHAPTER 6

Hajar sat in the room she shared with Megan, savoring the thrilling adventures of Kamikaze Kane. Mrs. Kerr gave Hajar a bit more free time than that of her fellow slaves. Instead of the endless list of tedious domestic duties, she replaced Yumi and ran the household. Now she was spending the lion share of her time searching for esoteric relics for Mrs. Kerr's still unnamed master plan. It was essentially the same job she did for Larry, but now she worked for an evil witch. It was all she could not to slit her own wrists.

"Library Volunteer Carol was right," she said softly. "These books are beyond great. Sure, a bit melodramatic, and some of Kane's gadgets downright silly, but the stories really suck you in."

Rubbing her eyes, Hajar bookmarked the page.

It had been nearly nine months since her forced conscription into Mrs. Kerr's little band of misfits. It had been without a doubt the most horrible time of her existence, but she did her level best to accept the situation. Constantly on the move, never staying in one place more than a few weeks, they had bounced across the country in such a bizarre fashion she was convinced that Mrs. Kerr was running from someone.

When she first met Mrs. Kerr, Hajar thought she was a heartless bitch with a sadistic streak a mile wide. Unfortunately, she was much worse. She never seemed to be happy unless she was causing someone else pain or humiliation. Hajar found that Mrs. Kerr enjoyed doling out punishments for the slightest violations as a way of enforcing her unquestioned command over her slaves.

While Mrs. Kerr was a walking, talking, blight on humanity, amazingly, she respected Hajar's boundaries—for now. However, Hajar knew it was only a matter of time before Mrs. Kerr found a way to take even that away.

Laying the book aside, Hajar rose from the bed. Moving to the ratty, second-hand dresser, she gazed into the mirror, slowly coming to grips with the new face staring back at her. Now completely Hajar, she found that Maggie Black was rapidly becoming a dim memory.

Gone was her beautiful raven hair. Cut into a short spike and bleached platinum blonde, it gave Hajar a punk look that was completely out of character. Never one for makeup, due to her tomboy upbringing, she now wore heavy eye makeup and bright lipstick. Even her dazzling green eyes were gone, hidden behind brown contacts.

Never caring for jewelry in the past, she now embraced it. Her ears bore multiple earrings while various rings graced her long elegant fingers. Around her neck, she wore a braided gold chain bearing a simple cross. Above the gold necklace lay a thin, black line, scarcely thicker than a single human hair and razor straight, encircling her throat. It was identical to that of her three companions and it was all that stood between her and freedom. Through the hated device, Mrs. Kerr could eavesdrop, track, and punish.

For all the impossible dangers Hajar had faced and beaten over the years, this obstacle was the toughest of all. So tough, in fact, that while she refused to admit it, Hajar's hope was eroding and she was actually entertaining the idea that she had finally met her match.

"My own dad wouldn't recognize me," she said as she fiddled with a stubborn lock of hair. A slight knocking from her bag attracted her attention.

Moving to her case, she withdrew THE MANY LOVERS OF THE PREACHER'S DAUGHTER.

~ Sup, Maggie, wrote Spooky. Silently the words appeared across the blank page.

Hajar wrote with her finger, well aware that Mrs. Kerr could hear any conversation and the last thing Hajar wanted was for her to find out about her one ace-in-the-hole, Spooky.

~ It's Hajar. Maggie is dead and you know it.

~ *Sorry, but you will always be my sweet Maggie. Hajar looks like a stoned hooker.*

~ I love you too. What do you have?

~ *I just wanted to congratulate the Blur Bandit on moving into the fifteenth spot on the FBI's most wanted.*

~ Yay. The whole thought makes me ill. Those poor people were terrified of me.

~ *You were a victim even more than they were and you know it.*

~ Still doesn't make me feel any better. Do the feds have any leads?

~ *Of course not. I have their computers telling them whatever I want them to hear. Right now, their main suspect is a career bank robber named Carl P. Feenklestein.*

~ Weird name.

~ *I made him up. I am such a stinker at times. Oh, by the way, I found someone who might be able to help translate* The Book of Xanadutha.

~ How is that possible? It is written in a Heavenly language.

~ *I don't question this stuff, I just report it.*

~ The name?

~ *Dr. Frances Kano. Seems the good doctor was some kind of occult expert who had ran across* The Book of Xanadutha *some years ago. My sources say he cracked the code, but lost the book before he could decipher it. I think it was Larry who snatched the book. Anyway, Kano has just been biding his time, tracking down leads on the book. He has made comments that the book leads to a power undreamt of by mortal man. It's a wonder he is still around, according to records he is in his eighties.*

~ Get me an address.

~ *903 Pauline Avenue, Somerset, Virginia. It should take you about nine hours to drive.*

~ Thanks, Spooky.

~ *By the by, got a lead on that collar you are wearing. You were right. They were developed by the Circle. Very expensive, very hard to make. Seven were stolen and a hefty bounty is offered for the thief, alive, dead, or undead . If nothing else, you could rat Mrs. Kerr out and let the Circle make her life hell for a change.*

~ And be a slave to the Black Circle? That is going from the frying pan into the fire. As bad as she is, Mrs. Kerr is the lesser of two evils.

~ *Figures. Just thought you should know, Maggie.*

~ That's Hajar. Got to go, bye.

Without knocking, Mrs. Kerr burst into the room.

"Mrs. Kerr, what can I do for you?" Hajar asked as she slipped Spooky into her bag.

"I was wondering if you had any leads on a translator."

"As a matter of fact, I do. Heard about an occult investigator in Virginia that seems promising. Rumor has it he actually cracked the book's code. His name is Dr. Kano."

"Never heard of him."

"This could be what you have waited for. With your permission, I thought I would grab Megan and pay him a visit."

Mrs. Kerr glanced at the book on her bed.

"You know, Hajar, I am impressed with your love of the written word. You must have read forty or so books since your addition to my family."

"It is an escape. I only wish Megan would take more of an interest, but I think she's a lost cause."

"What thrilling adventure are you working on here?" she said as she picked up the novel.

"It's about a guy named Kane—"

Mrs. Kerr let out an inhuman roar. "How dare you bring this filth into my house?"

"It's just a story."

"Is this just an irritation?"

Hajar fell to her knees as waves of agony slammed into her.

"*Slomatulan dee murtad doole!*" Mrs. Kerr intoned. The book burst into green flame that quickly spread to the bed. Still shaken, Hajar managed to smother the flames with a blanket.

"Never insult me like that again!" Mrs. Kerr hissed. "Do you hear me, Hajar?"

"What did I do wrong, Mrs. Kerr?"

Mrs. Kerr delivered a vicious, stinging slap to Hajar's face. "I never want to see anything—I repeat, anything—pertaining to Kamikaze Kane in my house, or my presence. If you disobey, I will give you a full day of punishment. Do you understand me?"

"Loud and clear," Hajar said slowly, holding her anger in check. Hajar didn't even think it was possible to mentally survive more than twenty minutes let alone an entire day. The very thought gave her an unsettling, unaccustomed emotion: *fear.* "Ma'am, may I take Megan and visit Dr. Kano?"

"Megan stays here. Leave early tomorrow, but check with me first before you go. I will have some last minute instructions. Now, clean up this mess."

"Yes, Ma'am."

Mrs. Kerr turned on her heel and left the smoky room.

What was all that about?

ოჯოჯ

Hajar tossed a few clothes into her bag and slung it over her shoulder. Trying not to wake Megan, she eased open the bedroom door and slipped out. To her surprise, at the end of the hall stood Mrs. Kerr, holding a garment bag.

"This is for you, Hajar."

"Thanks, Mrs. Kerr. What is it?"

"A way to help coax the code from Dr. Kano."

Hajar opened the bag and gasped at the shockingly scanty black dress.

"This is little bigger than a bathing suit, Mrs. Kerr. I thought I had made myself clear about boundaries."

"Why yes you did, my dear, however, it seems that there has been a shift in the balance of power."

"I don't understand."

"You're a brave woman and I have no illusions that pushed

too far you would die before violating your misguided moral code. What was it again? No murder, no sex, no corruption of faith."

"Where are you going with this?" Hajar asked as a cold knot formed in the pit of her stomach.

"You care for sweet Megan. I've watched as your relationship has blossomed over the past few months. It's almost like watching a mother-daughter relationship. That was a mistake. You cannot even entertain the thought of killing me now, because of what that poor child would suffer. She has just cost you what little control you thought you had. Checkmate, Hajar."

"Oh, no, Mrs. Kerr. Please, no."

"For daring to think you could dictate terms to me, I am going to break you, once and for all. You will seduce the good doctor to get his code on *The Book of Xanadutha*. Then you will take your gun and kill him. I expect photos and a severed finger as proof of his execution. After your cold-blooded murder, I'll find some appropriately humiliating way for you to renounce your faith. Do you have any objections, Hajar?"

The blood drained from Hajar's face. "No, ma'am," she said softly.

"I didn't think so. Get the information and don't dawdle. I eagerly look forward to our special time together."

CHAPTER 7

Doctor Gideon Elias Kane sat at a wide, mahogany desk in his study, writing the last of several letters. Although nearly eighty-three, he could have passed for a man twenty years younger. Dr. Kane maintained a rigorous physical and mental workout schedule that kept him in tiptop condition. Nevertheless, this morning's workout was to be his last.

With his usual bold flourish, he signed his name and dated the document. Lifting the silver Mont Blanc pen from the expensive parchment, he looked around the room and smiled.

This was his favorite room, his sanctum sanctorum, where happy memories were so thick and so prevalent that, at times, he thought he would have to brush them away from his face like a swarm of flies.

"I've had a good life, Ginny," he said. "Traveled around the globe several times, met a lot of fine people that I was proud to call friends. I'd like to think we did some good along the way. All that would have made for a pretty good life, but being loved by you has shown me how truly blessed I was."

Gideon recapped the worn pen and placed it carefully on the desk.

"I can't believe it has been five years. God, how I miss you, Ginny."

He took the letter and folded it with extreme care, making certain the crease was perfectly centered and razor sharp before sliding it into an envelope marked, *Marshall Kane*. Not bothering to seal the last packet to his brother, he placed it up-right on his leather-topped desk, leaning it against his favorite photo of his beloved wife, Virginia.

Mentally going over the list he had prepared, Gideon drummed his fingers on the desk until he was satisfied that he had left nothing out.

"Bags are packed. I guess I'm ready to go."

He pulled out a deep desk drawer, revealing a beautiful, matched pair of 1911 Colt .45s. The custom pair were a gift, made for him by a master gunsmith down in Tennessee whom Dr. Kane had helped out of a bit of trouble back in 1948. The guns were polished blue steel and perfectly balanced. Well-worn ivory grips, aged to a delicate patina, held the faded script, *G K*. They were as close to children as he and his beloved Ginny ever had.

Smiling, he selected one of the gleaming weapons, the one he nicknamed Lightning, and held it before him.

"How many scrapes have you two girls gotten me out of over the years? Probably end up gathering dust in somebody's gun collection or, God forbid, a pawn shop. What a shame I can't take you with me."

Carefully checking that the magazine was fully charged with his special, hand-loaded ammo, he paused and thought about his brother Marshall and the various nephews and nieces he would leave behind. Gideon felt a sharp pang of guilt.

"They'll get over it. Not like I have all that much time left, anyway. What I should be thinking about is the other side. Now, that, will be an adventure."

Inserting the clip, he racked the silky smooth slide for the last time. "Find out the truth in about three seconds."

"Gideon."

Gideon paused and looked up. Before the door, stood his Ginny. The smiling apparition was dressed in a pair of cream-colored satin lounging pajamas. Gone were the ravages of age. She looked like the voluptuous nineteen year-old girl he had first met back in 1946. Her long, honey-blonde hair was done up in the simple ponytail she favored.

"Ginny!" he cried at the sight of his beloved wife.

"Gideon, it is not yet your time. The fight has just begun and you are needed desperately. The snake that you thought was dead has returned. You are the forsaken pearl's only hope."

"Ginny, what does it mean?" he said as he leapt to his feet. "What is the forsaken pearl?"

Ginny smiled brightly. "They are here." Blowing him a kiss, she faded away.

A creak on the stairs outside his study door drew Gideon's attention. Seconds later, there was a sharp, loud knock on his door.

"Come in," he said, slightly puzzled at the politeness of the burglar.

The heavy oak door flew open, revealing a tall black man wearing a tan overcoat. His odd, dull yellow eyes highlighted the smiling stranger's painfully gaunt features.

"Professor Kano, I presume?" the man asked as he entered the study.

To Gideon's practiced ear, the man spoke with an undeniable Haitian accent. He assumed the intruder to be a *Vodou Houngan*, better known in distorted popular culture as a *voodoo witchdoctor*.

"I'm sorry, I didn't order any Haitian take-out."

"Very amusing, Dr. Kano."

"Sorry, I didn't catch your name," Gideon said.

"You may call me, Moge," the Haitian said with a small bow. "Please excuse the interruption, Doctor, but I am here to engage your services."

"Sorry, Mr. Moge, I'm retired. If you can see yourself out the way you broke in, I am a bit busy right now. Seems the ghost of my wife is trying to warn me about something."

"I never expected you to be so humorous, Dr. Kano. I'm afraid I cannot take no as an answer. Please gather your research on *The Book of Xanadutha* and come with us."

"Us?"

Pushing past the grinning Moge, were three huge fellows who looked like a trio of professional wrestlers. Ritualistic scars and tattoos covered their foreheads and cheeks. Kane noticed that their eyes had a strange, almost blank expression. They were dead bodies animated by the spirit of slave demons. Moge had left three more homicidal watchdogs outside to deal with anyone foolish enough to interfere with the kidnapping of Dr. Kano.

"Well now, isn't that just wonderful? I'm having one swell night, Mr. Moge. Ghosts, witch doctors, and now zombies. If only we had pizza, then it would be a real party. The only problem is, you and your muscle have the wrong house. My name isn't Kano."

"Take the lying fool," Moge said as the hideous smile dropped from his face. "I am tired of his silly prattle."

"Prattle this," Gideon kicked back from his desk and brought his .45 to bear.

CHAPTER 8

ajar parked half a block away from Dr. Kano's address, in the driveway of an empty house sporting a realtor sign in the front yard. The nine-hour drive was sheer hell as she alternated from fervent prayer and silently cursing Mrs. Kerr, to grasping at any straw that might get her out of this mess. Hajar felt like she was suffocating from the stress. Taking a deep breath, Hajar bowed her head and closed her eyes one last time.

Dear Lord, please help me. I'm in big trouble. I'm in a snare and, no matter how I try, I can't find a way out. Please free me from the cage Mrs. Kerr has put me in. While I would love to rip her head off, the whole thing I said about her mother and the Russian sailors was way over the line, but I was royally pis—mad. I am sorry. I've got a gutter mouth when I get mad, but then again you know that better than anyone.

Hajar took a deep breath.

Lord, what I'm about to do is terrible, but I have no choice. You know my heart belongs to you, but I'm about to soil myself with this Dr. Kano and commit murder. I ask for strength to find a way out. Please guide me and help me turn this mess around. In Jesus's name I pray, Amen.

Feeling better, Hajar checked the vanity mirror one last time. Satisfied she was good to go, she opened the door and slid out. Instead of the matching clutch, she pulled out her bottomless bag and slung it over her shoulder. She felt like a fish out of water in a dress and heels.

Cursing the spiked heels and the suffocating dress that made her feel like she was being squeezed by a hungry anaconda, Hajar wobbled and stumbled down the block until she found herself in front of the Kano residence, a rambling, three-story Victorian gingerbread house. An imposing, twelve-foot-tall black iron fence surrounded the property.

"Obscure occult research must pay really well. Would you look at the size of this place? It takes up half the block."

Looking up, she saw a light in an upper-floor window. A moving shadow proved that someone was home. Hajar jumped as several muffled gunshots rang out.

Springing into action, she kicked off her heels and tossed her bag over the fence. Taking hold of the cold, black metal, she easily scampered over the iron barrier, landing in the thick, carpet-like grass on the other side.

From out of the concealing darkness, three enormous creatures, each baring sharp-chiseled teeth, lunged at her.

"Great, zombies," she muttered. "Can't Kano have a Doberman like a normal guy?"

She sidestepped the first zombie and swung a terrific left hook at the second. The powerful blow landed with a dull thud on his jaw, snapping the creature's head to the side. The hook, capable of shattering a human's jaw, did not register the slightest bit of pain on the enslaved creature. Snarling its annoyance, it backed her against the fence.

"Aw, crap," she muttered, as the thing grabbed her.

She was lifted high then flung several feet away. Instead of landing with a bone-shattering crunch, she did a graceful mid-air flip and landed lightly on her feet. "Let's try this again, shall we, cuddles?" She held out her hand toward the forgotten bag. "Kali, come to Mamma!"

The mystic blade slipped through the opening of the bag and flew across the yard, coming to rest in Hajar's outstretched hand.

"I'm hungry," Kali whined.

"Dinner is served," Hajar said and met the zombie charge.

❧❦❧

Refreshed from dispatching the pitiful creatures, Hajar ran to the side of the house where she found a heavy wooden trellis leading to a second-story balcony. The bag, at her direction, had become a backpack. Slipping on the pack, she caught the lattice and swiftly clambered up as several more gunshots sounded.

Gaining the modest balcony, Hajar peered through double French doors and saw a terrific fight in progress. She watched as a bearded, older man delivered a stunning right cross to a tall, thin black man. As the skinny man fell back, a two-legged zombie mountain grabbed the older man and tossed him like a rag doll across the room and over a large desk.

Having seen enough, Hajar drew Kali and kicked the door inward.

CHAPTER 9

Gideon slid across his desk, landing hard on the floor beyond. White-hot pain flashed up his arm as he fumbled with the hidden compartment under his desk.

He looked up sharply as the balcony door burst open. Expecting zombie reinforcements, he was surprised as a tall, scantily clad woman, wielding a wicked looking kukri, rushed in.

"Stay down, Grandpa," Hajar ordered Gideon. "I'll take care of this."

"Grandpa?" Gideon spat.

Launching herself upon his desk, Hajar spun and executed a roundhouse kick to the zombie's head. In a spray of blood and saliva, his head snapped right. Stumbling back against a bookcase, the creature bared a mouthful of sharp, pointed teeth. Hajar leapt at the supernatural creature, thrusting Kali into his chest. A bright blue flash lit the room as two supernatural forces collided. The creature howled as Kali consumed its unnatural life. Within seconds, the zombie collapsed and promptly crumbled to ash.

Hajar turned as a wild-eyed Moge rushed at her, a wicked looking machete raised high over his head. She stumbled over the body of a dead zombie. Losing her footing, she fell back on the body-littered floor.

Moge gave a high-pitched yell of victory as he closed in for the kill.

Before she could react, two ear-shattering reports sounded

as Gideon shot Moge with a .357 revolver he had retrieved from the secret compartment in the desk. Moge gasped once and fell dead at Hajar's feet.

"Good shooting, Doc," Hajar said as she rose to her feet. "Doctor Francis Kano, I presume?"

"Francis Kano?" Gideon asked. "Not even close. I go by Gideon, young lady. Gideon Kane. Let me guess. You're here about *The Book of Xanadutha,* am I right?"

"Well, yeah, but how did you know?"

Gideon pointed his gun at her. "Drop the fancy butter knife sweetheart and grab a handful of sky."

"'Grab a handful of sky'?" Hajar chuckled. "Who are you, Tex Ritter?"

"I'm the fellah with the gun, sweetheart."

In response, Gideon pulled back the hammer on his revolver.

"Okay, okay, don't shoot, Tex," she said, lowering Kali to the floor.

'*Hajar, what are you doing?*' asked an incredulous Kali. '*You can take this dried up husk of a man easily. Don't surrender, I'm still hungry!*'

'*You're always hungry. I know I can take him. However, we aren't here to fight, Kali, but to make friends. We need the doctor, so for now, we let him think he's in charge.*'

"Now what, big boy?" Hajar raised her hands high above her head, giving Dr. Kane a good look at her scrumptious figure. "Looks like I'm all yours."

"Does your mother know you run around dressed liked that?"

"Excuse me?"

"People will get the impression you are...well, open for business, if you know what I mean."

"Umm...yeah? I think that's the whole point."

"Kids today," he said, waving the gun. "Not an ounce of modesty. Let's go, Lady Godiva."

"Where are we going?"

"Why, down to the kitchen for Mrs. Morrison's world-famous chocolate chip cookies and milk, of course."

"Excuse me, did you say, *cookies and milk?*"

"Yeah, zombie bloodbaths always make me hungry. Now march, blondie."

CHAPTER 10

Gideon took the pitcher of milk and filled Hajar's glass. Swallowing the rich cookie, she slurped down the ice-cold milk. "These cookies are simply wonderful."

"Mrs. Morrison is a wizard in the kitchen."

Gideon helped himself to one of Hajar's cookies.

"Doc, the cookies are great, but are the sexy-cuffs really necessary?" Hajar asked, indicating her arm. She sat at his kitchen table, her left arm extended over her head and attached to the hanging pot rack by a pair of padded, hot-pink handcuffs. "I mean, after all, I did help you upstairs. I'm one of the good guys—umm, girls."

"The silly cuffs are just a precaution," he said, "until I get to the bottom of why tonight, of all nights, I am so popular. The Haitian didn't have any ID. All I have is the name, Moge."

"Well, I don't know about the stiffs taking a dirt nap upstairs," she said, "or the three zombies I killed in the yard, coming to save your butt. However, I have nothing to hide. I will tell you whatever you want to know."

"We'll see about that, young lady. Now hold this in your hand," he said, producing a smooth egg-shaped stone.

"Excuse me?" she said, looking nervously at the strange stone in his hand.

"I'll demonstrate," he said, holding the stone before him. "I am Tarzan of the Apes."

To her astonishment, the white stone turned dull black, like a lump of coal.

"I will be eighty-four years old on April fifth."

The stone turned a deep emerald green.

"Now that you know how the game is played, doll, hold out your hand."

Swallowing hard, Hajar extended her right hand, palm up. Gideon placed the now white stone in her palm and she closed her fingers.

"Now, dear, I want to know who you are."

"Hajar."

The stone turned green with black stripes.

"That is not entirely true. While that wasn't a strike, it was a foul ball and in this game, it is your only warning. I want the pure, unadulterated truth, or I will call the cops right now."

"Okay, I am Hajar now. Nine months ago I was called Maggie Black."

The stone turned green and Gideon stiffened.

Maggie Black means black pearl, he thought. *Hajar means forsaken. Looks like the cryptic, forsaken pearl is sitting in my kitchen eating my cookies. I need to press her and see where this goes.* "Why the name change? Are you running from the law?"

"My former employer hired someone to kill me. His assassin, a witch, faked my death and turned me into her slave. She is the one who wants information about *The Book of Xanadutha*."

"Why?"

"Because she has it, but can't decipher it. I came here to seduce you and to get your research about the book."

"Is that why you are wearing an outfit that is scarcely larger than a soap pad?"

"Yes."

"What kind of hold does this witch have on you that would make you prostitute yourself?"

"I—I—"

"Don't sit there and stammer, woman! I want to know the absolute truth. Now answer me."

"She just does," Hajar said softly as she looked down in shame. "Look, I can't go back empty handed. I'll do whatever you want, just please give me the information on the book. Please?"

Hajar reached up with her free hand and began to slide the shoulder strap of her dress down.

"Stop," he said.

She looked up at him, her eyes glistening with tears.

Gideon pursed his lips. "Tell me, Hajar, how did you get on your boss's shit list?"

Hajar hung her head. "As crazy as it sounds, for the last three years, I have worked for a fallen angel named Larry. He called me his Paladin. I did good works on his behalf, mostly dealing with supernatural threats against humanity, in order to win Larry a pardon and help him regain his position in Heaven. I loved him like a father. I thought he loved me, too."

"I've heard of Larry and his Paladins, though I have never met one till now. What changed?"

Hajar's lip began to quiver. "Heaven made Larry a deal. Restoration in exchange for killing me. He didn't think twice before he threw me under the bus."

"Why does Heaven want you dead?"

"I've asked myself that question a thousand times a day for the last nine months and I still don't know why."

Gideon rubbed his beard thoughtfully. "That mystical kukri you used on the zombie, where did you get it?"

"Larry gave it to me to even the odds when dealing with boogers and spooks. Her name is Kali."

"That's Kali? *The* Kali, the embodiment of death itself?"

"The one and only. Before you get any bright ideas, Doc, only I can touch her without becoming her dinner."

"I have heard stories and rumors. I thought the demon blade created by the witch Layla was a myth."

"You saw her in action."

Gideon paced a bit, the entire time keeping his eye on the stone in her hand. "Hajar, what happens after you get what you came for?"

Tears welled in her eyes and she bit he lip. "I can't—"

"Tell me."

"She told me—to kill you," she said as the damn holding back nine months of pain crumbled. "She said to take a finger as proof of your death and her power over me. Then I'll go back to my private hell and let that sick, disgusting animal violate and humiliate me even further."

"Hajar," Gideon said as his heart went out to the devastated young woman.

"I know what to do." Her voice dropped to an eerily calm tone. "It's so simple. That bitch, Mrs. Kerr, will never use me to hurt anyone else."

"Did you say, *Mrs. Kerr*?" Gideon's eyes flew wide with shock. "Hajar, listen to me—"

Hajar ignored Gideon and carefully placed the stone on the table. Looking around, like one in a trance, she spied a knife block sitting on the counter across the room.

"So—*simple*," she said.

"No!" Gideon cried as she effortlessly ripped the steel-pan rack down.

The pots and pans made a terrific crash as they rattled across the tiled floor. Hajar lunged for the knives. Gideon picked up a saucepot and bounced it off the block, sending it skidding out of her reach. Hajar screamed and ripped the steel wrist cuff asunder. Tossing the entire rack at Gideon, she dove for a big butcher knife.

"Stop!"

Hajar gasped and pulled up short as Virginia Kane's spirit appeared in her path. The apparition shoved Hajar backward, where she tripped over a skillet and landed hard on her back, bewildered.

"What the—a *ghost*?"

Gideon tackled Hajar. Before she could use her superior strength, he locked her arm into an unbreakable *ude hishigi juji gatame* arm lock.

"Let me go!" she screamed.

"Calm down, girl. I want to help you."

"No one can help me. Please let me die and finally have peace."

"Ginny, honey, can you help me out? I need the stone."

The white stone rolled through the maze of scattered pots and pans to within reach of Gideon.

"Let me go!"

"Hajar," Gideon said. "Look at me."

She looked at Gideon through wild, red-rimmed eyes. Gideon held up the stone. "Hajar, I swear upon all I hold dear that I will free you and you will walk this earth unafraid of anyone ever again."

The stone turned an emerald green.

"I don't believe you!"

"Honey, I know this is a lot to ask, but you have to trust me."

"Trust?" she asked. "There is no trust. Trust is bullshit! I trusted Larry and look where it has gotten me. I will never trust anything that still draws breath."

"I'm sorry, baby," he said. "I can't begin to imagine the hell you've been through, but killing yourself isn't the answer. I want to help."

"No, only when I'm dead, can I finally be free of this miserable existence."

"Make you a deal, sweetheart. Talk to me for an hour and, if you think I am full of bull, I'll give you back the butcher knife. What do you have to lose?"

"I don't trust you. It's a trick."

"My show of good faith," he said as he released the unbreakable hold.

She leapt forward and snatched a knife from the block.

Gideon stood and, with a warm smile, held out his hand. There was something reassuring in his clear blue eyes that calmed her.

"Can I really trust you?"

"Only one way to find out. Take my hand, darling."

Hajar tossed the knife over her shoulder. Reaching up, she took his hand.

"This better be good, old man."

"It will be a game changer."

"Sorry about your kitchen," she said sheepishly.

"It happens," he said with a smile. "I'll send you a bill."

Hajar smiled in spite of herself.

His arm around her shoulders, Gideon led the distraught woman into his spacious, comfortable living room and gently settled her onto the sofa. "Hajar, earlier, you mentioned the name of the dog who sent you to me."

"Yes, her name is Mrs. Kerr."

Hajar could see fire flash in Gideon's eyes.

"She would not be Salome Kerr would she?"

"Yes, that is the bitch. Do you know her?"

"Unfortunately, yes."

"When Mrs. Kerr faked my death and enslaved me, she promised that if I went along with her plans, that once she had what she wanted, I would be released."

"Salome Kerr is a murderer and a liar—and those are her good points. She'll never release you until she has used you up and there's nothing left. When she's done with you, she'll kill you herself."

Hajar swallowed hard.

"That's why we must persuade Mrs. Kerr in a way that she can't resist. First, how does she control you?"

Hajar lifted her head. "The black band. It is some kind of obedience collar. Through it, she can speak to me and hear my conversations. She can also punish. I have never thought anything could hurt so much."

"A witch's collar," he said. "I was afraid of that."

"Hurts like sin."

"The collar opens the door to Hell itself. Contrary to popular culture, Hell isn't the grand kingdom of the Devil. It was created...*engineered*...to imprison and torment Satan and his fallen angels. To give them a taste of the misery they have caused others. Hurts like sin is a massive understatement."

"What kind of sick mind would come up with such a thing?"

"The Black Circle—who, fortunately, are the only witches who have them. I hear they give these baubles out in exchange for power. According to my sources, there are almost one hundred people walking around wearing these."

"One hundred? That's unbelievable. Who would want to be a slave?"

"Believe it, Hajar. Sad as it is, in exchange for a quick trip up the corporate ladder, or political power, you would be surprised at what people would give their souls for. Heads of states, executives in key industries, military leaders, even major actors, all under the manipulation of a gaggle of sadistic witches. I figure that once enough of these collars are in place, they will easily control the world's wealth, military power, even public opinion. It will be the beginning of the end."

"Can you remove it?"

"Sorry. Only the one who collared you can do that. As a rule, once they go on, they don't come off.

"Oh God," Hajar said. "It's hopeless."

"Difficult, yes, but not hopeless. The most intricate puzzle has a solution. The most convoluted lock, a key. We will beat this, girl."

In spite of Dr. Kane's optimism, a frustrated Hajar sat back and idly glanced around the living room at all the photos and mementos along the walls. One large framed photo on the wall caught her attention. It was of a laughing woman held aloft by four smiling men.

"Who is that?" she asked, pointing to the black and white photo.

"You met her spirit in the kitchen. That is my wife Ginny, hamming it up with the Choirboys."

"Your house is haunted?"

"No. Ginny's shade showed up right before I got popular with zombies, voodoo doctors, and half-naked Paladins."

"Choirboys?" Hajar couldn't understand why the name seemed so tantalizingly familiar.

"A nickname Ginny hung on them and, yes, it was meant to be sarcastic. Jim Longhenry, Clyde Loyd, Randy Vanderloski, and Harold David. God, how I miss them."

"Good guys, I take it?"

"Pack of degenerates. They lived to embarrass Ginny and me. We lived in dread terror of birthdays, Christmas, or any obscure holiday they could find. I remember one birthday in particular, the entire family was over, even the pastor of our church and his wife. Anyway, we were having a lovely dinner when in marches this dominatrix stripper complete with leather suit and whip, looking for a very bad birthday boy."

"Oh no, they didn't," Hajar said as she managed a smile.

"Oh, yeah. I think her name was 'Helga, Mistress of Pain.'"

"You made that up."

"You can't make up things like this. Poor Ginny was so flustered she actually took a gun and went to find them. Luckily, she cooled off before anyone was killed. Although, now that I remember it, Randy and Clyde did limp around for a while. While they were a burden that would have broken Job, when the chips were down, they would have moved heaven and earth to help me. The sexy cuffs were a memento of that night, until someone had to go Wonder Woman and break prisoner/interrogator etiquette by destroying them."

"Sorry about that. Next time, I'll meekly await my horrible fate."

"As long as we've learned something, I forgive you," Gideon said with a chuckle.

A realization slammed into Hajar's brain like a bolt of lightning and she experienced an epiphany. "You have got to be freaking kidding me," she said softly, looking at Gideon in utter shock.

"Excuse me? Hajar, are you all right?"

"Let me get this straight, Doc. You deal with the occult, your wife is named Ginny, and your four buddies are known as the Choirboys." Hajar turned and stared at Gideon as though he had sprouted a third eye. "Do you, by any chance, have a nickname?"

Gideon smiled. "It was a long time ago, but folks used to call me Kamikaze."

"You're Kamikaze Kane, the guy from those crazy books! Those wonderful, impossible stories were about you, your wife, and crew!"

"Guilty. I can't believe you have actually read those dreadful tales. They went out of print years ago."

"Dreadful tales? Are you crazy, they were great!" Hajar

stared at him in delight. It was if she had suddenly discovered that Santa Clause and the Easter Bunny were real. "You had a run in with Mrs. Kerr, didn't you? That's why Mrs. Kerr hates your books so badly."

"I kicked her ass in Book Four, stomped it in Seven, and dropped an anvil on it in Eleven."

"Oh my God in Heaven, you don't mean to tell me that *Mistress Ramona Fay* is actually Mrs. Kerr?"

"Unfortunately, yes."

"Unbelievable! For the last nine months I have been at the beck and call of the worst villain from the entire series? I think I am having a brain aneurism."

"My grease monkey mechanic, Harold David, who always fancied himself a writer, begged me to chronicle our adventures. Well, let me tell you, that the sneaky little twerp pulled a fast one. Selecting our most audience-friendly adventures, twisting a few locations, and mixing up the bad guy names, Harold sold them to a New York publisher. Since few outside our profession even acknowledge the things that go bump in the night, no one ever took them as anything other than silly fiction.

"Insult to injury, he used our real names. By the time Ginny and I found out what he'd done, Harold had skipped town. Those fifteen adventures have haunted me ever since."

"What happened to Harold?"

"Just before he went into hiding, he made a mint off of our sweat and married some Hollywood starlet. Mindy…something. Only contact since was a single Christmas card back in '60."

"What happened to everyone else?"

Gideon rubbed his bearded chin. "Mrs. Kerr always was a pain in my rump. Back in '76, she kidnapped Ginny and her kid sister to draw me into a trap. While I saved my wife and sister-in-law, that bitch killed the Choir Boys, using an explosive booby-trap meant for me.

"The last I saw of her was in a burning castle in Zaire. As the place was coming down, I shot her and made my escape. I was at peace because I thought I had killed her over forty years ago. The thought of that waste of skin still breathing while my friends lie dead...well, it pisses me off."

"I wished you'd been a better shot. You know, Gideon, I didn't think it was possible, but you have had adventures wilder than mine."

"I still got one more left in me, darling. Say the word and we'll kick the stuffing out of Mrs. Kerr. I'm still itching for payback."

"The word is given, Commander," she said with a bright smile. For the first time in months, Hajar embraced hope. "So why Mrs. Kerr's obsession with *The Book of Xanadutha*?"

"She thinks it can lead her to the Tree of Life."

"So what does she want to do with it?" Hajar asked.

"Eat from the Tree, it is rumored, and one can become a God."

"Can one?"

"Oh, I suppose anything's possible."

"Can you understand *The Book of Xanadutha*?" she asked

"As far as I know, I am the only one on Earth who can."

"Yes!" Hajar exclaimed. "We can use this to our advantage."

"How?"

"This is the plan," she said as she bounced excitedly off the sofa. "While you slip into the house to steal the book, you capture me and Mrs. Kerr's crew. You offer Mrs. Kerr the book and a translation in exchange for our freedom. Fat Lady sings and everyone is happy. What do you think?"

Gideon stroked his beard thoughtfully. "Why would I offer my dreaded enemy—who murdered my best friends, kidnapped my wife, and tried to kill me—everything she ever wanted on a silver platter for a group of total strangers? Wouldn't I just shoot her on sight?"

"'Cause you are...hell, I don't know. Let me think on that one."

"Now explain something else to me. Why would I have to subdue you and your friends if I'm supposed to save them?"

"That is the slick part of the plan. It gives us plausible deniability."

"Plausible deniability? Been reading Tom Clancy have we?"

"Guilty. Okay, we need an out, in case this goes south."

"It could spell disaster if they turn the tables on me. Why not just tell them the truth and get them to cooperate with the plan?"

"We can't. They're too afraid of Mrs. Kerr. They would never try anything so risky for fear of their collars. It would only take a single word to ruin everything."

"Can't I just break in when no one's home?"

"We're not allowed to leave the house. It all comes down to this—we, mostly me, need an alibi. You can't imagine the hell Mrs. Kerr would unleash on me if she found out I was working with her nemesis. Yesterday, she caught me reading one of your adventures and was so pissed she nearly set the house on fire."

"I see she still loves me, after all these years."

"Yeah, that torch is still burning bright."

"How about I lock you all in the cellar? Do you have a cellar?"

"Won't work. Roland is a shape-shifter. He turns into a God-awful tiger creature and you couldn't build a door strong enough to stop him. Come to think of it, chains wouldn't stop him either. Then there's Megan. She has a mental control that is simply phenomenal. She can open any lock, just by thinking about it. I once saw her create a perfect Winsor knot in a neck tie, all while sitting in the adjacent room."

"That could be bad."

"But not insurmountable for the great, Kamikaze Kane."

"Suck up. You do have the germ of a plan, girl, but there are holes you could drive a truck through."

"Why do you keep trying to rain on my parade?"

"Just playing the Devil's advocate. My Ginny used to do that when I would dream up one of my crazy schemes. It feels strange to be on this side of the fence, but it's better to find the holes now, than when the bullets are whizzing by. We just have to work out the fine details."

The smile fell from her face. "Oh God, I'm a fool," she

cried, as sheer terror gripped her heart. "Mrs. Kerr can hear us through my collar. She knows!"

"Calm yourself, girl," Gideon said with a smile. 'No hoo-doo device can detect squat in my house. I've taken precautions to keep supernatural snooping to a minimum."

"Oh, thank God," she breathed. "I thought we had screwed up.

"We have another problem to consider."

"What?"

"Apparently, Mrs. Kerr isn't the only one interested in *The Book of Xanadutha* or the services of the world renowned Dr. Fancies Kano. We may be up to our neck in trouble before we know it."

"Yeah, something's fishy about the timing, that's for sure. What's up with the alias, Dr. Kano, anyway? Even my source fell for that."

"I don't know. For some completely incomprehensible reason my name keeps changing on all official documents, phone records—heck, even my high school yearbook changes every few weeks."

"That's strange."

"Tell me about it. It started some thirty years ago, when I started getting mail for a Dr. Keene. Something's either trying to protect me, or is playing one massively elaborate prank. I've found, from the many years I have dealt with the supernatural, sometimes it's just best to keep your mouth shut and go with it."

Hajar screamed as the band around her neck sparked and glowed.

"It's Mrs. Kerr," Gideon said. "She lost you when you came into my house. Now she's trying to reestablish contact. Quick, girl, run outside!"

Hajar stumbled across the kitchen and out a side door onto a wide, concrete patio. Gideon, close behind her, paused long enough to rip a dry erase board from his refrigerator.

Once outside the protection of the house, Mrs. Kerr's voice thundered in Maggie's ears. "Where are you, you stupid *bint*?" she demanded.

"Doing what you told me to do," Hajar hissed. "Why did you stun me? I'm at the doc's house, and everything was going smoothly, then bam! Felt like I was getting a hicky from a swarm of killer bees."

"How did I lose your signal?"

"I don't know how you lost me—"

Using the dry erase board, Gideon wrote, *RADIO THEA-TRE... PLAY ALONG.*

"—could be because Kano's house is like a crazy muse-um—geezer has all this eerie looking stuff. Ever since I got here, he's been wearing out my ears about all the freaky stuff he's collected over the years."

"I see," Mrs. Kerr said. "His collection could be causing in-terference with your collar. It is unsettling to have you off my radar, my dear. After all, we have become so close. Don't go back into the house. I'll think of something else."

"Don't go back into the house?" Hajar said, looking at Gid-eon.

Quickly, Gideon wrote: *SEX STARVED. DO ANY THING FOR YOU.*

"But I have him where I want him," she said. "This guy is so desperate for a little loving, he has almost burned my dress off with his eyes. I have him following me around like a pup-py."

Gideon gave her a thumbs up. Wiping the board, he wrote more script for her.

"Look, Mrs. Kerr, one night with this poor sap and, tomor-row, we will be half way to understanding *The Book of Xana-dutha.*"

"I find your new attitude refreshing, my dear Hajar."

"Yeah," Hajar said quietly. "I guess I'm tired of fighting a losing battle."

"Excellent," Mrs. Kerr said. "I am curious about this mys-terious, Doctor Kano. What is he like?"

"Doctor Kano?" she asked as Gideon wrote out a brief de-scription. "An African American, looks to be about sixty-five," Hajar said, reading the board. "He's tall, but still shorter than me, and bone thin."

"I expect a full report on his demise tomorrow morning at seven sharp."

Gideon stepped back into the house and called out, "Hajar, honey, where are you? I found us a nice bottle of wine in the cellar."

"Sounds like show time, my dear. I suggest you don't exhaust him too much, Hajar."

"Yeah, I'll take it easy on Methuselah."

"Remember, seven sharp, or I will give you a wakeup call you won't like."

Hajar moved within the safety of the house and closed the door. She found Gideon picking up pots and pans.

"Oh, here, let me do that," she said.

"How did it go?"

"Hook line, and sinker," she said as she stacked the pots on the counter. "What's the plan?"

"Mrs. Morrison left half a pan of Lasagna in the fridge. I'll warm it up while you go to my bedroom and take off that dress."

"Excuse me?"

"That didn't come out right," he said. "I don't want to rape you, if that is what's running through your head. If I jumped into bed with every half-naked woman who showed up at my door, I would never get anything done around here."

Hajar smiled. "Get that a lot, Doc?"

"Not really, but a man can dream. Look, I never had the heart to throw any of Ginny's things away. You're about the same size, so go upstairs, take a long hot shower, and, once properly dressed, come down for supper."

"What's the matter, Doc? Don't like my outfit?" Hajar gave him a pouty lip and sultry pose.

"Hajar, darling, I am old, but I am not dead. Change, *now*."

She stepped in close and hugged him hard before turning and trotting up the steps.

"This is the most excitement I've had since Zaire," he said with a broad grin. "I should have tried to kill myself years ago. Zombies, half-naked women, and now my dead wife. This is just like the good old days."

Gideon picked up his phone and dialed a number he had hoped never to have to use again. "Cecil?" he said when the line was picked up.

"No, Professor, this is Mark, Cecil's grandson. I take it you need a house cleaning?"

"Yes. Upstairs, first door on right. Three bodies and a pile of dust."

"That will be five, Dr. Kane."

"Prices have tripled since last time."

"According to records, last time was twenty-five years ago. No one needed to erase DNA back then. It was a simple cleaning job."

"The house will be empty after noon tomorrow."

"A pleasure dealing with you, Dr. Kane. My grandfather spoke very highly of you. Does this mean we can expect future *business*?"

"I pray that this is the last, Mark." Gideon hung up the phone.

CHAPTER 11

ajar toweled dried her hair and hummed a happy tune as the morning sun peeked through the window blinds. Her situation was still dire, but for the first time in weeks, she felt genuine hope.

"I'm not exactly an off the rack kind of girl. I can't believe his wife—blonde bombshell, wise-cracking Ginny—was my size. The books said she was tall, luscious, and all woman, but my goodness, I'm six foot, six, and most of my clothes are special order. I'll bet back in the day when folks were shorter, she really stood out in a crowd."

Dressed in a silk, cream-colored blouse and dark slacks, she was beginning to feel almost normal, almost like Maggie Black. Hajar wrinkled her nose at the thought of her former, happy life that seemed like a half-forgotten dream.

"Thank you, Jesus. I was drowning and you have thrown me a rope named Gideon Kane. I never imagined for a moment that those crazy stories were true, let alone thought I would actually meet the man. Even if he is in his eighties, he is still more man than any guy I ever met. Tough as nails, but good as gold. He is a blessing. Thank you."

When Hajar heard the faint rattle of pots and pans downstairs, she decided it was time to retrieve Kali and her bag. Slipping down the hallway, she entered the study, where the night before they had staged a murder for Mrs. Kerr's benefit. Moge became the poor, unfortunate Dr. Kano and lost a finger in the deal.

Hajar skirted the gruesome mess, retrieving her bag from Gideon's desk. She turned to leave when a neatly folded piece of paper spun across the room like a Frisbee and struck her in the forehead. Alarmed, but finding no threat, she opened the note and blanched.

"Son of a bitch."

༺༻

Livid, Hajar stomped down the graceful, curving stairs and into the kitchen where Gideon was busy fixing breakfast.

"Good morning," he said cheerily. "I see you've retrieved your hoodoo pocket book and butter knife. Maybe you can explain—"

"Shut up, Grandpa!" she snapped. "Just shut up."

"Excuse me, young lady?"

"Explain this," she said as she thrust the note at him.

Gideon took the note and, without a glance, tossed it into the plastic garbage pail. "How do you like your eggs?" he said. "You look like a sunny-side-up kind of gal."

"That was a suicide note. *Your* suicide note."

"Thanks a bunch, Ginny," he said, looking up.

"Explain yourself, old man."

"Nothing to explain, Hajar," he said, putting down his skillet. "That's none of your business."

"I'm making it my business."

"Darling, you have to understand, before you and the undead Hardy Boys showed up last night, I was an old man who had out lived his usefulness. I had nothing left, but to slowly rot. Why not go out by my own hand, instead of wasting away in a nursing home?"

"But last night—I thought you were going to help me."

"I still am. Hajar, you have given me something to live for, a chance to help one last time. One last hurrah, if you will. Besides, damsels in distress are my specialty."

"Let's get one thing straight, old man. I am not now, nor will I *ever* be a damsel in distress, do you hear me? Granted, I may have had my share of tight spots, but I'm the one doing the rescuing and not the other way around."

Gideon laughed. "That was for calling me an old man. I thought that would push a button or two. You are just like my Ginny, God rest her soul. Both of you are real firecrackers."

"Listen, funny man, when I am free of this blasted collar, you will live with me. Gideon, you will never be alone, not as long as I can still draw a breath."

"That is very touching, but you are a young woman in the prime of life. Trust me, you don't want to hang out with an old codger like me. Why, you don't even know me."

"What I do know is that you are a killer guy and, when I needed help, you came to my aid."

"I haven't done anything yet."

"You will."

"Very well, I won't kill myself if you won't."

"You drive a hard bargain," she said, "but it's a deal. We will beat this thing. I have a good feeling about this."

"I have a feeling your breakfast is getting cold. Now zip your lip, *woman*, and eat."

Sticking out her tongue and making a face, Hajar sat down and Gideon placed a steaming plate before her.

"Good eggs."

"Thanks. By the way, I just want to say, that while painted Hajar is rather attractive, war paint free Hajar is simply breathtaking. I have never seen eyes that shade of green before."

"Yeah, Doc, I prefer this face too, but a little paint is better than a lot of dead."

"I understand."

"How did you get started?" Hajar asked. "You know, with all the supernatural mumbo-jumbo."

"When I left the military, I got it in my head to start an airfreight company. Scraping together every nickel I had, along with a few I didn't, I bought a long-range, military C-47 from the army. With the Choirboys, as my employees, I formed Wild Geese Freight."

"What happened?"

"Ran into a real mess in Southeast Asia...'46, I think it

was. We flew in some machinery to Richard Mosley, a rich American industrialist trying to set up shop as a rice grower. He was an insufferable, elitist snob, but his money was good."

"I know this one," she said with a smile. "*Book One. Vietnamese Terror.*"

Gideon rolled his eyes. "Yes. Anyway, Richard saw the rich land, complete with dirt-cheap labor, as nothing less than a money machine. Anyway, a few pesky shape shifters put an end to that dream. Killed half his workforce and burned down his canning factory, not to mention kidnapping his only daughter to use in one of their cannibalistic rituals. Me and the boys stepped in and put an end to their mischief, once and for all. Richard was so overjoyed to have his daughter back that he completely remodeled my plane. Made her a flying marvel. Well, for the time, anyway."

"So you and your men got a taste for adventure?"

"To the contrary, all we wanted to do was put the hellish incident behind us and forget that it ever happened."

"I don't understand. What changed your minds?"

"I started getting an avalanche of letters and phone calls, begging for our help. So, being the suckers we were, we came running."

"How did they find you? Did you advertise?"

"No," he said, wiping his mouth with a napkin. "Somehow, people in trouble, from all over the world, would dream of us and the address where to reach us, or my phone number."

"That's freaky."

"To say the least. We never understood who or what was behind it all, but it was an eye-opening revelation to find what a mess this world is in. That being said, for the next twenty-eight years, we helped people by dealing with spooky, hellish things like that. We got so busy from the get go that Wild Geese Freight's first job was her last. Mosley funded our humanitarian endeavors, partly out of gratitude, partly because I married his headstrong, extremely spoiled daughter. I should have quit, then and there."

A saucer rose from the table, shot across the room, and shattered against the wall.

"Even dead, Ginny still has a temper," Gideon said with a wink.

Hajar chuckled.

"Anyway, the letters came to an abrupt halt in April 1976, right after Mrs. Kerr murdered my crew. It was just as well. I'd lost my taste for adventure and fighting things that go bump in the night. I guess you might say I retired. My Ginny and I drifted into research. Why, I was even a professor for a while and picked up the title Doctor Kane. From time to time, we tracked down the occasional relic that was too dangerous to be left lying around. Funny thing is, I never thought I would miss it like I have. What about you, Hajar?"

"I was a kindergarten teacher when I got kidnapped by a five year old."

Gideon blinked. "Excuse me?"

"It was Larry's warped way of testing a new recruit," Hajar said with a smile. "Anyway, I passed and he offered me the job as his Paladin. I really hated being a kindergarten teacher." Hajar tossed her napkin at her plate. "I can't believe it's over. I was in danger constantly, but it was the best time of my life. How could he do this to me?"

"Hajar dear, it is time for your check in," Gideon said, checking his watch. "Remember what we worked out last night?"

"Got it."

෴

Hajar walked out to the patio and took a seat in a heavy, wrought-iron chair.

"Mrs. Kerr, are you there?"

Seconds later, her collar tingled. "Did we have a pleasant evening, Hajar?"

"Pleasant? I did what I had to and I have what you want."

"Did you find his research useful?"

"I don't understand any of it, but I think we hit the mother lode. Dr. Kano claimed to have cracked the code, but he didn't have the book to test his theory."

"I will be happy to test his theory for him," Mrs. Kerr said. "Is Dr. Kano available for consultation?"

"No. He was a sweet, lonely old man who never harmed as much as a fly, and once I had what I came for, I put a bullet in his brain."

"Any impressions you would like to share?"

"I feel dirty."

"It will pass. When I am through with you, Hajar, you will do whatever I ask, to whomever I ask, and you won't even blink an eye."

"Wonderful."

"You have a long drive before you, so leave now."

"I'm on my way."

CHAPTER 12

Hajar endured the long, monotonous drive with only stops for fuel. In the backseat of her Civic sat two file boxes filled with "research" on *The Book of Xanadutha*. It was actually back issues of Popular Science. In the trunk lay a small box that held the severed right forefinger of the mysterious Moge.

❧❧❧

Cleaning a side table to a high sheen was a mountain of a man with blond hair and piercing blue eyes. The big man would have been ruggedly handsome, but for the myriad of scars that crossed his face and neck.

He wore the simple white T-shirt and jeans that Mrs. Kerr favored for her family. "Well, would you look at what the cat drug in," Roland Gunn said as Hajar opened the front door. A lecherous smile creased the big man's face as his eyes devoured her.

"Don't start on me," she said. "I'm not in the mood."

"Speaking of moods, Mrs. Kerr has been stoked over your little trip. Never seen her so happy."

"Where is Mrs. Kerr?" Hajar asked.

"She said something came up and it will be late before she gets home. She said to tell you that she expects you to be waiting for her at the front door ready to decipher the book."

"Wonderful. Where are Megan and Yumi?"

"Megan has laundry and Yumi is knee deep in crapper detail."

"Okay. I'll be in my room."

"Need company?"

"Not, you, you big jerk."

"Now, don't be mad. I was only fooling around. What do you think of that shine?" he asked, indicating the table.

"You missed a spot," she said.

"Where?"

"There," she said as she coughed and spat upon the table.

Hajar smiled and waved the irate man off as she walked to her room to await tonight's festivities.

ୄୡୄ

The small, sputtering Ford pulled up the long drive to the isolated, two-story house. A lighted *Pizza Pirate* sign proclaimed the ten-year-old lime-green Taurus was an official delivery vehicle for the local fast food chain.

A bespectacled, elderly man, wearing an oversized windbreaker and utterly silly-looking plastic pirate hat, slowly toted two boxes up the front steps of the big house.

With shaking hands, he punched the doorbell several times.

The door flew open, revealing a scowling Roland. "I heard you the first time, old man," he snapped. "What do you want?"

"I—I got your order," stammered the shaking man. "That'll be $31.59."

"Yah got the wrong house old man."

"No—this has to be it."

"You don't listen so good, do you?"

The old man sniffled and was on the verge of tears. "If I wrote down the wrong address again, they'll fire me. I need this job."

"Look dude, how about I take it off your hands for say...fifteen bucks?"

"Make it an even twenty, and I'll throw in a side of breadsticks and soda."

"Done."

eɔeɔ

"Look at what this guy has for us to eat tonight," Roland shouted as he carried the pizza into the kitchen. Yumi, Megan, and Hajar soon entered the large, old-fashioned decorated kitchen.

"Delivery guy got the wrong house and we reap the rewards," Roland said.

"Hajar, when did you get home?" Megan asked as she embraced her friend.

"A little while ago. I needed to lie down."

"Hajar, I'm sorry," Yumi said. The small, wiry man was covered with a myriad of tattoos.

"It'll be all right," she said through her teeth.

"Dig in guys," Roland said. "We even got soda."

"No," Hajar said. "Let's make this a special dinner. You have worked hard today, so let me serve you in the dining room."

"Hell, yeah," Roland said. "Be nice to be waited on for a change."

"Are you sure, Hajar?" Megan asked.

"It'll be fun. Now go."

eɔeɔ

Pulling four water glasses from the shelf, Hajar set them on the granite counter. She looked around, to make sure she was alone, then removed a small plastic vial from her pocket. Into three of the four glasses, she poured an equal amount of the drug. Taking the large bottle of soda and an ice tray from the refrigerator, she dropped three ice cubes into each glass, before filling them to the brim and stirring each one quickly with a spoon. Then she moved to the sink, tossed in the plastic vial, switched on the garbage disposal, and destroyed the evidence.

Leaving out the ice, she poured soda into the fourth, drug-free glass. The she loaded up plates, pizza, and the tainted drinks and carried them out to her unsuspecting family.

CHAPTER 13

Hajar opened the side door and ushered Gideon into the house. Smiling broadly, she gave him a thumbs up. Carrying a big, stuffed duffle bag over his shoulder, he followed her to where Megan, Yumi, and Roland lay sleeping at the dinner table.

Gideon opened the bag and produced a handful of big yellow zip ties—the kind police use as handcuffs.

Together, Hajar and Gideon secured the gang to the sturdy wooden dining room chairs.

Gideon had his small dry-erase board, so the two could communicate without tipping off Mrs. Kerr. While Gideon secured Roland's ankles, Hajar took the board, wrote quickly, then flipped the board around. *You're my hero.*

Gideon turned red, which surprised and delighted her. She wiped the board then wrote, *My turn. Make it look good, old man.*

Gideon fished about in the bag and produced a heavy pair of police hinged handcuffs that gleamed dully in the room's dim light.

Hajar smiled and wrote: *What? Out of padded pink cuffs, Dr. Love?*

Gideon blushed furiously and rolled his eyes.

Hajar suppressed a giggle as she took her seat, slipping her hands behind her back and through the heavy wooden slats of the chair.

Gideon carefully encased her wrists in steel, making sure

not to pinch her skin. Satisfied, he began to bind her to the chair using five times the zip ties he had used on her companions. Soon, Hajar, even with her enormous strength, could not budge a muscle.

After checking to make sure her circulation was unimpeded, he produced a clear plastic tube and placed it to her lips. Hajar smiled and gave him a wink, before she drank the tasteless drug.

ↂↂↂ

"Hajar, wake up," Megan hissed.

Eyes closed, Hajar moaned and smacked her dry lips. "I feel...so funny..."

Megan managed to bump her chair into Hajar's. "Wake up!"

"What the—" Hajar tried to move. "What happened?"

"We got freaking blindsided," Roland snapped. Great beads of sweat rolled down his face as he strained in vain against his bonds.

"Change, you big douf," Hajar snapped.

"I can't," he said. "That thing on the table is screwing up my power."

In the midst of the remains from their half-eaten meal lay an evil-looking idol with glowing green eyes. About the size of a quart jar of pickles, the mystic idol radiated, vibrated, and pulsed, making those within the room feel odd and slightly woozy.

"I can't do anything either," Megan said. "We're dead."

"We have to get away," Hajar said. "Try and bounce your chairs. Maybe we can get out of range."

"How about we all sit still and enjoy each other's company?" Gideon emerged from the shadows. In his hand, he held a gleaming .45.

"Who are you?" Yumi snapped. "Why are you doing this?"

"You are that old fart who sold me the pizza," Roland said. "You set us up!"

"Way to go, hairball," Yumi said.

"Don't be mad, big guy," Gideon said. "I have a gift for you." With a grin, he plopped the cheesy pirate hat on Roland's head and snapped the elastic band under his chin. "That's for being an extra special customer."

Roland swore blackly and tried to dislodge the ridiculous hat, but it stayed locked in place, much to Gideon's pleasure.

"Your lovely boss and I go way back and I wanted to surprise her without any interference from her henchmen."

"Let us go," Hajar screamed.

"Listen to me." Gideon lowered his voice. "I've been searching for that hell spawn, Mrs. Kerr, for over thirty years and I intend that my pretty face will be the last thing she ever sees before I send her to hell."

"You can't do this," Megan pleaded as the color left her face.

"I could have just as easily poisoned the soda and pizza, but I'm not a murderer. Salome's death will be justice, not murder."

"You'll be killing us," Yumi said.

Inwardly jubilant, Hajar snarled, moaning her frustration and rage for the benefit of her companions.

Before she could voice her indignant outrage, approaching car lights, shining through the concealing curtains, told them they were about to have company.

The four captives exploded in a group cry for help. Hajar especially yelled with all her might. The sharp, unmistakable sound of a racked pistol slide brought instant silence.

"I want this little surprise party to go off without a hitch, so give me no trouble, and I'll give you no trouble. Understand?"

Three answered with a silent head nod. Hajar snarled in defiance.

Holding a finger to his lips, Gideon paused before Hajar and pressed the barrel against her forehead. "I said hush and I mean hush, or Mrs. Kerr will have company on the road to hell."

Hajar closed her eyes and gritted her teeth to keep from smiling.

CHAPTER 14

"What the hell's wrong with the lights?" Mrs. Kerr barked as she barged into the dark foyer. "Where's Hajar? I gave explicit instructions for her to greet me at the door. She will pay dearly for this." She paused and looked around. "Where is everyone? Last time I left them alone, I came home to a free-for-all. What are those idiots up to now?"

Her fiery anger growing by leaps and bounds, she charged into the dining room. "Bloody hell?" she said as she beheld her slaves' dire situation.

Hajar screamed a warning, but it was too late. Mrs. Kerr grunted as she was slammed into from behind. Gideon grabbed the woman and bashed her into the wall, twice, before tossing her into the dining room, where she landed in a crumpled heap.

"*Dome triesioo,*" she cried, but to her dismay, the spell fell apart in the spiritual dampening field.

Two more meaty blows connected, stunning the helpless witch and removing all resistance. Quickly and efficiently, her hands were drawn behind her back and zip-tied together. Dragged to her feet, Mrs. Kerr was dumped into an armless chair. Sputtering useless incantations, she was lashed tightly into place.

"Comfy?"

"Release me, or you will pay," she screamed.

With a sharp "snick," the lights blazed to life and the captives squinted against the harsh glare.

Gideon stood by the light switch, a smile playing at his lips. "Hey, sweetie. Remember me?"

"Oh my God!" Mrs. Kerr breathed as her eyes grew wide with sheer terror. "Kane, it can't be you. You're dead. I killed you."

"I'm touched that you remember me, Mrs. Kerr. How long has it been?"

"Please, let's talk about this."

Kane strode across the room and gave Mrs. Kerr a savage right to her nose. "How's that for dialog, baby?"

"Please don't kill me, I beg of you. I'll give you anything. I have money—"

Kane slammed a left into her jaw. "You know, I forgot how much fun it is punching you in the face."

"Please, no. Quit hitting me. Let's talk about this. We can reach an agreement!"

"Agreement? You killed the best friends I had in the entire world, not to mention you tried to kill my wife and myself. What do we possibly have to talk about that doesn't end with your death, you sadistic bitch?"

"Please, no."

"Don't worry. This won't be quick. I'm going to savor the experience." Wearing a big smile, Gideon walked over to the table. "I really hated to use up my last Ganish, but this is a special occasion, and I didn't know what devilish powers any of your minions might have up their collective sleeves. I know, from my surveillance, that Conan the Barbarian here is a shape shifter, mercenary, and lousy tipper. Mr. Sulu, while a snappy dresser, is a hired killer and general thug, with an addiction to body art. Love the swimming koi by the way. Hannah Montana—I don't have a clue, but she's cute as a button. If you're working for this snake, you must have something really nasty up your sleeve. This brings us to our last contestant, as well as the loudest one in the bunch. She's a very naughty girl who did her level best to spoil our little reunion, Mrs. Kerr. I hope you give her a proper reprimand for trying to be a party pooper."

He gave Hajar a smirk, receiving a black response. "Temper, temper," he said. "Do you kiss your mother with that mouth? Anyway, Miss Gutter-Mouth here is better known to the FBI and America's Most Wanted, as the Blur Bandit. Here's a woman of phenomenal strength and skill who, instead of leading a productive life, has decided to take the low road by robbing banks. I really hate thieves."

Gideon bent down and looked Hajar in the eye. "While you're very easy on the eyes and easy to dismiss, after seeing the results of your bloody little rampage in Idaho, you are without a doubt the toughest badass of the bunch. Still, I'm at a loss at what hoodoo gives you your athletic ability."

"Go to hell," Hajar snapped.

"Care to give me a hint, Mrs. Kerr?" Gideon asked.

"Go fish," Mrs. Kerr snapped.

"You're a bit tall—outside of a college volleyball team, that is—but otherwise a completely normal-looking woman who incorporates physical skills and reflexes that would put an entire Olympic Team to shame. Your reflexes are scary fast and you're stronger than five strong men, not to mention your superb fighting skills. From what I've observed, you're as dangerous as a platoon of Devil Dogs. Back in the day, some fifty-eight years ago, I was *something*. But on my very best day, you would have been a handful.

"The Ganish here seems to have zero effect on your strength and, frankly, sweetheart, that scares the hell out of me. Good thing I gave you the deluxe spa treatment, just in case." Gideon pinched her cheek playfully. "Bad as you are, don't you just make the cutest-looking damsel in distress, though?"

Enraged by his intentional jab at her personal pet peeve, Hajar dropped the playacting, let loose with a verbal barrage, and strained with all her might to get at Gideon.

"I love you, too," he said, patting her on the head. "Write when you get to the supermax, doll.

"And that leaves just queen rat herself—the main event of tonight's show. I hate to give away the ending, but it's a killer."

"You can't kill me," Mrs. Kerr screamed. "I'm unarmed, tied to a chair. What happened to your Christian values? What would Jesus think of cold-blooded murder?"

"Funny you should bring up the whole, cold-blooded murder thing. Remember the Choirboys?"

"But that was years ago. What about turning the other cheek?"

Gideon chuckled and took out his .45, the one he named Lightning. "This is for the best friends I ever had," he said, bringing up the gun muzzle and pressing it hard against the center of Mrs. Kerr's forehead. "May they rest in peace, while you fry in Hell, where you so richly belong. Say goodnight, Gracie."

The family shouted and cried in terror as Gideon's finger rested upon the trigger.

"Am I missing something here?" he asked, frowning. "Normally, anyone who knows you, wants you dead, Mrs. Kerr."

"Why don't you ask them?" Mrs. Kerr said as she spit out a bloody tooth.

Gideon lowered the hammer on his pistol and holstered the weapon. Without taking his eyes off Mrs. Kerr, he moved to the table. Cutting the strap that kept her chair locked to the table, he spun Megan around.

"Please don't kill, Mrs. Kerr, I'm begging you. If she dies, the pain won't stop. The pain won't ever stop!"

"What's your name, darling?"

"Megan."

"A very pretty name, for a very pretty girl. Okay, Megan, honey, what are you talking about? What pain?"

"If we don't do what she says, she hurts us with our collars. If she dies, the pain won't ever stop."

"What did you do to them, you snake?"

Mrs. Kerr gave him a ghastly smile of dripping blood and broken teeth. "They all wear witch collars that are linked to me. I own them and, if I die, they will suffer unimaginable hell."

"That's inhuman!"

"It's effective."

Gideon took up a glass from the table and shattered it against the wall near Mrs. Kerr. "Release them."

"No."

"If you value your life, let them go."

"You kill me and they're the ones who'll suffer, you big Boy Scout."

Gideon stalked toward Mrs. Kerr.

"Lay another hand on me, Kamikaze, and I'll do this."

The captives screamed in utter pain.

"Stop it, you monster!"

"Very well," Mrs. Kerr said. "Looks like we have a Mexican standoff, Kane."

"Looks like. How do we resolve this?"

"Die."

"Besides that."

"They're mine and they'll damn well stay that way until I die. The most you can do for these pathetic fools is to walk away and let them go back to serving me."

"I have an alternative plan," Gideon said after a moment of thought.

"Oh really? And what would that be?"

"I get you the Tree in exchange for your servants' freedom."

Mrs. Kerr gasped. "How did you know about that?"

"Who you talking to? I have known about your silly obsession with the Tree since '59. Besides, while I was waiting to kill you, I rummaged around looking for something to read. By the way, the owner of the *Illustrated Karma Sutra* should be ashamed of yourself."

All eyes fell on Roland, who gave a toothy smile.

"Anyway, I just went through a couple of boxes of twenty-dollar words strung together about *The Book of Xanadutha*. They just confirmed what everyone already knows, that the book's a road map to Eden and the Tree of Life. Oh, by the way, I used all that boring, dry-as-dust research to start one hell of a barbeque out back—after I discovered the secret location of the Tree of Life."

"Sorry bastard," Mrs. Kerr cried. "That was for me!"

"I love our little pet names. Do we have a deal or not?"

"You'll do this—for me?" Mrs. Kerr asked. "I don't understand. You know full well what the consequences would be if I eat of the fruit."

"*Possible* consequences. It could turn you into a God, or give you indigestion. Rumor aside, no one really knows the truth."

"It *is* the truth, you moron. I would trade every life on this miserable rock in space for a chance to transcend mortal existence."

"I know you would. Unlike you, I have come to cherish life in my old age. It's a gift greater than all the treasure in the world…well, except yours. You, I consider a cancer that would be best for everyone if I cut it out."

"Why would you do this? My slaves are scum, nothing more than killers and outcasts. You said so yourself. They're not worth the effort."

"I disagree. A few rough edges, perhaps. Nevertheless, as much as you deserve death, I won't let them take the fall with you. I just don't have it in me."

"You're pathetic."

Gideon grunted in response.

"Very well, Kane. I accept your offer. Go get the Tree and I'll release them when you get back."

"I was born at night, but it wasn't last night. You perform the ritual of Hammurabi and release them to me. This road's going to be rock hard and I could use some help."

"They're yours. However, the ritual is out of the question."

"Can't say I didn't try to be reasonable."

Gideon took out his cell phone.

"What are you doing?"

"Plan 'B.' Calling a friend, of a friend, who knows someone in The Black Circle. I'm going to rat out the thief who stole their witch collars. In case you're wondering, that would be you, Mrs. Kerr. The evidence is sitting around the table. I shudder to think what they'll put you folks through—most likely white slavery sex trade for the women and forced work camps for the men—but at least you'll be alive and free of this snake.

"Mrs. Kerr, on the other hand, will no doubt get a taste of

the business end of one of those damn collars she loves so much. Ironic, don't you think?"

Megan began to cry.

"Okay, you win!" Mrs. Kerr cried. "I'll perform the damn ritual and you can take them with you, however, I keep the book as insurance."

"Disable the tracking and eavesdropping capabilities."

"No."

"I didn't ask. I believe that the Circle, in time, can also use this to their advantage. I have it on good authority that a crack hunter/killer team is, as we speak, searching for you."

Mrs. Kerr twisted her head and gritted her teeth. "Very well. I can still punish them if you even think about double-crossing me, Kane. I want daily updates or else."

"Fair enough."

Gideon picked up the Ganish and looped a cord around its fat neck. Taking it over to Mrs. Kerr, he slipped the loop around her neck. Taking her by the back of the chair, he slid Mrs. Kerr into the far corner.

In a flash, Roland transformed into the were-beast, ripping apart the plastic cuffs and tearing the plastic hat from his mis-shapen head.

Part tiger, part man, and entirely terrifying, he shattered the table and gave an ear shattering roar before resuming his human form. He took a serrated knife and cut the ties on Yumi's wrists.

The bindings holding Megan simply fell off without a sound.

"Shit," Roland cried as Kali swooped into the room barely missing his head. Falling in a spinning arc, she severed, in one stroke, the plastic ties and the handcuffs encasing Hajar's wrists.

"Are you all right, Hajar?" Megan asked.

"I am now, sweetie, but I'll be on top of the world after I kick Kane's ass."

"I just bought those cuffs," Gideon said as he tossed her the key. "Some people have no regard for the property of others."

Hajar kept silent, but her eyes bored holes through Gideon

as she unlocked each half of the broken cuffs. Reaching down, she picked up Kali and cut her legs free.

"What should we do?" Megan asked.

"Rip his throat out," Roland snarled.

"Gideon Kane's your new boss," Mrs. Kerr said. "As much as I hate to admit this, he's one hell of a leader. Go with Kane and do whatever he says, whenever he says it, or you'll answer to me. Find my prize, and I'll free you. Screw this up, and I'll make damn sure you pay dearly."

"Looks like we do what Mr. Wonderful says," Hajar said. "But when this is over, old man, we're going to go a round."

"Yes, you must definitely make your mother proud," Gideon said.

"My mother's dead, for your information."

"Died of shame, no doubt," Gideon said.

Hajar started to respond when Gideon silenced her by drawing Thunder. "Listen up, people, pack a bag, grab a weapon or two, and meet me out on the front porch in fifteen minutes. The clock's ticking." Holstering his weapon, he wrote furiously in a small leather notebook. "Mrs. Kerr, the Ganish will last about an hour or so and should keep you out of trouble while we take our leave. You'll meet me at this airfield and, there we'll perform the ritual," He tore a page from the notebook and handed it to here. "Time and date are at the bottom."

Mrs. Kerr threw back her head and laughed.

"What's so funny?"

"The great Kamikaze Kane working for me. How does it feel to be my bitch, Kane?"

He leaned in and whispered, "Feels like this."

In one smooth motion, he drew Lightning and fired. The big bullet ripped through the black leather shoe and the side of Mrs. Kerr's foot before splintering the floor.

She screamed from the excruciating wound.

Gideon laughed as he turned and walked out.

CHAPTER 15

Gideon Kane's Baja Gold, 1970 GTO rumbled into a parking space in front of the Travelers Rest Motel, followed closely by Hajar's Civic. Gideon emerged from the immaculate classic car and stretched his back.

"Cool car, Doc," Megan said. "I love the way it rumbles."

"Thanks, Megan. I always had a weakness for muscle cars."

"Can I ride—"

"*You* are riding with me," snapped Hajar.

"But, Hajar—"

"No, buts, Shortstack." Loudly tapping her nail on the metal top of her car, she gave Gideon a look that would freeze lava.

"Are you all right, Hajar?" he asked.

"I'm fine. Just fine."

"Oh shit," Yumi and Roland said in unison.

They both knew that when Hajar said she was fine, all hell was about to break loose.

"Dr. Kane," Yumi said. "I just want to thank you for getting us away from that monster."

"You're welcome, son."

"He ain't done nothing yet, but drug us and make us look like a bunch of rookie retards," Roland snapped.

"But I gave you a nifty hat to make up for it," Gideon said. "Yo, ho, ho!"

Roland took a step toward Gideon and opened his mouth,

but Yumi grabbed him by the arm. "Do you like swabbing toilets and waiting on Mrs. Kerr hand and foot?" he hissed.

"No," Roland said through clenched teeth. "I guess he did give Mrs. Kerr a taste of her own medicine. Popping a cap in her foot, now that was funny as hell."

"Why don't you four go and get us a table at the restaurant while I book some rooms." Gideon turned and walked to the office.

"Good, I am starving," Roland said. "But hell will freeze over before I eat pizza again."

"Coming, Hajar?" Megan asked.

"Go on, Shortstack. I want a few words with Mr. Wonderful first."

"Hajar," Yumi said. "I know you're still pissed, but let it go. Doc has given us our best chance of getting away from Mrs. Kerr. Don't mess this up."

"Save me a seat, Shortstack."

Hajar then turned and stalked after Gideon.

ᴇᴔᴇᴔ

Hajar found Gideon alone in the motel office, looking at a brochure for a haunted hayride. A small sign on the neat counter said the clerk would be back in ten minutes.

"Good. I think we need to talk," he said, as he replaced the flyer in a rack.

She walked up to him and stabbed her finger into his chest. "You want to talk, old man? I was thinking more along the lines of taking you out back and kicking your sorry ass."

"If I didn't know better, I would say you were miffed at me, Hajar," he said with a grin.

"Miffed?" She grabbed him by the lapel of his sport jacket, pulled him close, and smiled. "It worked. Thank God in heaven, it worked."

"All we did was get past a rough spot in the road. We still have a whale of a journey before us."

"I'm out of that hellish house and that's a major victory."

"Fortunately for us, your rather fragile emotional state didn't surface."

"To what fragile emotional state are you referring, Dr. Kane?" she asked, her tone tinged with frost. "Are you saying I'm crazy?"

Gideon smiled and took her face in his hands. "Betrayed by Larry and delivered into the hands of Mrs. Kerr was like dropping you into a mental meat grinder. Face it. You were cracking under the strain."

"I wouldn't say cracking...*exactly*."

"Really? I think we both remember the knife incident in my kitchen."

"Let's keep that little tidbit under our hats, shall we?" she said, rolling her eyes. "Okay, I'll admit I've been a bit on edge, but I feel much better now, thanks to you."

"Hajar, I think it would be a good idea for us to not appear too chummy. The last thing we need is for Mrs. Kerr to suspect we're in cahoots. She still has control of those collars."

"Yeah, I thought of that, too. Roland or Yumi could use that against me if things go south." She let out a deep, noisy breath. "You're just way too slick for your own good, old man."

"I'm glad that's settled," he said with a smile, "but you call me an old man again and I'll take you out back and kick your pretty ass."

"Bring it on," she said softly. "Why can't I find a good guy like you?"

"You will. He just won't be as good looking."

Hajar snorted and playfully punched Gideon in the arm. "One last, *small* point I need to clear up."

"What's that?"

Quick as a striking serpent, she lashed out and slapped him hard across the face. The blow sounded like a gunshot in the tiny office.

"Ow!"

"That little love tap was for being a total smartass and calling me a damsel in distress."

"You folks need a room?" asked the wide-eyed night clerk as he entered the office.

"Do it again and I really will kick your old, wrinkled ass," she snapped. "You got me, old man?"

Hajar strutted past the confused night clerk and pushed through the door.

"Still want a room, mister? Your lady seemed kind of mad."

"Oh that?" Gideon said as he rubbed his stinging jaw. "Don't worry about it. That was just foreplay."

CHAPTER 16

A re we lost?" Yumi asked from the front passenger seat of the GTO.

"Unfortunately, I know exactly where we are," Gideon said. "Desperate times call for desperate action."

"Excuse me?" Yumi asked. "Did you say something about desperation?"

"No, just thinking out loud." Gideon rubbed his still sore jaw and chuckled. "Hajar has a punch like a ton of bricks."

"Tell me about it." Yumi took off his Wayfarers and shoved them into his shirt pocket. "I only wanted to make a little time with the new girl—ease the tension, if you know what I mean. Anyway, she about ripped off my head, just before she tossed me through a window."

"That's nothing," Roland said. "I merely made an innocent comment about her boobs being nice and squeezable, and that bitch broke my nose. Can't she take a compliment?"

"She'll make a man a good sparring partner one day," Gideon said.

"How much farther to this stupid museum of yours?" Roland asked. "I hate boring museums. Hey, Doc, why don't you just drop me off at the local strip club and pick me up later? Can you spot me a hundred or so?"

"Shut up, Hairball," Yumi said. "We got a job to do."

Roland crossed his arms and slipped into a dark mood. "Can you at least put on some music? Something from this century please?"

"Sorry, my portable Victrola is in the trunk."

"Is that a digital player?"

Yumi laughed.

"Have patience, Mr. Gunn, we are almost there," Gideon said.

"With all due respect, Doc," Yumi said. "Before the GPS had a nervous breakdown and quit, it didn't have a listing for Bulls Gap, Pennsylvania. In fact, I can't even find this highway on the map."

"I know. Just trust me."

☙☙

Gideon eased the GTO off the mysterious highway and down a single-lane gravel road where he crossed an abandoned set of railroad tracks. Ahead of them, a small unpretentious sign proclaimed, *Bulls Gap, Pennsylvania. POP: 359.*

Gideon drove down the tree-lined street, passing The Blue Bird Diner, Fancher's Family Barbershop, and Margo's Funeral Parlor, before pulling into the first of three parking spaces dedicated to the Bulls Gap's Museum of Milking History.

"Lord Jesus, please be with me," he said before switching off the engine.

"You've got to be kidding me," Roland exclaimed, staring in shock at the museum. "Is this a joke, Doc? We traveled all this freaking way for this hole-in-the-wall tourist trap?"

☙☙

Hajar and Megan pulled into the spot next to them and, like Roland, stared in puzzlement at the small benign structure.

"The old man has gone freaking bonkers," Megan said. "I think someone has spiked his Geritol."

"Amen."

"Hajar," Ginny said, appearing beside her.

Hajar jumped, but Megan didn't seem to see or hear the apparition.

"This is very, very bad. Don't be fooled by the silly façade.

This is a hellish place. Whatever you do, don't let Gideon go in alone, and be prepared for the fight of your life."

Hajar's right hand fell to her pistol, while her left checked to make sure Kali was ready for action.

'*Time to eat?*' Kali asked.

'*I sure hope not.*'

∽∾∽

The Bulls Gap's Museum of Milking History was a single-story, brick storefront that had a life-sized, hot-pink plastic cow standing by the door. Hanging from its neck was a hand-lettered sign that said, *To miss the world famous Milking Museum would be a cow-tastrophe! Tours by appointment only.*

Hand on the car door lever, Gideon glanced into his rear-view mirror, where his eyes met Roland's ice-hard glare.

"Do we have a problem, pumpkin?" Gideon asked, turning around in his seat.

"I let Mrs. Kerr push me around because I had no choice. You, on the other hand, ain't shit. Just an old fart that used to be somebody back in the caveman days. If anybody's going to be calling the shots around here, it's me."

"After carefully considering your offer, Mr. Gunn, I must decline. My counter offer is for you to kiss my ass."

Yumi snickered.

"Yumi, since you seem to be the only adult in the group, I'm leaving you in charge. Keep everyone here with the cars while I go in. I think it would be safer."

"What do you mean, safer?" Roland asked. "This is a freak-ing hick milking museum for crying out loud!"

"A precaution," Gideon said. "Evil hides behind smiling faces. Better safe than sorry."

"Evil hides behind smiling faces?" Roland cried. "Where did you get that little gem of wisdom from? A fortune cookie? We're smack in the middle of downtown Dogpatch USA! You better tell me what you're hiding, before I lose my temper."

"Think on this, cupcake," Gideon said as he surprised Roland with the back of his hand.

Roland let loose with a black stream of profanity as he and Gideon faced each other, nose to nose across the seat.

"I've killed men for less," screamed the humiliated Roland.

"We have work to do, youngster," Gideon said, "and I don't have time to teach a cull like you a lesson in manners. So stow your piss-poor attitude before I lose *my* temper."

"Let's go, Grandpa! The only lessons being taught 'round here will be by me."

The sound of a cocked hammer made Roland flinch. Out of the corner of his eye, he glimpsed the barrel of gun.

"You heard the man, hairball. Now back down or I'll put you down for good," Yumi said. "Doc's trying to help us, you moron."

"You believe him all you want. Me and the girls don't trust him one bit. He's up to something. Nobody sticks his neck out for strangers—not unless he wants something big in return. Before this is over, me and you are going to go a round, old man."

"Yes," Gideon said. "I'm afraid we will, Mr. Gunn."

⎯⎯

Gideon, holding two large, roughly shaped gold coins, stood before two coin-operated parking meters.

"What are those?" Hajar asked.

"Coins hammered from the gold used to ransom Montezuma."

"Of course, they are," she said, "and I'm the Queen of England."

"If you don't mind, please move your royal highness back to the cars."

Scowling, Hajar walked back to the GTO where Yumi and Megan joined her.

"Dear Lord, give me the strength to carry this quest through to the end," Gideon prayed quietly. "In the name of Lord Jesus Christ, let it be."

He put one coin into each of the meters and turned the handles three times. As he finished cranking the parking meters, the shops along the street for eight city blocks shimmered, like a heat mirage in the desert, and then vanished.

Instead of the line of typical, small town businesses, a single, colossal building now stood before them. Hajar and her crew stood in shocked awe before the now imposing Bulls Gap's Museum of Milking History. The daunting art nouveau structure, built entirely of pink Tennessee marble, was fifty stories high and a full mile square. The beautiful building was flawless, except for several ugly scorch marks radiating up the side on its eastern most section.

"What happened to the crap-hole town?" Megan asked as she popped her gum noisily. "Where did this building come from?"

"Two things," Gideon said.

"What's that?"

"Don't say crap-hole and, for goodness sake, spit out your cud."

Rolling her eyes, Megan turned her head and spat a massive wad of bubblegum into a garbage can.

"Do not budge from this spot," Gideon said. "I'll be right back. Probably be running, so you be ready to move out in a hurry."

"No way, Doc," Hajar assured him. "We're coming along."

"It's too dangerous. Now be a good girl, do what I say, and stay here."

"Did you just tell me to be a *good girl*?"

"I'm sorry, lost cause, isn't it? Stay put, toots, and I mean it."

"I'm not taking my eyes off you, *old man*," Hajar said. "For all we know, you may just go out the back and leave us high and dry."

"I'm not trying to ditch you. I'm trying to protect you!"

"Hello? It's a freaking milking museum!" Roland said. "How dangerous can it be?"

"One that just appeared out of thin air?" Gideon asked. "One bigger than the Pentagon? That doesn't make you wonder if something is a bit off?"

"It's still a milking museum," Roland muttered.

"Stay here," Gideon said.

"Not happening, you old fart," Hajar said, "so get used to the idea."

"All right," Gideon said. "If you behave, that is. Now remember, *children*, we go in together and we come out together. No sightseeing and, for goodness sake, *do—not—touch—anything*. Got me?"

"Yes, *Daddy*," Hajar said. "We'll be real good. So let's go before you wet your diaper."

"Have you ever heard of a woodshed, young lady?" Gideon said. "Looks like you're long overdue for a visit."

"Yeah, yeah, we got it, Grandpa," Roland hissed. "Let's get this over with."

Instead of going up the wide, marble steps, Gideon led them down the street and around the windowless structure to a massive bronze door set into the side of the building. The ten-foot-tall door was masterfully formed into the face of a woman with flowing hair.

"Why are we going this way?" Megan asked.

"Because this is the real front door. Hold on and I'll—"

"I got it," Megan said. "Alarms and security systems are my specialty."

She walked up to the heavy side door and gingerly placed her hand on the door handle. Frowning, she pulled and the ponderous door silently swung open. Down a short, black-and-white linoleum clad hallway, they could see various implements in the history of gathering milk from a *Bos taurus*. Crude, hand-lettered signs hung from brown twine, informing visitors as to what they were looking at.

"Way to go, Megan," Roland whispered. "That was quick."

"I—I didn't do anything," she said. "The alarm is off and the door was already unlocked."

"No, sweet child," Gideon said. "There isn't an alarm, and the doors don't need locks. Besides, you opened the wrong one."

"What do you mean the wrong one?" Megan asked. "It's the only door here."

Pushing past the girl, Gideon closed the door, caressing the cheek of the bronze face. To the group's surprise, the mouth opened wide. Gideon placed his hand inside. After a few seconds, he removed it and the face smiled. The door opened of its own accord.

This time, however, instead of a corridor devoted to milking machines, there was a long, marble-lined passage. A few yards away stood a man in a long, dark coat, leaning on a twisted, black cane. The tall, painfully thin stranger had a mass of dark hair and fine, pale skin. Perched upon his hooked nose was a pair of round, deep blue glasses set in frames of gold.

"Stop," the stranger said. "You're banned from this place, Gideon Kane. Dare to enter, and you will all die."

"Who's that?" Megan asked. "And what did you do to get banned from a milking museum?"

"I did something *utterly* disgusting," Gideon said.

"That was awful," Hajar said. "I feel violated."

"Time to be serious, woman," Gideon scolded. "What we have before us is one of the museum's watchmen. Hajar, have you still got that fancy butter knife with you?"

"It isn't a butter knife, you old coot. Her name is Kali."

She produced Kali, who appeared as a seventeen-inch-long, razor-sharp kukri.

"Here, place this around the haft," he said, giving her a small beaded bracelet. "It will hide Kali from *her*."

"From whom?" she asked as she carefully wrapped the beaded loop around Kali.

"You'll see. Now remember, girl, do not for any reason pull Kali or she'll happily kill you and take Kali for her own."

"Who is *she*?" Hajar demanded.

"Just do it."

Hajar nodded her head slightly as she re-sheathed Kali.

"I go in first, then Yumi, Megan, Roland, and Hajar brings up the rear. Keep a sharp lookout and don't touch anything. Once past the main watchman, if we're careful, perhaps the building won't release its watchdogs."

"I ain't afraid of a few mutts," Roland said. "After the long drive, I could use a snack."

"The only snack around here will be you," Gideon snapped. "Now, let's go."

"This is no milking museum," Yumi said. "What is this place?"

"A depository," Gideon said.

"You mean like for hemorrhoids," Roland asked. "It's a freaking big one."

"That's a *suppository*, you idiot," Hajar said.

"Thank you, Hajar," Gideon said. "It's a depository of unique knowledge and priceless treasures."

"What about the watchman up there?" Roland asked.

Gideon unsnapped his holster. "Leave that to me."

"Vlad," said a disembodied, soothing feminine voice. "Allow them to enter."

The tall man changed into a black mist and dissipated.

"Did you see that?" Megan asked.

"Shush, girl," Gideon hissed. "Please give your mouth a rest, darling, I need to think."

cococo

The group wandered into a virtual maze of glass-encased objects. Looking up, they could see tiers upon tiers of items, all carefully arranged and neatly labeled.

A small army of strange creatures scampered back and forth, tending the glass cases. The creatures were about the size of a large, hairless chimpanzee with snow white, extremely wrinkled skin. The creatures' most striking feature was their large, jewel-like azure eyes.

They wore identical, light gray tunics and leather harnesses that contained various tools and devices, only a few of which were recognizable. Many had special glowing backpacks that allowed them to defy gravity and soar silently to the uppermost cases.

While the energetic activity seemed like complete chaos, it was actually a meticulously organized, systematic cleaning of the entire library.

"What the hell are those things? *Monkeys*?" Roland asked.

"I've been about everywhere and I never even heard of white apes, let alone ones wearing clothes before."

"They're not monkeys. They're called Setiis," Gideon said, "and they're a lot smarter than you are, Mr. Gunn. They're worker drones who take care of the place. Don't interfere with their duty and they'll leave you alone."

"Gideon Kane?" asked a disembodied female voice. "This is a surprise. You were explicitly warned not to come back."

"I know. I have a request, Alexandria."

"A request? Of *me*? Are you serious?"

"I want to borrow something."

"Neither a borrower nor a lender be."

"I thought that, because of our colorful history, you would make an exception for me."

"Our history wasn't one of sunshine and roses. You threatened to kill me and burn my collection to ash, as I recall."

"I did, didn't I?" he said with a chuckle. "Perhaps, it was the fact you kidnapped and tried to clone me. A thing like that makes a fellow kinda grumpy. Be that as it may, I could have destroyed you, but I let you live."

"Yes, you did. In hindsight, perhaps I did overstep my bounds."

"I'm willing to forget the past and start over, if you are."

Before them, an ethereal woman appeared. Her face was the same as the image on the outer door. She was tall, with flowing silver hair, unnaturally flawless skin, and deep blue eyes.

She wore a light blue silk robe and everyone noticed that Alexandria's feet did not touch the ground. "Your colossal nerve has always intrigued me, Gideon Kane. Leave your companions here and come with me. We'll discuss your proposal in my private chambers."

"Wait a minute," Hajar said. "*This* is the Library of Alexandria?"

"Yes, it is," Gideon said. "Do not move from this spot until I come back."

"Do not fear for your companions, Kane," Alexandria told him. "I will grant your people safety within my domain. They are free to look around my collection, but they must not touch anything."

"Wait a minute," Yumi said. "The Library of Alexandria was destroyed by Julius Caesar in 48 BC."

"Apparently, this is not the same one," Gideon remarked.

ロンロン

Hajar swallowed hard. *Book Five, The Scrolls of Doom.*

The Library of Alexandria was disguised as a flat iron museum in Squall Falls, Montana. In the story, the library collected the most unique items on the planet. Alexandria was a vast and ancient alien computer, originally created to document humanity, but her benign creators were destroyed eons ago by a supernova. Without anyone to keep her electronic ass in check, she got this crazy obsession with things and became the biggest klepto on the planet.

Every major painting, sculpture, historical artifact—anything, is here. Heck, in the basement is the real Statue of Liberty. She even kept genetic material samples of living organisms. The book hinted that the entire history of life on planet Earth, both plant and animal, is preserved here.

In the book, Alexandria got tired of collecting inanimate objects and adding to her DNA database. Hal 9000 here got the bright idea to collect unique people and wanted to make Kamikaze part of her living collection. However, Ginny and the Choirboys came running to the rescue. Gideon triumphed and could have destroyed her, however, he figured Alexandria did mankind a service because, in her own twisted way, she safeguarded humanity's treasures.

They made a deal and he told her that if she tried it again, he would put an end to her, even if it did mean destroying her priceless collection.

Hajar gazed in awe at the wonders around her.

I always thought this was the most farfetched of all the Kane books, but it is real! I am totally freaking out!

ロンロン

Hajar watched Gideon and Alexandria in the distance. She saw Gideon come to a stop at a case, one set apart from the others. From her angle, Hajar couldn't see its contents. To her surprise, she saw Gideon lean over and gently kiss the surface of the glass. A Setii came rushing up to Gideon, jabbering in a high-pitched squeal, apparently giving him a piece of his mind. The strange beast then began wiping the glass furiously. Gideon chuckled at the creature's antics before he and Alexandria walked through an arched opening and heavy, double bronze doors closed behind them.

Curious about Gideon's reaction, Hajar traced his path to the lighted case that sat by itself. She gasped when she stood before the display.

It wasn't some grand artwork of a master artist. It was no more than two simple, rough-hewn beams of wood fixed in the shape of a cross. The sinister handy work of Roman laborers and Hebrew slaves to punish and execute prisoners.

The three, square-headed holes, two in the cross beam and one situated low on the vertical, were stained a reddish brown. At the top of the cross was a notice written in three languages. Hajar couldn't read the words, but she knew them by heart. *Jesus of Nazareth, the King of the Jews.* A chill ran though her very soul at the horrific device upon which her Lord had died.

ℰ◦ℰ◦

While Hajar stood at the foot of the Cross and meditated, Yumi gawked in wonder at such priceless artifacts such as the Ark of the Covenant, the Ten Commandments, da Vinci's personal notebook, and a pristine #1 Action Comics.

Roland and Megan, on the other hand, were bored within five minutes.

"Hey, runt, let's see if there is a gift shop," Roland said.

"Sure."

CHAPTER 17

Alexandria led Gideon into a plush, book-lined chamber where she directed him to a luxurious, high-backed chair.

"I never thought I would see you again, Kamikaze," she said. "The situation must be desperate for you to come to me."

"Yes," Gideon replied. "I guess you could say that. You see, I have a quest before me—probably the most important of my life."

"What do you seek?"

"The Tree of Life."

"It is a myth, or I would have it here."

"No, it is real all right, protected even from your fancy alien detection equipment."

"I see. I suppose, you would like to peruse my reference material to help with your search?"

"No."

"I don't understand," she said. "What do you want from me?"

Gideon let out a sigh. "Truth is, I'm not a young man anymore, Alexandria. The journey thus far has me worn out and we haven't even begun the hard part yet."

"What can I do?"

"Let's not play games. I need the Tear of the Phoenix."

"Like I said before, this isn't the borrowing kind of library. Besides, whatever benefits the Phoenix grants are short lived.

It will kill you and, from what I understand, the death isn't pleasant."

"The Tear of the Phoenix will give me the strength I need to finish this mission, and that is all that matters."

"It is a one of a kind item and far too valuable to let out of my sight," she said.

"Figured you would say that," he said. "How about I rent it for a while."

"What could you possibly have that I—"

Gideon pulled a ring from his pocket.

"My wife's wedding ring."

"That is the ring Caesar gave Cleopatra," she gasped. "I have searched centuries for it. I offer a counter proposal, Kane. The ring and the Tree when you find it."

"You can fight Mrs. Kerr for it when I find it, because she's the one I have to give it to."

"Salome Kerr?" Alexandria wrinkled her nose. "You certainly have lowered your standards in acquaintances since last we met. I detest that vile woman."

"It's complicated. In the meantime, this ring is more than enough to rent the Phoenix. Do we have a deal?"

Alexandria leapt from her chair and paced back and forth. "If you take the Phoenix, it will be lost when you die."

"I give you my word," Gideon said. "I will see to it that Hajar returns it to you. She is—*was*—a Paladin. Her honor is beyond reproach."

"Deal," Alexandria cried, snatching her prize from his hand. "This way, Kane. I have to warn you, though, the process does sting a bit."

"Doesn't everything these days?"

దుంజుం

As Gideon and Alexandria bargained, two black vans pulled to the curb before the Blue Bird Diner.

"Now remember, Curry," Duncan Figg said. "We want Dr. Kane alive, but feel free to kill the rest."

"Yes, sir."

"I can't stress enough for you and your men to be careful with the collection. The entity known as Alexandria takes offence if her acquisitions are disturbed in any way, and, buddy boy, let me tell you, the woman has a temper. In fact, if you so much as touch one bauble, I will have to look for other hired guns. You get me?"

"Don't worry, Mr. Figg. We are professionals here to do a job and get out. We'll nab the old man for you, and his crew will be in Hell ten minutes before they know they are dead. Piece of cake."

The doors slid back and disgorged twenty black-clad mercenaries, along with one, handsome, well-dressed man in a dark sport coat.

Figg removed his sport coat, tie, and Rolex, whereupon he laid them in the van's passenger seat. Taking a big duffle bag, he pulled out a large, plastic container.

"Line up, gentlemen," he said, removing the container's lid.

Curry covered his nose and turned away.

"Yes, it is revolting," said Figg, "but it will keep you alive until you are able to snatch the good doctor."

"What is it?"

"Little bit of this, little bit of that, and a lot of dreams," Figg said with a smile. "It will keep you and your men hidden from Alexandria and her minions. Be warned, the concoction only lasts an hour. Pulling up the sleeves of his expensive, custom-made dress shirt, Figg dipped his hands into the red goo and, in turn, marked each of the soldiers before smearing the last of the exotic potion on himself.

ဢၜဢ

Like Gideon before him, Figg stood before the mystic parking meters. He placed two extremely rare Roman coins into the meters and the library appeared.

Figg snapped his fingers and the soldiers flowed silently past him. Resembling a big city swat team, the group of hired killers rushed up the steps of the museum and into the Milking Hall of Fame. Following a diagram of the building, they made their way to the back of the whimsical, *Cows in Heaven* exhibit.

Figg, with expert precision, drew an elaborate design upon the wall. Stepping back, the marked section of wall shimmered and faded away. They were in.

CHAPTER 18

Helloooo, beautiful," Roland said. "Kid, do you see what I see?"

"A guitar?"

"Calling this a guitar, is like calling Mona Big Rack Gerson, just a stripper."

"Okay, if you say so."

"This is Jimi Hendrix's Stratocaster! Says at the bottom that he played it at Woodstock. I have hit the jackpot."

"I heard of him," she said. "Set his guitar on fire, didn't he?"

"Yeah, he was so cool," Roland agreed. "Hendrix was a southpaw. However, he used right hand guitars restrung for left hand play. He played them upside down. You know, Kid, I play a little. Not as good as Jimi, but still damn fine, if you ask me. Bet I could really be good if I had Jimi's very own axe."

Roland measured the distance to the door and weighed his smash-and-grab's chances of success.

"I know what you are thinking," Megan said, "and you better get it out of your head right now, hairball."

"You know, Megan, if you could see your way free of helping me—"

"No way! You heard what Alexandria said. No telling what she will do to us."

"You're right, Kid," he said. "I was just thinking out loud."

"Did you hear that?" she asked.

"Hear what?"

"Nothing, I guess. Hey, let's look around some more."

"You go ahead, Kid. I want to drool over the axe a little while longer."

☙ ❧

"Excalibur," Hajar said, as she gazed upon the gleaming, mythical sword. "This place is amazing."

Turning she came face to face with Ginny.

"Will you quit doing that?" Hajar hissed. "You scared the bejesus out of me."

Ginny smiled. "What do you desire, Hajar?"

"I want free of Mrs. Kerr, I want Larry to pay—I want my life back."

"I like you. You remind me of myself."

"Ginny, why are we here?"

"Don't waste his sacrifice."

"What's he doing?" Hajar asked as she suddenly got a very bad feeling. "I mean—this is my fault. We have to stop him. I can't let him suffer on my behalf."

"What is done is done."

"What can I do?"

"Be there for him. Cherish him. Love him. I want you to be his."

"Really?" Hajar asked. "Now there is a new twist to the story. A ghost is trying to fix me up with her eighty-three-year-old husband. You haven't been talking to Spooky have you?"

Ginny smiled.

"You don't want him to be alone, do you?" Hajar asked.

"It is certain."

"That's sweet. You must have loved him very much."

"Yes."

"I promise he will never be alone."

Ginny smiled.

To Hajar's ears came the faint, unmistakable, sound of a man crying out in pain.

"Gideon," Hajar called out as the cry rose in volume. Her hand fell on Kali, but Gideon's warning rang in her ears.

"It has to be," Ginny said.

"What is he doing?"

"What has to be."

"Mrs. Kane, talk to me so I can understand."

"You will see."

"In Heaven, does everyone talk like a frigging Magic Eight Ball?"

"Signs point to yes."

"Oh great, a smartass ghost."

"We are of a kind."

Hajar heard her cell phone chime. To keep in contact, Gideon had provided his team with non-traceable "burner" phones. She snatched the phone free and saw that she had a text from Megan.

Hajar scanned the text and groaned. "Oh, no."

ᘒᘒᘒ

Megan wandered aimlessly through the seeming endless maze of glass-encased treasures. Pausing to sit on a padded bench, she watched as several of the library's weird looking minions set a golden chalice on a marble stand. One creature manipulated a strange looking device, which looked much like an electric screwdriver. Suddenly, a seamless glass case appeared around the finished display.

From where Megan sat, she could see hundreds of the creatures fussing with the collection from arranging new displays to cleaning. Absorbed as they were in their work, they paid zero attention to Megan.

She looked up and beheld Vlad staring at her from a few feet away. The creature looked at her and licked his dark red lips. She could see raw hunger shining brightly in his red eyes. Several of the Setii saw the approach of the vampire and stopped their work to watch.

"It was a mistake to leave the safety of your companions," Vlad said in a thick Romanian accent. "I haven't had fresh, *soul-warmed* blood in over one hundred years—not since I was trapped within this hellish place."

"You're breaking my heart," Megan said, as she fiddled with her music player.

With a wolf-like snarl, he took a step toward her. He opened his gaping maul, exposing a mouth full of unnaturally sharp, white teeth.

Megan gave the foul creature a bored look and brought up her palm.

"Boo, Count Chocula," she said. "Now go away before I get mad."

Vlad gave an unaccustomed look of terror before he hissed and backed quickly away.

"Vampires are soooooo over rated," she said.

The Setii erupted into wild, high-pitched laughter and fell about the polished floor. They mocked the vampire, relishing his misery. Adding salt to the wound, the aliens did an impromptu spoof of a scene from *Dracula*.

"I hate this infernal place," muttered Vlad as he vanished into a black mist.

Megan settled back and listened to her ever-present MP3 player while the still chuckling Setii went back to work.

"Waiting is always the worst part," she said, settling back.

Two songs later, a pair of soldiers grabbed her from behind. A gloved-clad hand covered her mouth, stifling a scream, as she was picked up and carried away.

CHAPTER 19

ajar looked at the text and groaned.
~ *Hajar, as you must have surmised, we have your young friend, not to mention, you and your cohorts are out gunned and surrounded. There isn't a need for anyone to get hurt. Turn over Dr. Kane, and you and your friends can walk away. You have three minutes to decide before we start hurting poor little Megan.*

Clicking off her phone, Hajar found Yumi taking cover behind the statue of Michelangelo's David. Squatting next to him she asked, "Got the text?"

"Yeah. This is all we need."

"Where is Roland?"

"Don't know," he said, checking his pistol. "From what I saw, we are in a bad spot. Must be up against twenty or more and I have only twelve rounds. We need to move, no way to defend against so many."

"Outside," Ginny said.

"I won't leave Gideon."

Yumi looked at her sharply. "What happened to you? I thought that you despised Doc?"

"Without the old man, we are dead."

"Well, getting ourselves killed won't help anyone," Yumi said. "If we can, we have to fall back to a better defensive position. I noticed some large statuary to the west that should even the odds."

"No!" Ginny said. "Outside, now!"

"But Gideon—"

"Can take care of himself," Ginny informed her.

"Well, Megan can't!" Hajar hissed.

"Megan can't what?" Yumi asked.

Hajar thought a moment. "You ready to get off the bench and help the home team—*Alexandria*?"

"She is here?" Yumi asked. "You can hear her?"

"Yes, she is. I can hear her with my special...umm, Paladin hearing. And she wants to help, don't you, *Alexandria*?"

Ginny smiled and faded away.

ℰᴐℰᴐ

Figg and Curry stood with five of the mercenaries, next to a case containing Beethoven's hand written copy of the Fifth Symphony.

"The clock is ticking, Hajar," shouted Figg as he glanced at his watch. "You have five seconds...four...three..."

"Okay, okay, don't hurt her, we are coming out!" cried Hajar.

Figg and Curry smiled.

"Megan, looks like your friends do care about you after all," Figg said.

Megan grunted harshly.

"I can't believe anyone is that stupid," Curry said. "This is going to be a snap."

Several yards ahead, Hajar and Yumi came out of hiding with their hands raised high over their heads.

"Now, this was far easier than I imagined," Figg said with a chuckle. "Curry, let me remind you and your killers here not to use firearms. When they are close, stun them with the tasers, then take them outside, and finish them off."

"Yes, sir," he said. "But what if things get difficult? I still don't see Dr. Kane or that...what was his name, Roland something."

"You heard me," Figg said. "No firearms, period."

Three of the soldiers produced tasers and took aim at the approaching pair.

"Where is the other one? Gunn, I believe he is called?" Figg called out.

"Don't know," Hajar said. "My guess is, he ducked out the back door the minute he saw trouble. You ask me, I always thought he was a coward."

"And where is, Dr. Kane?"

"Behind those doors over there," Hajar indicated the doors with a nod of her head. "He is talking with Alexandria."

"If this is some trick," Figg said, "I'm afraid that poor Megan will be the one who pays."

"No trick, whoever you are. Now give us Megan like you promised and we will walk away."

"Sorry, Miss Hajar. I have changed the terms of the deal." Figg nodded to Curry.

e⁄ɔe⁄ɔ

Megan stood wide-eyed as she heard a voice whisper in her ear.

"Okay, kid," Ginny said. "Dissemble."

Under the stifling hand, Megan smiled at Ginny's instructions and closed her eyes. Soon, beads of sweat dotted her face as she concentrated with all her might.

The three taser-toting soldiers turned and promptly shot each other. Their voices were raised in a chorus of grunts as they exchanged thousands of volts before falling unconscious to the floor.

Their plans shattered, the rest of the soldiers ignored the edict handed down by Figg and drew their machine guns. They were in for quite a surprise.

Their magazines, all sixteen, ejected as one, while the bolts on their weapons, seemingly of their own accord, yanked back, sending chambered rounds spinning away. The clatter of falling pins and bouncing springs mixed with the soldiers shocked dismay as their weapons fell apart. Within half a second, Megan had disarmed the entire squad.

"Now, hairball!" Yumi cried.

With a blood-curdling roar, Roland sprang over a glass case

and into the helpless rank of mercenaries. The grotesque beast, a mixture of human and saber-toothed tiger, ripped into the evil men. With enormous strength and speed, Roland ripped two soldiers to shreds, seconds after contact. Chaos ensued as the yelling and cursing soldiers resorted to using knives and makeshift weapons against the enraged were-beast.

Ignoring Figg, Hajar pounced on the hapless soldier who held Megan, slamming him into a wall. One punch later found him slumped on the floor.

You all right, Shortstack?" Hajar asked.

Megan walked over and kicked the fallen man, several times in the head. "I am now," she said, breathing hard.

"There are too many," Hajar said. "Let's grab Gideon and get out of here."

While Hajar took care of Megan, Yumi snatched up a fallen knife and flew at Figg. "Call off your men!" he demanded.

"No," Figg said with a smirk. "*Goeiin ghton!*"

Yumi gasped as the weapon in his hand suddenly glowed red-hot. Dropping the scorching blade, Yumi stumbled back.

"Looks like you and your friends are out of your league."

Roland laughed as he sent soldiers running in all directions. Seeing Yumi in trouble, he bounded across the carnage and arced high into the air.

Figg looked up and, with a wave of his hand, spoke, "*Hek-ali mockius!*"

Roland's guise as the beast vanished and he came crashing down at Figg's feet. With a wave of his hand, Figg slammed Roland into Yumi as if he were a puppet on a string.

Figg laughed. "You should have run while you had the chance."

"No, you should have," Gideon Kane said.

Gideon grabbed Figg by the shoulder and jerked him about to face him. Before Figg could hurl a deadly incantation, Gideon slammed a boney fist into his throat.

Figg, gasping and grunting, stumbled back into the wall.

"Can't speak and you are no better than one of us normals, are you?"

Figg fumbled and produced a small pistol. Drawing his .45

with speed that would have made Wild Bill Hickok proud, Gideon shot Figg square between the eyes.

"I really hate warlocks," he said.

Roland and Yumi looked up in shock at the elderly man, who not only saved their lives, but who easily bested a powerful warlock one-on-one.

"Don't just lay there, move!" Gideon shouted.

Firing his pistols with deadly accuracy, he killed three soldiers as they rushed at them armed with wicked looking high-tech tomahawks.

Hajar was fighting with two knife-wielding mercenaries when Gideon came rolling up and shot both of her assailants.

"I didn't need your help," she spat.

"I know, but I got what we need, doll," he said, grabbing her by the arm. "Time to blow this joint."

"I thought you were in trouble?" she whispered. "I heard you yelling."

"No time to talk. Move, woman, before Alexandria drops a bomb on all of us."

ৎৣৎৣ

A soldier had re-assembled a pistol and pointed it at Hajar. Gideon tackled her just as he fired. The 9 mm round, missing its mark, traveled two feet before shattering a protective glass cube. Yumi slammed a foot into the soldier, knocking the pistol from his hand.

"Oh, no," Gideon yelled. "Run!"

ৎৣৎৣ

"Get those weapons put back together!" Curry shouted.

"Sir, Figg is dead," said one of the men. "This mission is busted."

"According to Figg, Dr. Kane is worth his weight in gold," Curry said. "We snatch him and we can sell him to the highest bidder. Now move your butts before they get away."

With practiced skill, the ten remaining mercenaries quickly

reassembled their weapons and soon were in hot pursuit through the maze of glass cases.

A brief, but bloodcurdling scream brought Curry and his men to a halt.

"Where is Matt?" shouted one. "He was right here!"

"Never mind about Matt," Curry ordered. "What is that?"

Blocking the squad's path, a smoky apparition rose before them. The hideous thing appeared as a woman with wild, dark hair and black eyes. Intertwined with her wiry black hair were a myriad of hissing, green snakes, making her look like a Gorgon. Her gaunt, almost skeletal frame was covered with scaly, bleached white skin. In her hand, she bore a golden scythe and blood red chain.

Being men of few words, they opened fire. The thing laughed as their bullets passed harmlessly through her, shattering an entire row of priceless artifacts.

"Kill them," Alexandria screamed. "Kill them all!"

The Fury lashed out with her red, glowing chain and cut one soldier in half. Soon the library was awash in their blood as the survivors threw away their weapons and ran for their lives. One of the hapless soldiers slammed into and shattered a glass case that held a simple wooden staff. The staff flipped into a knot of mercenaries trying to re-locate to parts unknown. The simple staff, upon contact with the ground, promptly turned into an angry, twenty-foot long, king cobra. Three soldiers-of-fortune died, victims of the staff with which Moses had led the children of Israel.

છળછ

Gideon led the way as Yumi and Hajar, half-carrying, half-dragging Megan, finally made the entry hall of the museum.

"Girl, your ass needs to start exercising," Yumi said.

"And stop smoking," Hajar added as she stopped to catch her breath.

"You guys take all the fun out of being young," Megan said. "Somebody want to tell me who was talking in my ear back there?"

"Perhaps, your guardian angel?" Hajar suggested.

"Alexandria," Yumi said as he gave Hajar a narrow gaze.

"Yeah, that was her all right," Hajar said. "Anyway, Short-stack, you did great!"

"Face it, guys, I rock," Megan said.

"W—where is Roland?" Gideon gasped as he tried to catch his breath. "I'm too old for this."

"I thought he was behind me," Yumi said.

"Here he comes," Megan said. "What is that in his hand?"

"Oh no, he didn't!"

"Yes, he did," Megan said.

Roland charged the group at full speed, giving out a tremendous rebel yell as he waved the legendary 1968 Fender over his head.

"What did you do?" Gideon exclaimed.

"Kept this little beauty from rotting away in a dusty hole, old man! I know Jimi would want me to have it."

The heavy bronze door to the museum slammed shut with a deep, resounding boom. Not one, but three of the vengeful Furies floated above the sea of glass, leisurely moving in on the small group. Vlad, along with three of his fellow un-deads, moved along the corridor, a look of raw hunger etched upon their hideous faces.

"Furies," Gideon gasped. "She just had to send in the Furies."

"Don't forget the vampires," Yumi said. "We can't fight them. All we can do is run."

"Aw nuts," Gideon said. "I didn't see this coming. Looks like this adventure is over before it began. I am sorry."

"Help Megan get the door open," Hajar said, drawing Kali. "I'll take care of these bitches."

"Hell yah!" cried Kali.

Hajar paused and looked Gideon in the eye. "Who's the damsel in distress now, old man?"

"You have weird issues, you know that, woman?"

Emitting a yell of pure joy, Hajar rushed the supernatural terrors.

While Yumi and Roland protected Megan, Gideon watched

helplessly as Hajar fought alone. It galled him to let someone else fight while he stood by. However, he was soon mesmerized by her beauty and grace as she dealt death.

Graceful as a ballerina, Hajar spun and dodged, weaving Kali about her like an impenetrable shield. Vlad and his unholy companions died, screaming, in a blaze of brilliant blue light.

"I never saw anyone fight with such skill," Gideon muttered. "She's the most graceful, beautiful thing I ever saw."

"She is a vision," Ginny said.

"To say the least," he said, not able to take his eyes off Hajar's deadly dance.

To his amazement, Hajar not only fended off the daunting Furies, but actually struck down two of the devils. Kali in Hajar's hands was more than a match for the worst mythic terrors Alexandria could produce. Gideon could see why Larry had picked her to be his Paladin.

"Megan did it," Roland cried as the huge door swung open. Selfishly, he pushed past Yumi and knocked Megan down in his rush to freedom.

Hajar backed down the corridor, fighting the last remaining Fury, as she stepped up her attack. After a terrific battle, Hajar cut the creature down and dove through the opening before the door slammed shut behind her. The face on the bronze door transformed into one of utter rage.

CHAPTER 20

Woooohooooooo!" Roland cried as he danced around with his prize Fender. "Now that is what I'm talking about!"

"You are a fool!" said Yumi.

Breathing hard and sweating profusely, Hajar slid Kali back into her sheath and began to giggle uncontrollably.

೭⁄ɔ೭⁄ɔ

When Kali fed, she consumed her victim's life force, drawing in the living energy, but as voracious as she was, some was always wasted. The overflow entered Hajar, healing any injury and creating a brief, yet intense, euphoria beyond that of any drug. Hajar called it the *death-rush*. It had saved her bacon a few times, but the tremendous rush it brought was a danger in its self.

This was why Hajar used Kali only in emergencies, as she was always fearful that the death-rush could become an addiction. She had never killed many beings as powerful as the vampires and the Furies. The rush hit her like a tidal wave.

೭⁄ɔ೭⁄ɔ

Gideon rushed to Hajar's side. "Are you all right, Hajar?"

"I'm fine, old man." Hajar giggled. "How about you?"

"Are you...*stoned*?" he asked.

Hajar laughed. "It will wear off in a bit, Giddy. You're Giddy and I'm giddy! Isn't that funny?"

"Roland, you big turd!" Megan spat. "You almost got us killed!"

"You can't blame this on me! Those snake-haired things were after the mercenaries. Probably just came after us by mistake."

"Yes," Gideon said, "they were hunting the warlock's men, but when you lifted the Stratocaster, you put a target squarely on our backs. If it wasn't for Hajar, we would all be dead."

"Let's hear it for Hajar!" Hajar cheered. "Hip, hip, hooooooorah!"

"I'll have what she's having," Roland said, "only make mine a double."

Gideon glared at him. "Mr. Gunn!"

"Thanks, Hajar," Roland said with a big grin. "I owe you one. Okay, chief, you satisfied now?"

Gideon groaned and clutched his chest. The fresh, crescent-shaped incision in his chest burned like the surface of the sun.

"Gideon!" Hajar cried as the high suddenly wore off.

Gideon shook violently, as if in the throes of an epileptic fit before collapsing.

"Looks like we need another old guy," Roland said with a laugh.

With a wild yell, Hajar rushed Roland and smashed her fist into his nose.

Roland fell back, his nose spraying blood as his stolen guitar flew through the air. Yumi, with an amazing leap, caught the Fender before it hit the sidewalk.

"You'll pay for that," Roland spat as he swung a right at her head.

Hajar dodged the wild haymaker and snapped his head back with a stunning left jab. She dropped down and swept his legs out from under him. Grunting sharply, Roland slammed hard on the sidewalk.

"Behave yourselves!" came a deep voice.

"What the Hell?" Hajar exclaimed.

Instead of the tired, eighty-three year old man, there stood an energetic, twenty-five-year-old Gideon Kane. Gideon ripped off his now too-small shirt, exposing his well-muscled chest and arms.

"Oh, that is much better," he said, stretching.

"Wow," said Megan.

"I'll have a big glass of that," Hajar agreed as her eyes devoured the ruggedly handsome man.

"Nice," Ginny said with a grin.

Gideon looked at Roland for a moment. "Yumi, why don't you take the ladies back to the car? Roland and I are going to have a word of prayer before we go one step further on our mission."

"Suits me just fine, old man," Roland said, wiping the blood from his nose. "I been itching to settle a few things with you, anyway. Now, when I whip your ass, nobody can say I took advantage of a broken down old man."

"Impressive transformation, Dr. Kane," Yumi said, stepping close to Gideon. "But hairball there still outweighs you by about twenty-five pounds. I will be more than happy to assist."

"Thanks, but I got this," Gideon said. "Keep an eye out for any more surprises from Alexandria."

"If Doc wants to commit suicide," Hajar said, "it's none of my business. I'm going to the car."

Gideon nodded. "I will see you all at the car."

"Very well," Yumi said. "After you, ladies."

���

As Hajar and her crew walked out of sight, Roland took off his shirt and tossed it next to his stolen guitar. "I'm going to enjoy kicking the shit out of you."

"You know, Roland, there is always a bad apple like you on every squad. That pain in the rump who thinks of themselves before the goals of the team. This poor attitude of yours will end tonight. You will be a team player and support the goals of this team or, so help me, I will give you back to Mrs. Kerr."

"In other words," Roland said, "you mean I should cow

down to you and what you decide? With Mrs. Kerr, I didn't have a choice, but you, it ain't happening."

With a wild yell, Roland Gunn rushed Gideon.

ოჯოჯ

The ponderous library door swung open before Roland. Standing in the doorway was Alexandria, her face twisted with rage. Roland, his right eye terribly discolored and swollen, extended the Fender before him. "Sorry," he said, through clenched teeth. "Temptation got the better of me."

"I should kill you for this," she said.

"You have your property back undamaged," Gideon said. "Be satisfied with that."

"Very well, Kane."

Alexandria accepted the guitar and Roland stepped back. "If I ever catch you setting foot anywhere near my collection, Mr. Gunn, you are a dead man."

"Yeah—I got you," Roland said as he backed away.

"Kane," Alexandria said. "Thank you for returning the guitar. I knew it wasn't you who stole it. You are an honorable man."

"You still tried to kill us all."

"Several artifacts were damaged. What can I say? I lost my head."

"That was an understatement."

"I expect you to keep your word and return the Phoenix to me as well."

"You know I will."

"God speed," she said. "I want you to know, Gideon Kane, that on the day you die, I will mourn."

"Sorry, but with our history, I find that hard to believe."

"It's true. You would have made a fine addition to my collection," she said with a sly smile.

ოჯოჯ

"Here they come," Yumi said. "Been almost an hour. I

thought, for a moment there, they had killed each other."

Hajar snorted. "I wish. That would have been the best thing to happen since we started this little adventure."

Megan crushed out a cigarette "Does Roland have the guitar?"

"No, he doesn't," Hajar said. "And it looks like's he limping."

"Pay up, ladies," Yumi said with a smile. "Let me see those lovely green portraits of presidents."

Grumbling, Hajar and Megan each forked over a dollar bill.

"You know, Hajar," Megan said. "Got to admit, the old fart is much easier on the eyes now."

"Young or old, he's still a dirt-bag," Hajar said. "Even if he is much easier on the eyes, he's still a double-dealing, low-down, weasel."

"He's young and so am I."

Hajar gave Megan a sly wink. "Put it out of your head, jail-bait," she said with a smile. "I deserve a shot at the new and improved *after* version."

"Jailbait? You can kiss my jailbait ass, you Amazon cow turd!"

Hajar put up a halfhearted defense while Megan tried to take a poke at her. Hajar couldn't help but laugh. As a fighter, Megan was more of a danger to herself than her opponent, looking more like a demented windmill than Muhammad Ali.

"Thumb to the outside, Shortstack," Hajar said as she sparred with Megan. "You don't want to break your thumb."

"Don't tell me what to do! I'll fight any way I want to, you long-legged mule!"

Megan smiled when Hajar's feet slid together and her shoelaces intertwined.

"What the—" Hajar yelped as her shoelaces tied themselves into knots.

While Hajar's attention was on her feet, Megan tackled her and both hit the ground, laughing.

"That's not fair," Hajar said as Megan pounced on her.

"Ladies, please give this a rest," Yumi moaned. "Feels like I'm back in high school. No, make that grade school."

Roland opened the door to the GTO and crawled into the back seat. Moments later, he tossed a shirt to Gideon. "Here yah go, Doc."

Gideon slipped the black tee shirt over his head. "Thanks."

"Doc, we found the merc's vans down the street," Yumi said. "Liberated some top of the line assault weapons and a ton of ammo."

"Good," Gideon said. "They won't have need of them and Alexandria's minions will just melt them down."

Yumi slid into the front seat of the GTO.

Gideon glared at Hajar and Megan. "If you girls are through roughhousing, we need to find some food and a place to rest. We have a long drive ahead of us."

"Yeah, Doc, I think Hajar has learned her lesson. Next time, I won't take it so easy on you." Laughing, Megan walked away with an exaggerated, cocky strut.

Hajar smiled. "I want a rematch."

Without looking back, Megan waved her hand over her shoulder.

"So, Giddy," Hajar asked as she untied her laces. "What happened? Did Alexandria have the fountain of youth squirreled away in the back room?"

"No, just a two edged sword," Gideon said. "And stop calling me, Giddy."

❧❧❧

"Tell me, hairball," Yumi asked, "did the good doctor get in a lucky punch?"

Roland looked at the grinning assassin and took a deep breath. "No, Yumi. I am a fighter. Hand to hand is my specialty and I am really good at it. I have fought hundreds of men on every continent, except Antarctica, but I ain't never fought anyone like Doc Kane."

"How good was he?"

"He is in a league by himself. I really and truly think he could whip Hajar's ass."

"Damn," Yumi said. "He's *that* good?"

"And then some. He knew what I was going to do before I did. I felt like a five-year-old fighting Bruce Lee. The fight lasted about three minutes."

"You could have resorted to the beast."

"That's how come I got the shiner and the limp."

"If the fight was over so quick, what took you so long?"

"We had a talk," Roland said. "Well, he did most of the talking. I'm here to tell you, Yumi, Doc is the *man*. I have served under many a seasoned commander over the years, but Doc puts them all to shame. You'll laugh, but I would follow the Doc to Hell and back—or until something better came along."

☙❧❦

"Hajar, I know a good place to eat and rest for the night," Gideon said. "You and Megan go on and meet us there. I need to buy some clothes that fit. I'll give you the address and we'll rendezvous later at the restaurant. Got a slip of paper?"

"Umm, in the car. Come on."

Gideon followed her back to her Civic.

"I got a napkin," she said.

"It'll do."

Gideon wrote on the napkin then carefully tore it in half. Giving her the top section with the address, he nonchalantly let her see the bottom half, before slipping it into his pocket.

It read: *We have a spy.*

CHAPTER 21

You have disappointed me, Kyle," Simone Ravenwood said to the young man sitting before her desk. "I gave my word that the shipment would be delivered on the fifth. The order did not arrive until the tenth. Explain yourself."

"Mrs. Ravenwood," said the chubby, balding, profusely sweating shipping manger. "The shipping company went on strike. There was no way to foresee this. It's not my fault!"

"Do you like working for my company?"

"Oh, yes, ma'am!"

"Never let this happen again, Kyle. If I give my personal word about a shipment, by God, it will be there on time, even if you have to deliver it yourself! Understand me?"

"Yes, Mrs. Ravenwood!"

Simone smiled. "I hear that you have another child on the way."

"Yes, my Mandy is three months along," he said, beaming with pride.

"Congratulations," she said. "How many does this make?"

"Four. We have three boys and would love a little girl."

"Excellent."

"Nice office," he said. "Is that a crystal ball?"

"Get back to work and don't let this happen again."

"Yes, Mrs. Ravenwood."

"Give my love to Mandy and the kids."

As Kyle beat a hasty retreat from the office, Simone touched a button on her office intercom. "Howard, I think that

Kyle Ladd has dropped the ball for the last time. He needs a rest. Arrange it."

"Heart attack or stroke?"

"Surprise me," Simone said. "Make damn sure to make it a real showstopper of a funeral. We have a reputation to uphold, after all."

"Yes, Mistress."

Simone Ravenwood was CEO and chief executive officer of Happy Time Amusements, a small toy and novelty company that had just branched out into the lucrative children's television market. Their latest product was Pansy Panda. The cheaply made, yet expensively priced toy was taking the market by storm and would soon have its own TV show.

The small older woman straightened her tailored gray business suit before tossing her cell on the enormous teak desk that held all the normal business accoutrements—appointment book, computer, crystal ball, calendar, etc.

On the far corner of the desk sat the plump, perpetually smiling Pansy Panda.

"How many times have I told you to sit on the shelf?" she asked. "I hate the way you watch me! Now go before I have you cast out."

"Sorry," the minor demon in the stuffed bear said, before leaping off the desk and waddling back to its shelf.

"I hate the creepy things, but have to admit, though, Pansy Panda dolls are bringing in a ton of cash."

Simone was more than the CEO of a second-rate toy company. She was foremost the leader of the Black Circle, the most powerful coven of witches in the world. The coven used Happy Time Amusements as a front in which to launder money from their more unsavory pursuits.

"Samantha should have reported in by now," she said aloud, idly tapping her long nails upon the desk.

Leaning back in her chair, she glanced at the gold mounted crystal ball. The bowling-ball-sized chunk of clear quartz slid across the desk, coming to rest before her. Across its surface floated the words: *Mistress Ravenwood, are you there?*

"Samantha, your report is overdue," Simone muttered. "I

was beginning to think your true identity had been discovered. How is my dear friend Salome Kerr?"

My apologies, Mistress. You dear friend Mrs. Kerr is an insufferable, horrible woman who deserves a slow, painful death. Since the former Paladin has joined our ranks, she has tightened security and it has been harder to get a message away.

I still do not understand your interest in keeping the pig alive. It is a clear-cut case. Mrs. Kerr stole your collars and she must die. I never understood why you wanted me to pretend to be her slave.

"That is my business and not yours. You will play your part and be a good girl until I say otherwise. Your reward will far more than compensate for any inconvenience."

Yes, Mistress Ravenwood.

"I am curious about Maggie Black—excuse me, *Hajar.* How is the poor girl holding up? For anyone else, the betrayal by one so close would be soul crushing. Add to that, Mrs. Kerr's own brand of misery must be wreaking mental havoc of biblical proportions. Has she broken yet?"

As a matter of fact, Mrs. Kerr is no longer in charge of us, Mistress.

"What? Explain."

Mrs. Kerr was confronted a few days ago by an old nemesis, going by the name, Gideon Kane. Seems Mrs. Kerr had murdered a few of Kane's friends back when disco was king and Kane has a long memory. In a rather brilliant move, the old boy caught us flatfooted with a drugged pizza. Before we knew what hit us, Kane had Mrs. Kerr strapped to a chair with a cocked .45 Colt to her head.

"How could you let this happen? Is Mrs. Kerr dead?"

I am ashamed to admit that I was blindsided like a rank amateur. However, for all his apparent skill, Kane turns out to be a fool who fancies himself "a good guy." The numbskull felt sorry for Mrs. Kerr's slaves and, instead of righteous, well-deserved revenge, made a deal with the devil. In exchange for the release of her slaves, Kane agreed to deliver, believe it or not, the mythical Tree of Life.

Have you ever heard of anything so ridiculous?

"My God." Simone settled back into her chair. "Where are you now? Are you still with Mrs. Kerr?"

We left Mrs. Kerr behind. Right now, I am at The Star-Bright Motel, a crap-hole in beautiful downtown Hoobidton, Pennsylvania. Mistress, life hasn't been dull since our change in management. A few hours ago, we were in a firefight at Alexandria's Library.

"*The* Alexandria's Library? Have you been drinking?"

As crazy as it sounds, I was there. It seems that Kane and the mysterious Alexandria have a history. From what I gathered, he almost destroyed her once.

"You gathered wrong, because that is impossible! The entire might of the Black Circle would be helpless before her."

Nonetheless, I heard Alexandria admit to it.

"What happened there?"

Kane made Alexandria some kind of deal, the exact extent is unknown, but old man Kane is now super-hot, young man candy Kane.

"Please try to control yourself. What turned it into a fight?"

Your associate Duncan Figg and two dozen mercs showed up and tried to snatch Kane. Alexandria slaughtered them and almost wiped us out, too. Fortunately, Hajar was on our side or you would not be getting this report.

"Figg? Are you sure?"

I got up close and personal. It was Figg all right. Mistress, who is this Kane? How could someone with his skills and connections fly under the radar?

"I don't know, Samantha but, by God, I will find out."

I did an internet search on this Kane and nothing came up but a series of out of print, adventure books written by a Harold David back in the 1950s. From the descriptions of the plots, I suspect they were fictionalized accounts of Kane's exploits.

"That could tell us something about whom we are dealing with."

Say the word and Kane won't know what hit him.

"Absolutely not! You will follow Kane and support his

mission. In fact, get close and learn all you can. He must never suspect you."

Understood, Mistress. You don't really think he has a chance of finding this Tree do you? I always thought it was no more than a silly Christian myth.

"Myth or not I want to see where this goes."

Understood.

ↄ⁄ↄ℮ↄ

As the crystal's mystic energies abated, Simone's cell rang.

"Yes?"

"Mistress," Howard Valdez said, "I have the forecasts for the upcoming fiscal—"

"Forget it. I want the board assembled—now."

"Yes, Mistress. However, I believe Mr. Moge and Mr. Figg are out of town."

"Way out of town."

"Excuse me?"

"Never mind, have the board ready in an hour."

Chapter 22

Simone burst through the tall double doors of the extravagant conference room where the three remaining council members awaited her.

While the exact number of their followers and disciples was in question, it was known to exceed that of the United States Marine Corps.

Wearing her warmest smile, Simone took her chair at the apex of the gleaming stone table. The council members bowed slightly before taking their own places. Two chairs sat conspicuously empty.

"Welcome to Salt Lake City, my brothers and sisters of the Circle," Simone said.

"Thank you, Mistress," Thomas West said. The small, delicate man with watery eyes and a nervous demeanor spoke with a pronounced New England accent. "Don't you think it is a bit reckless to set up our headquarters in a bastion of Christianity? Aren't you afraid of spiritual reprisal?"

"Hardly. Whether or not this is a bastion of Christianity is debatable. While the Mormon faith has a considerable following, mainstream Christianity considers Mormon doctrine to be an abomination—a perversion of Christian tenets. The general population, however, sees the Mormons as God fearing, sober, moral conservatives, which is precisely the demographic we are after. Besides, I personally adore our Mormon workforce. They are honest hard workers who have been instrumental to our success."

"I don't think our employees would be happy if they knew that they worked for a godless coven of witches," Thomas said with a smile.

"Nonsense," Simone said. "Everyone knows that witches don't exist."

The council laughed.

"Mistress Ravenwood," Thomas West said. "You will be happy to know that Pansy Panda has exceeded our wildest expectations and sales are through the roof."

"We're not here about some silly stuffed doll," Simone snapped, "or plastic dog poop, whoopee cushions, or any of the other junk we peddle here. This is Circle business. I apologize for the short notice, however, I felt it important to personally address certain concerns I have."

"What concerns might that be?" asked Alistair Broome.

"There is a certain, special project I have been working on. It has come to my attention that some of you have...inadvertently...stumbled into it. Back off. This is my show alone."

The council looked at Simone and smiled.

"Now that, that is settled, you are dismissed."

No one moved.

"We have concerns about the Tree," Mei Xue said.

"Concerns, Mei?" Simone asked. "About a tree? I am not a gardener."

"Don't play games with us," Alistair snapped. The squat Brit looked more like a truck driver or longshoreman, than one of the most powerful warlock leaders on the planet. "Our spies have confirmed that you are on the trail of the Tree of Life."

"This path leads to disaster, Mistress Ravenwood," Mei Xue said. The small, elegant Chinese woman was known for her exotic beauty, her voracious appetite for female lovers, and her odd habit of using a long old-fashioned cigarette holder. "Such an endeavor brings into question your ability to lead this cabal."

"I would be careful if I were you, Mei," Simone growled. "I may take offense and I'm sure you wouldn't want to open that door."

"I hate to say it, but Mei is right," Thomas said. "Granted, under your leadership we have reaped substantial financial benefits, but this time you have gone too far."

Simone stiffened. "Risk is all part of the game."

"You should have consulted us!" Alistair's face was flushed with anger. "This could ruin everything!"

Simone sighed. "Brothers and sisters, I am doing this for us—for the greater good of The Black Circle."

"And if my poor old granny had wheels she would be a wagon," Alistair said. "You want the Tree for yourself. You know it and we know it."

"Ah, Alistair, as always," Simone said, "you are as subtle as a sledge hammer."

"Alistair is right," Mei said. "We don't want your thirst for power destroying everything we have built."

"Looks like I have some explaining to do. Yes, I am going after the Tree of Life."

Mei slammed her fist on the table. "Duncan and Moge must have found out about your plan and you had them killed to hide your intent."

"Duncan and Moge are dead," Simone agreed, "but not by my hand. Apparently, their spies were better than yours were and they found out about my little treasure hunt weeks earlier. It appears that they paid the price for their greed."

"You have lost me," Thomas said. "If you didn't kill them, who did?"

"Yes," Mei said. "Bring us up to speed on your plan and don't leave out any details."

"Very well. You are all familiar with Salome Kerr, I take it?"

"Yes, that fool broke ranks with us years ago," Alistair said. "Some think that the strain has been too much for her mind to bear. What about her?"

"About three years ago, Mrs. Kerr stole seven of our brand new witch collars. It took some time, but my investigators eventually figured out that she was to blame. I sent an assassin to kill her and return our property, but certain reports as to her intent fascinated me, so I turned her killer into a spy by allowing her to become one of Mrs. Kerr's slaves. Mei, I think you know her, Samantha Jordan."

Mei smiled. "Sam is the best—in many ways."

"This is pointless," Alistair said. "Just kill the fool and be done with it."

"It may interest you to know that Salome Kerr is in possession of *The Book of Xanadutha.*"

Mei gasped. "How did Mrs. Kerr obtain the book? I have spent years—spent a fortune searching for that damn book. I was beginning to think the book was no more than an old wives' tale."

"Oh, it is real. Mrs. Kerr obtained the book as payment for killing the Paladin."

"The Paladin?" Thomas cried. "That is all we need! Larry will seek revenge and that unpredictable angel is more than we can handle. I say we turn Mrs. Kerr in and let Larry deal with her."

Simone chuckled. "It was Larry who hired Mrs. Kerr to kill Maggie Black. Seems that Heaven has thrown open its door to Larry, the only stipulation being that poor Maggie had to take one for the team."

"Why?" Thomas asked. "It makes no sense."

"Who cares?" Alastair asked. "We are the ones reaping the benefits of this deal. Larry is gone and Maggie Black is dead. No more interfering with our plans. It is definitely a win-win situation."

"Unfortunately, for some strange reason, Mrs. Kerr did not kill Maggie Black. She faked her death and made her a slave instead."

"Collars do give a whole new outlook on life," Mei said, blowing a ring of animated smoke.

"Yes," Simone said. "Maggie is now Hajar. Mrs. Kerr uses her to rob the occasional bank and to be her muscle. I find it ironic."

Mei snorted. "My, how the mighty have fallen. I love it when a self-righteous twit is corrupted and turned to the dark side."

"This is all very interesting," Alastair said. "However, what does this have to do with the Tree?"

"Mrs. Kerr is working with a partner who can decipher the book's cryptic writing. It has been confirmed that the book is indeed a map to the location of Eden. As we speak, they seek the Tree."

"This is astounding," Alastair said. "What did you plan to do about this, Mistress?"

"While my spy feeds me information, I have men close by. When they get close, I will swoop in and take the prize away from them. Duncan Figg tried to interfere and paid the price with his life. I order all of you to stand down and let me take care of this matter."

"Figg wasn't the only one, Mistress," Alastair informed her. "I happen to know that Moge also knew about the Tree. Seems he and a few of his Zombie abominations have been missing for a few days. My psychics confirm that he is dead."

"If we keep our heads, the Tree and all its benefits will be ours," Simone said.

"Haven't you overlooked something, Mistress?" Thomas asked. "The reason no one seeks the Tree is because it is being guarded by a hellish, invincible sentry. Besides, it is said that to tread in Eden will invoke the wrath of Heaven. I think we all remember Noah and the Flood. I, for one, live much too well to throw everything away on a pipe dream."

"Afraid?" Simone asked. "I thought you were bolder than that?"

Thomas blotted the sweat from his upper lip with a hand-kerchief. "This is suicide! *You* should walk away before this explodes in *our* faces. If the legends are to be believed, the Nephilim did indeed find the Tree of Life—and were wiped out, along with almost every other living thing on this planet. We should be happy with what we have and leave well enough alone."

"Regardless of how well we live and how much money we stockpile, one day we will die. The Tree is a cosmic conduit of raw power. We will walk this world as eternal Gods, and that is worth any risk. Besides, it is Mrs. Kerr who will incur any wrath if this goes south. Once she has done all the heavy lifting, we take the prize. What could be simpler? When all is said and done, the seven billion souls that crawl around on this miserable rock will be our slaves."

"I am in." Mei took a drag and slowly blew a long cloud of smoke. The smoke magically turned into a perfect representation of the Earth. "For such a prize it is well worth the risk."

The counsel chuckled at the bright lust shining in her eyes.

"However, I don't think I am ready for you to be a God, Mistress," she said.

"What's the matter, Mei, don't trust your beloved leader to share with the council?"

"I trust my *beloved* leader, but let's face it, we of the counsel are not exactly the sharing type. How many of our brothers and sisters have died so we could sit in these chairs? We must work together or not at all. What say you, Mistress?"

"Agreed. It is the only way."

"I say we use our combined resources to safeguard the former Paladin and her troop," Alastair suggested.

Mei nodded. "At a discrete distance."

"Yes," Alastair said. "They will be as safe as a baby in his mother's arms. That is, until we have what we want."

"I am glad that we are finally seeing eye-to-eye on this," Simone said.

"Where is Mrs. Kerr's group?" Astaire asked.

"That little secret stays with me alone," Simone said. "I will keep you abreast of information. Now get out and be prepared to travel."

Chapter 23

Drinking in the dark aura, born of the crimes committed within the confines of the richly appointed chamber, Simone Ravenwood meditated while she awaited *him*. The room suddenly grew bone cold, its temperature dropping several degrees in mere seconds. Simone smiled as she saw her breath condense before her.

"Is that you, my Lord Aesir?" she asked.

"Who else would it be, Simone?"

"The plan is working perfectly."

"Did you have any doubt?"

"No. However, I had hoped that the council would not get wind of it."

"It was only a matter of time. I know that they can be difficult, but perhaps they can be of use."

"They are pack of dogs," Simone said. "They will probe for any weakness, trying to find a way to seize the prize for themselves, just like Duncan and Moge tried to do."

"Then you must exercise your authority and control them."

"Like trying to herd a dozen cats."

"That is not my problem."

"How did I know you would say that?"

"Whatever trouble, whatever difficulty, will be worth it when Eden is discovered. There will be a new era ushered in, a new authority, while the old authority will pass away in fire and disgrace."

"We will find it, my Lord."

"Yes, you will," Aesir said, "and you, Simone Ravenwood shall be a God."

"Which raises the question of why would you give it to me, instead of keeping it for yourself?"

"I am one of the old Gods, blindsided by my own petulant child. Selfish, greedy, and arrogant, he is clever, though. He created a mystic prison that feeds on my supreme power. However, the key to my freedom is the Tree. Take the Tree and I will be released back into the universe. Then this world and all who dwell upon it are yours."

"Yes, my Lord."

"Just be sure that when you find the Tree you will not touch the fruit until my arrival."

"It will be good to finally see the face of my Lord. That is, unless you want to give me a sneak peek now?"

"You will see my glory when the time is right and not a second before."

ඏඏඏ

Simone pursed her lips in frustration. Aesir's identity might be a mystery, but one thing was for sure, he was indeed powerful. He had first come to her when she was sixteen years old, living in Sage, Kansas. Back then, she was plain old Lucy Etta May Hickey, the only daughter of a Bemis Tractor sales representative, Ed Hickey and his homemaker wife, Mary.

She would never forget the night he first spoke to her. She was out walking in the fields, looking for her lost calf. Lucy was terrified by this unseen voice in the night, but his voice was so soothing, his words so compelling, that she thought he was an angel from heaven.

For two years, he came to her at night and seduced her with promises of power beyond her wildest dreams. Finally, to show her dedication and devotion to her new lord, she murdered her parents while they slept.

After an innocent drifter paid for her crimes, Lucy Etta May Hickey became Simone Ravenwood and slipped away into the rancid world of darkness and witchcraft.

It was Aesir who had guided her down the road that led to the Black Circle and her eventual leadership. Unlike the story she had concocted, it was Aesir who had given her the secret of the obedience collars. Simone was fabulously rich, powerful, and she knew without question that she owed her entire life to Aesir. He asked only one thing, that she pour the Circle's last ounce of energy into securing for him the Tree of Life.

e/ɔe/ɔ

Mei Xue rode in the back of her limo, mulling over what Simone had told them. She couldn't get the image of *The Book of Xanadutha* out of her head. It was a ripe plum that had eluded her for too long.

Mei's phone chimed, interrupting half dozen ideas for stealing the book. Picking up the phone, she saw a text message that read: ~ *Mrs. Kerr's people will be at The Star-Bright Motel, in Hoobidton, Pennsylvania for another 14 hours. Act before it is too late.*

Mei clicked a button and called her assistant.

"Andrea dear, it seems that opportunity has landed in my lap and I must leave town for a bit. I know this is short notice, but I need a double for me at Thomas's suite at the Fremont Hotel in an hour. As usual, he and blowhard Alistair throw a conspiracy party whenever Simone passes gas. Use the girl I used at the Vanderbilt affair. I know she isn't perfect, but she is available. Have her smoke a lot, be bitchy, condescending, and disagreeable, and those two twits will never know the difference."

e/ɔe/ɔ

An hour and thirty-seven minutes later, a small airliner, suffering apparent catastrophic hydraulic failure, crashed into the posh hotel killing all fifty-three passengers. It took out the top five stories, including Thomas West's penthouse suite. There were no survivors, above the second floor.

CHAPTER 24

With the scent of strawberries filling the steamy shower, Hajar worked the shampoo through her hair. Rinsing away the rich, foamy lather in the second-rate motel's dismal water pressure proved to be a challenge and, for once, Hajar was glad for her hair's painfully short length.

Relishing the soothing, hot water, her mind drifted.

Gideon and the others are at the local greasy spoon, giving me some much deserved alone time. Now if Gideon wanted to stay behind and scrub my back—well, that would be even better. I don't care if he is eighty-three, damn, he's hot.

Turning off the shower, Hajar pulled free a scratchy white towel with the absorbent properties of a sheet of polypropylene and began to furiously towel dry her hair. Sliding back the plastic curtain, she stepped blindly onto the cheap bath mat. Pulling the towel down, she discovered that she stood toe to toe with Mei Xue.

Before Hajar could react, Mei, using her cigarette holder, blew an odd, white smoke into her face. Gasping in surprise, Hajar drew in the spell. Instantly, her body froze. While her mind was untouched, she could not make the smallest muscle move, let alone cry out. Unable to control her body, she fell forward.

Exerting strength beyond her delicate-looking five-foot frame, Mei caught the toppling woman and cradled her in her arms like a child.

"You are a pleasant surprise, Hajar," Mei whispered. "From your exploits, I was expecting a brute that resembled a Russian weight lifter. You are simply gorgeous." She carried the help-less Hajar from the steamy bath where she laid her gently on the bed.

"Don't worry, Hajar," Mei continued as she lightly stroked the curve of her face. "I don't want your life. I merely want to make you an offer without you beating me to a bloody pulp. I know about your little quest and I want the Tree of Life for myself."

Unable to speak, Hajar rolled her eyes, making Mei smile.

"Heard that before, have you, girl? Nevertheless, while my brothers and sisters will try and steal your prize and leave you dead, I offer you payment in the form of sweet retribution against the bastard angel who let Mrs. Kerr make you a slave."

Hajar's eyes widened.

"That got your attention. Hajar, I know your story. I know that you burn with the desire to give Larry a taste of the humil-iation he heaped upon you. If you are interested, come alone to Room 205 after the others go to bed. Do not breathe a word of this to anyone, especially Gideon Kane or I rescind my offer. Here is a small token of my goodwill. There is a Black Circle spy in your midst, so trust no one."

Mei looked down at Hajar and bit her lower lip. The undis-guised lust in her eyes made Hajar blush. "If I knew you looked like this, I would have kidnapped you years ago. Any-way, beautiful, the paralysis will only last a minute or two longer and leave you with no ill effects. Remember, room 205 and don't forget to bring Kali."

Mei tucked the blanket about Hajar's body as one would tuck a child in for the night. With a sly smile, she kissed Hajar's lips lightly before quickly slipping from the room.

Like the lifting of a fog, the paralysis melted away, leaving Hajar beyond furious. Ripping the blanket away, she leapt from the bed, intending on chasing down the seductive witch and breaking her in half.

Hajar's cell buzzed angrily on the cheap nightstand.

Snatching up the phone she barked, "What?"

"Hajar," Megan said, "I forgot what dressing you wanted on your salad."

"Italian, Shortstack. You know that."

"You sounded pissed when you answered the phone. Anything wrong?"

"Um, no, honey. I didn't mean to snap at you. I was in the shower was all."

"Sorry about that. Be back in a few."

Hajar turned off her cell. She mentally struggled over hunting the witch down, but her offer was tantalizing. Slipping on her clothes, she felt a small smile playing at the corners of her mouth as she entertained the idea of payback.

CHAPTER 25

Hajar silently moved down the darkened breezeway, expecting a demon or some other nasty surprise to spring out at her.

Calm down, girl. If she wanted to, the witch could have killed me this afternoon and I could not have lifted a finger to stop her. Damn, catching me flatfooted like that, in the shower of all places, really pissed me off. Worse, I didn't care one bit for the way she was ogling me.

Hajar stopped at room 205. Swallowing hard and fighting her guilt, she paused to lightly rap upon the door when it sprang open.

The room lights were out. However, the chamber was illuminated by the soft glow of dozens of flickering candles.

The cheap motel furnishings were gone, replaced with an enormous bed covered with luxurious coverings of mink and ermine. Beside the bed lay a low table that contained delicacies and rare chocolates, along with a bottle of vintage champagne cooling in a silver bucket of ice. It looked less like the dangerous demon-haunted lair of a witch who wanted her head on the wall and more like the bed chamber of a seductress. Hajar shuddered. She would have much preferred the former.

What I wouldn't give for the right guy to go to all this effort for me. Instead, I get the treatment from an evil lesbian witch. Is my life screwed up or what?

Warily, Hajar entered and the door closed behind her. Mei sat back on the bed, wearing an expensive negligee and smoking, using a long old-fashioned jade cigarette holder. A smoky halo encircled her long raven hair.

"I am still pissed at the *Psycho* shower scene, lady. A text message would have sufficed."

"I thoroughly enjoyed our brief time together. The water glistening on your flawless skin will haunt my dreams forever."

Hajar blushed and her green eyes flashed with anger. "Keep it up and you'll be haunting this room forever, sweetie."

Mei laughed.

"Nice room. You must have sprung for the Traveler's Rest Presidential Suite."

"Where are my manners? Care for a drink, an appetizer, or perhaps a cigarette?"

"Nasty habit. Don't you know it is against the law to smoke in motel rooms? You could smoke meat in here."

"You don't indulge in the pleasures of tobacco, Hajar? I am surprised. Life is too short not to experience it to the fullest."

"I don't care to indulge in the pleasures of emphysema or lung cancer, either."

"Enough small talk, Hajar. My name is Mei Xue. You may call me Mei, beautiful."

"Sorry, sweetie I don't know what you expected, but this girl don't swing that way—*ever*. Now what is this deal you were talking about?"

"I don't know if you or your intrepid leader, Kane, realizes it or not, but Heaven will notice when you get close to the Tree of Life. They will send someone to persuade you to stop. When they realize that you are not dead, that person will no doubt be your former boss, Larry."

"How can I stop him?" Hajar asked. "Even Kali can't kill an angel."

"She can with a boost," Mei toyed with her slim cigarette holder. The witch produced a small glass vial of dark purple liquid. "This poison can kill even one from the heavenly realm, if combined with the power of Kali."

Hajar eyed the vial and pursed her lips. "As much as I want Larry to pay for what he has done to me, I can't give you the

Tree. To be free of this damn collar, I have to give it to Mrs. Kerr."

"I do not have a problem with that," Mei said with a sly smile. "I merely ask to be there in the critical moment before she enters Eden. Between your release and her taking the Tree, is all the window of opportunity I need. To do this, I must know your precise whereabouts at all times. You will carry my mark."

"You want me to carry a GPS tracker?"

"I was thinking of something a bit more esoteric."

"You are with the Black Circle, aren't you?"

"With the Black Circle? My dear, girl, I am Mei Xue of the Dark Counsel. I am second only to Mistress Ravenwood herself."

"Then forget it! Mrs. Kerr is one thing, but what hell will the Black Circle put us through? I have a feeling that we would go from the frying pan into the fire. I think I will stay with the devil I know."

Mei removed her smoldering cigarette from the holder and crushed out the butt in a heavy glass ashtray. "Honestly, it would make your time with Salome Kerr seem like a trip to Heaven. Many on the counsel are just itching to pay you back personally for the trouble you and your boss Larry have caused them over the past few years."

"That's former boss."

"Whatever."

"And how does this make me want to help you?"

"I weary of the Circle and always looking over my shoulder to see who is gunning for me. I want to stage a coup and destroy the organization once and for all. For that, I need the Tree."

"With you as the most powerful witch on Earth? What then, world domination?"

"You make me sound like a James Bond villain," Mei said with a laugh. "I have always had a live and let live attitude. The 'normals' would never have a clue that anything has changed, but esoteric evil would be far less organized without the Circle's lust for power."

"Your brothers and sisters won't like this."

"No. In fact, I think they already suspect I have turned on them. Anyway, Hajar, do we have a deal?"

"How do I know this isn't a trick? Witches are masters of the double cross."

"I get nothing but a horrible death if Larry kills you, now don't I, Hajar?" Mei rose from the bed, her striking form accentuated by a sheer, black nightgown. "I am risking everything I have worked for, including my very life, to give you your shot at revenge, and all I want in exchange, is to merely know your whereabouts. I offer you an opportunity that you will never otherwise have."

"What kind of a mark?"

Mei smiled brightly. Opening a ratty looking carpetbag, she produced a small amber jar.

Hajar backed away. "Whoa, now. How do I know that isn't some kind of love potion or mind-control drug? I don't need another master."

"Such potions are very limited in their effectiveness. Besides, they severely lower the subject's IQ. The road ahead is treacherous and you will need to be at your sharpest if you are to even get close to the Tree."

Hajar thought a moment, then sighed. "All right, Mei, you have a deal. Give me the bottle."

"Not so fast, beautiful." Mei removed the glass stopper. "I am taking the lion's share of risk. I deserve a small pleasure in return."

"Excuse me?"

Mei took a long swallow of the potion, carefully recapped the jar, and put it away.

"I have dreamed of your sweet, luscious lips all day. This deal will be sealed with a kiss."

To Mei's utter shock and delight, Hajar scooped the witch up in her arms and delivered a passionate, soul-stirring kiss. Caught off guard, Mei intertwined her arms about Hajar's neck and pulled her close as the mystic potion flowed into Hajar. After long moments, their lips parted, leaving Mei panting.

"Wow," Mei whispered.

"Just so you know, Mei," Hajar whispered back, "I still don't swing that way, but for a chance to get even with that sorry, rat bastard, I would have rocked your world. However, the deal was for a kiss only, and I gave you a smooch that made your knees sweat. Now pay up, witchy woman."

Mei gave her a narrow gaze and slowly slid her arms from Hajar's neck. "You are beautiful, smart, and utterly cruel. Just the way I like my lovers."

"You like cruel? If I have time later, I'll drop by and beat the hell out of you, but for now, the clock is ticking."

Mei laughed. "Produce Kali."

Hajar pulled Kali from her bag.

"Feed me the witch thing," whined the mystic blade. "I am hungry."

"Hush," Hajar hissed.

"Hold the blade out before you, right side up," Mei ordered.

Hajar obeyed.

Mei chanted in a singsong voice as she lit a thick, black candle. Holding the candle under the blade, her voice rising to a high-pitched tone, Mei bathed Kali in fire. Mei took the vial and let fall a single drop of the purple fluid.

Kali screamed, catching Hajar by surprise. It took all of her might to hold the blade steady as Mei, still chanting, motioned for Hajar to turn the mighty blade. Another drop of poison and Kali became wild, thrashing about in agony.

"What have you done?" Hajar cried, as the enchanted blade grew red hot, glowing crimson in her hands.

Ignoring Hajar, Mei calmly finished her spell and then blew out the black candle. The tremendous heat vanished and Kali returned to normal.

"It is done," Mei said. "It is up to you now, Hajar."

"One last thing, Mei. Who is the spy?"

Mei affixed a fresh cigarette to her holder. Sitting back on the bed, she casually lit the cigarette. "Samantha Jordan is the serpent in your midst. Be careful, beautiful. She is the best deep-cover assassin the Circle has. If she even suspects you are on to her, she will kill you all."

Oh God, not Megan.

Returning Kali to her bag, Hajar turned and left room 205 without looking back.

Mei drew deeply on her cigarette and slipped on a long, chocolate trench coat. With a wave of her hand, the room illusion vanished and the drab motel room returned to normal.

"Good fortune, Hajar. I am truly sorry for what I have done to you, but a debt must be paid. If only we had met under different circumstances."

Tracing a circle on the carpet, Mei chanted a small incantation and, stepping into the portal, disappeared.

CHAPTER 26

Her mind reeling, Hajar slipped through the shadows of the sleeping motel.

So, little sweet Megan isn't who she says she is. Betrayed again. Damn it, I must be the sucker of the year. I'll never trust another human being as long as I live. Not to mention, I just frenched a walking ashtray. Before going back to the room, I need to down a large bottle of Listerine.

Feeling thoroughly disgusted over the revelation of the spy and at her own dealings with a witch, Hajar nearly ran into Ginny.

Hajar looked upon the beautiful apparition and beheld a single jewel like tear rolling down her crestfallen face.

"Ginny, honey, I can explain."

Ginny turned her back and promptly disappeared.

"Explain what?" Gideon asked as he emerged from the darkness.

"Nothing."

"Kind of late for a stroll isn't it? Especially since we have a long drive ahead of us."

"I went to the vending machine—you know, for a soda."

"Where is your drink?"

"What's with the third degree?" she snapped. "When it comes down to it, old man, it's none of your damn business what I do. If I want to take an early morning stroll buck-naked wearing a red rubber clown nose, that's my business, so get off my back."

Unperturbed by her outburst, Gideon stepped in close and got a whiff of an almost forgotten scent. "Have you taken up smoking as well?" He grabbed her by the shoulders and shoved her into a concrete block wall. "Where is she?"

"Where is who?"

"Mei Xue. I know the stench of her brand of cigarette like the back of my hand. It is her private, one of a kind stock. What have you done, woman?"

"It is none of your business!"

"You are right," Gideon snarled as he stepped away. "None of this is my business. I wash my hands of you and your problem. Give my regards to your crew, I'm going home."

He turned on his heel and, while Hajar watched in shock, quickly descended a set of stairs and sauntered toward his GTO.

"Wait," she hissed. "You can't go. We need you!"

Gideon didn't respond, but pulled a key ring from his jeans.

"Oh no you don't," she muttered as she raced along the second floor.

Taking a mighty leap, she landed between the GTO and Gideon, slamming him hard against the side of the car.

"You can't go. We need you—*I* need you, damn it! You promised to help me."

Gideon reversed the move and put the surprised Hajar on the ground. "You look here, *woman*. I don't have the time for lies or half-truths, especially when the silly girl I am sticking my neck out for is making under the table deals with the Black Circle. Now spill it or I am gone."

Hajar swallowed hard and looked down at the pavement. "You're right, Gideon. I did make a deal with Mei Xue."

"I knew it." He slapped the fender of his GTO. "Give me the details."

"She wants the Tree."

"What a surprise. What did she offer?"

"She supercharged Kali in exchange for a way to track us."

"Supercharged Kali? I don't understand. Kali can deal with almost—*shit*." Gideon closed his eyes as if physically struck. "You want to kill Larry."

"I owe him."

"Let it go."

"He has to pay! Don't you understand?"

"Do *I* understand? Sweetie, I swore revenge on Salome Kerr before you were born. When I laid eyes on that sadistic devil, it was all I could not to rip her head off, but I laid it aside to help you. I expect you to do the same with Larry. Call it a lesson learned and move on with your life."

"What's the matter, old man? Aren't you even going to give me the spiel about digging two graves and serving cold dishes?"

"I signed on to free you from Mrs. Kerr, not help you with a blood vendetta, especially one that has less going for it than a snowball in Hell. It ends now or I walk."

"You can't do this to me! You will help me, Gideon. I'll make you!" She leapt at him and threw a wild haymaker. "You are not going anywhere, old man!"

"Here we go again," he said, dodging and weaving.

Back and forth, across the mostly empty back parking lot of the motel, they fought. Enraged, Hajar fought with all her power, if not her skills.

Gideon, on the other hand, calmly responded with a series of expert defensive parries, knowing full well that, if she connected, with her sheer power, it could be the end of him. He refused to strike the furious woman, hoping that she would eventually run out of steam and regain her senses.

Unable to break through his superb defense, and her mindless frustration, Hajar cried out, "Kali, come to Momma."

The deadly blade flew through the night air to her hand. "Hajar, tasty as he probably is, Gideon is your friend," Kali said. "Are you sure?"

Screaming in rage, holding Kali high, Hajar rushed Gideon.

He simply stood his ground, crossed his arms, and ignored his concealed Colts. "You want me dead? Go ahead and save us both some trouble."

Oh God, what am I doing? she thought suddenly as her blind fury vanished.

She stopped Kali in mid-strike. With a wild, primal scream,

Hajar spun like a hammer thrower and launched the blade two hundred and fifty yards across the parking lot and deep into an empty wooded field where Kali plunged into a towering oak. In seconds, the tree crumbled and died.

"You done?" he asked.

"I don't know what happened. I am s—sorry," she said. Her chest heaving and her body shaking with nervous energy, she stood, with her head down, before him in shame.

Gideon gently gathered the broken woman into his arms and held her close. He was mildly amazed at how comfortable he was with the strange girl whom he had just met. As he held her, in a way, it was if he held his own sweet Ginny. Whether he wanted to admit it or not, he enjoyed holding Hajar.

Hajar embraced him tightly, her pain drained out in a torrent of tears and sobs.

"Let it out," he cooed as he stoked her sweat damp hair.

"Please don't leave me, Gideon. You are all I have."

"I'm not going anywhere, sweetheart. As long as you need me, I'll be here."

"I still despise the ground Larry stands on, but revenge isn't worth loosing you. You are the first good thing to happen to me since the world fell apart."

They held each other, enjoying the warm embrace and, for a few precious moments, the world did not exist outside of each other's arms.

"I feel better, Gideon, thanks. Your beard tickles, by the way."

"That's my girl. You know, Hajar, we do this a lot. Since I have known you, we have fought more than Ginny and I did in thirty years of marriage."

"This was the last meltdown, I swear."

"I know. Now, what did Mei say to you?"

Hajar wiped her eyes on her sleeve.

"Other than wanting me to be her girlfriend, she gave me some kind of potion to keep track of me. Oh yeah, she said that our spy was a Black Circle assassin, Samantha Jordan. I still can't believe Megan could be a cold blooded killer. That little shit really snowed me."

"I always thought of myself as being a fair judge of character. Megan just doesn't seem the type, but I have never known
Mei to lie."

Hajar squinted at Gideon in the gloom.

"You and Mei have history?"

"We have butted heads a few times over the years."

"I must have missed the book called, *Kamikaze Kane and
the Chain Smoking Lesbian Witch.*"

"That's a ridiculous title. Besides, Mei is not strictly lesbian. She can be very charming, but don't let her sweet smile
fool you, underneath, Mei is a real monster."

"Charming? Sweet smile?"

"Let's just say, Mei and I have an understanding. I leave
her alone and she does the same with me. What I don't understand is that she obviously knew we're together and yet she
still approached you."

"Together?" Hajar asked with a mischievous smile. "Don't
flatter yourself, old man. You should be so lucky to get a real
babe like me."

"You know what I mean."

"So again, how *well* do you two kids know each other?
When you speak of Mrs. Kerr, I can hear your blood boiling,
but Mei is different. It's almost as if—hey, wait a minute.
When you say you know her, you aren't speaking as in *bibli-
cally* knowing each other, are you?"

On the outside, Hajar smiled and appeared to be joking,
however, she was deadly serious. The mere thought of Gideon
and Mei being more than sworn, gun blazing, hate-the-ground-
you-walk-on enemies unsettled her. What she would never
admit was that deep down, there erupted a small, yet intense,
flame of jealousy.

"Drop it, Hajar. You know? The longer I know you, the
more I want to turn you over my knee."

"Is that what you're into, old man? Did you turn Mei over
your knee, too?"

"That's disgusting, even for you."

Hajar giggled.

"Oh no," he said as his eyes grew wide.

"What's the matter?"

"Something has just occurred to me. How could I have been so blind?"

"What's wrong, tell me."

"Listen to me very carefully, because this is critical. Mei didn't touch you, did she?"

Hajar gazed into his deep blue eyes. "No. She wanted to play house, but this girl is not into witches."

"Are you sure? I have to know."

Hajar winced in embarrassment. "Okay, there was one little thing, but it was nothing."

"What was it, girl?" he asked, taking her by the shoulders.

"Okay, she delivered the potion with—a kiss—sort of."

"Oh no." He closed his eyes as if in pain. The reaction sent a spasm of dread through Hajar. "Anything, but that," he continued. "Oh, Lord, what have you done?"

"It didn't seem like *that* big a deal."

"Lips only or with tongue? You better tell me the truth. It may be the only way to save you."

Hajar swallowed hard. "There may have been *some* tongue."

"Quit beating around the bush, this is life or death important!"

"Okay, I gave her the full treatment—damn near gave her a tonsillectomy! What is it, Gideon? What did she do to me?"

"Hajar, honey, I hate to say this, but—" Gideon took a deep breath and let it out. "Mei has *cooties*." He threw his head back and roared with laughter.

For a moment, Hajar stood before him, stunned, not comprehending what just happened.

"That wasn't funny. Oh, you miserable, sorry old asshole, now I really am going to kick your ass." Looking over his shoulder, she paused. "Gideon, it looks like we have an audience."

Behind them stood a ragged crowd of bleary-eyed, disgruntled motel guests.

Wearing a wife beater and stripped pajama bottoms, the irate motel manager marched up to Gideon. "I run a nice place here, mister. Take that crazy, loud mouthed drunk woman and get out before I call the cops!"

"Loud mouthed?" Hajar exclaimed.

Gideon grabbed her as she took a step toward the small man. She suddenly clutched her midsection and let out a moan.

"Hajar, what's wrong?" Gideon cried.

"I feel sick. Oh God, I feel like I am on the receiving end of a nuclear-powered cramp."

While Gideon had his hands full with Hajar, Roland, Yumi, and Megan rolled up to the former Iranian national motel manager.

"Oh Lord give me strength," Gideon muttered as he tended to the ill woman, praying his new crew wouldn't kill anyone.

Hajar broke out in a clammy sweat. Just when the pain became unbearable, it was gone, leaving her feeling weak and washed out. "Oh thank God, the pain's gone," she whispered softly. She knew that it was the potion she ingested from Mei and she silently prayed that it wasn't poison.

Gideon scooped her up into his strong arms. "I am taking you to a hospital."

"I am all right now, put me down. We have to stop Roland from starting a fight," she said, even though she loved being cradled in his strong arms.

∽∾∽

"I don't like your attitude, Sudamm." Roland stood toe to toe with the cowering man. "Call the cops and you had better call an ambulance, too, wiseass."

"And the fire department," Yumi said. "This dump looks like it is about to go up in smoke at any moment."

"Yeah," Megan said.

The small pudgy man blanched in fear.

"Stow that crap," Gideon said as he set Hajar down. "We're going. Come on children, we've out stayed our welcome."

"You crazy bitch!" Roland pointed a thick finger in Hajar's face. "Doc's our only chance out of this mess, so leave him alone!"

"Get off me, hairball. I am not in the mood."

"Hairball, for once, is right," Yumi said. "I am getting tired of your silly tantrums. You need to grow up before you blow this for all of us."

"Lay off, her!" Megan yelled. "She's been through more than we have."

"I don't need your help!" Hajar snapped at Megan.

"I was only trying to help you."

"Help someone else. I have to pack." Hajar held up her hand and, out of the darkness, Kali flew into it. She promptly turned and stalked off to her room.

Dumbfounded, Megan looked as though she were about to cry. "What did I say?"

"It's all right, honey." Gideon put a comforting arm around Megan's shoulders. "Just give her some space."

"Okay, Doc."

"Megan, how old were you when that rat Mrs. Kerr kidnapped you?"

"Fourteen. Why?"

"Oh, I was just thinking about your poor mother and what she must be going through. I swear I'll get you back home."

"I know you will, Doc."

Gideon glanced down at the emerald green stone concealed in his hand and frowned.

CHAPTER 27

W
e have arrived," Gideon said as he rolled to a gentle stop on the cracked asphalt. Setting his parking brake, he switched off the purring 455. After being asked to leave The Star Bright, they drove south all day, and now an angry red sun dipped low over rolling cow pastures and wooded fields. They sat parked next to the crumbling hanger of an abandoned airfield that was losing a battle with kudzu.

"Welcome to Tennessee, gentlemen."

"Open the door, Doc," Roland said. "I got to water the Volunteer State,"

Shaking his head, Gideon opened the door and Roland made a beeline to the weed choked rear of the dilapidated building. Yumi popped open his own door and slid out.

Closing the car door, Gideon took a moment and looked into the rearview mirror at a face he had not seen for fifty-eight years. On the way, he had found a barbershop. Along with a haircut, he had shaved off his beard, much to Hajar and Megan's approval. He absentmindedly ran a hand across his smooth, youthful face as the image triggered a flood of memories.

He opened the glove box and extracted a folded paper. Pulling a pen from his shirt pocket, he quickly signed the document. "Take good care of her, Virginia."

He laid a gentle hand on the wheel and thought of all the great times he'd had in this car. Patting the leather wrapped wheel for the last time, he opened the door and eased out.

As Yumi stretched, Hajar parked next to the GTO and shut off her engine.

"What do we have here, Doc?" Roland asked as he buckled his belt. "Another secret museum?"

"No," Gideon said, rising from the car. "I need a piece of specialized equipment for the next leg of the journey." He took out his smart phone and hit speed dial.

"It is about time you showed up." Mrs. Kerr emerged from the shadows. Her face was puffy and swollen and she was walking with a cane. "I have been here in this God forsaken place for hours." She took out a bottle of pain pills and popped one, swallowing it without water.

Everyone, but Gideon, cringed. "Do you have the articles?" he asked, replacing his phone.

"It's all here," Mrs. Kerr said. "I have the hanger prepared to perform the ritual, as you requested." She paused. "Now there is the face I had come to despise over the years. Nice makeover, Gideon. How did you accomplish your return to youth?"

"Tear of the Phoenix."

"My, you are resourceful. I thought those things went the way of the Dodo."

"Makes finding the Tree of Life a bit easier."

"My, you *are* dedicated. Never would have thought a man of your...*misguided*...moral convictions would have used such a dark, magical thing."

"I'm glad I've brightened your day. How's the foot?"

"You suck."

Gideon grinned.

"Where did you find the Tear of the Phoenix?"

"None of your business."

"Hajar?"

"The Library of Alexandria, Mrs. Kerr," she said with her head down.

"Oh my God," Mrs. Kerr said. "Where is it hidden?"

Gideon pulled out his pistol. "Want me to perforate anther shoe, Mrs. Kerr? Or how about a kneecap this time?"

"Ma'am?" Hajar asked.

"Never mind, my dear. We'll talk later."

Hajar breathed a small sigh of relief.

"Megan, how has Kane been treating you?"

"Good, Mrs. Kerr. Doc's a great guy."

Megan screamed and clutched at her throat as her collar blazed bright orange.

Mrs. Kerr chuckled as Megan thrashed about on the ground in agony. "Children should be seen and not heard."

Mrs. Kerr's laugh was cut short by Gideon's stunning right cross. She landed hard on the cracked parking lot.

"She's just a child, you monster!" he cried. "Turn it off, or, so help me God, I'll break you in half!"

"You'll pay for that, Kane!" Mrs. Kerr snarled, as blood gushed from her nose.

Gideon took a step toward the cowering woman.

Mrs. Kerr flinched. "Stop him!"

Gideon heard the unmistakable sound of guns clearing holsters. Glancing back, he saw Roland, Yumi, and Hajar with guns drawn down on him.

"Well, don't just stand there, looking stupid," Gideon sneered. "You heard your master, shoot me! Send me to my final reward, I dare you!"

Hajar brought her pistol up, the muzzle less than a foot from Gideon's left temple. A smile played across her beautiful face. "Payback's a bitch, old man."

"No!" Mrs. Kerr shouted as she trigged Hajar's collar.

Hajar screamed as her gun bucked and roared, the shot flew wide of its intended target, shattering the quiet Tennessee night.

Gideon laughed. "You can't get your precious Tree of Life without me, can you, Mrs. Kerr?"

Mrs. Kerr rose from the ground, climbing up her cane, and wiped the blood from her face. "Put those guns away, you fools."

Gideon picked up Megan. "You all right, girl?"

"I am now," she said. "Thanks, Doc."

"Don't mention it," he said with a grin.

Hajar lay on the ground with her eyes squeezed shut, soaked in sweat. Ginny knelt down, smiling at her.

Hajar nodded slightly.

"Enough of this foolishness," Mrs. Kerr said. "Let's get this ritual started so I can be on my way. I have wasted enough time."

"What ritual?" Hajar asked as she reholstered her Glock.

"Gideon doesn't trust me to keep my word to release you when he delivers the Tree to me."

"Insurance," Gideon said. "When dealing with double-dealing witches, you always need insurance."

Mrs. Kerr smirked. "Double-dealing? That hurts my heart, old friend. This way."

ᘓᕩᘓᕩ

Roland and Yumi slid back the door of the large, decaying hanger. The air was full of stale oil, rust, and the cloying scent of kudzu blossoms. A few scattered camp lanterns revealed a complicated chalk design drawn on the cracked concrete floor.

"Great. More hoodoo," Roland said.

"You will appreciate this hoodoo, Mr. Gunn," Mrs. Kerr said.

"Before we begin," Gideon said. "Let me check the articles."

Mrs. Kerr handed him a sack with various items. "As I expected."

"I'll prepare the mix while you gather the blood," Gideon said.

Megan gasped. "Did he say *blood*?"

"Yes, he did, child." Mrs. Kerr produced a lancet and a pack of alcohol wipes. "I need a sample from each of you. Don't be squeamish. It's for your own good."

Gideon tossed Mrs. Kerr a small, silver bowl.

Yumi stepped up and held out his hand. "No use arguing."

Mrs. Kerr poked his finger. "When I have gathered your blood, I will place you on the mandala. You will not move until the ritual is complete."

Soon, Hajar, Megan, Roland, and Yumi stood patiently within the mystical circle. Gideon poured a black powder into the silver bowl and Mrs. Kerr mixed it carefully.

"From now until the ritual is complete, no talking, no murmuring, no whispering. Only silence will be tolerated. Do you understand me?" Mrs. Kerr asked.

All four nodded their heads.

One by one, Gideon dowsed the lanterns. As the last died, hundreds of hidden candles blazed to life.

"Let the ritual of Hammurabi begin," Mrs. Kerr said.

കൗരൗ

For close to an hour, while Mrs. Kerr chanted in a high, singsong voice, she used the bloody mix to draw a pattern upon her face. Moving to the center of the mandala, she poured out the bloody remains of the bowl. The circle glowed a bright neon yellow. Each of the witch collars glowed as well.

"I, Salome Kerr, swear, upon forfeiture of my very essence, that the moment I have the Tree of Life, my power over my slaves is no more. I will release Megan Franks, Roland Gunn, Yakusho Shimura, and Hajar. Let it be."

The glow faded and Mrs. Kerr stumbled back. The blood on her face was gone and her skin was ashen.

"Satisfied, Kane?" she asked.

"Yes," Gideon said. "Now get out. My crew and I have to get your prize."

"What just happened?" Hajar asked.

"Your overgrown boy scout of a leader has made sure that I have no choice but to release you."

"I don't understand," Roland said.

"Simple," Gideon said. "Once we hand Mrs. Kerr the Tree, she loses all control over you. You're free."

"What if Mrs. Kerr decides to forget the deal," Yumi asked.

"Then I die, and your collars fall off, anyway," Mrs. Kerr said. "One way or the other, you are free. Now if you will excuse me, I must be on my way."

"Mrs. Kerr, you might want to be on your guard. Seems the Black Circle has been sniffing around."

"How do you know, Kane?"

"Had a run in with a witch named Moge, and another one named Figg who gave us trouble at Alexandrian's place. Hope they weren't friends of yours because we killed them. I also got the impression that Mei Xue herself might be tailing us."

Hajar stiffened at the sound of Mei's name.

"Oh no, this is bad," Mrs. Kerr said. "They know. God in Heaven, how do they know?"

"Anything you want to confess?"

"I can assure you, that it wasn't me. However, Kane, you are wrong about Mei. I heard it through my sources that she and the rest of the dark counsel were killed in an arranged accident. Seems Simone has cast off her favorites and taken sole rein of the Black Circle. I would watch my own back if I were you, Kane. Simone wants the Tree for herself and, if you value their lives, she had better not get it."

"Yada, yada, yada," he said.

Mrs. Kerr turned and walked toward the door.

"See you around—*Ramona*," he said.

The witch turned, her eyes flashing fire. "Don't you *dare* call me that! I hope Harold David fries in Hell fire for slandering me," she screamed.

Amid Gideon's laughter, Mrs. Kerr pushed through the door and was gone. Moments later, the engine of a car and the squeal of spinning tires could be heard.

"I think you hit a nerve, Doc," Yumi said. "Nice going."

"If you are through day dreaming, Hajar, we need to make plans," Gideon said.

"Don't get your panties in a wad, old man," she snapped. "I'm coming."

"Doc," Roland said, extending his hand. "I just want to thank you. I know I suspected you, but you're on the level."

"Yes," Yumi said. "That was first rate, Doc. For the first time, I can see an upside to this mess."

Megan surprised everyone as she pushed past Roland and hugged Gideon hard. Tears of gratitude rolled down her face.

"Thanks, Doc," she said softly. "For the ritual thing and for standing up for me."

Gideon placed a fatherly arm about her shoulders. "You're welcome, Megan."

"Ah, come on," Hajar said, slipping on her tough-girl facade. "Let's not open the champagne and swap spit just yet. We still have to the find the damn Tree."

"But, Hajar, what he did for us," Megan said, wiping her eyes. "Aren't you at least grateful? He's not what we thought. Gideon's a killer guy."

"Yeah, Gideon's a real sweetheart. I still wonder what's up his sleeve. I know we won't like whatever it is."

"But Hajar—" Megan began.

"Okay, okay! If you're going to bug the crap out of me. Tell you what, Doc, you find the Tree, get us all free, and I'll be real grateful. Hell, I'll even marry you."

"Marry—*you*?" Gideon stared at her in mock shock. "You really do hold a grudge, don't you, Hajar? You are bound and determined to make the rest of my life hell."

Fighting a smile, Hajar gave him the finger.

Yumi laughed and Roland clapped Gideon on the back.

"So, where are we headed, Doc," Roland asked.

"To the Great Smokey Mountains National Park."

"Why?" Yumi asked.

"We have to pick up another item before our real journey begins."

"Sounds like we have to steal something," Hajar said.

"I wish snatching something was all it was." Gideon said. "But this caper is probably going to get as hairy as the museum."

Hajar sighed heavily. "You know what, old man? You helping us is liable to get us killed."

"You're welcome," Gideon said. "Megan, honey, would you run out to the car and get my maps?"

"Sure thing, Doc," she said, hurrying out the door.

"Let's get these lanterns lit, gentlemen," Gideon said, moving away from the mandala. "Take them out to the end of the runway. Hajar, you follow me."

"Where we going?"

"We're going to drive our cars to the start of the runway."

Gideon's cell began to vibrate.

"We have to hurry," he said.

CHAPTER 28

Fifteen minutes later, Hajar's Civic and Gideon's GTO were in place, their high beams illuminating the airstrip. At the other end, they could see the bouncing lanterns held by Yumi and Roland.

Momentarily hidden from prying eyes, Hajar hugged Gideon hard then, fighting back tears of gratitude, she moved away before anyone spotted her. She leaned against her car when she heard the deep-throated rumble of twin Pratt & Whitney engines coming in low over the trees. Looking up, she saw a heavily modified silver and white C-47B sail over her head, seemingly appearing from nowhere. Powerful twin search beams lighted the airstrip as the big plane touched down in a sharp squeal of tires.

"What is that?" Hajar shouted over the roar.

Gideon leaned against the GTO, his eyes misty. "A dear old friend," he said softly, giving Hajar a wink. "Let's go."

℘℘℘

The C-47B taxied to the end of the weed-choked runway. With a flourish, the pilot spun the aircraft around, pointing her nose back the way she had come, before shutting down the twin engines.

Running up and wearing a big smile, Gideon gave the pilot a small salute. Moments later, the side hatch popped open revealing a small red-haired woman dressed in a vintage flight jacket. Pausing long enough for a set of air-stairs to unfold to the tarmac, she bounded toward Gideon.

"What has happened to you?" she cried as she leapt into his arms. "You look like you did in Dad's old pictures!"

"Had a whale of a makeover, Virginia. You might say it was magic."

"But you warned the whole family that, under no circumstances, were we to ever go near hoodoo. You said that if we did, you would make us wish we had never been born."

"Nevertheless, it had to be done, darling. If it would make you feel better, you can call me a hypocrite."

"Hypocrite," Virginia said softly as she hugged him tightly. "I haven't seen you in five years, not since Aunt Ginny's funeral."

"Sorry."

"Sorry? That all you got? You had better do better than sorry. Not a single word in five years! You cut the entire family out of your life. Do you know how much that hurt us? It almost killed Dad. Sorry, won't cut it."

"Sorry is all I got," he said.

"Then on top of everything else, out of the blue, I get a summons to bring the *Ginny K* to an abandoned airstrip in the middle of Podunk, Tennessee. I thought you had given up on crazy adventures?"

"Sorry—I mean, Ginny's death—I wanted to be alone. I should have called. It's good to see you again, Virginia. How are Bob and the kids?"

"Fine. Brandy and Kate miss their crazy Uncle Kamikaze."

"And how is Marshall?"

"He's getting old. All he talks about is his older brother who won't come around anymore."

"I see that you have taken good care of the old girl," he said, looking up.

"Don't you dare try to change the subject. You got some explaining to do, mister."

"Sorry, don't have time, sweetie. Just have to believe me that it's important."

"Make time," Virginia said, wiping her eyes. "Now what foolishness has you flying off on another adventure?"

e/ɔe/ɔ

"Who's the babe?" Roland asked. "She's got some age on her, but she is still plenty hot. She sure is friendly with the Doc."

"She is attractive," Yumi said, "but I never cared much for redheads."

"Ahem," Megan said, giving Yumi the stink eye.

"I never cared for natural red heads," he corrected. "Your hair color is, umm, much more attractive to say the least."

"That's better. I wonder what hair color Doc would like?"

"Probably likes blue-haired little old ladies," Roland laughed while Megan turned red.

Hajar didn't say a word as she stared, awestruck, at the vintage airplane gleaming in the lantern light.

It's her! In the flesh and looking like a million bucks! It's the real, honest-to-God Ginny K! In the books the Ginny K was a rocket powered autogyro—whatever the crap that is. I feel like I've fallen into the pages of the Kane chronicles and have become a character myself.

e/ɔe/ɔ

"Virginia, I would like you to meet some friends of mine," Gideon said. "Kids, this is my niece, Lieutenant Colonel Virginia Kane of the United States Air Force. Virginia, this is Yumi, Roland, Megan, and Hajar."

Surprised, Virginia gasped as she looked at Hajar. "Sorry for staring, Hajar. For a minute, with your height and the blonde hair, I thought you were my Aunt Ginny."

Hajar put her hands on her hips "That's one job I don't want."

Virginia's eyes narrowed at the remark. "So, are you the idiots who have talked my Uncle into another harebrained adventure? He's almost eighty-four-years-old, for God's sake."

"Look here, missy," Gideon snapped. "Since when do you speak to me in that tone of voice? Whether I am twenty, or a million, you will show proper respect."

"Sorry, Uncle."

"That's better."

Roland gave a loud wolf whistle. "Now *that*, is one hell of a babe."

Gideon looked around and saw Roland shining a flashlight on the nose art of the plane.

The plane sported a bathing suit clad, blonde bombshell pinup girl looking over her left shoulder. Scrolling up one side in fancy scrip were the words: *GINNY K.*

"Uncle!" Virginia said as Gideon pulled away from her.

"You look here, Mr. Gunn," Gideon said, coming nose to nose with Roland. "You will treat my wife with the proper respect she deserves. You got me, mister?"

"Yeah, Doc, I didn't mean any harm, honest. That was your wife? You were one lucky man. You know? From this angle, she does sort of look like Hajar."

"No, she doesn't!" Gideon snapped. "No one, much less, Hajar, was like—will *ever* be like—my Ginny. She was my life and now she's gone. Killed—no, *stolen* from me by a stupid, drunken teenager!"

He looked up at the smiling, artistic rendering of his wife and angrily wiped the tears from his eyes.

"What are you four looking at?" he barked at Hajar, Roland, Yumi, and Megan. They were stunned at his outburst, but he wasn't through. "Get your gear out of the cars and stow it away—now!"

Gideon caught a sad, almost pained look in Hajar's eye as she quickly turned away and headed for her Civic.

"I'm sorry," Virginia said, placing her arm around his waist." Aunt Ginny was a great lady."

Gideon glanced around, curious as to where the shade of his dear wife was lurking. "The best."

"If you are set to do this…whatever it is…you'll need a pilot. I'm coming along. I've got some leave—"

"Out of the question. You have a family and a career. You

can't be caught up in another harebrained scheme of mine."

"Must I remind you, that you don't have a pilot's license anymore."

"The absence of a piece of paper can't take away hard won skills."

"Be reasonable, Uncle."

"You be reasonable. Is the lady ready to go?"

"Like talking to a stubborn mule!"

Gideon smiled.

"Yes, Uncle. Topped off her tanks in Bristol. Other than a general route, you were kind of vague, so I guessed at provisions. I stocked the *G-K* with enough MREs and water for a couple of months. Included three dirt bikes, just in case taxi service is unavailable."

"Good thinking," he said. "How about weapons?"

"Got five fully automatic battle rifles and even liberated a couple of highly illegal SAWs. Packed enough ammo to take down a small country. I even added a couple hundred rounds for your fancy pop guns."

"That's my girl. Got the fuel dumps ready?"

"Cost you a pretty penny, by the way, but yeah. Fuel prices are steep, but so is the price for pump jockeys to look the other way." Virginia pulled a map from her jacket and handed to him. "Got them marked."

Gideon smiled and kissed her lightly on the forehead. "Kiss your girls for me," he said. He fished his car keys out of his pocket. "The Goat is yours. I always wanted you to have it, so when you are fishtailing around Milligan's Curve, think of your old Uncle Gideon."

"I learned how to drive in that car."

"Yeah, still I remember how you *borrowed* it and went cruising when you were fourteen."

"I couldn't sit down for a week," she said with a smile.

"She's all yours, Virginia. The signed title is in the glove box."

"You're not coming back, are you, Uncle?"

"No."

"I don't understand—"

"Let's not make this worse than it should be, Niece. I love you. Tell Marshall...I am sorry."

With tears in her eyes, Virginia stepped back, clutching the car keys. Gideon stood ramrod straight and gave her a smart salute. Virginia returned the salute, then turned and walked toward the waiting GTO.

"I love you, too, Uncle," she said softly, opening the car door.

დიდ

As Hajar pulled baggage from the Civic, a small voice whispered in her ear.

"Hajar, go to the hanger," Ginny said. "I need you."

Gideon smiled as the GTO's tail lights disappeared down the dusty road. Glancing over at the hanger, he saw Ginny framed in the doorway. She motioned for him to join her before stepping back into the darkness. He entered the hanger, the still-lit flickering candles chasing away the worst of the darkness. Ginny stood near the mystic chalk circle.

"This is kind of romantic," he said.

"I'm here," Hajar said as she entered the large room.

Gideon looked at Hajar and frowned. Ginny approached her and smiled.

Ginny pointed at Gideon without taking her eyes off Hajar. "I have to go. Let me say goodbye."

"What do want me to do?" Hajar asked.

Ginny moved forward and, to Hajar's shock, moved into her. Hajar felt a momentary panic as the icy cold of another soul took over her body.

"Thank you, Hajar," Ginny whispered.

"I'm afraid this is the end of the road, husband," Ginny/Hajar whispered. "I can't go any farther, but Heaven likes you and has allowed me to say a proper goodbye."

"You can't leave me, Ginny," he said. "The last five years have been sheer Hell on Earth."

"I know," she said. "You could storm the gates of Hell without batting an eye, but you could never take being alone.

Trust me, you big lug, I have been working on that. You and
Hajar will make a great team, so don't do anything stupid to
mess it up."

Ginny/Hajar rushed toward him and embraced him.

Gideon covered her mouth and face with desperate kisses.
"Ginny, I love you so much."

"I love you too, you big lug. Trust me, Gideon Kane, you
will never be alone again."

Gideon and Ginny/Hajar kissed desperately, saying a final
farewell.

"He is all yours, sweetie." Ginny slipped out of Hajar's
body. "Take good care of the big lug."

With a small giggle, she was gone.

Hajar regained her body, but continued to passionately kiss
Gideon as if her life depended on it. At last, Gideon pulled his
lips away, but still held her tightly.

"Ginny's gone, isn't she?"

"Umm, yeah." Hajar blushed. "Sorry about that. I got carried away."

"I did, too." Then he pressed his lips to Hajar's and drank
deeply.

〜〜〜

A full thirty minutes after Hajar returned to the *Ginny K*,
Gideon entered the plane, stepped into the rear cargo door, and
closed the hatch behind him. Their eyes did not meet as he
fussed about the hatch.

"It's good to be aboard again," he said, patting the door.
"Have you missed me, girl?"

He stopped and looked back at his sullen crew. All but
Hajar stared at him grimly.

"Where's the morale officer when you need one?" he said
with a smile. No one laughed or even smiled at his attempt to
lighten the mood. "I want to apologize for my pissy behavior,
back there," he said. "Especially to you, Mr. Gunn. You meant
no disrespect and I acted like an ass. I'm sorry."

"We remember you telling Mrs. Kerr about your wife and

the anniversary of her death," Yumi said. "We understand."

"Oh. I forgot about that. Still no excuse."

"Sorry won't cut it." Megan rose from her seat and held out her arms. "I need a hug or this could scar me for life."

"We can't have that, now can we?" Gideon smiled and opened his arms. Megan rushed into his arms, and, after a lingering embrace, reached around and squeezed his butt. "Hey!" he exclaimed as his face glowed crimson. "Hands off my bum, youngster."

Megan giggled and dodged as he swatted at her.

"Hey, that looks pretty good," Roland said with a chuckle. "I think I'll have some of that action." He reached out and also grabbed Gideon's butt. "Solid. You must work out,"

Gideon swatted away his hand and unsnapped his holster. "Next wisenheimer that grabs my derriere gets it right between the eyes."

"Looks like I'm safe," Hajar said as she crossed her arms.

Gideon and the rest of the crew exploded into laughter.

"Get ready for takeoff, you pack of degenerates," Gideon ordered, suddenly realizing that, for a moment, they reminded him of The Choir Boys.

"Care if I ride shotgun, Doc?" Roland asked.

"Not at all."

"So, Doc, is this a C-47A or B?"

"I'm impressed, Mr. Gunn. The *Ginny K* is a C-47B. Do you fly?"

"I am the best unlicensed pilot you ever met, Doc. I have flown everything you could fly in the bush, but I never flew anything near as nice as this baby."

"She is a special lady who has never let me down. Let's get her prepped, copilot."

"Rodger that," Roland said.

After extensive checks, Gideon was satisfied and turned over the engines. "One last thing," he said. In a tradition that he hadn't preformed in twenty-eight years, he opened his cockpit window and pressed his fingers to his lips. Reaching out, he caressed them against the eternal smiling lips of the image of his Ginny.

CHAPTER 29

I t sure is beautiful here," Hajar said, looking out the motel window at the picturesque river and surrounding forest. "Look alive, guys, Mr. Money's back."

The door opened and in walked Gideon, carrying two plastic bags. "Good," he said. "All my rats are together in one hole."

"What'd you get, Doc?" Megan asked.

"Why, Megan, you look particularly pretty today," Gideon said. "Breakfast. Plus, I got you a new T-shirt. I got us all new T-shirts."

Megan beamed at his comment while Hajar and the rest smiled. Gideon doled out the bright shirts. "Put them on, please. Then we can eat."

"Cades Cove is one of my favorite places," Gideon said. "You know, I grew up about an hour from here. Over in Hamblen County."

Roland looked suspiciously at the big biscuit. "This isn't opossum, is it?" he asked. "'Cause if it is, I'm allergic."

Yumi chuckled. "No, it's called vittles. Isn't this supposed to come with a mess of collard greens and a side of fatback?"

"It's called rude behavior and is liable to get two Yankee wiseacres a whooping by a good old boy from Tennessee," Gideon said with an exaggerated southern twang.

Hajar and Megan retuned from the bathroom, sporting their new look. Roland tossed them each a wrapped biscuit.

Gideon cut off the price tags and slipped the white T-shirt, complete with the bright orange power T, over his head. "Much better," he said. "We need to blend."

"I got a problem, old man," Hajar said.

"And that would be?" Yumi asked.

"I'm from the great state of Alabama. Working for a satanic witch bent on replacing God and ruling the world is one thing, but wearing orange and white is crossing the line."

Gideon chuckled. "I'm sure the spirit of the Bear will forgive you, this one time."

"Doc, you call *this* blending?" Megan asked, pulling at her garish, bright orange top. "They can see this color from space."

"Believe it or not, little girl, in East Tennessee, this is going native."

"Great," Yumi said. "Let's get this operation over before someone sees me."

"One more time," Gideon said. "Let me hear the plan."

Megan moaned. "Oh—not again!"

"You and Hajar go in after the thingamabob," Roland said, "while we cover you." He smiled as he patted the huge Stihl chainsaw that sat on the floor. "This is going to be fun."

"Did you get gas?" Gideon asked.

The smile fell from Roland's face. "Umm...I will by the time I need it."

"I picked up a can when I bought the shirts in Gatlinburg. Already mixed and in the trunk of your rental car."

"Thanks, Doc," Roland said.

"Big dummy," Megan said, playfully punching Roland in the arm.

"The kid, hairball, and I are to suppress any police and/or ranger response," Yumi said. "To give you time to find the relic."

"Yes, but remember, no one gets hurt," said Gideon. "You hear me?"

"Loud and clear," Yumi said. "You want to do this the hard way. This operation would be foolproof if you'd let me do my job the way I see fit."

"I like you, Yumi, but your complete disregard for human

life is appalling." Gideon shook his head. "Those park rangers are only doing their job. A job where they're overworked and underpaid, I might add."

"Their bad life choices are not my problem," Yumi said.

"So help me, if you harm one hair on their heads, Yumi, you'll answer to me," Gideon growled.

"Don't worry, Doc," Megan said. "I'll keep him in line. If he gives me any trouble, I'll swat him upside the head."

Yumi looked at Megan and rolled his eyes, before slipping on his sunglasses.

Megan sat on the bed next to Roland and began munching on a ham biscuit. With undisguised puppy love, she watched as Gideon tacked a map of the park to the wall.

Roland's mouth formed a particularly evil grin. "Megan and Gideon sitting in a tree," he sang. "K-I-S-S-I-N-G. First comes love, then comes marriage, then comes the cops to lock Gideon up because Megan is underage!"

Roland fell back on the bed and laughed as Megan turned several shades of crimson. She stood, turned, and glared at the laughing man. The crumpled sheet, on which he lay, came to life and, to his dismay, wrapped itself about him tightly.

"Hey, what's going on?" he cried.

Megan launched herself at the helpless man, punching and kicking, while he struggled to untangle himself.

"Now *that* is funny," Yumi said.

"Megan," Gideon said. "Much as I hate to say this, let the boy go."

"All right, but he started it," She delivered one last vicious kick before the sheet released Roland.

"Can't you take a joke?" Roland spat as he threw the sheet to the ground.

"She puts up with you," Hajar said.

"All right, listen up, *children*," Gideon said. "Fortunately for us, there are few roads in and out of this area. If things go south, there only the two main roads, here and here," he said indicating the map, "and those are only two-lane roads. With the prevalence of cell phones, there is no way we can slip in and out without the alarm being sounded. So we will do the exact opposite and make as big a commotion as we can. The more witnesses we have, the more confusion there will be. I need the three of you to give me a first rate, flashy diversion. It will draw the rangers away from the loop and give Hajar and me time to work."

"Yeah, Doc," Yumi said. "A few carefully felled trees and we have a parking lot from here to Gatlinburg. That should considerably slow down any police response."

"I need you to keep them busy for about an hour or two. After we retrieve the Key, we will rendezvous in the meadow where we landed the *Ginny K*. She's only five or six miles away along this hiking trail here. Hopefully, by the times the smoke clears, we will be long gone."

"What's the story with this, Key?" asked Roland. "And how did it end up way out here in the sticks?"

"*The Book of Xanadutha* gives the location of an ancient storehouse of knowledge created by the Nephilim. Within this archive is the exact location of the Tree of Life."

"The archive is located within Cades Cove?" Yumi asked.

"That would be too easy," Gideon replied. "Like I said, *The Book of Xanadutha* gives the location of the archive—as it was ten thousand years ago. Unfortunately, the world ten thousand years ago was vastly geographically different than today. My best calculations place the archive within an area slightly larger than the combined size of Texas, New Mexico, and Arizona."

Hajar frowned. "We could spend an entire lifetime looking for that."

"A lifetime and then some, but a bit of knowledge I came across years ago will come in handy. There is a device, hidden within the cove, which if brought into the general vicinity, will pinpoint where the archive is located. The text I read called it The Key of Solomonan. I have known where the Key was hidden for decades, but since I didn't have a clue where to look for the archive, it wasn't worth the trouble to retrieve, until now."

"What do you mean, it wasn't worth the trouble to retrieve?" Hajar asked.

"Some misguided soul, over a hundred years ago, built a two story log cabin over the entrance to the cave that contains the Key. I don't think the Friends of the Smokies will be very happy when we're done."

CHAPTER 30

Gideon gunned the BMW F800GS and relished the motorcycle's raw power. It had been years since he had been on a bike and it made him feel like a kid again.

"Last time I was on a motorcycle I had to mix the fuel," he mumbled. "Boy, that was a long time ago. Things have certainly changed over the years. The Triumph I had looked like a motorcycle, not like a machine from outer space. If this thing had wings, I bet it would fly."

Hajar strode up to Gideon then paused to adjust the straps on the big, black backpack she wore. She looked at the powerful motorcycle with undisguised lust.

"Nice bike, old man."

"Thank you."

"If you were a gentleman, you would carry the bag and let me drive the bike."

"Hajar, Hajar, Hajar," he said, giving her a wink. "Ride behind a woman on a motorcycle? There are some things a man just can't do."

"Why, you male chauvinistic piece of..."

He smiled and gunned the throttle drowning out her lengthy, animated rant.

Rolling her eyes, she swatted him hard on the helmet, making him laugh. He dropped the mirrored visor into place. Hajar slipped on her own helmet and slid onto the back of the bike.

She had no sooner wrapped her arms snuggly about his waist than they were roaring out of the motel parking lot.

ℰↄℰↄ

The cool, early morning ride up the curving, inclined road was like going back in time for Gideon. For a moment, it was forty years ago and the two supple arms about his waist belonged to Ginny. Hajar snuggled close, her warm body becoming one with his, and Gideon admitted that she felt mighty good. She would playfully caress his chest and he would squeeze her hand. She felt a bit too good, and his mind began to wander.

Come on, Gideon, you have to focus on the mission, he thought. *As much as I hate to admit it, Hajar drives me crazy. I've met countless beautiful women over the years, but none have ever made an impression like this wild, unpredictable girl. I never thought I'd ever again have feelings for anyone like my Ginny. God, Hajar feels so good. I can't get her off my mind. I'm a fool to think about things that will never be. I'm living on borrowed time. I'll be lucky to live long enough to free Hajar and her friends, let alone have any kind of future. Besides, Hajar's young enough to be my great-granddaughter. Damn the Phoenix to Hell! In restoring my youth, it has made me as randy as a goofy, hormone-crazed teenager.*

Gideon forced his mind off the beautiful woman, who held him close, and began running through the batting averages of the 1975 Cincinnati Reds Baseball Team. Eight times through the roster, his desire waned—a bit.

Deep within his chest, he felt an ominous warmth begin to stir. While not painful, it brought him back to the grim realization that time was running out.

Half an hour later, they entered the Cades Cove area and made a beeline for the *loop*.

The loop was an eleven-mile road that gave park visitors a taste of what life was like in the Cove before it became part of the National Park. The narrow, one-way road was often bumper to bumper as, more often than not, guests of the Cove would leap from their vehicles at the slightest sign of a deer or the occasional black bear.

Ignoring the sign that proclaimed the loop was closed for

yet another hour, Gideon and Hajar slid past the simple barrier and raced along the empty, winding road.

"This is Alice," Hajar said into her headphone. "Let the games begin, Caterpillar."

"Rodger that, Alice." Yumi gave Roland the signal. His adrenalin up, Yumi smiled and opened a black, waterproof twin rifle case they had confiscated from Duncan Figg's hired killers. "Hello, my beautiful ladies. My name is Yumi and, together, we are going to kill a lot of people today."

The large-wheeled case held two exotic, state-of-the-art long-range sniper rifles. An olive green .338 Lapua Magnum lay beside a black .50 BMG. He extracted the smaller scoped rifle with the green plastic stock and unfolded the attached bi-pod. Inserting a ten round magazine and racking the polished, oversized bolt on his rifle was like music to his ears. Yumi took ambush position beside a stone, moss-covered bridge, eager to unleash hell.

He spoke into his microphone. "White Rabbit, you are a go. Please don't screw this up."

"Caterpillar, you're just jealous because my saw is bigger than yours," Roland said.

"Knock it off, you freak, and do your job, White Rabbit," Megan said.

"You heard, Cheshire Cat," Gideon said. "Step on it."

"Rodger that, Mad Hatter," Roland said. "Consider it stepped on."

"We got a problem, Mad Hatter," Yumi said, looking through his Leupold scope. "Got a couple of civilians near the choke point."

"We're committed," Gideon said. "Shoo them away if you have to, but under no circumstance are you to hurt them."

Accidents do happen, thought Yumi. *Often, they are tragically fatal.*

CHAPTER 31

Big Jim Griswold smacked his lips as he polished off the last of bit of bacon from his breakfast. "That was mighty fine, Carla," he said to his wife. "This mountain air really gives me an appetite."

Carla smiled and poked his prodigious belly. "You must be a real mountain man then," she said, taking his plate.

Jim laughed and patted the small blonde woman affectionately on the head.

The couple had stopped at a small roadside picnic area to have a meal before spending the day at the park.

Stroking his chest-length, gray beard, Jim smiled and savored the moment. Leaning back in his folding chair, he lit his pipe and opened a crumpled local newspaper while Carla cleaned up.

"I just love this place," he said. "It's so peaceful and removed from the mess the rest of world is in."

 espes

With the big chainsaw slung over one shoulder and a black duffle over the other, Roland walked to within a few feet of Jim. Throwing up his hand, Roland gave a friendly wave. "What's up, Snuffy Smith?"

"Huh?"

Roland smirked and pointed at Big Jim's ample belly. "Is it going to be a boy or girl?"

Jim angrily exhaled a cloud of smoke as Roland passed by him, laughing.

Scowling, Jim looked on as Roland walked toward the road. "Yankees ought to stay up north where they belong," Jim snorted.

Roland trotted across the road and scrambled up the steep bank to where three enormous oak trees stood. To Jim's amazement, Roland fired up the chainsaw and began slicing at the base of the tallest tree.

"Hey!" Jim shouted. "This is a national park, you dang idiot! You can't do that!"

Amid a spray of sawdust, Roland laughed at Jim's rants. Moments later, the old growth tree crashed to earth, effectively blocking the narrow road.

"Carla, call the rangers," Jim shouted. "I'm going to teach this guy some manners."

"Now don't lose your temper, Papa."

"Too late, Mama. Too dang late."

Roland was three quarters through the second tree when a line of five bullets struck the tree next to his head, sending large chunks of stinging bark flying into his face.

"What the—" he cried. Looking across the road, he saw Big Jim snap a fresh clip into his AK-47.

"Stuffy this, Yankee!" Jim said, taking aim.

"Oh crap." Roland feverishly tried to finish cutting the tree. "I got a freaking redneck with an AK! Need some help here, Caterpillar!"

"I'm on it," Yumi said as the crosshairs of his L96A1 settled on Big Jim's enormous head. Even though he was nearly five hundred yards away, for Yumi's uncanny accuracy with a firearm, it was an easy shot. Yumi took a breath and held it as he gradually brought pressure on the trigger. "Consider his melon thumped."

"Gideon said nobody was to get hurt!" Megan screamed as she shoved Yumi from behind, throwing off his aim.

The shot just missed Big Jim's head. So close in fact, that the man felt the wind off the .338 Lapua Magnum round as it passed a hair's breadth in front of his bulbous nose. The powerful sniper round shattered both the driver's side and passenger side windows of Jim's formerly mint, Ford F-100 pickup truck.

"Good God Almighty!" Big Jim shouted as he dropped his AK and ran for the cover of the trees.

Roland dropped a second tree and began working on the third when three ranger patrol cars shot past Yumi and Megan's hiding place. Roland's makeshift roadblock had already made the busy road a hopeless morass, as twenty frustrated drivers found that they were stuck, unable to turn around on the narrow road.

"Not good," Yumi spat. "We figured on more rangers responding. Go take care of the rest, Shortstack."

"I'm on it," she said. "Remember not to hurt anyone, or Doc will be mad."

"Yada, yada, yada! Don't worry, they won't be harmed."

Yumi switched rifles and drew a bead on the patrol cars with the enormous Barrett.

The cars, lights and sirens blaring, slid to a stop as Roland, covered with sawdust, finished felling the third and final tree. Before the officers could exit their vehicles, Yumi sent three armor piercing rounds deep within the engine blocks of their cars. Realizing they had walked into an ambush, they piled out and began using their useless cars as shields.

Yumi chuckled. "This is like a shooting gallery."

At this distance, he could stand in the middle of road without fear of their pistols. He sent a few rounds into the tires before taking apart their light bars. The park rangers were not prepared for this turn of events and leaped from their interceptors, scrambling over the fallen trees for cover.

Pinned between Roland, who had abandoned his chainsaw in favor of an M-16 battle rifle, and Yumi, the rangers decided to rethink their position. Firing a few covering rounds from their pistols, they joined the mad rush as park visitors abandoned their stranded vehicles and ran back toward Gatlinburg.

"Alice, Mad Hatter," Yumi said. "Red Queen is on the run."

CHAPTER 32

Gideon and Hajar left the road, cutting across country, making their own shortcut through an open meadow. Bounding over a sparsely wooded hill, he brought the bike to rest beside the secluded, two-story, Carter Cabin.

To their dismay, a family was taking pictures by the open front door. Wasting no time, Hajar leapt from the bike, pulled her pistol, and fired twice into the air.

The Dobbs family of Springdale, Georgia, broke into a mad, screaming run for the parking lot that lay half a mile away.

"Was it something I said?" she asked innocently as she removed her helmet.

Gideon pulled off his own helmet and chuckled. "You do have a way with words, Hajar."

Hajar slipped off the bottomless backpack and tossed it to him.

"Stand guard in case we have more visitors," he said.

He ran inside the one-hundred-and-fifty-year-old structure. Pausing by a main support beam just beneath a giant carved heart that proclaimed the undying love of *KN* to *CN*, he placed five bricks of plastic explosive. Quickly, he wired blasting caps into the C-4 and armed the system.

Moving outside, he grabbed Hajar by the arm and, together, they ran for the cover of a massive oak. Once shielded, Hajar slammed Gideon against the wide bole and kissed him as he squeezed the detonator.

The big cabin that had sheltered generations of Carters was, in mere seconds, reduced to smoldering splinters by the high explosives.

"You really know how to make the earth move, big man," she whispered.

"No time for fooling around," Gideon said as he flew past her. "Come on, woman!"

Threading their way through the burning wreckage, they stood at the gaping maul of a cave that lay several feet below the main floor of the cabin. Gideon produced a flashlight and, throwing caution to the winds, disappeared into the inky blackness of the cavern. Hajar felt a distinct chill, looking at the mountain witch's former abode, and drew Kali, before following Gideon's lead.

'*I smell breakfast*,' Kali said.

"Great," Hajar said as she stepped into space.

The low, soot-blacken ceiling forced the tall woman to stoop forward as she sought to catch up with Gideon. Her boots echoed eerily on the steeply descending stone floor as she followed his distant, bouncing light.

"Wait up!" she yelled as the cave branched sharply to the left. Rounding the corner, she discovered that Gideon was nowhere to been found. "Where are you? I don't need to get lost down here!"

Gideon appeared from an almost hidden cleft in the rock wall.

"Sorry," he said. "I got ahead of myself."

With Hajar at his side, he traced markings on the floor and walls.

"So what is the witch's story?" she asked. "And how did she come by this Key thing?"

"No one knew her real name, but she came to be known as Granny Cabal. For a mountain witch, she was powerful, and only the most foolhardy sought her out. They said that she kept a vast treasure hidden in her cave. A treasure, it was said, that could unlock the wisdom of the ancients."

"The Key?"

"Not exactly. The tale I told our people was a cock and bull story."

"What?"

"We have a spy, remember?"

"Megan, yeah, don't remind me."

"Perhaps—perhaps not. For all we know, they may all be spies. In any case, I don't want the real story about *The Book of Xanadutha* to get out until I am ready. You, silly sexy woman, are the only person I trust."

"Thanks...I think. You mean to tell me *The Book of Xanadutha* isn't a map to Eden?"

"Hajar, *The Book of Xanadutha* isn't a book at all. It is an alien device that can breach time and space. With that little beauty you can travel to each of the infinite universes."

"Excuse me?"

"Look, the book is the most dangerous device on Earth because the doors it can open, open both ways. Creatures beyond your imagination would love to drop in and ravage Earth."

"How do you know this?"

"Because, back in '51, I used the damn thing to stop an alien invasion. Afterward, I did everything I could think of to destroy the device, but the godless race who built it made it indestructible. Believe it or not, the boys and I managed to place it at the center of a hydrogen bomb test. The blast wiped out an island but didn't put a scratch on the book. So we did the next best thing. Made up a bunch of wild tales about its 'heavenly language,' removed its power supply, and hid it in a library."

"Weren't you afraid that someone would find it?"

"Why? Without its power, it's a fancy paper weight."

"But Mrs. Kerr wanted it to find Eden."

"Sweetie, Eden isn't on this Earth...well, not exactly. It's in a bubble dimension. Half a second separates it from this world. On Earth, but as unreachable as the farthest star."

"My head hurts," she said. "Then why did we just blow a log cabin to kingdom come?"

"Because this place, two hundred and fifty years ago, is where I stashed the battery."

"Time travel? You're pulling my leg."

"I used the device. Once I removed the battery, I had just enough power for a return trip home. How else could Ginny's wedding ring be the one Julius Caesar gave Cleopatra? Ginny was very…appreciative of my effort."

"You're slick, did you know that?"

"I've been told."

"Do you know what this means, Gideon?"

"Don't even think about it."

"Why not? We can go back and make this whole mess never happen. I can warn myself—you can save the Choirboys!"

Gideon let out a breath and a sad expression crossed his face. "Don't you think I've thought about this at least ten thousand times? Going back doesn't change our time. It creates a split, and a new, completely independent time line branches off. Your situation, here and now, is untouched because you have already lived it. Once you have knocked off Mrs. Kerr, or warned yourself of the ambush, you will instantly come back to the point in time where you started with nothing to show for your effort."

"Shit," she said. In frustration, she sent a small loose stone clattering down the long passageway.

"Sorry," he said, caressing her cheek.

"For your information, I would have gone back to when Larry recruited me and given him a terminal case of heartburn."

"Good to know."

"So once we get the alien battery, we can open a portal to Eden?"

"In a way. You see Eden is a special place. While any other destination in the multi-verse can be reached by merely dialing up the right number, so to speak, you must be standing on a particular Earth point to reach Eden and the Tree."

"Of course, it wouldn't be easy."

Gideon chuckled. "That would just take all the fun out of it."

"Where is it?"

"For now, I need to keep that under my hat."

"I thought you trusted me?"

"With my life, doll. However, we both know that if Mrs. Kerr commands you to tell her, you will, because you have no choice. I can't have Mrs. Kerr knowing the location until the very last minute."

"I understand."

"Let's get the battery and blow this place. The opening is up ahead."

With Gideon taking the lead, they traveled down the rocky, uneven floor, pausing at a spot that appeared as a blank rock wall. He reached out his hand and, to her amazement, his hand disappeared.

"Nice trick."

He took her by the hand and they entered the mysterious camouflaged opening.

After traveling a hundred feet, and three hairpin turns, the dank cave walls gave way to gleaming gold.

The slightly angled walls were covered with deeply etched hieroglyphics that emitted a bluish glow, dispelling the gloom. Maggie thought that the weird glyphs were oddly similar to Egyptian drawings found in tombs. She dismissed the thought, as rural Tennessee couldn't have been further removed from ancient Egypt.

"Is that gold?" she asked.

"Yes, pure gold."

Hajar reached out her hand to the gleaming, slightly glowing wall. "Ow!" she cried, pulling back a finger oozing blood.

"You pricked your finger," he said, taking her hand. Unfolding a pocket square, he held pressure on her finger.

"Funny, the wall looked smooth, but it felt like a needle got me."

"I think you'll live."

The glowing walls began to pulsate wildly and, seconds later, a low moan reached their ears."

"Was it like this last time you were here?"

"No." Gideon finished with her slight wound and then drew his weapons.

She could feel a dark, oppressive presence in the new

chamber. It felt as if fear itself had taken on a tangible form that one could physically touch. Hajar warily moved forward, holding Kali before her, while Gideon, half a step ahead, held both Thunder and Lightning, cocked and ready.

"What is this place?" she asked. "It feels evil."

"A remnant of a dark world long gone, this place was constructed by the Nephilim, before the Great Cataclysm, better known as Noah's flood."

"Nephilim?" Hajar asked. "You mean the children of women and angels?"

"Yeah, the scourge of the antediluvian world."

"This place looks Egyptian."

"Much older than Egypt. This place was one of two holy places built by the dark wizards who did the Nephilim's bidding. This is either Khoorum or Thalamus. That's why I stashed the battery here, I figured that buried deep under a national park in a cave equipped with spiritual shielding, the battery would never have been found."

"If you say so," she said. "It looks like a new ride at Dollywood."

"You know, Hajar, you and my Ginny have the same way with words."

"Thanks."

"I didn't mean it as a compliment."

Hajar stuck her tongue out at him.

"Anyway, as I was saying, this chamber is the last surviving section of a temple complex devoted to their blasphemous deities. As I recall, I stashed the battery in a stone box I found up ahead. What I don't get, is where that glow is coming from."

"Was it this oppressive then?"

"No, and that worries me even more. Keep a sharp eye out for trouble."

"Gideon!" Hajar cried as the passage ahead filled with a rolling black mass. The mass had dozens of evil yellow eyes and bright flashes of white, needle-like teeth.

"Crap," Hajar said.

"Demons," Gideon corrected.

'*Lunch,*' Kali said.

Before the pair could defend themselves a deep, thunderous voice rang out. "*Gettor! Gettor dayior somger, daye.*"

The demon hoard dissipated like a morning mist in the hot sun.

"What the hell was that?"

"I don't know, girl, but I think we'll find out. Let's go.

A few hundred feet in, the golden passage opened up into a colossal room lined in sheets of shimmering gold. Fifty feet above their heads floated a fiery globe of deep blue that illuminated the vast chamber. In the center of the room lay the large stone vault where Gideon had hidden the battery. Standing next to the vault was a huge figure nearly twelve feet tall.

The giant looked like a Viking chieftain, dressed for battle in glittering scaled armor. His massive, hairy arms were bare, with the exception of stylized metal bands at his biceps and wrists. His eyes seemed unnaturally bright green. As he contemplated his guests, he stroked the huge reddish-brown beard that fell to his chest.

"As I live and breathe," Gideon whispered. "Nephilim."

"That's crazy," she whispered. "I can't believe that a dead race of giants is hiding out under a log cabin in a national park."

The giant, except for his proportions, looked completely human. A smile crossed his broad features and he glided toward them.

"Do you see what I see?" Gideon asked.

"You mean the freaking giant?"

"No, that the freaking giant isn't real. Look closely. He's slightly transparent." In a sign of good faith, Gideon holstered his guns and stepped forward. "I am Gideon Kane, and this is my friend, Hajar. We mean you no harm."

The giant stopped two feet away, put his hands on his hips, and looked down on Gideon. The creature's smile turned into a deep scowl and he drew back a fist.

"Look out, Gideon!" Hajar screamed.

The giant lashed out with a massive fist. Gideon spun right, dodging the brunt of the blow, but was still shoved several feet away, where he lay stunned. Hajar leaped at the creature and slashed with Kali only to find the sword passed harmlessly through him, as though the giant was made of insubstantial mist.

Reaching out a thick hand, he touched her between the eyes. Hajar felt a massive electrical shock course through her, but she kept her feet. The giant chuckled at her as he stepped back. "Think that was funny, did you?" she snapped. She prepared for a second assault when the creature spoke.

"Peace."

"Peace?"

"I am Diolefin and I mean you no harm."

"You nearly killed my friend, you giant asshole!"

"Friend? How can that be? He is only a dwarf, and dwarfs are beneath our contempt."

"Dwarf?"

"Is he your pet or slave?"

Gideon staggered over to Hajar.

"You all right?" she asked, not taking her eyes off the grinning giant.

"That old boy packs a wallop, but I've had worse."

"The next time you dare approach me, I will kill you, dwarf."

"Who are you?" Gideon asked.

"Screw that, *what* are you?" asked Hajar.

"Why, I am Diolefin, of course."

Hajar snorted. "Oh yeah, that clears up everything."

"He is a simulation." Gideon looked about the great room. "Oh my goodness. This isn't a temple—it's a computer."

"Computer?" she asked." How hard did he hit you?"

Gideon wiped a bit of blood from his mouth. "I'm serious. We're looking at a ten-thousand-year-old artificial intelligence."

"Your dog is quite correct," Diolefin said.

"So you are the world's first calculator, or video game?"

"I am the great machine created by the mighty Nephilim scientist Borate, the warlock Herah, and commissioned by the last Emperor, Raa. I was to be the final solution."

"A machine created by the combination of science and dark magic," Gideon said. "How is it you speak English?"

"I listened to your world as it slowly recovered from the great disaster. I know your worthless people better than you do."

"I never read about him in the Bible," Hajar said as she gripped Kali tighter.

"What is your specific purpose, Diolefin?" Gideon asked. "Final solution to what problem?"

Diolefin gave Gideon a smirk.

"You heard Old Yeller, what's your purpose?" Hajar demanded.

"You'll pay for that," Gideon whispered.

"To rid the world of the dwarf infestation, of course."

"Of course," she said. "How, exactly?"

"I would have been released into their technology and would have used their own machines against them. Unfortunately, before I was brought to bear, disaster struck and my people were destroyed. I thought my advent would be a mere act of revenge. However, with your coming, I see my original purpose is still valid."

"So you sat here twiddling your thumbs all this time?"

"No. I was dormant for thousands of years until the spark of life came to me two hundred and fifteen years ago."

"The battery," Gideon said. "When I stashed the battery here, the power seepage triggered this Nephilim death machine."

"Way to go, Gideon. That's like throwing a lit candle into a bin of bottle rockets."

"I have a question, Diolefin. Why do you treat Hajar with respect, when I am a no more than a dwarf dog?"

"The gulf that separates the two of you is as wide as that of an amoeba and a God. I can't understand why she even acknowledges your existence."

"Why?" Gideon asked, although the truth was becoming chillingly clear.

"You are human, dog, and she is Nephilim."

"Excuse me?" Hajar asked. "Gideon, tell this guy he is full of sheep dip."

"I wish I could," Gideon said as he turned and looked closely at Hajar. "Why didn't I see this before? Your unnatural speed, strength, and stamina are well beyond that of a trained athlete. It is as obvious as the nose on your face."

"This isn't funny, Gideon. I was raised in Alabama and I know for damn sure that Travis Smith wasn't an angel by any stretch of the imagination."

"No, it's not funny, but it is true, nonetheless. You are a Nephilim."

"I will admit that she is a mere sprig of a Nephilim, a terribly stunted midget, but her blood is absolutely pure."

"Stunted midget? I am six foot, six!"

"Next to him, you're a midget, sweetie. When you pricked your finger on the wall back in the tunnel, HAL 9000 here must have taken a blood sample."

"This is insane."

Gideon's eyes flew wide as an idea was born. "Quickly, ask him where Lagrangian point, zero, zero, zero is located."

"Answer the man," Hajar said as her head swam with confused thoughts of who or what she really was.

Floating before them, a transparent globe appeared. And although the landmasses were skewed, it was definitely the Earth. A bright point appeared in the southern hemisphere.

"Latitude and longitude please," Gideon asked as he produced a small leather clad notebook and pen.

Rolling his large eyes, Diolefin told him the precise coordinates, pinpointing the glowing spot.

"Excellent." Gideon tucked away his book and pen. "Let's grab the battery and scram, sweetheart. Without power, this thing will return to dormancy."

"Enough useless banter," Diolefin said. "Release me and let me fulfill my reason for being, last Daughter of the Nephilim. The blood of your ancestors demands it!"

"Can you imagine this thing loose in the world?" Gideon said.

"Release me!"

"How do I release you?" Hajar asked.

"Hajar, what are you doing?"

"Silence, dog!"

"I am getting awfully tired of being called a dog by a glorified abacus."

"Remove the Spark of Life and place it in the chamber," Diolefin said. The simulation pointed toward a tube that rose silently from the floor.

"You can't open the vault lock, can you?" Hajar asked. "You don't have any hands to manipulate the mechanism."

"No. You will do it for me."

"I don't care if I'm a Nephilim, or green blooded Martian, no way am I going to let you kill everyone I know."

"I will trigger a nuclear war and melt down every nuclear reactor. However, fear not. I will keep you safe within this chamber, Hajar. When the radiation levels have dropped, you can go out and take this dead world for the Nephilim."

"By myself? Not big on biology are we?"

"I have a DNA database of the Emperor and his command staff. I will impregnate you and you will bear the children of our great leaders."

"How romantic. I get to be a baby machine for a bunch of stiffs who have been dead ten thousand years. I'll pass."

"You betray the blood of your ancestors. I honor them by forcing you to fulfill your destiny."

Gideon flew through the air, spinning several times before slamming against the far wall.

"If you care about your pet, Hajar, you will release me or I will pull him apart."

"Don't you dare, woman," Gideon cried as he staggered to his feet.

"You don't tell me what to do, old man," she screamed. "I'll save you if I want to!"

Diolefin laughed as Hajar ran to the vault and released the intricate lock, before she ripped off the stone lid. Lying on an old green army tarp was a rectangular sliver of silver metal about twelve inches long and one inch wide.

"Ahhhhhh yesss," Diolefin cooed as the lifting of the

shielding stone lid gave the machine a rush of energy. The walls and the suspended globe of blue fire doubled in intensity. "Place the spark in the chamber."

Gideon watched helplessly, trying to find a weakness when a thought occurred to him. With a look of grim determination, he pulled Thunder and Lightning.

Diolefin laughed. "Your weapons have no effect on me, dog. I am invincible."

"Outside, maybe, but, old boy, we are standing in what basically is your heart."

"What?"

Gideon sent a volley of fire at the walls. Diolefin flickered and screamed. He lashed out in rage and Gideon grunted as he was toppled off his feet.

"Way to go, old man," Hajar said. Laughing with joy, she spun around the room, slashing the walls with Kali. The walls exploded outward as Diolefin begged and pleaded for mercy. Finally, after half the room lay in smoking ruins, the simulation of the giant vanished.

The battery safely in the backpack, Gideon planted plastic explosions in the vast Nephilim computer.

"That thing must never see the light of day," he said as he wired the bricks.

Hajar sat down and watched Gideon rig the bomb. Her mind was reeling from the revelation of her incredible heritage.

"That'll do the trick," Gideon said as he held out his hand and pulled her to her feet.

"I have been called a freak my entire life. I guess this proves it."

"That's nonsense."

"You heard what Diolefin said. I'm not human. I'm a *thing*."

Gideon grabbed Hajar hard by the shoulders. "Look here, woman. Nephilim is human. You are human. You just have a special ingredient that makes you unique and extraordinary. Think of it like this. Brownies are good, but brownies with walnuts are better."

Hajar laughed. "You don't do this a lot, do you?"

"Was it that obvious?"

She drew him close and kissed him. "Thanks, just the same, Gideon."

"You can thank me like this anytime, beautiful," he whispered.

"So what are we going to call this adventure?" she asked as she wrapped her arms around his neck. "I've got it. How about *Kamikaze Kane and the Nephilim Computer of Doom that Almost Destroyed the World*?"

"Tell you what, doll. I'll keep quiet about your episode in my kitchen, if you'll keep my little screw-up here under your hat. Deal?"

"With all our little secrets, you'd think we were on the verge of a relationship, old man."

"Just like a dang stunted Nephilim woman to go and ruin a perfectly good adventure by talking all gushy."

"When this is over, I am never letting you out of my sight again."

"I'm counting on it. Now move your freakish ass. We have to go," he said, taking her by the hand.

They flew through the cavern, the spot under the incision on Gideon's chest becoming hotter as the tiny demonic creature stirred. The warmth now felt like a severe case of heartburn. The creature was growing faster than Gideon had expected. The weeks he had hoped for now looked like a mere few days.

He was never one to complain, but inwardly he railed at the unfairness of it all. He wanted to live. He wanted Hajar, but he knew that the death in his chest was growing by the moment.

His life was essentially over. However, he prayed that he still had time to perform the last act and free the woman he loved.

CHAPTER 33

The pretty, blonde reporter took a sip of water as the camera operator adjusted his Sony. The uncomfortable-looking police officer at her side nervously swallowed and fiddled with his tie.

"Relax, Captain," she said with a grin. "You'll do just fine. Isn't that right, Mickey?"

Her cameraman, Mickey Falla, gave him a thumbs up. "Let her rip, Elsa."

"This is Elsa Phillips, reporting for Action 13 News. I am here with Captain Dale Sonora of the Joint East Tennessee Task Force. Captain Sonora, can you tell me what your organization is doing here today?"

"Yes, Miss Phillips," he said with a deep Southern accent. "We have special tactical units from five East Tennessee Counties in a joint training exercise, basically to brush up on the latest tactics and equipment. If, God forbid, the need arises, such as a disaster or malicious action, we can work as a single body."

"Malicious action? You mean an act of terrorism?"

"Yes, as well as search and rescue in the case of a natural disaster. We have learned much from the lessons of Katrina and the tornados that hit Tuscaloosa."

"When you say tactical units," she asked. "Is that another name for SWAT teams?"

"A rose by any other name," Captain Sonora said with a grin.

"How many police officers are involved?"

"Just over one hundred officers, including six canine units."

"I'm sure that the people of East Tennessee will sleep much better knowing that such a polished group stands ready to respond. I am Elsa Phillips for Action 13 News."

"And...we're done," Mickey said.

"Thank you, Captain Sonora," she said. "You did great. I loved the, 'rose by any other name.'"

"Thanks, Elsa, but, please, call me Dale."

"Captain Sonora, we got a situation," said a short, red-faced officer wearing sergeant's stripes. The police officer grabbed the captain by the arm and began to pull him away.

"What is it, Jerry?"

The sergeant spoke quickly in hushed tones.

"Get everyone ready. We're going to respond," Captain Sonora said.

"What's going on, Dale?" asked Elsa.

"We have a situation at the Park," he said. "Sorry, Elsa, I can't talk now, please excuse me."

"Did I hear the sergeant say that there was a shooting at the park?"

"Look, Elsa," the captain said. "We don't know the particulars, but keep a lid on this and I promise I will give you first shot at the story—if there is one."

"Well, I—"

"Corporal Johns, show the TV people out—*now.*"

After being politely, but firmly, escorted from the building, Elsa walked down the parking lot of the Justice Center toward the Action 13 News van.

Stay calm, Elsa, she told herself. *I'm the only reporter here. This is my story. I just don't understand what has stirred the hornet's nest.*

She looked around the empty parking lot before ducking behind a single story generator shed. Hidden from the unwanted view of prying cell phones cameras, she produced a pack of cigarettes and lighter from her shoulder bag.

"I know you, don't I?"

Elsa turned and beheld an older, distinguished looking female police officer approaching her. The handsome woman looked oriental with short, silver hair. Elsa's eyes were drawn like a magnet to the brightly shining captain bars adoring the police officer's starched white shirt.

"Excuse me?" Elsa asked.

"You're that reporter from Channel 13, aren't you?"

"Guilty," Elsa said with a dazzling smile.

"Captain Vicki Orrick," the cop said, sticking out her hand. "My wife is a huge fan of yours. Could I convince you to give me an autograph?"

"Your *wife*?"

"Well, *partner*, if you will. Mind if I bum a smoke? I'm supposed to stop, but…well, you know."

"Yes, I do." Elsa gave the captain a cigarette and soon both women were leaning against the building, indulging their guilty vice.

"About that autograph?"

"Sure, Captain," Elsa said, producing her pen and a slip of paper with the Channel 13 letterhead.

"Just make it out to Connie, if you don't mind."

"Could you give me a hint at what's going on?"

"Well, you didn't hear it from me," Vicki said, looking around to see if they were alone. "But all hell's broken loose in the park."

"Excuse me?"

Captain Orrick exhaled a long cloud of smoke. "An armed force has isolated Cades Cove and is shooting the place up. The situation is more serious than a hefty bag full of Rottweilers."

"Cades Cove?" Elsa asked. "Why? There's nothing there, but a bunch of…*nature*!"

"Who knows?" The captain shook her thick mane of hair. "Who knows why a fellow would blow up a federal building or shoot up a school full of kids? All I know is that we are co-ordinating with the local national guard. We are going to heli-copter a first response team into the park and put a stop to this foolishness before any more good people get hurt."

"Oh my God," Elsa said as the thrill of an exclusive, major network story danced before her eyes.

"Now mum is the word," the captain said. "I can trust your discretion, now, can't I?"

"Don't you worry about that, Captain Orrick," Elsa said sweetly. "You have my word as a professional. Will you excuse me, please?"

Elsa dropped her cigarette to the asphalt and crushed it out before she turned and walked around the corner of the building. Once out of sight of Captain Orrick, she broke into a full sprint for her news van.

As Elsa passed out of view, the captain wadded up the autograph and tossed it into a nearby trashcan.

"I'm so good, it's a shame," Mei said. She dropped the cigarette in disgust. "What a foul, disgusting habit."

Producing one of her own slim cigarettes, she fixed one in her long holder, which appeared in her left hand. Mei drew in the noxious, acrid smoke as if her life depended on it.

"Now, let's see if we can give that luscious Hajar's band of misfits a helping hand."

Chapter 34

Now, Mrs. Kerr, I promise, we'll take very good care of you," Dr. Thornton said.

"Thank you, Doctor." Mrs. Kerr settled back into the reclining dental chair. "Sorry about the short notice."

"Now don't you worry about that, dear," said Mary Sue Thornton, the dentist's wife and dental assistant. The short, plump woman with the perpetual, sunny smile clipped a bib into place around Mrs. Kerr's neck and lowered the surgical light fixture. "You poor thing," she said softly and patted her lightly on the arm. "What is this world coming to when a person isn't even safe in her own home?"

"I know what you mean," Mrs. Kerr said. "I thought he was going to kill me, but thank Jesus my family wasn't home at the time. I shudder to think what might have happened to them."

"That lowlife did a number on your teeth," the dentist said as he stepped behind Mrs. Kerr and checked the dental x-rays on the wall mounted light box. "However, I think…"

Almost a minute of silence ensued.

Mrs. Kerr sat up in the chair and frowned. "You think what, Dr. Thornton?"

"I think you have some explaining to do, Mrs. Kerr," Larry said as he spun the chair around.

"Oh God in heaven," she screamed.

"He is the last person you want to summon, witch."

Glancing around, she found Dr. Thornton and his wife frozen in place, like a video recording set on pause.

"I paid you handsomely to do a simple job. Why is Maggie Black still breathing?"

"She got the jump on us," Mrs. Kerr said. "She took over my people and now we work for her. Calls herself Hajar and even changed her looks to blend in, I swear to God. Look at what she did to me when I crossed her. The woman's a monster!"

"Where is she?"

"She wants you dead, Larry, for trying to kill her."

"Now how did she find out that little tidbit of information?"

"She beat it out of me. The woman's a walking nightmare! She shot me in the foot. Please, for the love of God, help me. She's waiting to ambush you, so you have to strike first. Don't give her an opportunity to get in the first shot. If you give her a chance, she'll kill you, then she'll come after me!"

"Where did she find so potent a weapon that could hurt moi?"

"She had it with her—I swear to God!"

"Where is Maggie?"

"Cades Cove, Tennessee. She has a partner that's as dangerous as she is. His name is Kane. They'll kill you on sight, so watch your back."

"If I find you have been lying to me Mrs. Kerr...well, you know what I will do."

"I swear!"

Larry disappeared.

"Got to get out of here," Mrs. Kerr mumbled. To her horror, her body refused to move. It was as if she were superglued to the chair itself.

"We—are ready to begin—Doctor," Mary Sue said. Her eyes were glassy and her voice slightly off.

"I have to go, you fools," Mrs. Kerr said. "Help me get out of this damn chair!"

"Gas—Doctor?"

"No—this is only—a simple tooth extraction. She won't need numbing—or anything to dull the pain." Doctor Thornton spoke in the same dull monotone voice as his wife.

"Tooth extraction?" Mrs. Kerr screamed. "What the hell are you talking about?"

"Your—teeth are all bad—and have to be removed—*now*. You should have flossed—young lady."

"I don't have a single cavity, you blind fool." Mrs. Kerr suddenly began to sweat as her heart was gripped by terror. "Oh no, Larry."

The blood draining from her face, Mrs. Kerr looked at the metal tray of instruments Mary Sue wheeled next to her and began to cry. Along with the rusty dental tools, were an assortment of greasy hacksaws, hammers, and pliers.

"Pry her jaws apart—Mary Sue," Dr. Thornton said as he selected a large ball peen hammer from the tray. "Now don't worry—Mrs. Kerr—this won't hurt a bit."

CHAPTER 35

Keep working, hairball," Yumi said as he checked the drum on his battle rifle.

He stepped back from Roland and their preparations to defend the blocked mountain road.

Roland set a fifty-caliber sniper rifle on a bipod and inserted a charged magazine. The pair was now dressed in camouflage after ditching their *please-shoot-me-first* bright orange shirts that Gideon had given them.

Yumi's collar buzzed slightly.

"Mr. Yumi," Mrs. Kerr said. "You have a big problem headed your way."

She sat in the parking lot of Dr. Thornton's office. Despite a few shots of Novocain and a handful of Percocets, her mouth was swollen and throbbing from eight extracted teeth.

Mrs. Kerr, in an inspired move, had used the rinse wand to snap the Thorntons out of their hypnotic trance before they killed her. The horrified doctor had given her drugs and attempted to fix the mess he had made, but the damage had been done.

"Mrs. Kerr, your voice is distorted," Yumi said. "Did you say problem?"

"Massive…police…response…one royally pissed angel."

"Nothing we can't handle," Yumi said. "It will take time for them to hike up the mountain from Gatlinburg, or should I say the Great Smoky Mountain parking lot. Once they see our dug-in position, they'll take the time to negotiate."

"Listen!" she snapped. "Kane didn't count on a SWAT convention going on in Pigeon Forge. They're loaded for bear and, once helicopters arrive from the local national air guard unit, they're going to drop in behind you."

"How do you know this?"

"Some stupid TV reporter just released their plans on TV. You have to get that Key and get out of there—now."

"We're past the point of no return," Yumi said. "From the smoke, Doc has already blown the cabin and is in the cave."

"That much I surmised, Mr. Yumi," she said. "I still want my prize and only Kane can get it for me, but I can't have Hajar spilling the beans to her former boss, or we are all dead. I want that bitch buried long before that ever happens, you hear me?"

"Yes, ma'am," Yumi said, "but it will take time. They're miles from here."

"Not my problem. Just do it. Do it now."

"Okay. How many cops are coming? Can you at least tell me that?"

"Over...one hundred."

"Great. What are you going to do to help us?"

"Are you serious? That's not the way this works, Mr. Yumi. I thought you had figured this out by now? Go kill her."

Yumi groaned as her voice vanished.

"Roland, we have a situation."

"How bad?"

"Got a division of airborne cops on the way and, if that wasn't enough misery, we're going to have Hajar's former boss breathing down our necks. This plan has just fallen into the toilet."

"Figures," Roland said.

Yumi wiped the sweat from his brow and picked up his AR-16 carbine. "Mrs. Kerr wants Hajar dead before Larry shows, so I have to leave you here."

"Yumi, my little buddy, you worry about Hajar," Roland said, clapping the smaller man on the shoulder. "I've got a crackerjack plan to slip past the cops."

Yumi groaned. "When it rains it pours."

Roland opened a map of the cove and spread it out on the ground. "Go get pimples and meet me here," Roland said, marking a spot along the loop with a pencil.

"What are you going to do?"

"No time to explain," Roland said, slinging his leg over a dirt bike that was a twin to Gideon's. "You're just going to have to trust me."

Without looking back, Roland started the bike and roared away.

ɛ⁊ɛ⁊

Sitting in the back of her car, Simone Ravenwood munched on a corndog and sipped a diet soda. Her crystal ball began to pulsate. Gobbling down the nitrite-sicle, she plopped the ornate crystal ball onto her lap and peered into its swirling depths.

Mistress Ravenwood, are you there?

"Yes, I am here, Samantha. What do you have to report?"

Mistress, have you heard about the trouble in the national park?

"Yes, my dear," she said. "I take it that this is your little band's work?"

Yes. We are running out of time. Unexpected law enforcement response will soon put an end to our plans. We need help.

Simone smiled.

"You are in luck. I am in Gatlinburg. You worry about the relic and I will take care of the police."

Thank you, Mistress, you have never let me down.

"Does Mrs. Kerr suspect that you aren't quite as innocent as she was led to believe?"

Mrs. Kerr is a fool.

"What about your teammates?"

Putty in my hands.

"Don't underestimate them, Samantha. Hajar was a Paladin and—"

I know Hajar is somewhat formidable, but Gideon Kane is the one I worry about.

"Doctor Kane has taken the Phoenix," Simone said. "He is, as they say, a 'dead man walking.' Now, put him out of your mind and focus."

Forgive me.

"Of course," Simone said. "Now be a good girl and trust your mistress."

It will be done.

᎒᎒

Yumi burst through the door of the ranger station to find Megan listening intently to a large shortwave radio.

"Where are the rest of the rangers?" he asked.

Megan giggled, "Sleeping off the prescription M&M's I gave them. She tossed him a big prescription bottle of Hacion.

"Where did you get this?"

"I have my ways," she said with a sly smile.

"We have to go," he said. "The feds are about to drop on us like a cartoon anvil."

"Yeah, it's all over the radio. So what's your plan?"

"Umm...not my plan. It's Roland's."

"You've got to be kidding me? You listened to that big douf Roland?"

"I was out of options."

"What's the plan?"

"Hairball didn't say. Just to meet him at this place on the loop." Yumi showed her the rendezvous spot on a huge wall sized map of the Park.

"Take one of the ranger's cars and get there," he said. "I'm going to hang back and slow down any pursuit."

Yumi was sweating profusely as he checked his rifle.

"Don't worry, Yumi," Megan said as she laid a reassuring hand on his shoulder. "It'll be all right. You'll see."

"Why are you so calm?" he asked.

"Umm, we just have to trust in that gorgeous hunk, Gideon. He won't let us down."

Yumi laughed. "Roland's right, you know. Gideon is much too old for you."

"We'll see," she said.

"Get going, girl, and pray that Roland can come through for once."

Megan ran out the door and soon was driving toward the loop in a ranger vehicle.

"Hajar, it looks like your luck has run out," Yumi said as he checked his ammo. "What the hell?" he said as he beheld the empty magazine. "I loaded that myself."

"I can't let you shoot poor Hajar like a rabid dog, Mr. Yumi," Mei said from the radio speaker. "She has a mission to perform for me first. If you start now, you may get out of the building before the police arrive."

Suddenly, the ranger station went dark. Yumi lit a match and found the door and windows gone, replaced with a seamless wall.

"No!" He ran to the spot where the door had been and slammed his fist into the hard wallboard. Looking around the room, he leaped upon the desk, removed a few ceiling tiles, and pulled down the thick yellow insulation batting. Sticking his head into the opening, he found a small, thin aluminum-ridge vent grate on the far gable. He grabbed hold of a truss and pulled himself up into the crawl space. Working his way down the dusty, blazing-hot attic space, he turned and kicked out the entire section of thin plywood making up the gable.

Dropping to the ground, Yumi found, to his chagrin, that all the vehicles parked around the station or in the adjacent store parking lot had flat tires.

"Great, just great," he spat as he jogged toward the campground several hundred yards up the narrow road.

Chapter 36

Hajar climbed out of the splintered remnants of the Carter cabin. She shouldered the backpack containing the battery, while Gideon stayed behind and placed the last of his charges.

She laid the pack to one side of the BMW, before returning to the mouth of the cave. As Gideon appeared, she leaned over to help him up. "The coast is clear," she said.

Gideon paused and took out his detonator. "Take cover," he said and counted to ten before squeezing the device.

The ground shook and a thick column of choking dust and flying rubble erupted from the entrance.

"That should take care of Diolefin once and for all."

"I don't hear sirens. Looks like our crew has kept Johnny Law off of us, Gideon."

"They did well," he said.

"My, my, you just never know who you will run into in the middle of the woods," Larry said.

Hajar and Gideon turned sharply to find the smiling Larry leaning against a tree.

"Larry," Hajar breathed. "Oh, no."

"This entire time I thought you were dead, Maggie, or should I say Hajar? In a moment, you will be."

Gideon stepped between Larry and Hajar. "You got something to say, you say it to me."

"Well, as I live and breathe." Larry walked toward the pair. "The world renowned, Doctor Gideon 'Kamikaze' Kane in the flesh. You know, Doc, you look pretty good for a eighty-three-year old fart. Don't tell me that this stupid girl has pulled your old Geritol-swigging butt out of retirement? I think you've finally picked a fight you can't win."

Gideon moved nose to nose with the powerful angel. "If I have, you're going to have to prove it, bird-boy," he whispered.

"If it's a pissing contest you want, you got it, has-been."

"Gideon, no! I can't let you get hurt because of me," Hajar said as she stepped out from behind him. "Larry, if you want to kill me, I can't stop you. But please at least tell me why? What did I do wrong? I loved you. You were the best friend I ever had and I can't believe it was all a lie. Did you know that I'm a Nephilim?"

"Very well. You did a good job for me so that's the least I can do before I send St. Peter a new arrival. Yes, I knew you were a Nephilim. That was what made you so valuable to me, and that's why Heaven put a target on your back. Can't have you starting another race competing for the planet, now can we?"

"Where did she come from?" Gideon asked.

Larry let out a deep breath of frustration. "A fool angel named Tarrazonne came to Earth. The dimwit found himself a whore that he, in his lust, thought he loved. I forget her name, but anyway, they had a child, you. Before Heaven could respond and destroy the child, I saw an opportunity to help myself, so I took it."

"What opportunity?" Gideon asked.

"All my previous Paladins had one major defect—they were flimsy humans. Humans break easily. I figured that a Nephilim female would be sheer hell on wheels. I uglied you up a bit and gave you to Travis Smith to raise. Along with stunting your growth, I kept you weakened, unable to reveal your true prowess until after I recruited you."

"You mean this is my real face? I grew up thinking I was the ugliest creature in five states."

"Six, actually," Larry said. "It was a mask to hide your true identity and to keep people away."

"It worked," she said softly. "I thought that when you made me your Paladin, you had made me beautiful."

"I just revealed the beauty under the beast and took credit for it. Unfortunately, for you anyway, Heaven figured it out."

"You used me, my entire life," she said quietly.

"Yes, I did," he said with a broad smile. "It's what I do, baby girl. Think of it like this, you were my get out of Hell free card and it worked better than my wildest dreams."

Hajar felt as though her heart had been ripped to shreds. Larry was her anchor, her best friend, a second father, and it was all a lie.

"Please, help me," she said in quiet voice. "Please, for the love of God, help me."

"I never saw you as a whiner," Larry said as he flashed a bright smile. "Suck it up and take your medicine like a man—I mean, Paladin—okay, sweetie?"

"How could you do this?" Gideon asked as he clenched his fists. "She loves you. In the short time I have known her, I have found Hajar to be a rare and special jewel. I won't let you treat her like trash."

"Oh, don't tell me an old dog like you has gotten himself all smitten?" Larry threw back his head and laughed.

Gideon's reaction shocked both Hajar and Larry. Enraged, Gideon Kane did the unthinkable and backhanded Larry squarely across the face. The slap sounded like thunder. "Hajar is a good woman and she sure as shooting doesn't deserve the likes of you. You deserve the Hellfire that's waiting for you, you grinning bastard. If I could, I'd send your sorry ass there now."

The cocky, perpetual smile disappeared from Larry's face. His eyes radiated an unearthly glow as his face twisted in rage.

"Oh, no." Hajar had never seen her boss lose his temper before. "Gideon, run!"

With amazing speed, Larry snatched Gideon by the throat and slammed him like a ragdoll against an oak tree. "You dare to strike me, you insignificant ant," he said. "I could kill you with a thought!"

"Kiss—my—Tennessee ass," Gideon gurgled as Larry ground him into the unyielding tree.

With his left hand, Gideon pulled out Thunder and emptied the clip into Larry's face. It only made Larry smile.

"Like I said, you bit off more than you can chew, Kane. But, hey, to show you how nice a guy I am, since you love the stupid bitch so much, I'll send you both together to Happy Land."

"Larry, for the love of God, stop. You're hurting him!" Hajar cried.

"Hurt him?" Larry snapped. "I'm going to kill him."

Hajar swallowed hard and raised Kali high. Kali, for once, was as silent as a crypt and seemed to weigh a ton. Hajar's sweaty hand shook as a hard knot formed in her stomach. Regardless of the pain he had caused her, she didn't want to hurt Larry. "You want to kill me, fine, here I am, but leave Gideon out of this."

Larry laughed. "Make me, you coward."

Eyes blurred by tears, Hajar leaped forward and, with a wild scream, plunged the poisoned Kali deep into Larry's back, driving her to the hilt in the wild Hawaiian shirt.

She heard Kali scream, just before the world exploded into a flash of blue. The spiritual shockwave tossed her several feet away. The ground rumbled and swayed greatly, the sharp tremors being felt as far away as the Cumberland Plateau.

Hajar staggered to her feet, only to find Larry crying out in abject agony. Gone was his human guise and before her writhed a being with skin the color of molten bronze. Buried to the hilt, Kali screamed in agony as well.

"How could you do this to me?" he screamed. "I was so close to Heaven."

"I'm sorry. You were hurting Gideon."

Tears of pain and sorrow flowed down her face. As she watched, his bell-like cries got weaker. Finally, Larry collapsed and lay still upon the red Tennessee clay. In seconds, he breathed his last and became a fine white ash, which quickly dissipated, leaving only a faint outline of ash.

"Oh God, what have I done?" Hajar whispered.

"Uhh…" Gideon grunted.

"Gideon, are you all right?" she asked as she ran to his side.

Gideon looked around in a daze. "How long have I been out?"

"A second or two at the most."

"I could have sworn—been a rough day. Between Nephilim supercomputers and pissed-off angels, I've taken a beating."

"Yeah," she said as tears flowed down her face. "I feel your pain."

"Where's Larry?"

Hajar leaned over and kissed Gideon lightly on the lips. "In Hell, where he belongs."

She helped Gideon get to his feet, amazed that bones were not broken and that all he showed was some serious-looking bruises. Gideon reached out to the tree trunk and steadied himself.

"Are you all right?" she asked.

"Next time I decide to bitch slap an angel, please just shoot me. It will save us both a lot of trouble."

"Gideon, that was the stone-cold, ballsiest thing I ever saw. You really are Kamikaze Kane."

"If you mean by 'stone-cold, ballsiest thing,' I'm stupid, yes, I agree. Feel like I was run over by a truck—twice."

He noticed the heartbreaking look in her misty eyes. "I'm sorry, Hajar. I know how much Larry meant to you."

"Do me a favor, babe, never mention that creep's name again, okay? I made the right choice."

"You got it. We need to go. Where is your butter knife?"

"Kali's gone. I think the contact with Larry was too much and they died together. I will miss the creepy thing."

Retrieving the battery and his weapon, they climbed aboard the motorcycle, and, with Hajar driving, roared off down the winding trail.

ॐ

Mei Xue appeared near the vestiges of the Carter cabin as Gideon and Hajar disappeared over a hill in a cloud of dust.

Mei left a pungent smoky trail as she approached the angelic remains.

"Well done, Hajar," Mei said. She stirred the fine angelic ash outline with the toe of her shoe. "Because of you, I am one tantalizing step closer to my prize. I had no illusions as to your pain, but I didn't think you would have taken it this far. I would have bet real money against you killing him."

Drawing on her ever-present cigarette, she blew a smoky kiss at the ash and it completely disappeared.

Snapping her fingers, the ravaged cabin exploded in reverse. Far-flung stones, boards, down to even the tiniest splinters, came together, reassembling the cabin—once again hiding the secret of the Nephilim and leaving no trace that Gideon or Hajar had ever been there.

"To the Friends of the Smokies, you are welcome," Mei said as she sauntered down a side trail.

CHAPTER 37

Reminiscent of television images of the Vietnam War, several Blackhawk helicopters, escorted by an Apache gunship, landed half a mile from Yumi's position.

Exploding a few carefully placed smoke grenades, in order to slow down pursuit, proved to be in vain. The joint taskforce quickly swept through the campground and rescued the drugged park rangers. Coordinating with the national guard, they began a meticulous hunt for Gideon's crew.

"That's not playing fair," Yumi said as he watched the heavily armed attack helicopter sweep along the fields, sending herds of whitetail deer stampeding in terror.

His assassination of Hajar foiled by Mei, Yumi barely had time to fell a few trees to slow down response on the loop, but the arrival of the nimble, heavily armed gunship ruined what was left of his plans.

"We can't fight that," he muttered. "All we can do now is escape."

☙❧❧

"Caterpillar, we are back from the Rabbit Hole and we have the Magic Mushroom," Hajar said. "How is your dance with the Red Queen?"

"Glad to hear it, Alice," Yumi said. "Change of plans. Meet us at the car park, two miles up from your location. Cheshire Cat should already be there."

"What's the problem?"

"Unexpected response from the Red Queen," he said. "She's being a real bitch."

"What do you mean?"

"Red Queen bypassed the road from Gatlinburg. She has landed over a hundred heavily armed troops from helicopters and is sweeping the park with an AH-64D. They've already cut off our exit. That bitchy enough for you?"

"Pretty much," she said. "Where's White Rabbit?"

"In route. White Rabbit has a plan."

"Oh, no. As if things couldn't get any worse."

"Rodger that, but we are out of options."

∽∾∽

Simone Ravenwood sat at a small table in Room 301 of the Dew Drop Mountain Motel. With the curtains drawn, a spell had been cast over the seedy motel room, making the space as dark as pitch.

A detailed map of Cades Cove lay before her, illuminated by a single red candle. While she chanted and moaned, the air in the room became dank and oppressive.

Weird sounds, uttered by unnatural spiritual creatures ripped from nightmares, crawled and slithered around her. Focusing inward, she funneled her dark power toward the beleaguered Cove.

∽∾∽

Hajar, Gideon, and Megan stood by a stolen ranger cruiser, trying to figure a way out of their mess. The deep, booming, chop, chop, chop of the distant prowling Apache didn't help their concentration.

"Hey, you guys hear that?" Megan asked.

"Thank you, Jesus!" Hajar said at the familiar deep rumble of twin Pratt & Whitney engines. Sailing low over the trees, the *Ginny K* settled down on the open, rolling meadow.

"I don't believe it," Gideon said as Roland poked his head

out of a side widow and waved. "Let's go, ladies. Our ride is here!"

"Thank Jesus for me," Megan said.

She and Hajar jumped into the cruiser.

Astride the dirt bike, Gideon followed behind the car. Hajar drove down the grassy embankment and bounced over the trimmed grass of the field. Roland taxied the big plane around, pointing the nose toward a long stretch of rolling runway.

Breathing a sigh of relief, Gideon saw Yumi bounding over a hillock on a stolen motorcycle, racing for the *Ginny K*. Gideon had never left a man behind and, regardless if the entire US Army was after them, he wasn't about to start now.

Unfortunately, Gideon and his band weren't the only ones who saw the plane land. The pilot of the Apache gunship also saw the C-47B and changed course to investigate.

"What's that?" Gideon asked, watching tremendous fingers of an inky-black cloud sweep across Gregory Bald and roll down the valley toward them. "That isn't natural. We have to get out of here!" As he neared the plane, he was shouting orders. "Leave the bikes. We have to go, now."

A tremendous clap of thunder shook the valley and the wind suddenly began to whip the trees about.

Moments later, the *Ginny K* picked up speed and bounded down the gently sloping field. As she left the ground, they saw the gunship dead ahead, moving to block them.

"Aw crap, Doc," Roland said.

"Hold on," Gideon said. The big plane banked sharply and darted into the sky. "He can't shoot at us without express permission from his superiors, and I know for a fact, he can't keep up with the *Ginny K*."

ℰᎧℰᎧ

Colonel Bob "Cowboy" Ellis was flying across the park at tree level when he saw the *Ginny K* coming in for a landing.

"I'll be damn," he said. "Cute trick using an old DC-3, but that big antique stands out like a sore thumb. Every airport from here to Timbuktu will be on the lookout." Bob thought about his brace of Hellfire missiles. "I sure would love to turn that big goony bird into a pin wheeling fireball—send a message to those damn towel heads that old Uncle Sam is tired of taking shit, but it ain't worth throwing away my career."

He turned and began a pursuit. He tried to send a description of the distinctive aircraft, but his radio inexplicably died.

"Aw great, typical substandard military contractors," he spat, banking right. "They won't get away—what was that?" There was a loud bang and his aircraft shuddered slightly.

"Aw Hell! It's hail! Big ass hail at that!"

Suddenly, without warning, the sky was full of baseball size hail, falling at terminal velocity. Thousands of the deadly, icy missiles slammed into the gunship at over one hundred miles an hour.

Bob valiantly tried to land, but his aircraft was swatted from the sky and sent sliding into a stand of oak trees. As the expensive piece of government hardware burned, and the only witness to the *Ginny K*'s escape lay dead, the savage storm vanished.

ဆဝဆ

"Looks like a freak weather incident has given Mrs. Kerr's motley crew a chance to escape, Howard," Simone said as she opened the drapes, letting in bright sunlight and dispelling the last of the fading spell. "Pity about the army pilot."

Howard smiled.

To Simone, human life meant nothing and she was guilty of hundreds of murders and deaths. While polished and sophisticated on the outside, inwardly she and her coven were little more than soulless animals.

"It is a shame you must personally address the needs of this rag tag band."

"A price I must pay."

"Perhaps disbanding the Dark Counsel was a bit premature."

"Are you questioning my decisions, Howard?"

"Of course not, Mistress Ravenwood. I merely point out

that the burden has fallen squarely on your shoulders. With running the company, the strain must be terrible."

"That's why I want you to take the reins of Jolly Time, until this business is finished."

"Thank you for your trust in me, Mistress."

"You've earned it. Just don't drive the company into the ground."

"Where's their quest taking you, now that you have saved them from the local authorities?" Howard asked.

"Patience. My informant will let us know when she can."

"You put a lot of faith in this spy of yours, Mistress," he said. "Who is your informant?"

"Samantha Jordan," she said. "You remember little Samantha, don't you? Last year she infiltrated the Kennan P Walker High School in St. Louis."

"Ah, yes," he said. "She dealt with the bogus satanic group who was bringing too much unwanted attention our way. The local police thought they'd all committed ritual suicide. Nice work."

"Yes, she's more than a match for anyone in Mrs. Kerr's group, and that includes the ex-Paladin."

"If you say so, Mistress," he said. "However, in a fair fight, my money's on Maggie Black. Her skills are second to none."

"Samantha doesn't fight fair. She fights to win. Besides, Maggie Black's no more. She is Hajar now,"

Howard looked at Simone for a long moment. "Mistress, I know this may be none of my business, but why do you want to find the Tree of Life so badly?"

"If my plan works as I hope, being the head of the Black Circle is small potatoes. I will be a new eternal god and shall unite this world under my leadership. No more petty bickering among nations, no more hunger, no more disease. I shall make this world a paradise—as long as the world's population gives me the proper obedience and unwavering devotion."

"Six billion, *obedient* subjects?" Howard asked. "Interesting. I believe that will be a first."

"I find that the current population's a bit excessive and rife with trouble makers who have silly, misguided ideas about personal freedom. My first act, as God, is to make a definitive example. I'm not greedy. Five hundred million loyal servants are more than enough."

CHAPTER 38

Gideon, Yumi, Roland, Megan, and Hajar shared a table in Big Mamma Shirley's Home-Style Restaurant, Gibbons, South Carolina's, finest, and only, eatery.

"Hajar, way to go," Roland said. "Offing an angel? I knew you were good, but shit. Damn, that had to be one hell of a rush!"

Hajar hung her head and looked like she was about to cry.

"What's the matter? You ain't going all soft, are you?"

"Leave her alone, you big jerk," Megan said. "Hajar has been put through a meat grinder. Cut her some slack."

"Killing an angel—one who'd betrayed and tried to murder you must have had some satisfaction?" Yumi asked.

"I feel sick," Hajar said.

"You did save the doc," Roland said.

"Stop it. Now I really am sick."

"Simmer down, children," Gideon said as he perused the single-sheet, plastic laminated menu.

"Bite me, you old fart," Hajar snapped. "If we didn't need you, I would have left you nailed to that tree."

"If I didn't know better, I'd think you're getting sweet on me, Hajar," Gideon said. "Too bad I have higher standards."

Hajar gave Gideon the finger.

A pretty, very well-endowed blonde waitress in skintight jeans and an equally snug pink T-shirt carried a tray of drinks to their table. Along with the beverages was a large bag of frozen corn.

"Hey, darling." Roland grabbed a long-necked beer from her tray. "We like our food a bit warmer than that."

"Ha. Ha," she said dryly. "Now here, sugar," she said to Gideon, "put this on the nasty bruise. It must hurt something awful."

"Thank you, Rhonda." Gideon took the makeshift cold compress and pressed it to the ugly bruise encircling his throat. "This is very kind of you."

"You bet, sugar. You sure you just want to drink plain old root beer? I can spice it up a little—make you feel a lot better."

"The root beer's fine, thanks."

"Now if you need anything, and I mean *anything*," she said, bending over and giving Gideon a good view of her ample cleavage. "You just holler, sugar."

"I—I'll keep you in mind."

"So, Rhonda, is penicillin on the menu as a chaser?" Hajar asked.

"I don't think so, but I'll check with Shirley."

"You do that, *sugar*," Hajar said.

As she left, Roland leaned in close to Doc and batted his eyes. "Can I get you anything else, *sugar*? Coffee, tea, or me?"

Gideon turned beet red. "Nice girl. Very pretty eyes."

"Oh, did she have eyes between her boobs?" Hajar asked. "I must have missed that."

"She had *eyes*?" Roland asked. "I must have missed *that*."

Gideon smiled and raised his glass. "To Mr. Gunn. Thanks to your quick thinking, we are one step closer to our goal, instead of rotting in a jail cell."

The rest of the group raised their glasses and it was Roland's turn to glow crimson.

"Yeah, even a blind pig finds an acorn every once in a while," Hajar said.

"Quit trying to butter me up, woman, I told you, we're through."

"Bite me, hairball," she said with a smile.

"And now to Miss Black." Gideon stood and raised his glass. "She saved my bacon twice today, and I really appreciate it. Thank you."

"That's not me anymore," she said. "I'm Hajar."

"Hajar means forsaken. By God, I swear that you will never be forsaken again."

"To Maggie," Yumi said as he stood and raised his beer.

"Maggie," Roland said, following suit.

"Maggie," Megan said, raising her soda high. "Mrs. Kerr and her stupid name for you can go straight to Hell."

"Amen," Gideon said. "Ladies and gentlemen, I present to you the return of Maggie Black."

"Okay, I'm Maggie," she said softly. "Thank you."

"Oh, you ain't going to *cry*, are you?" Roland displayed a wicked grin. "That's it. You've definitely gone all girly girl on me!"

"I am about to make *you* cry," Maggie said, dabbing at her eyes. "I need to go to the restroom."

Megan stood, threw her bag over her shoulder, and followed close behind Maggie as she bolted for the rear of the dinner and the restrooms.

"I'll never understand why women travel in herds to take a wiz," Roland said with a chuckle.

"One of life's great mysteries," said Gideon. "And why are women never the right temperature?"

Yumi giggled.

"How's that hicky the angel gave you?" Roland asked.

"Hurts like sin, but it won't kill me."

"Where we going now, Doc?" Yumi asked. "More rural cabin demolition or secret museums?"

"No, we have all the relics we need, but the next leg is rather long, I'll explain when the girls get back."

"So, Doc," asked Roland, "Been dying to know how you came by the nickname, Kamikaze."

"You don't want to hear about that," said Gideon. "It's ancient history."

"Oh come on, Daddy," Roland said. "Tell us a story."

"Shoot a few of my countrymen down during the Great War, did we?" Yumi asked. The small Japanese man did not smile.

"No, nothing like that," Gideon said. "I earned my wings

just days before the war ended and never saw any action. I was stationed in San Diego, flying a sweet F4U along the coast on a routine patrol. Maybe the hydraulics sprung a leak…I don't know…but the controls locked up tighter than my dad's wallet. Even the throttle was locked wide open. I was headed straight out over the Pacific at four hundred plus miles per hour and couldn't do a thing about it.

"While I was still close to land, I slid back the canopy and hit the silk. As it so happened, a minesweeper, the *USS Rodger P. Gibson*, was a couple of nautical miles to starboard. They saw my predicament and, after changing course, headed to pick me up. As I'm floating down, I see my plane take a hard right and head straight for the *Gibson*. I know this sounds funny, but the way it acted, it was as if someone was aboard the Corsair, flying it. The *Gibson* saw the Corsair and took evasive action, but my plane actually made two course corrections and struck the minesweeper squarely amidships. Substantial damage, but fortunately no one was hurt."

"It wasn't your fault," Roland said.

"That didn't matter. Someone one had to pay."

"What did they do to you?" Yumi asked.

"The reaming to end all reamings. While, publicly, the board of inquiry found me not guilty, they made it clear, privately, that my flying days for Uncle Sam were over. To throw salt into the wound, I got stuck with the moniker, 'Kamikaze.'"

Roland leaned forward. "If I was you, I would just say I shot down a butt load of Japs, instead of that lame-ass story."

"But it's the truth," Gideon protested.

"A cool lie in the hand is worth two pitiful truths in the bush," Roland said. "And you can take that to the bank."

"What?" Yumi asked. "Are you delusional, hairball?"

"Chicks dig war heroes, guys," Roland said. "When I meet a girl in a bar, I captured Saddamm Hussein single handedly."

Gideon rolled his eyes. "You have no shame."

Roland grinned. "Maybe, but I never go home alone."

ℰℐℰℐ

Megan pushed through the restroom door, hopped up on the sink counter, and lit a cigarette while Maggie wiped her eyes.

"Thanks, Shortstack," she said giving the girl a hug. "That meant a lot to me."

"Good, now tell me why, since Pennsylvania you've been treating me like shit. You won't talk to me, and when I say anything, you bite my head off. You don't even bitch at me for smoking."

Maggie looked at Megan and considered her options. Mei had told her the spy was Samantha Jordan and Megan, being the only girl in the group beside herself, Maggie had taken it for granted that she was guilty. However, Gideon had privately expressed doubt. Besides, Megan was well...*Megan*. No one was that good an actress.

Could Mei have simply lied to throw them off and have them fighting amongst themselves? She was a witch and that was the antitheist of integrity. Maggie took a deep breath, climbed out on a swaying limb, and made a decision. "I guess I hit rock bottom and I took it out on you. I thought the whole world was out to get me. I'll never doubt you again, Shortstack. Forgive me?"

Megan carefully set her cigarette on the tiled counter, before leaping off the sink and into Maggie's arms. Her eyes filled with tears as she hugged Maggie tightly. "We're good."

"Hey, girl, don't go all soft on me. What happened to the hard-core juvenile delinquent I first met?"

"Shut up," Megan as said she wiped her eyes. "Maggie, when Mrs. Kerr gets what's coming to her, please, swear you will never leave me."

"You got it."

Jubilant, Megan retrieved her Marlboro.

Maggie plucked the Marlboro from Megan's mouth and crushed the offensive cigarette under her heel.

"Hey!"

"The smoking stops now. You'll finish high school and get a college education."

"I thought I was getting a cool aunt, not a nagging mother!"

"Get used to it. Oh, and you will start going to church."

"You're crossing the line."

"And you'll wear a dress."

Megan thought a moment. "Okay, I'll go to church, but you can forget the dress."

Maggie gave Megan a hug. "Deal. Now let's go, before Rhonda tries to rape Gideon."

"Gideon's mine," Megan snapped. "How about we take Ronda-slut out back and jack her up?"

"No," Maggie said. "If Gideon wants a double dose of the clap, he can have her. Serves him right."

℮ℑℯℑ

As Rhonda set down a plate of food before Gideon, the front door opened and in walked three, very large rough-looking men. "Oh great," she moaned. "The McKinney boys. I thought they were still in jail. Shirley won't be happy about this. That pack of white trash broke the place up about a month ago and put poor Shirley in the hospital."

The three men took a table between Gideon's crew and the restrooms.

Yumi glanced at them. "Now that looks like trouble."

"Yeah," Gideon agreed, "but then again, could be just what the doctor ordered."

"Huh?" asked Roland.

"Trust me."

At that moment, Megan and Maggie exited the restroom.

"Well, lookie here, boys," Don McKinney said through a set of rotted yellow teeth He grabbed Maggie by the arm. "Hey, honey, you want to party?"

"You want to brush your teeth?"

"Smart ass bitch!"

"She's a real queen," Tim McKinney said. "I never saw a prettier girl in my whole life."

"I ain't interested in her face," Chuck said. The hulking man sported a short mohawk and mean black eyes. "Get our food to go. These two whores are coming home with us for desert."

"Oh, *hell,* no." Roland stood. "I'm going to see the color of their redneck blood."

"Sit down, Mr. Gunn," Gideon said with a wink. "Think of this as a dinner and a show."

"Huh?" Roland asked. "Ain't we going bust these jokers up?"

"They're messing with *Maggie.* Let her blow off a little steam."

Roland snorted. "Got you," he said, sitting down. "It's their funeral."

"I love to watch a professional work," Yumi said and took a fork full of salad.

Gideon gave Maggie a big grin and a thumbs up.

"Let's go, whore," Don said as he grabbed for her arm.

Maggie reached around and snapped Don's wrist, before breaking Chuck's hooknose with a shattering, roundhouse kick.

Tim jumped up, but a look from Megan made the plastic condiment container before him explode, sending a thick stream of ketchup into his face, blinding him.

"Megan," Gideon said sharply. "Get over here."

"She needs help!" Megan said.

"Now, young lady," Gideon ordered as he dug into the steaming bowl of pinto beans. "Sit down and eat your food."

Megan threw up her hands in frustration, but did as Gideon ordered and took her seat.

A few minutes later, Maggie stalked up to the dinner table and the grinning trio of men.

"Thanks for all the help, guys," she said, plopping down in a chair before her burger and fries.

"What's the time, Yumi?" Roland asked.

"I got eight minutes, three seconds."

Roland grinned. "Pay up suckers."

Grimacing, Yumi and Gideon each produced a dollar and tossed them at Roland.

Maggie glared at them. "Not only didn't you help me, you have the nerve to bet against me?"

"Betting and losing," Gideon said. "By the way, we weren't

betting against you, Maggie. We were betting on how long it would take you to take care of those redneck clowns. I figured you would have taken no more than five minutes. You must be out of shape or I just overestimated your skills."

"Out of shape, old man?" she said. "Overestimated my skills? Really? I still got enough left to break you in half."

The three men laughed.

"What's the matter with you jerks?" Megan asked.

"That's what happens when you get a group of men together," Maggie said. "Their IQs, along with their maturity, drop to the level of the Three Stooges."

Laughing, Yumi snatched a heavy, old-fashioned glass sugar canister off the table and threw it at Maggie. She ducked and the cylinder sailed past, shattering against Tim's forehead as he drew a bead on Maggie's back with his 9 mm. Grunting, Tim collapsed into a heap with his brothers.

"Thanks," Maggie said.

"Why soitenly," Yumi said in a fair impression of Curly.

"What's so funny?" Megan asked as the men laughed.

"Go ahead and eat, toots," Gideon said. "We will give this trash the bums rush."

Gideon paid Shirley for damages, while Roland and Yumi tossed out the McKinney boys and encouraged them not to come back, for which Shirley was very grateful. The plump, older woman was all smiles while Gideon filled her hands with cash.

"Sorry for the ruckus, ma'am."

"Don't you worry about it," she said, patting him on the arm. "Them punks are always coming in here and busting my place up. I can't believe they got beat up by a girl. They'll never live it down. You and your people are always welcome here."

Rhonda slid up to Gideon and pushed a slip of paper into his hand. "I get off at nine," she whispered. "My trailer's a little ways down the road. Here's the address. I'll show you the time of your life."

"As much as I would love to, darling, my fiancé has a bit of a temper."

Gideon, Shirley, and Rhonda looked back at the table where Maggie was giving Rhonda the stink eye.

"You mean—you and her—"

"Yes," Gideon said. "She's my sweetie. Maggie's good as gold, but she has a jealous streak a mile wide. Why, she darn near killed a girl over in Roan County just for talking to me."

Rhonda turned white and looked as if she was about to faint.

"Even if I had a shotgun," Shirley said, "I wouldn't want her coming after me."

"Umm—let's just forget the whole thing, okay, sugar?" Rhonda said. "Seems I suddenly have a bad headache."

❧❧❧

Gideon rolled a map out on the table.

"Nepal?" asked Yumi.

"Yes," said Gideon. "Machhapuchare Mountain Range."

Yumi rubbed his face. "The forbidden mountains?"

Gideon nodded. "You got it."

"What makes it so forbidden?" asked Maggie.

"It's sacred to the Hindis," Yumi said. "No one is allowed to set foot on the mountain."

"It's also where we will find the archives that will give us the location of Eden."

"How hard is this going to be?" Roland asked as he chewed on a toothpick.

"The mountain is treacherous and should only be attempted by experienced climbers. Anyone here have any climbing experience?"

The group gave him a blank stare.

"Great," Gideon said, tossing a pencil on the table.

"Too bad we can't just shoot our way in," Roland said.

"Well, if the mountain doesn't kill us, which it probably will, there's an army division located here at Pokhara. Let me tell you one thing, Mr. Gunn, these old boys don't mess around."

"Well, if it was easy, anybody could do it," said Maggie.

"Amen," Gideon said.

"Oh, man, I hate the cold," Roland said.

"Where are we going, exactly?" Yumi asked, looking closely at the map.

Gideon leaned back in his chair. "We won't know until the Key locates it. It could be in a valley or, for all we know, on a mountain top."

Roland snorted. "With our luck, it will be on the mountain top."

"Looks like we're going to do some shopping," Megan said. "I wonder if I can get a pink climbing outfit? You like pink, don't you, Gideon?"

"We don't have time to enroll in mountaineering school," he said. "I guess we'll have to train on the way somehow."

"Is anything about this job easy?" Roland asked.

"Guess not," Gideon said.

CHAPTER 39

While the *Ginny K*'s fuel tanks were topped off and supplies loaded, Gideon slipped into the empty office of the manager of Appalachian Flying Services, locking the door behind him. He walked over to the cluttered desk and sat down. Sitting back in the squeaky desk chair, he looked out the window as the *Ginny K* was serviced.

He watched Maggie, Megan, and Roland horsing around near the right wing and smiled. "Can't believe how proud I am of that bunch of clowns. They are like the Choirboys."

Gideon rubbed his chest. It felt warm, warmer than it should, but the sharp pain he'd felt in the lair of Diolefin was thankfully gone. Since the ass whipping he had received at the hands of Larry, the Phoenix was no longer painful, but the heat was still there and, probing the spot under the crescent-shaped scar, he felt a hard lump that was gradually getting larger.

He chuckled. "This has been a hoot of an adventure. I couldn't have picked a better one to exit the stage on. Moreover, the Phoenix here will ensure I go out in a proper blaze of glory. Never thought that I'd meet a Nephilim, let alone be infatuated with one. Heck, I'm crazy about her. I just want to sweep her off her feet and head off to Tahiti or some out of the way place where no one will ever find us. Which brings up another interesting point. If Heaven is so dead set against the Nephilim getting a toehold on Earth again, and Maggie is such a terrible threat, why has no one else come after us? They must know Larry's dead and, to me, that would put an even larger target on Maggie's back. This is very strange. I think there's more going on than meets the eye."

He pulled out his smart phone and punched in a number.

"This had better be important, Kane," Mrs. Kerr said.

"Watch the pissy attitude, Mrs. Kerr. I'm not one of your slaves that you can bully. Now listen to me carefully. We're on the last leg of this journey and the prize is within sight. Unfortunately, it seems that your friends, the Black Circle, have been tracking us as well."

"Yes, the freak hailstorm back at Cades Cove smacks of their modus operandi."

"Your friends in the Circle know full well what we're after and will try to take the Tree, after we do all the dirty work. You have to be careful and put them off our trail. Now listen, I'll give you everything I have, and you can rendezvous with us later."

"If this is one of your tricks—"

"For my friends to be set free, you have to receive the Tree, remember? Trust me, I want that more than you know. However, I don't want to have to fight a bunch of witches to do it."

"I see," Mrs. Kerr said.

"I'm sending you the information on our final destination, so pack your bags."

Gideon turned on the airport manager's computer terminal and plugged in a slim flash drive. A few keystrokes later, he pulled the drive from the machine and turned off the computer.

"I know this may sound strange coming from me," Mrs. Kerr said, "but good luck, Gideon Kane."

Gideon hung up without replying.

CHAPTER 40

The massive, intercontinental Boeing 747-8 airliner sat parked at a tiny mountain Nepalese airport. The state-of-the-art craft was the private flying palace of the Black Circle's mistress and should not have been able to land on the rough, painfully short runway that was barely suitable for puddle jumpers. Nevertheless, if Simone wanted to land on a postage stamp, the pilot team would make it possible, whether through natural skill or unnatural dark arts.

The airplane sat in the dark, patiently awaiting the arrival of the slower, antiquated *Ginny K.*

Simone switched off her e-reader, closed her reading glasses, and rubbed her eyes. "If even a third of this silly pulp drivel is true, Samantha's correct. Gideon Kane is one hell of a man. But a rocket powered, autogyro? Give me a break."

She gazed out of the airplane window at the harsh, icy landscape and the heavy, falling snow.

"Nepal in winter. A vacationer's paradise."

Moreland Quomet, Simone's newest assistant, entered the luxurious cabin with a bottle of wine and paused by the door. "I thought a little wine would make those dreadful tales more palatable, Mistress."

With a nod from Simone, he moved to her desk and filled her goblet with spiced wine.

"Leave the bottle, Moreland."

The slightly built, impeccably dressed man with thinning blond hair placed the aromatic canister on her desk.

"Moreland, is everything arranged?"

"As well as it can be. I have a crack mountaineering team standing by under the guise of a newly formed climbing company. It was short notice, but I have some of the best in the world under contract. If anyone can get Kane and his inexperienced group up the mountain, it is them."

"I don't care if they have to strap them to their backs and carry them."

"Yes, Mistress."

Simone smiled as she sipped her wine and allowed herself to daydream about her future glory. The ornate crystal ball on her desk began to hum.

"Our intrepid band of adventures should be close to landing, in Spain," Moreland said. "Too bad they don't have a more advanced aircraft."

Mistress Ravenwood... The words floated across the surface of the mystic orb.

"Go ahead, my dear," Simone said. "How was your flight?"

Mistress, we have a problem.

"My forces stand ready here in Nepal," Simone said as she gave Moreland a smile. "We think we have solved the problem of your inexperienced group tackling the mountain range."

Mistress, listen to me! Doc has pulled a fast one.

"What do you mean, he pulled a fast one?"

Apparently, he knows that he has a spy in his group and has fed us false information about the location of the archives.

"What?" Simone said softly. "You mean you aren't on your way to Nepal?"

Not unless Nepal is located in South America.

Moreland stood by impassionedly as Simone smashed her wine cup against the bulkhead and uttered a black, ungodly, stream of profanity.

"Listen to me," she snapped. "I have too much invested in this to let that insipid Salome Kerr walk away with the prize. Do you hear me?"

Yes, Mistress.

"Does Kane suspect you?"

Doc has an eye on everyone, but I think I'm the least of the suspects. He probably thinks it's either that idiot Roland or the former Paladin.

"The Paladin—really?"

Even though Doc's trying to help, Miss Black still bears a fierce grudge over being blindsided by an eighty-three-year-old man. I would not be surprised if, when all is said and done, she tries to kill him over her bruised ego. She's a woman ruled by blind passion and not her head. I can't believe someone so unprofessional survived this long.

Simone paused at her window and, for a moment, watched the snowfall while she mulled over the situation. Even with her advanced aircraft, there was no way she could get to Kane before he delivered the Tree of Life to Salome Kerr. She grudgingly admitted that Gideon Kane was even better than the books alluded.

"Samantha dear, we've been played from the beginning. Kane knows full well that we're tracking him, so drop the ruse. I want you to hold them until I get there with my men. It would be nice if you had all the pertinent information when I arrive."

I'm open to suggestions.

"If I may?" Moreland asked. "Your agent could trigger a fuel dump. With the proper instruction, it could look like an accident. After all, they're flying an antique, and accidents do happen. That would force them to turn back and scrounge for fuel. That would be the perfect opportunity to take control of the situation."

"Moreland, I'm giving you a raise," Simone said. "Give her the directions and tell the pilot to get this plane ready to fly home. I and my soldiers are staying here so have them start off loading their equipment."

"Yes, Mistress," said Moreland.

Simone paced about the cabin.

"Have Salome Kerr picked up. She no doubt knows where Kane is headed."

"What if Mrs. Kerr is stubborn?"

"Don't kill her, is all I ask, but I must know exactly where Kane is going."

"It will be done, Mistress," Moreland said.

"Samantha, dear, I want to meet Kane. He seems like an utterly fascinating man. The rest, well, I don't care for riffraff, if you know what I mean."

It will be done, Mistress.

Chapter 41

Gripping a small ratchet and socket, Samantha Jordan carefully loosened the access panel that would uncover an obscure, yet vital wiring harness within the *Ginny K*. If the information from Mistress Ravenwood was correct, she could dump the fuel from the main tanks, leaving only a small auxiliary tank untouched.

Her companions were up front in the spacious, modified cockpit, which gave a spectacular view, as well as insulation from the ever-present roar of the engines, thus giving her a small window of opportunity in which to work. In spite of the unlikely event that someone would hear her, due to the drone of the *Ginny K*'s engines, Samantha took extreme care not to make a sound.

With a sigh of relief, she felt the hinged compartment pop open. Samantha took a pair of needle nose pliers and a tiny flashlight from her small bag. With a smile, she shined the light into the deep cavity. Instantly, the smile disappeared from her face

Instead of a bare wiring harness, there was a stainless-steel sleeve clamped together with specialized, non-standard screw heads.

"How am I supposed to—"

"How are you supposed to do what?" Megan asked as she peered over Samantha's shoulder. "What are you doing, Yumi? Gideon will have a cow when he finds you messing with his precious plane."

Samantha/Yumi dropped the needle nose pliers back into her bag.

"You deaf? I asked what you are doing."

"See for yourself," the spy said as she shoved the bag into the girl's face. Megan stumbled and fell back hard into the bulkhead. Yumi produced a small, silenced .22 and shot Megan twice between the eyes.

"So much for the fuel dump. Looks like I have to take them out now."

"Hey, Megan, I—" Maggie began as she entered the cabin. Horrified, she watched Megan slide down the curved fuselage, leaving behind a bright smear of blood.

Spinning around, Yumi pointed the gun at Maggie, but squeezing the trigger only produced an impotent click as the weapon jammed.

Enraged, Maggie flew across the intervening space and slammed into Yumi, sending the murderer reeling. Before Yumi could recover, Maggie aimed a haymaker at her. Yumi was quick and the crushing right cross barely grazed her jaw, however, the blow still felt like a sledgehammer. Yumi stumbled and fell hard against the bulkhead.

"*Commo gouno yupal!*" she cried as she spat blood.

Maggie felt herself enveloped in an unseen, irresistible force. Suddenly, she was yanked off her feet and slammed into the bulkhead, two feet from the rear cargo door. Struggling with all her might, Maggie fought to get free, but she was effectively pinned off the deck.

Yumi got to her feet and laughed at Maggie's struggles.

"You'll pay for that," Yumi said, as she wiped the blood away from the corner of her mouth. "You knocked loose two fillings and nearly broke my jaw!"

Maggie, puzzled by the decidedly female voice with which Yumi now spoke, opened her mouth and screamed, "Gideon!"

"Oh, no," Yumi said as Gideon burst through the cabin door. "*Commo gouno yupal!*"

Gideon made it halfway into the cabin before he too was swept off his feet and pinned to the opposite bulkhead from Maggie.

"He killed Megan!" Maggie cried.

"Fight it, girl," Gideon said. "Yumi can't hold both of us for long."

He was right. Already, great beads of sweat were rolling down Yumi's forehead and the strain was reaching critical.

"Listen to me, you two," Yumi said. "This isn't personal. I didn't want to kill Megan, but she surprised me. If it'll make you feel better, she didn't suffer."

"You talk like she was a rabid dog," Maggie spat. "She was a human being! She was my friend!"

"So you're the spy," Gideon said. "When I get down, I'm going to teach you the error of your ways."

"I'm afraid you won't get the chance, Doc. Yes, you're right. I'm a spy for the Black Circle. I have to hand it to you. Very clever of you diverting the coven toward Nepal when, all along, you were headed for South America. I can't let you give the relic to that bitch Mrs. Kerr. Help me find the Tree for my master and I promise you riches and power beyond your dreams."

"Go to hell," Maggie snapped. "I swear to Jesus, you will pay for Megan."

"Megan, Megan, Megan," Yumi said. "You act as if that obnoxious brat was someone of worth. She's gone, so get over it."

"I'll kill you."

"Let's suppose I play ball?" Gideon asked. "I know where we're going and you don't. What's that worth to you?"

"Gideon," Maggie snapped. "What are you doing?"

"Release Roland and Maggie from the collars they wear and I'll lead you to the Tree."

"Honestly, Doc, if it were my call, I'd do it in a heartbeat. I've grown close to our little band of misfits. However, I'm just a little Indian in my tribe. I'm afraid that Mistress Raven-wood would never give up such valuable assets. Especially Maggie."

"No!" Maggie yelled. "I'll never serve you!"

"Don't waste my time, Maggie. You robbed banks for Mrs. Kerr because of the collar. You'll serve us just as well."

"You know full well that the only reason I'm helping Mrs. Kerr is to release Maggie and her friends," Gideon said. "I'll never let that pack of degenerates get their hands on the Tree and leave my crew enslaved."

As she was unable to hold both Gideon and Maggie, Yumi's disguise melted away and she reformed into a slim woman of medium height, with brown eyes and shoulder length auburn hair. Yumi was gone and in her place stood the witch, Samantha Jordan. "You make this hard on me, Doc. I'll make you a fair trade, Maggie's life for the location of the Tree."

As Maggie and Gideon struggled, the spell that gripped them weakened. With a gesture, the big hatch opened and swung outward from the *Ginny K.* The cabin was filled with the deafening roar of rushing wind.

"No," Gideon screamed as his hand slowly moved to the .45 on his hip.

"Give me the location or we will see if Paladins can fly."

Maggie redoubled her efforts, but the powerful witch slid her slowly toward the open, whistling hatch.

"No, please, Yumi, or whatever your name is," Gideon cried. "Don't do this! I'll do whatever you want, just don't kill her."

"The location."

"Very well. Listen carefully."

Reluctantly, Gideon gave Samantha the exact location supplied to him by Diolefin.

"You have what you want witch, now please, let Maggie go."

"Sorry, lover," Samantha said. "I could never control both of you. It will be much easier to handle you alone. By the way, my name is Samantha, Samantha Jordan. I have a feeling we're going to be the best of friends."

With a short, sharp scream of effort, Samantha flung Maggie out the opening.

His will, magnified by sheer rage and desperation, Gideon managed to break the witch's spell and grab his .45. He fired once, shattering Samantha's right kneecap. The evil woman went down in a screaming heap as Gideon rushed past her.

Grabbing a parachute from a rack, he leapt through the open hatch of the *Ginny K* and dropped out of sight.

Gun in hand, Roland burst into the cabin and took stock of the situation. Near the open hatch, lay a pale and shaking Yumi, trying desperately to open a first aid kit. His bloody right trouser leg was ripped apart, exposing an ugly gunshot wound. Slumped near the open hatch lay Megan. Roland had seen enough of bodies in his time to know that the girl was dead.

"What happened?" he cried as he bent down beside Yumi. "Where's Doc and Maggie?"

"Dead," Yumi spat when Roland popped open the medical kit. "That little tramp there did it."

"Pimples?" Roland asked as he irrigated the wound.

"She was some kind of witch—heard Maggie scream—that little monster used her hocus pocus and tossed both of them out of the plane."

"But why?"

"She must work for those witches who are chasing Mrs. Kerr," Yumi said. "They're trying to stop us."

"Sorry little bitch. Now hold still, this is going to hurt."

"I drew my gun, but she shot me first. Blew my knee out. She should have killed me—that was the one mistake she will never make again."

"Calm down, buddy," Roland said. "I'll splint your knee then we will sort this cluster out."

Pale and in excruciating pain, Yumi grabbed Roland by the front of his shirt. "We can't give up. We have to find Eden."

"If you wanted to find Eden so bad," Roland whispered, "why did you snuff the only hope we had of finding it?" With an inhuman snarl, he lifted the wounded spy off the deck. "Megan don't carry a gun and I know the sound of Doc's .45s like the back of my hand, asshole. It was the Doc who gave you that limp—didn't he?"

"My, you're far smarter than I gave you credit for," Samantha said as the guise of Yumi vanished.

"Damn, you're a skirt—and a fine looking one at that." Roland moved toward the open hatch. "Can you fly, sweetheart?"

"Go on, Roland, toss me out, but with Doc and Maggie gone, I'm your only hope."

"Big talk. You're stuck with me in this mess."

"Not at all. The people I work for created the collars and can remove them. I was sent to kill Mrs. Kerr, but that mission evolved into keeping an eye on her. In the immortal words of the Road Warrior, 'You want to get out of here, you talk to me.'"

"A woman who quotes the Road Warrior can't be all that bad. What's the plan?"

"Land at the nearest airfield and let me contact my people, then hopefully we can find a doctor."

Roland laid Samantha gently in a reclining seat and carefully bandaged and splinted her wound.

"Would you mind terribly tiding up?"

Pausing a moment, Roland looked at Megan's lifeless body. Moving to the small body, he gently lifted her and stood before the open hatch. "See yah in hell, kid," he said as threw her from the *Ginny K.*

CHAPTER 42

Maggie plummeted from the *Ginny K*, her short life flashing before her eyes as the green carpet of thick, steaming jungle rose up to meet her.

Never thought I'd go out like this. Please, Lord Jesus, accept me into your kingdom—

A heavy weight slammed into her, knocking the breath out of her and cutting short her last prayer. Strong hands pulled her around and she came face to face with Gideon.

"Hold on tight, sweetheart!" he yelled against the roar of the wind.

"Thank you, Jesus!" she yelled. "That was quick."

Overjoyed, she wrapped her strong legs and arms tightly around him. He pulled the ripcord and the massive, orange-and-white-striped parasail opened, yanking them upward and slowing their descent.

They were still plunging toward an inhospitable jungle while all their supplies sailed away, but they were alive and, for that, Gideon thanked God.

He sighed in relief that he had Maggie and that she was safe. When Samantha threw her from the plane, he felt as if his heart had been ripped out and tossed out the cargo door.

Could it be that Maggie meant far more to him than he'd admitted? He didn't care about her dazzling beauty. It was who she truly was that made him feel like living again.

He relished the sparkle in her beautiful green eyes, the way she smiled. Even her smartass comments made him want to do more than solve one last case. For the first time since Ginny died, he felt truly alive and he wanted to stick around. He wanted to be with Maggie.

Looking down, he smiled at her head, which was buried in his neck, her eyes tightly closed. He could feel the hammer of her terrified heart beating against his chest. He placed a hand on her head and stroked her hair.

Maggie smiled and squeezed him tighter.

~∞~

Guiding the parachute toward the impenetrable canopy, Gideon looked for an opening and found none. While their air speed had slowed considerably, landing in the rainforest canopy would be dicey at best.

With the canopy coming up fast, he held Maggie tight and braced for impact as a giant kapok loomed before them.

"Get ready, Maggie. This is going to leave a mark."

To their surprise, the trees vanished, and before them lay a massive reddish-stone spire. About to be flattened like a bug on a windshield, Gideon yanked on the parasail controls and they banked sharply left. Throwing out his legs, he ran along the curving, cracked, and pitted surface. Breathing a prayer, Maggie and Gideon finally slid past the tower, landing hard in the red dust fifty feet from the base.

"Did we make it?" she asked as she raised her head and looked around.

"I wouldn't swear to it." He gingerly rose to a sitting position. "But I think so."

Maggie rose and promptly tackled Gideon. Pinning him to the ground, she covered his mouth with her own and kissed him deeply. "Thanks, handsome," she said, brushing away a stray lock of his hair.

"Don't mention it."

"You are one in a million, Gideon Kane. You just jumped out of a freaking airplane to save me."

"What can I say? I like having you around, doll."

She smiled. "The real-life Kamikaze Kane puts the fictional

one to shame. Not to mention that you're far sexier than I ever imagined."

"That's nice. Now get off me, woman. We have to find Eden."

"You sure know how to kill the moment."

Gideon chuckled.

"So what happened to the freaking rainforest?" she asked as she gained her feet and offered him a hand up.

"We fell through an illusion," he said, taking her hand, "and an impressive one at that. Seems that someone wanted very badly to keep these ruins hidden."

Surrounding them, spreading out for miles, lay the ruins of an ancient, jungle-choked city.

"You know anything about this place?" she asked.

"No, darling," he said. "I have been through this region several times in my travels, but never heard a whisper about this place."

"What now, fearless leader?"

"Maggie, what have you got on you?"

She turned out the pockets of her cargo pants, producing a few coins, a pack of gum, and a big folding knife.

"I feel naked without Kali, but I haven't had time to get a replacement."

Gideon carried four spare magazines along with Thunder and Lightning, a snub-nosed stainless steel .357, three energy bars, a Swiss Army knife, a big-bladed folding knife, a green plastic cylinder of lifeboat matches, a small flashlight, and a braided watch fob containing twenty feet of 550 paracord. A side pocket, held the mystic battery.

"What, no duct tape?"

"In my other pants, along with my life raft."

"I'm surprised you don't rattle when you walk, sweetie."

"I don't have a bottomless pocketbook. I learned the hard way that it pays to be as prepared as possible. You never know when someone might throw you out of an airplane."

"Point taken. On the bright side, looks like we found our spy."

"Yeah and got blindsided. I was pretty sure Yumi was the

wolf in sheep's clothing, but I never thought for a moment he was actually a woman."

"That witch killed Megan. Almost killed me, too."

"If it'll make you feel better, Maggie, Samantha's one kneecap short of a complete set. She may have gotten away with the *Ginny K* and all our supplies, but I made her pay for it."

"Swear to God, Giddy, round two will be different."

"I know. For now, we have to focus on the problem at hand. We need water."

"It is hot. This place makes Alabama in the summer seem downright chilly."

Gideon took off his double-holstered gun belt and handed it to Maggie.

"What's this?"

"I'll admit they aren't as exotic as Kali, but they saved my skin a few times over the years."

She gingerly took the prized set of legendary weapons and slipped them around her waist. "You are going to let me borrow Thunder and Lightning?"

Smiling at her excitement, Gideon adjusted the holster to fit her slim waist. He kneeled before her and carefully strapped each holster to her thighs.

"How does that feel?"

"Feels like fresh squeezed, one-hundred-percent awesome!"

He rose and stepped back, laughing. "They suit you."

"Wow," she said as she quick drew both renowned guns savoring their balanced weight and feel. "I swear I'll take good care of them, Gideon."

"I know you will, Maggie, but you misunderstand. The girls aren't a loan, they're yours."

"But—"

"No buts. You know, I was anxious, thinking that when my time was up, the girls would end up in some seedy pawnshop. Now I can rest easy, knowing that they'll be put to good use."

"What will you do for a weapon?"

"I've still got my .357. Now let's go before we melt—"

"If I didn't know better, I'd say you were stalking me, beautiful."

Guns drawn, Gideon and Maggie whirled around and found Mei Xue lounging on an eroded, horrific statue. Dressed in tiger-striped camouflage, she blew an impressive series of smoke rings.

"I should have known you would be lurking nearby," Gideon said.

"Hajar, you are looking particularly sexy," Mei said. "Our time together will haunt me forever."

"Nothing happened and you know it. And for your information, my name's Maggie."

"Have it your way—Maggie," Mei said. "Nothing sexual happened between us." She followed the statement with an exaggerated wink.

Maggie turned crimson as Mei laughed, relishing her discomfort.

Gideon turned and gave Maggie a steady gaze. "Is there something you want to share with the class?" he asked.

"One smartass word, Gideon Kane, and you will get shot with your own gun."

"Gideon, it's been too long. Come here and give me some love." Mei bounced off the stone and gave Gideon a warm embrace. "I am so sorry to hear about your lovely wife. Virginia was a genuine lady."

"Thank you, Mei," he said. "Good to see you again, old friend. Now what is this place?"

"Welcome to the legendary city of Ophir."

"*The* Ophir—from the Bible?" he asked.

"Is there another?"

"Simply amazing," he said, looking around. "All this time it has been here in the Americas. What happened here and why is it shielded?"

"Another mystery for the dashing Kamikaze Kane and his stalwart band of cohorts to solve," Mei said.

"Yeah, yeah," Maggie said. "It's a pile of damn bricks. Now how come you two are so damn lovey-dovey? Did you hit your head when we landed, old man? She's a freaking Black Circle witch!"

Gideon and Mei laughed at the outburst.

"Looks like someone has been bit by the green eyed monster," Mei said.

"I'm not jealous."

"Oh, don't worry, Maggie," Mei said. "My heart will always be yours."

Maggie clenched her fists and rushed toward Mei. "Bitch."

Gideon stepped in and caught her.

"Come on, Gideon," she said, not taking her eyes off the smiling Mei. "If you can tear yourself away from your girlfriend, we need water. If there is a city, there must be a river or wells."

"There's a stream, but it's just chock full of nasty bacteria that would make you wish you were dead. There is water, shelter, and food back at my camp. Please, be my guests."

"Why should we trust you, Mei," Maggie asked.

"It seems our paths have converged. You help me, I help you, and, if we don't all die, it's happy ever after."

"Hell no," Maggie snapped. "Come on, Gideon, let's go."

"I think we should hear her proposition."

"Really?"

"Mei offered water and food. How can we refuse?"

"Then it's settled," Mei said. "We have much to discuss over dinner. If you're sweet to me, Hajar, I'll let you sit next to me."

"The name is *Maggie*."

Gideon chuckled.

"What's so funny?"

"Oh, nothing, but if you want to sit with Mei, you better stow the attitude."

⌀⌀⌀

Gideon and Maggie found Mei's idea of "roughing it" hilarious.

What looked like a circus tent was set up in an open stone-paved plaza. The enormous, brightly colored canopy covered the entire campsite, providing shade from the blistering Amazon sun. Sheer white mosquito netting that looked like lace cascaded from the canopy, providing protection from the voracious bloodsucking insect population.

Within the covered compound were two top-of-the-line tents equipped with real wood frame beds and Egyptian cotton sheets. A hefty generator sat some ten yards away, silently churning out electrical power to a large, stainless steel rotisserie grill that was busy roasting twin capons and assorted vegetables. A slightly humming refrigeration unit, the size of a restaurant refrigerator, fully stocked with cold drinks, milk, and meats, sat close by.

"Wow," Maggie said. "Looks like a Sharper Image exploded in here."

"Looks like you haven't changed a bit, Mei."

"I have found that it's possible to camp without being reduced to barbarity."

"Something smells good," he said.

"Dinner will be ready in a few moments. Now wash up and I'll set the table. Do you still have an affinity for that dreadful root beer?"

"Dreadful? I'll have you to know that they serve root beer only to the most pious souls in heaven."

"You've just made the case for Hell, Gideon," Mei said. "You'll be happy to know I acquired several bottles, just in case your taste buds were still impaired."

Maggie pulled Gideon aside. "Again, why are you so chummy with Mei and how come she knows so much about you? She's an evil, soul-sucking Black Circle witch, for crying out loud."

"I can still hear you," Mei said.

"Good."

"Maggie, like I said before, Mei and I go way back…what was the year?"

"Chicago 1949," Mei said. "You tried to shoot me in the head, as I recall."

He chuckled. "At the time, you were trying to chuck me out a window at the Drake Hotel."

"Good times," Mei said, blowing a stream of smoke.

"Are you two nuts?"

Gideon and Mei laughed.

"Maggie, while we've had our little differences over the years, Mei is one of my dearest friends."

"Yes," Mei said. "Remember that party where the Boys hired the stripper with the whip? Helga...something."

"You were there?" Maggie asked.

"Of course. Who do you think hired her? The look on Ginny's face was priceless."

He frowned. "You? This entire time I thought it was Clyde Loyd."

"I know," Mei said with a laugh. "Poor Clyde. Ginny almost shot him. It was glorious."

"But, Gideon, she's an evil witch. You hate witches."

"We all have our little faults," Mei said.

"Are you really going to cast the first stone, Maggie?" he asked.

"I—I'm about to have a break down."

"Sit down, Maggie," he said. "I need to explain a few things."

She reluctantly took a seat in a plush folding chair. "This better be good."

"You're right. I despise witches, but Mei isn't a witch."

"So you're telling me she's a lesbian who just happened to infiltrate the most dangerous coven in the world?"

"She isn't a lesbian either."

"Oh come on. Mei nearly sucked my tonsils out."

"Mei isn't female."

"You're a dude?" Maggie asked, giving Mei the once over. "That's one hell of a makeover."

"Not exactly, Maggie," Mei said. "While I am a male, I'm not a human male. I'm an Oki."

Maggie moaned. "My head hurts. What the hell is an Oki?"

"I suppose it would be best if I showed you," Mei said, laying aside her cigarette holder.

In an instant, Mei became a nine-foot-tall, towering nightmare of teeth and slimy gray tentacles.

In spite of herself, Maggie leapt to her feet and pulled Thunder and Lightning.

With a smile, Mei resumed her human form and lit another cigarette. "As nice as it is to be myself again, I can't hold that form for more than a few seconds. What you hairless monkeys think of as magic is actually advanced tech I smuggled from my world. Magic is so...odious."

"I don't understand," Maggie said.

"It's like this, Maggie," Gideon said. "Mei was a despot on his world."

"Ouch," Mei said. "Let's just say I made a few mistakes and had a great number of enemies. The misguided public blindsided me and I was deposed. Instead of execution, as would be the expected punishment on your world, I was sentenced to exile on a primitive, completely alien world of hairless monkeys."

"If you're a dude, why do you look like a chick?"

"While my people would never execute me, they relished humiliating me. Unfortunately, my reputation was used against me. I am what you would call a womanizer."

"Horndog is what I would call him," Gideon said.

"Now that's funny," Maggie said. "They gave you a taste of your own medicine."

"Be that as it may," Mei said. "Locked in this form was hell, but eventually, after many years, I overcame my nausea at the thought of touching the repulsive, hideous females on this planet. Even without a certain...appendage...I still had a damn good time."

Maggie grimaced in horror. "I smooched that...that, God awful thing?"

"We both know you enjoyed it, sweetie. You have such soft, responsive lips."

"I'm going to be sick."

"I told you that Mei was a monster," Gideon said.

"Really, Gideon?" Mei asked. "A monster? I'm far more civilized than you ever thought about being."

"You said she had cooties," Maggie said, "but—damn!"

"Cooties? Gideon Kane, keep this bashing up and no hazelnut cheesecake."

"I take it all back," Gideon said. "Your cheesecake is to die for."

"I know what this is," Maggie said. "It's so damn clear. I'm either asleep, or in a psyche ward hooked up to a morphine drip. How else would I be smack in the middle of the Amazon, talking to the fictional hero of a pulp novel and a lesbian witch who's really a chain-smoking alien politician who also makes a killer dessert?"

With a wicked grin, Gideon reached over and flicked her ear.

"Ow! Why did you do that for?"

"Does that feel like a dream?"

"By the way, Maggie dear," Mei said. "I'm not doing anything as vile as smoking. My special cigarettes and holder recreate the atmosphere of my world, allowing me to survive in this toxic, oxygen-nitrogen soup you call an atmosphere."

"Wait a minute," Maggie said. "The books! I got it. You're Talconoiur, the Martian from Book Seven, who Gideon made an honorary Choirboy. You were the alien who kept calling Earth people scum, while you helped Gideon stop the invading army of Golem."

"Martian, *indeed*," Mei said. "I hope Harold David fries in hell for calling me one of those green-skinned cockroaches. Still, it was my finest moment."

"Without your help, dear friend, we would be knee deep in Golem invaders. Those little bastards are worse than cockroaches."

Maggie laughed.

Mei rose from his chair. "Enough talk, human scum. We will eat first, then we have plans to make."

CHAPTER 43

Gideon's right, Mei, you make the best cheesecake in the free world."

"Thank you."

Mei leaned back in his chair. "Gideon, my friend, the hammer is about to fall. Mistress Ravenwood and about two hundred crack troops will arrive sometime late tomorrow. The crazy bitch thinks I'm dead and no threat, but I still have spies deep within her organization."

"I was afraid of that. With any luck, Mrs. Kerr will get here before that happens."

"Mrs. Kerr is with them."

"Fantastic," Gideon said as he tossed his napkin on the table.

"Seems Mistress Ravenwood made her a deal and now they're working together."

"She'll kill Mrs. Kerr the minute they get within sight of the Tree."

"Mrs. Kerr knows. She also knows that Mistress Ravenwood will kill her instantly if she doesn't cooperate. Talk about being between a rock and a hard place."

Maggie frowned. "Wait a minute. I thought you wanted the Tree as well?"

"No. I want *The Book of Xanadutha*. With that, I can finally go home."

"You can't go home," Gideon said. "Your people will exile you again, but this time to a worse place."

"Ah, you see, my friend, I have received word that the political climate has changed and the people are thinking that they were wrong to reject my benevolent rule."

"But we need the book," Maggie said.

"Use the book to breach Eden, then after Mrs. Kerr has freed you, I will use it to go home. It's a win-win."

"Why did you go to such lengths to convince me you wanted the tree?" Maggie asked.

"Because you were still under Mrs. Kerr's influence," Gideon said. "That's why I never told you the truth about Mei. Remember, you told her about Alexandria's place and would have given her the street address if I hadn't stopped you."

"Okay, I get it. I'm getting sick and tired of being left out of the loop, but I get it. What now?"

"We'll work together," Mei said. "It will be just like old times, my friend."

"It will be fun."

Maggie gaped at them. "Fun? Let me get this straight. We have to sneak in and rescue that bitch Mrs. Kerr under the noses of two hundred trigger-happy mercs, not to mention that we don't know how far away the *Ginny K* is. It could take weeks to just find the landing field."

Mei laid a map upon the table. "We are here," he said, indicating a spot on the plastic coated surface. "The *Ginny K* is forty-three miles away—here." He circled it with a small marker.

"Forty-three miles through the thickest bush I've ever seen," Maggie argued. "Make it a solid month."

"The bad guys won't show up until tomorrow, right?" Gideon asked.

"Yes."

Gideon nodded. "I'm going to check it out."

"What are you talking about?" Maggie asked.

"A dress rehearsal before the big show tomorrow," Mei said. "Luck favors the prepared mind."

"How close can you get me, Mei?"

"A mile would be the safest and not draw attention."

"Good," Gideon said. "Let's not waste any time. Be back in an hour, Maggie."

"No way are you going without me. I need to pay that Jordan bitch back for killing Megan."

"Precisely why you are staying put. You killing Samantha will tip the Black Circle's hand and we don't need that right now. Now don't argue. Just stay here and rest up for tomorrow's fire fight."

Maggie crossed her arms and snarled, but settled back in her chair. Although obviously unhappy, she made no further comment.

Mei drew a circle on the ground. Giving Gideon a small pendant, Mei stepped back. "You have precisely an hour before you are brought back. Lose the charm and it's a long walk."

Gideon gave Mei a wink before he entered the circle and vanished.

"While you're waiting, Maggie, would you care for a shower?"

"Shower?"

"Of course. Doesn't that bring back fond memories? We met in a shower. If you like, I would love to wash your back and a few other things."

"If you like, I would love to shoot you," Maggie said, much to Mei's delight. "Right between the tentacles, *Cthulhu*. Nice show you put on at the motel. I thought you had really put some kind of witch curse on Kali. What did you really do?"

"A little lethal tech from my world," Mei said. "The satanic chanting was actually a series of nursery rhymes I learned as a child. All joking aside, Maggie, did your quest for vengeance bring you peace?"

"God, no. I feel ill and hollow inside. When faced with the opportunity, I didn't want to kill Larry. All I wanted was an explanation. I wanted him to tell me it was all a terrible mistake and I could wake up from this nightmare. After he was through, I felt like he had kicked me in the teeth. He was mean, meaner than I had thought Larry could be. Now that I think about it, it was like he was trying to goad me into lashing out at him. Nevertheless, as painful as it was, I didn't have it in me. I would have gladly let Larry kill me and be done with it."

"But you *did* strike him down?"

Maggie wiped her eyes. "He would have killed Gideon. In this entire mess, Gideon's the only one who stood up for me—a total stranger he'd just met. He's beyond wonderful. I didn't kill for revenge I killed—"

"To save the man you love?"

"What?" Maggie looked at Mei, as though the very thought had delivered a physical blow.

"Don't 'what' me, Maggie Black. I see it in the way you look at him, the way you touch him. You have it bad."

"I just met him. Besides, you're from another planet. What do you know about how humans feel?"

"What has that got to do with the price of tea in China? People are people, regardless of where they're from. We still grasp for power, for faith, and for love."

Maggie gave him a long, thoughtful look. "You mentioned showers?" she asked after several moments.

"Yes, of course, let me get you a towel."

"By the way, Mei. Thanks to you, I now shower armed."

⸎

Gideon drew a diagram on the graph paper while Mei and Maggie looked on. "The *Ginny K* is parked at this small plantation. Roland made a mess of the manioc fields, but made it down intact."

"Wonderful," Maggie said. "Is he a prisoner?"

"No. Samantha was in the main house, while I watched Roland removing what was left of the farmers and crew. They were torn to shreds, so I figured it was all him. I counted ten bodies as he piled them up and doused them with gasoline.

"Samantha hobbled out on a makeshift crunch and marked the clearing in front of the main house. Poor woman looked like she was in pain."

"Good," Maggie said.

"Roland brought her some freshly killed chickens and a few goats. She used the blood to create what looked like a big mandala. I estimated it was around fifty yards across."

"What was the design?" Mei asked.

Gideon carefully drew the mystic symbol.

Mei shook his head. "She's making an astral bridge. That's where the Black Circle's hired guns are coming through."

"That still leaves them forty miles away," Maggie said.

"Where's the best place to defend your front door?" Gideon asked.

"It's as far down the road as you can," Mei said.

"I figure we can separate Mrs. Kerr from the pack with a little diversion then bring her back here," Gideon informed them. "I don't think they'll be expecting us."

"No, Samantha thinks she killed us." Maggie ran a brush through her damp hair. "While they're running around chasing ghosts, we will be long gone. Good plan, old man."

"We merely have to wait for them to show up," Gideon said.

"What kind of diversion are you talking about? We don't have much on hand, sweetie."

"More than you think. The *Ginny K* is more than a fine aircraft. Years ago, I came up with a crazy idea to use her as a big bomb if things got out of hand and we didn't have a chance of survival. Ginny called it the 'spoilsport option.' Thank the good Lord, things never got bad enough to use her. She's wired with the latest plastic explosives, situated under special panels, making the old girl a very large antipersonnel mine."

Maggie chuckled. "You think too much, old man. Thank God."

"Rest, my friend," Mei said. "When they activate the bridge, I'll wake you." He turned to Maggie. "You should rest, too. I think it will be an interesting night and, if I don't miss my guess, tonight you'll finally be free."

"Gideon, I need to tell you something," Maggie whispered as she stepped close and wrapped her arms around his neck.

"What did I do, now?"

"Shut up, old man," she said softly. "Gideon Kane, I could

live a dozen lifetimes and never meet anyone like you. Old man, you are one of a kind."

"I hope you mean that in a good way."

"Hush," she whispered. "I want to spend the rest of my life with you, and not in some sleazy, shacked up way, although that does have its merits. I want you as my husband. Will you please marry me?"

Gideon gave her a sad smile and caressed her face. "Flattered as I am, darling, I might as well tell you now. While it would be an honor to share my life with you, I don't think I have more than a day left in me."

"What?"

"When I first agreed to help you, I was old and worn out. I didn't have the strength to start this quest, let alone see it to the end. That was the reason for our little excursion to the library, where I talked Alexandria into giving me the Tear of the Phoenix."

"What's the Tear of the Phoenix?"

"It is a rare creature that, in exchange for a nurturing host, will grant a small period of rejuvenation."

"Come again?"

"It makes a dried up old man young again."

"This is a good thing. I don't see—"

"The Phoenix grows rather quickly and, when it is ready to be born, the host is consumed in a fiery blaze and reduced to ash."

Maggie felt her heart in her throat. "You mean, you die?"

"Yes, and nothing on this Earth, can stop it."

"Why would you do this?"

"For you, Maggie Black. I had out lived my purpose and, for a man like me, that's a fate worse than death. Then along came this knife-wielding, half-naked woman who gave me something to live for."

"But you're going to die!" she moaned as tears welled in her eyes.

"Darling, we all die. It's how we live that matters. I have a home built on that heavenly shore and I'll be more than all right. All I have is one last earthly chore and when I set you free, then I can go to the Lord with a smile on my face."

"Gideon—I—" Maggie hugged him hard, overwhelmed by his selfless act. "The offer's on the table, old man," she whispered. "Whether it's a thousand years, or a single day, I want to spend it as your wife."

Gideon looked at her in shock. "It would be my honor to marry you, Maggie."

He kissed her and, sweeping her up, cradled her in his arms.

"Well, isn't this just the sweetest thing?" Mei said. "While my authority and jurisdiction, on this world anyway, is below that of a bum on the street, on mine I was the Law. I can't have you two degenerates cavorting under my tent in sin." He straightened. "Gideon Kane, do you take this gorgeous, incredibly sexy woman who keeps leading me on, to be your wife?"

"Absolutely."

"Maggie Black, in your haste to avoid becoming an old maid, will you forego all my charms and pledge yourself to this pitiful excuse of a man, forever?"

"Amen," Maggie said.

Mei stepped forth and kissed Gideon lightly on the forehead. He then, in turn, kissed Maggie. Placing his hands on their heads, he whispered a prayer and stepped back. "With the authority I had, and will have again as supreme ruler of the Oki, I pronounce you as one entity," he said. "That will be one thousand Kronars, please."

"Take a check?" Gideon asked.

"Go make some noise with your wife, you deadbeat."

CHAPTER 44

From the cover of the jungle, Maggie and Gideon watched the farm as Simone Ravenwood's mercenaries made camp.

"Gideon, I see that rat Mrs. Kerr," she said. Lowering her binoculars, she pointed to the barn.

"Yes, you're right," he said. "That means that Simone and the book are in the main house."

"Who goes after what?" she asked.

Gideon lowered his Steiners. "Free Mrs. Kerr and you two skedaddle back to Mei's camp. Before the *Ginny K* blows, I should be able to walk in and snatch the book right out from under their noses. They won't know whether to cry or wind their watches when we get through, sweetheart."

Maggie leaned in and kissed him.

"As much as I hate to say this," he said softly. "We need to focus, Mrs. Kane."

"I can't believe I married such a sexy party pooper."

"I'll give you twenty minutes to spring that rat. When you hear the engines of the *Ginny K* fire up, you'd better be getting out of Dodge in a hurry."

"Rodger that, Commander," she said. Giving him a tender kiss, Maggie disappeared into the night.

CHAPTER 45

Gideon moved through the night like a ghost. Slipping past the patrolling mercenaries, he pulled out his cell phone and punched in a special number, starting a countdown.

"Goodbye, girl. We've had one hell of a good time, but it looks like the end of the road for us all." He gasped as a sharp spasm tore through his chest. He could feel heat stirring deep within. "Yeah, definitely the end of the road."

He ignored the growing ache and headed for the farmhouse. Crossing the compound, he found an empty tent and appropriated an ACU military uniform blouse and pants. He blended in easily and moved quickly toward his goal.

Fortunately for him, the soldiers were far from crack warriors. They were sloppy and ill disciplined—little more than hired murderers who liked to shoot guns and push people around. No one gave him a second look as he took up a position next to the big stone house.

Peeking through the windows, he spied Roland and Samantha as well as an older woman who he assumed was Simone Ravenwood. Simone paced the room and seemed to be giving Samantha a royal chewing out.

Gideon smiled. Checking his watch, he steeled himself.

Suddenly, the twin Pratt and Whitney engines sputtered to life. He stepped to the door, pushed through, and yelled, "The plane! They're stealing the plane!" Quickly, he slammed the door and retreated back into the shadows.

Like rats deserting a sinking ship, Simone's crew rushed from the building.

"Stop them!" Simone screamed as, off in the distance, the powerful engines settled into a full, smooth drone. "Do not kill Kane. I want him alive!"

Grabbing their guns, the soldiers swarmed the beautiful plane as it began to roll slowly toward them.

Simone backhanded Samantha. "So, Kane's dead, is he?"

Samantha stumbled back and fell to the earth in a sprawl. She whimpered, clutching her ruined knee. "Mistress, please, I have served you well over the years."

"Then serve me in Hell."

At a discrete nod from Simone, a solider stepped forward and shot Samantha in the head. Dispassionately, the soldier put away his pistol and looked at Simone.

"Well?" she snapped. "You made the mess, now clean it up."

The soldier reached down and, grasping Samantha's lifeless body by the shirt collar, quickly dragged her away.

"Doesn't anyone around here think for themselves?"

෧෨෬෭

Gideon walked around and entered the house through the main entrance. Locking the door behind him, he looked specifically for Simone's room.

"God, what animals," he said as he beheld splotches of bloodstains where the owners met their deaths. He ran up the creaking staircase and found a large room equipped with all the comforts of home.

"Must be the place." He ransacked her personal belongings. Her e-reader lay open to *Book Eight of the Kane Saga, The Blood of the Vampir,* and it made him laugh. "She's sicker than I thought."

Under the bed lay a great molded-black-plastic case. Pulling out the nearly bulletproof container, he found *The Book of Xanadutha* nestled in a molded foam liner.

Sounds of gunfire outside made him look up just as a form

separated from the shadows and pounced. Gideon sidestepped Roland's clumsy attack. Grabbing the case, he swung it around, clocking Roland under the chin.

Stunned, Roland fell back and slammed into the door. "I would know your scent anywhere, Doc. Trying to pull a fast one, are we? Well, think again, cause it ain't going happen."

"Listen to me, Gunn," Gideon said. "I'm trying to help you. Tonight, you can be free."

"I don't need your help, Grandpa. Simone removed my collar, which is a hell of a lot more than you ever did. She even promised to let me personally kill Mrs. Kerr when she has the Tree. How can a guy, who has taken Mrs. Kerr's shit for five years, pass that up? Move away from the book and surrender. I do admire you, Doc, so I promise your death will be quick and painless."

"Do you really want to fight me again, boy?" Gideon moved slowly to his right away from the bed and took up a fighting stance.

"You're tough, and I'll never forget the ass whipping you gave me, but you had room to maneuver. In this cracker box, I have the advantage."

"Well, don't just stand there, talking me to death, boy. Let's dance."

Roland's eyes turned red and, with a roar, he transformed into the beast. Gideon stood his ground, a small smile playing at the corner of his mouth. As if propelled by a hydraulic ram, the beast sprang, his razor sharp claws extended forward to rip Gideon to shreds.

Gideon sidestepped the creature's charge with the grace of a matador. Roland's momentum sent him crashing through the room's only window, his frightful roar replaced with a high-pitched shriek.

"Some fellahs just never learn," Gideon said as he heard a heavy thud and a woman scream out in pain. The black case in hand, he used the alien device and disappeared.

CHAPTER 46

Roland crashed through the window with a shriek of surprise. In a cloud of glass shards, he slammed into Simone, sending the small woman rolling across the stony ground. Roland came up fast and transformed quickly back into his human guise.

Two soldiers helped Simone to her feet. She was not happy. "I'll have you skinned alive for that, you fool!"

"Doc's after the book!" he yelled. "I tried to stop him, but he tossed me out the window."

The soldiers stormed into the house, but found Gideon and the book long gone.

"No!" Simone screamed. "They'll try to rescue Mrs. Kerr next. Do not let them if you wish to live."

"Yes, ma'am," said the captain of her bodyguards.

With a slight nod, the entire contingent flew to the barn.

"Gideon Kane used that stupid plane of his as a diversion," she screamed. "When you find him, Roland, bring him to me."

"You want me to go after Doc by *myself*?"

"You're a freaking shapeshifter, for God's sake!"

"Doc's…well, he's dangerous."

"He gets away with my book and I will show you how dangerous I can be."

Roland swallowed hard then transformed and bounded into the darkness.

The soldiers set up a skirmish line before the slowly rolling plane, laying down a deadly stream of fire at the landing gear.

The tires blew immediately and the plane turned sharply to port.

"Aw, screw this," said a particularly gruff and sociopathic mercenary named Ernesto.

He fired his AK-47 at the cockpit. Ripping holes in the aluminum and shattering the windows. The beautiful image of Virginia Kane was soon a bullet-ridden mess. Ernesto was joined by the bulk of the soldiers who surrounded the plane and began to riddle the fuselage and engines indiscriminately.

"Stop, you fools!" Simone cried. "I want the pilot alive."

With a wave of her hand, both engine cowlings crumpled as if pinched between giant fingers. Amid screeching metal and flying sparks, both engines gushed coolant and belched thick, black smoke, before they died. The once elegant and beautiful *Ginny K,* who had carried Gideon Kane and his crew on many victorious missions, had finally met her end.

Weapons ready, the soldiers crunched across a carpet of spent shell casings as they moved in to capture the pilot—or to recover a body.

In a protected armored case, concealed under the pilot's bullet-ventilated seat, a timer reached zero, just as the first soldier entered the plane.

The tremendous explosion lit up the jungle for miles as the DC-3 dissolved into a cloud of fire and deadly shrapnel. The hapless soldiers were obliterated and the substantial radiating shockwave destroyed all the plantation's buildings, including the barn and house. The red-hot metal shards fell like rain.

Simone and her entire gang of mercenary thugs lay dead in the smoking ruins.

CHAPTER 47

Mrs. Kerr nervously paced the small windowless tack room. The light from a single kerosene lamp gave the chamber a smoky flickering light.

"I can't believe I'm so close and yet so far from my goal. Damn Simone to hell!" She turned as she heard a heavy thump against her door. The chain rattled and she heard the sound of the padlock being removed. "Looks like my time is finally up," she said grimly. It was then that she heard the unmistakable cough of the *Ginny K* as her engines came to life.

"Mrs. Kerr, I presume," Maggie asked as she poked her head into the room.

"Hajar? How is this possible? They said you were dead."

"You want to talk, or do you want to go?"

"How? We're surrounded by Simone's thugs."

Maggie slipped into the room and closed the door. "I have this," she said, showing the pendent around her neck. "This doohickey will whisk us away from this place."

"Astral travel, excellent. However, I'm not going anywhere without *The Book of Xanadutha*."

"Gideon is taking care of that. He'll meet us at the camp and give you the way into Eden."

Mrs. Kerr smiled as she gazed at the pendent.

"Do you only have the one?"

"Yes, but don't worry, it can carry both of us."

"Are those Kane's infamous weapons around your hips?"

"Yes, he let me borrow them after I lost Kali."

"Killing an angel is an impressive feat, Hajar. I take my hat off to your deadly prowess. With that being said, give me Kane's guns—now."

Having no choice, Maggie removed her coveted weapons and handed them over to Mrs. Kerr.

Grinning, Mrs. Kerr removed the pistols from the holsters and slipped one in each of the main pockets of her jungle jacket. "My, I couldn't ask for better souvenirs of my victory than Kane's very own weapons."

Maggie bit her lip and fought the urge to throttle the evil woman.

"Give me the pendent, Hajar."

"Mrs. Kerr—"

"If I have to ask again, you won't like it."

Maggie surrendered the jewel-like device.

"I take it that all I have to do is concentrate and the device will take me to your camp?"

"Yes, Mrs. Kerr. Gideon will meet us in a great amphitheater at the center of a ruined city."

"A lost city? How dramatic."

"Mrs. Kerr, we have to go. The *Ginny K* is rigged to blow and give Simone a very bad day."

"A typical Kane ploy," Mrs. Kerr said. "Have a seat in the corner, Hajar. I'm afraid I'm going to leave you behind. If you make the slightest move to escape, I will make you wish you were never born."

"But the bomb—"

"Sit."

Obediently, Maggie moved to the corner and sat down.

Mrs. Kerr moved toward the door.

"Why are you doing this?"

Mrs. Kerr paused. "When I get the Tree, you'll be free and I'd rather not have my head bashed in. If you happen to escape Simone's men, Kane's booby trap, and somehow navigate through this green hell back to civilization, look me up. I'll let you work for me again. No one ever cleaned a toilet like you, my dear."

"What about Gideon?"

Mrs. Kerr laughed. "Once Kane gives me the Tree, I'll kill that infernal Boy Scout with his own guns. Don't you find the irony delicious?"

"Please, for the love of God, don't hurt him, Mrs. Kerr, I beg you!"

"Seems someone has fallen under Kane's dubious charm. That will make his demise all that much sweeter."

Mrs. Kerr slipped through the door and closed it behind her. Maggie grimaced as she heard her chain and padlock it securely.

That bitch! I have to get out of here. I have to warn Gideon.

Maggie gave Mrs. Kerr time to leave before she pulled out her knife. Using the thick spine of the blade and working frantically, she popped out the door pins. Then she heard the angry sound of automatic weapon fire and black oaths of a few soldiers.

As the last pin fell to the ground, the roar of the *Ginny K* filled her ears. Ripping the door away, she escaped the storeroom. She was quickly through the loft and slid down a ladder to the dirt floor. Sprinting with all her might, she flew out the gaping rear door of the barn.

A dark shape rose in the moonlight to block her way. It was a soldier, who fortunately brought up a shovel instead of a rifle to kill her. Before the hapless mercenary could brain her, Maggie threw a haymaker without losing stride. The punch connected with a crunch of bone and spray of blood. She flew past without looking back, trying to reach the safety of the jungle.

Two more steps and she stepped into an unseen pit that gaped before her. Gasping, she fell hard into the freshly dug grave. As she landed on the still warm, body of Samantha Jordan, the night exploded.

Protected from the brunt of the thunderous concussion by the barn and the walls of the grave, Maggie grunted as something heavy slammed into her, nearly knocking her out. Her vision fuzzy, she beheld the blacked, deformed face of Virginia Kane. The aluminum nose section, containing the smiling pinup, had struck Maggie in the back. Fighting to stay conscious, she slid underneath the metal shield, as a deadly rain of red-hot shards fell around her.

After what seemed like an eternity, she crawled out of the grave. When she saw a figure walking toward her, Maggie struggled to rise and meet the new threat. Then it dawned on her that the figure was too small to be a soldier. The small figure walked up to her and smiled.

"M—Megan?"

Megan Franks stood before her in the moonlight. Covered with dirt and bleeding from the bullet wounds to her forehead, Megan was a ghastly sight. The moonlight glinted off the deep red blood that wound its way like a river, cutting a channel through the dirt and grime of the spirit's face.

Maggie gasped and her eyes rolled back as the world went dark.

CHAPTER 48

Mrs. Kerr hobbled down the broken cobblestone path toward the great sunken amphitheater at the center of Ophir. Her swollen mouth and foot throbbed mightily, but her sheer joy dulled much of the pain.

Standing on the wall that encircled the complex, that was easily the size of a modern sports arena, she spied Gideon on the broad grassy floor of the stadium. Shaking with joy, she patted the hard outlines of the .45s in her pockets. "It's Christmas morning," she whispered. "And I'm finally getting everything I deserve."

Clutching *The Book of Xanadutha* to his burning chest, Gideon watched his dreaded enemy stumble down the cracked and round granite steps. Every breath was agony as he felt the massive lump grow and expand.

"I have to admit, Kane, that, for once, you're a sight for sore eyes. Thanks for the timely rescue. Now that the pleasantries are over, I have an appointment with Godhood to keep."

"Where's Maggie?" he asked. "So help me, if you've hurt her—"

"Relax, Kamikaze," Mrs. Kerr purred. "I left Hajar back at Simone's compound so that she wouldn't get any wild homicidal ideas once she was free. Now where's the Tree?"

"Her name's Maggie and you would do well to remember that."

Gideon produced a smooth egg-sized stone from his pocket and handed it to Mrs. Kerr.

"Why, as I live and breathe," she said, "a Kopi Truth Stone. What's the matter old friend, don't you trust me?"

"We both know the answer to that, *old friend*. What did you do with Maggie?"

Rolling her eyes, she held the stone in her open palm. Producing a flashlight, he illuminated the Kopi Stone.

"I took her gun and then shot her in the head."

Gideon gritted his teeth as she cackled at her own morbid joke, but he was relieved when the stone turned a dull black, indicating that she was lying. "The truth," he said.

"The truth is, my old friend, is that I didn't want my devoted employees turning on me when their collars come off. I left her locked in the barn, not a single hair of her lovely head harmed in anyway."

He breathed a sigh of relief as the stone turned an emerald green. Gideon took the Kopi stone and slid it into his pocket. "You left her in that den of snakes? That's forty miles away."

"We both know that Hajar—Maggie—is a match for an army of mercenaries and, I have to admit, she's probably the most resourceful woman I've ever met. She will, no doubt, escape that big bomb you left behind as well."

"Granted," Gideon said.

"Okay, Kamikaze, now that your precious Maggie is safe and sound, where's my prize?"

"Stand in the circle I drew," he said. "It will protect you if this goes south. Whatever you do, don't move from the circle."

Mrs. Kerr noticed that the circle glowed and pulsated with a bluish glow. Barely able to contain her excitement, she moved over to the intricate two-foot-diameter circle and stepped inside.

Keeping a wary eye on his nemesis, he tried to act nonchalant, but the pain in his chest was unbearable. The incredible, fiery throbbing was consuming his torso and slowly moving to his extremities. Weak in the knees, he walked to the center of the round field on sheer willpower alone.

He connected the exotic battery to the spine of *The Book of Xanadutha*. As the book began to glow and build a charge, he pressed his hands into the identical, misshapen hand grooves cut into the front and back panels. Taking a deep breath, trying to take his mind off the pain consuming him, he concentrated, connecting with the spirit embedded within the device, and requested his destination.

The book glowed brightly in his hands, so much so that she had to shield her eyes from the dazzling light.

"Come to me, Eden, so that I may partake of the Tree and live," he said.

Mrs. Kerr looked up nervously as black clouds rolled across the moon and terrible flashes of lightning lit up the sky. The wind began to whip and whistle through the dead city.

Looking over Gideon's shoulder, she saw the air itself split apart. She gasped as she beheld a massive, glorious tree standing one hundred yards beyond the open portal. The twisted, sliver-tinged limbs reminded her of a delicately crafted bonsai tree, only on a massive scale. Dwarfing even a mighty redwood, the tree was surrounded by a three-foot-tall, intricate, silver fence.

The tree's strange crimson red leaves moved, as if having a life all their own. To her delight, golden, pulsating fruit hung thick in the branches, each able to bestow Godhood.

"I can't believe that it's an actual tree," she said as she beheld the beautiful creation. "It is so beautiful and all mine."

She moved from the circle and stood at the edge of the portal, her eyes bright with desire.

"Let—them—go," he said.

"Yes, of course," Mrs. Kerr said. "I now fulfill my blood oath. I release my hold over Roland Gunn, Yakusho Shimura, Meagan Franks, and Hajar. I command their collars to release their hold. They are now free."

Smiling, he closed his eyes in relief. His last mission was accomplished and Maggie Kane, the woman he loved, was free.

Gideon suffered a spasm of agony that sent him to his knees. He felt like a flaming knife was being slowly pushed through his chest. Holding tightly onto *The Book of Xanadutha*, he fell to the ground.

Grinding his teeth against the white-hot pain that enveloped him, he sought to protect the device and keep the field it projected from collapsing.

"What's the matter, old friend? Feeling a bit under the weather?" Mrs. Kerr chuckled at her old adversary. She pulled a .45 from her right pocket, leveling the gun at Gideon's head. "Give my best to your beautiful wife, Ginny."

๛๛๛

Maggie awoke and stifled a scream. She was looking into the weather-eroded face of a squat, ancient gargoyle. The gargoyle and its twenty brothers guarded the once grand entrance to Ophir.

"Megan, I owe you big time, honey."

She moaned, feeling like a tackling dummy for the Crimson Tide. Crawling to her feet, she noticed something glinting atop the reddish stone of the statue. As she picked up the small diamond earrings that she had given Megan for her birthday, Maggie's eyes filled with tears.

"Thank you, Megan. I love you, Shortstack."

Suddenly, in the distance, Maggie saw a great glowing sphere appear.

"Gideon," she breathed. "I still have time."

Ignoring her injuries, she ran with all her might toward the light, threading her way down rubble-strewn streets and alleyways at breakneck speed. Without warning, her throat felt as if it was on fire. Blinded by the sharp pain, she ricocheted off a crumbling brick wall.

Reaching up, to her surprise, she felt a slim metal necklace encircling her throat.

The witch collar. Gideon did it!

Grasping the infernal device with both hands, she pulled with all her might, ripping it apart with a savage growl. The hateful thing felt like ice in her hands and sparked with a dull, greenish glow. She threw the shards away and watched as it melted like frost on the stone.

She was free.

"Got to save Gideon before it is too late."

With a new surge of energy, she vaulted a low wall, but then she heard the unmistakable report of Gideon's .45. Three shots in rapid succession echoed through the dead city, then silence.

"Please, God, no."

CHAPTER 49

"Is that you, Salome?" Mei asked.

Mrs. Kerr turned quickly to find him walking toward her.

"You're too late, Mei!" she screamed. "The Tree is mine!"

"Don't be silly," he said as he blew a cloud of smoke. "Move out of my way before I cut you down, you ridiculous buffoon."

Mrs. Kerr turned the pistol toward Mei and fired three times. With a snarl, she plunged through the portal with Mei hot on her heels.

Mei paused before Gideon and smiled. "Goodbye, my friend, and thank you."

Mei dropped his cigarette holder near Gideon and, with a bright smile, entered the exotic world.

Two dozen steps beyond the opening of the portal, Mrs. Kerr began to choke and sputter as her lungs burned and her eyes watered.

"What's happening to me?"

With superhuman effort, she struggled on. Falling over the low fence, she crawled to the bole of the mighty Tree.

"Beautiful, isn't it," Mei said. His human form gone, he glided toward Mrs. Kerr on a wriggly stalk of tentacles.

"It's not—supposed to be—like this," she stammered as the alien atmosphere drew the life from her. "What in God's name are you?"

"Oh, don't mind me, Salome. I am just going native." Standing before the gilded fence, Mei stretched out an impossibly long tentacle and plucked a juicy, bowling-ball-sized fruit.

"That's mine!" Mrs. Kerr screamed.

"The fruit of the G'nash is one of the great delicacies in the universe, but it isn't worth dying for."

"T—this—isn't the Tree of Life?"

"Of course not," he said, bringing the fruit to a gaping maw of jagged teeth whereupon he took an enormous bite. "It's a common shrub that grows on my world."

"A silver fence for a common shrub?"

"To keep people away from the tree's root system, my dear woman. It's quite voracious, you know."

Mrs. Kerr screamed as several white tendrils burst from the ground and wrapped around her legs and torso. The crushing, hungry roots made her think she was caught in a nest of anacondas.

"Aconda goo to shree tooka!"

"Oh, by the way," Mei commented. "Magic doesn't work here."

Mrs. Kerr drew Thunder and Lightning only to have them snatched from her grasp by Mei. He tossed the pistols through the still-open portal to Earth.

"Those are Gideon's property, not yours, you bitter old woman."

"Help—me—for God's sake. Kane tricked us both! You can't let me die. I'm a witch like you! Please, help me get back to Earth."

"You mean, Kane and *I* tricked you and, yes, I can let you die with a smile on my pretty face. Salome, you are a blight that leaves nothing behind, but pain and misery."

"Help me!"

"Too late. I'm afraid you were dead the moment you stepped into my world. The beautiful air, I enjoy and thrive in, is quite poisonous to humans. It will kill you long before the roots have a chance to crush and consume you. For future reference, Salome, when you seek the Tree of Life, make sure you pick the right one before you plunge headfirst. Now, if you will excuse me, I have a world to run."

Mei tossed the core of the fruit aside and slithered away to the distant, glittering city, leaving Mrs. Kerr to her death.

"I hope you rot in Hellfire, Gideon Kane!" she screamed, using her last breath to curse the man who had ultimately bested her.

CHAPTER 50

As his pistols slid to a stop beside him, Gideon removed his hands from the book and collapsed. Soaked with sweat and wracked with pain, he tried to remove the battery, but it proved to be stubborn in his weakened condition.

"Gideon!" Maggie cried.

He looked up and smiled as she bounded down the stone steps like a gazelle. "You *are* resourceful," he said.

"Where did she shoot you?" she asked as she kneeled beside him and cradled him in her arms. "Oh, God, you're burning up."

"She didn't shoot me. It's the Phoenix. I guess this is the end."

Maggie cried as she held him close and prayed for a miracle.

"You're free, my love. You must hide the book, so it can't unleash hell upon this world. Remove the battery and throw it into the ocean."

"I will."

"How very touching."

Gideon and Maggie looked up and beheld Alexandria standing a few feet away. She looked precisely as she had in the library, even floating a foot off the ground.

"I didn't think you could leave your house of horrors," Gideon said.

"I have learned a few things since our last encounter, Kane. Now give me the book."

"Don't let her get it," he whispered.

Maggie grabbed for the book, but it was snatched from her grasp by an invisible force.

"Thank you for the gift, Kane," Alexandria said. "No longer will I be stranded on this backward world. This device will give me the universe and beyond."

"I thought you gave up the Phoenix a little too easily," he said, gritting his teeth against the pain. "Been using the little critter to track us, have you?"

"When you dangle a prize like the Tree of Life before me, how could I resist? However, *The Book of Xanadutha* is the real trophy."

"You have what you want, now please take the Phoenix away!" Maggie cried.

A smile creased Alexandria's perfect features. "I have looked forward to watching you die, Kane. The look of pain on your face is so titillating."

"You have what you wanted because of Gideon, now, please, heal him," Maggie said.

"Don't waste your breath, Maggie," he said through clenched teeth. "I'm done."

"With nothing to bargain with, your time's up, Kane. Unless, that is, sweet Maggie here will trade me the mystic weapon she used to make mincemeat out of my security."

"I—I don't have Kali anymore. There must be something else I can do? Take me. I'll work for you, just let Gideon live."

"Maggie, you can't," Gideon hissed. "I won't stand for it. I didn't go through all this just to see you serve a new master."

"It's my decision."

"Actually, it's mine," Alexandria said. "Pity. But without that wonderful blade, Paladin or no, you have no value to me."

"I am a Nephilim, surely you could use me?"

"Amazing," Alexandria said. "That would explain much. Using your DNA, I could create a marvelous force to safeguard my treasure. I'll take you up on your offer of service, Maggie Black, however, I make one small change. Kane still dies."

"*What?*"

"Sorry, Kane, looks like even your vast reservoir of luck has finally run out. Don't worry, Maggie, I'm a benevolent master and you will be the instrument to bring your race back from the dead."

Maggie screamed at the smiling apparition.

"Vent, if it will make you feel better, child. You should be honored to witness my triumph. The ultimate acquisition, along with my most dangerous enemy dead at my feet. This day will be remembered long after the world has turned to dust."

Alexandria held the book before her and a shimmering portal appeared. As Maggie glimpsed a gorgeous land, more perfect than a dream, a column of a thousand Setii, formed, behind her, dressed in weird armor and armed with weapons thousands of years beyond humanity.

"Go into Eden and retrieve my prize," Alexandria ordered. "The Tree of Life is mine."

Abruptly, a large man, nearly eight feet in height and sheathed in golden armor blocked the portal.

"The angel of the Tree," Maggie whispered. "Wow."

Unlike the drawings and depictions of winged warrior angels dressed in Roman or Greek styled armor, the angelic armor appeared extremely sleek and hi-tech. Close-fitting and transparent, the armor looked like golden glass. Maggie thought the wingless warrior angel seemed more like something from a big-budget sci-fi movie than from the Bible.

"Looks like you have provoked the Guardian of the Tree of Life," Gideon said. "If I were you, I would take my space monkeys and run."

Alexandria laughed. "We both know that my technology is thousands of years beyond anything on this miserable planet. A creature in a silly suit will not stop me. Kill it, my children."

The Setii unleashed a violet-hued stream of energy at the Knight of God. The angel took the brunt of the energy beam that could have bored a hole completely through the Earth herself and...*smiled*.

"That's not possible," Alexandria said. "Nothing could have survived that blast."

"Told you to run," Gideon said.

Taking hold of Gideon, Maggie gained her feet and ran, trying to escape the battle. Their way was blocked as a shimmering, translucent wall appeared. The Setii produced a force shield while they quickly rearmed with another weapon.

The angel laughed merrily as he drew his own weapon and returned fire. The force shield, which could have withstood the entire nuclear arsenal of NATO, shattered before his God-conceived weapon. Within seconds, the clearing was a mass of dead and dying Setii. For the first time in her ten thousand years of existence, Alexandria was out of her league and hopelessly out gunned.

Setting Gideon down, Maggie dashed at Alexandria and tore the book away. Realizing defeat, Alexandria screamed in frustration before vanishing.

"Gideon, I got the book!" Maggie cried. With a loud snap, Maggie ripped the battery loose and tossed it away.

"Good girl."

"Why isn't the portal to Eden dissipating?"

"This isn't good," he whispered.

The Guardian of the Tree held out his hand. Gideon and Maggie rose from the ground and flew toward him. Maggie heard the angel laugh as they entered Eden.

CHAPTER 51

Maggie and Gideon burst into blessed air, free of the stagnate rot of Ophir, and from dense night into bright, warm sunshine.

Above them, the sky was a deep, cloudless blue. At a glance, she saw lush, well-tended plants and flowers in full bloom. Clouds of colorful butterflies flitted across the plain.

Looking around for her husband, she found the Guardian, complete in exotic golden armor, standing over Gideon. Gideon convulsed violently as plumes of steam rose from his body.

"Gideon!" she yelled. Looking up at the angel, Maggie pleaded, "Please, help him."

The angel removed his helmet. He was breathtakingly handsome, with curly blond hair and dazzling topaz eyes. Tossing his helmet aside, he removed his gauntlets and dropped them beside his helmet.

"You know," Aesir said, "I really thought it would work this time. If I were a gambler, I would have bet that, this time, I would have succeeded."

"Succeeded at what?" Maggie asked.

"Mei told me that Simone Ravenwood was crazy obsessed with the idea of the Tree of Life," Gideon said. "That idea came from you, didn't it?"

"Very astute of you, Gideon," Aesir said. "I thought that having Simone and her bully boys use the dimensional device was foolproof. But through a bizarre series of events, that I still can't wrap my head around, Salome Kerr ended up with the device. I figured that just as long as someone found the Tree, it would still be a win for me, but then you two messed the whole thing up. I am very disappointed."

"I don't understand," she said. "You *know* where the Tree is—I mean, you guard the Tree."

"Oh, yes, it's just over the hill behind me," he said. "Let me explain. You see, Maggie, I am the most powerful warrior angel ever created by the Father. My purpose in life was war and I was the best. Look at the splendid armor created just for me. It can withstand the power of an exploding sun. In theory, the only weapon capable of penetrating it belongs to Michael himself, however, I myself don't subscribe to that theory."

"It is very pretty," Maggie said.

Aesir snorted. "Pretty? Hundreds of millions of rebellious creatures, most of which your feeble imaginations could not even begin to describe, have fallen before my might. Ahhh…those were the days. Life was good when I could kill. Then came that cursed day when you talking monkeys fell for Lucifer's lame ruse, spit in God's face, and ate from the Tree of the Knowledge of Good and Evil. On that day, I got a call directly from the Father. I figured the Old Boy had learned His lesson and was going to turn me loose on that pair of ingrates. Instead, He enclosed Eden in a dimensional bubble. He then ordered me to protect the Tree of Life at all costs from Man."

"Bet that didn't sit well with you did it, Aesir?" Gideon asked.

"Correct," Aesir said. "With all my gifts—with all my power—He makes me a security guard for an overgrown bush! Can you believe that?"

Maggie stifled a laugh. "Shocking."

"I wanted to walk out but, as we all know, the sin of rebellion is a capital crime."

"The ass I used to work for rebelled," she said.

"Do not compare me to that fourth-rate angel, Larry! He is a weak fool whom I could kill with a wave of my hand! If I didn't know better, I would say he was behind the catastrophe! This smacks of his twisted handiwork. Oh, if only I could get my hands on him, I would wipe that insufferable smirk off his face once and for all."

"Don't bother," she said quietly. "Larry's dead."

"You goaded the original Nephilim into seeking the Tree," Gideon said.

"Like I said before, Gideon Kane, you are astute."

"Wait a minute," Maggie said. "You've have lost me. For what possible purpose do you want someone to find the stupid Tree?"

"It was one of the reasons God destroyed the world," Gideon said. "With no one left alive, there wouldn't be a reason to post a guard."

"Bingo," Aesir said. "Unfortunately, that goody-two shoes Noah found grace in the eyes of the Lord."

"You would kill everyone?" Maggie asked. "Just to get out of Eden? This place is a freaking paradise."

"Even Paradise gets old, Maggie," Aesir said. "This is my fifth attempt, by the way."

Gideon shuddered.

"Do you want to save your husband?"

"Yes, I'll do anything."

"Walk over the hillock behind me. There you will find the Tree of Life. Pluck a fruit and eat your fill. Then and only then, will I save your precious husband."

"Don't do it, Maggie," Gideon cried.

The powerful Angel grabbed Gideon and lifted him high.

"Maggie, do as I say, or I will rip poor Gideon apart before your eyes."

"Gideon!" She launched an attack that would have killed an ordinary man.

Aesir laughed at her assault. Knocking her down, he grabbed her by the throat and lifted her up off her feet.

Gideon cried out in pain.

"I am your only option, Maggie. Now be a good girl and do as I say."

"No—don't."

The angel slammed Gideon down on the ground.

"Leave him alone, Clarence," she screamed.

"Really? Clarence? The longer you stall, the more poor Gideon suffers."

"Okay, Aesir, I am going."

Aesir released his grip on Maggie. Landing on her feet, she turned and slowly walked up the steep grassy slope.

"What are you going to do, Aesir?" Gideon asked.

"When your beloved touches the Tree, I will do my job and kill her, but the very action of a human touching the Tree will invoke an automatic response from Heaven. Man will be erased forever and I will be free of my servitude."

Gideon rose to his hands and knees when, deep inside his mind, the voice of Larry spoke. *'It's show time, Gideon Kane. So be a good fellow, and don't blow it.'*

Suddenly, Gideon was no longer in Eden, but found himself back in Cades Cove, Tennessee. Larry held Gideon by the throat.

What is going on? Gideon thought. *Didn't I just do this?*

He could see Maggie frozen in mid-step behind the Angel, Kali raised high in her hand. Larry looked at Gideon and smiled. "Baby girl is cute as a button when she's about to dish out mayhem, isn't she?"

"Huh?" Gideon asked. "What's going on?"

"We interrupt this donnybrook," Larry said, "to bring you, Gideon Kane, a special announcement."

"I don't understand."

"Don't talk, just listen," said Larry's soothing, hypnotic voice. "That you're remembering this, means that you're in Eden and Aesir is being an ass. Do not think about it. Do not hesitate, but strike now. Your life, my baby girl, and the entire world depends upon it. Now take this and have fun."

Larry stabbed a finger deep into Gideon's chest.

While the repressed memory exploded in his mind, time seemed to slow for Gideon. To him, everything moved as if in slow motion.

As Aesir watched Maggie, Gideon looked down at his chest and ripped open his shirt. The tremendous, blistering pain vanished. Instead of a terrifying demonic creature, a golden rod pushed its way through his chest incision. Reaching up, he grasped the warm, golden shaft and pulled it free, the bloodless wound miraculously sealing itself.

Gideon held in his hand the bladeless haft of an artfully designed sword. Overjoyed, he clutched the legendary angelic weapon tightly. As though it had read his mind, the ethereal blade appeared, making Gideon wince at its dazzling brilliance. The heavenly sword looked as if it had been forged from a living bolt of lightning.

Gideon drew back and plunged the weapon into Aesir's armored belly with all his might. The otherworldly weapon sliced through the spiritual armor, as though it were made of paper.

Eyes wide with both pain and disbelief, Aesir screamed in horror. Maggie, at the crest of the hill, slowly turned.

In shock, having never tasted pain before, Aesir fumbled and tried to pull his own mighty weapon, but Gideon twisted his sword, causing Aesir to cry out. Aesir's own weapon fell to the thick, carpet-like grass. He shook his head from side to side, his beautiful blue eyes now wide with fear.

"Mercy," Aesir muttered.

"Go to Hell."

Gideon pulled the weapon upward, slicing through the mad angel's chest and exiting through his head. Strange, silver blood, looking very much like quicksilver, bathed Gideon's face and chest as Aesir fell dead at his feet.

Gideon's skin drank in the silver blood much like water into a sponge. He felt euphoric as the raw power surged through his body.

Looking down at the fallen angel, he smiled in relief. Aesir turned to dust, leaving behind his shattered armor.

Time abruptly returned to normal speed.

Maggie took a quick look at the Tree then flew down the slope and leapt into Gideon's arms. He laughed as she covered his face with kisses.

"Oh, now you two have done it."

Gideon and Maggie looked up and beheld another angel standing before them.

The angel was flawlessly handsome with the same topaz

eyes as Aesir, but his hair was black as pitch. However, he looked less angel-like than Larry and his beach bum attire did.

The newcomer was powerfully built and dressed in a dark-blue, double-breasted pinstriped suit. In spite of the warm weather, a cashmere overcoat and matching scarf were draped over his broad shoulders like a cape. Perched on his head, cocked at a slight angle, was a broad-brimmed white fedora, which made the stranger looked like a gangster from the thirties. All that was missing was a Thompson submachine gun and a pack of Lucky Strikes.

"We don't want any trouble," Gideon said, brandishing his weapon. "Just show us the way home."

"It was self-defense," Maggie cried. "Aesir brought us here and tried to kill us."

"Calm yourself," said the stranger in a smooth, rich baritone. "Aesir had it coming. Now be a good kid and give me back my weapon before you cut your arm off."

"*Your* weapon?" Maggie asked. "Prove it."

"We haven't been introduced, doll. My name is, Michael. I think you have heard of me."

"Oh, man," Maggie whispered. "The Big Cheese himself?"

"Yeah. The Big Cheese himself," Michael said with a smile. "Anyone tell you that you have a unique way with words, doll?"

"Yes," Gideon said, giving her a homicidal look. "We've been trying to work on that."

"Anyway, against my better judgment, I loaned my gat to this pain-in-the-rump fallen angel acquaintance of yours. He said it might come in handy. I guess he was right. No sense of style, but a very smart fellow. Now, Gideon Kane, are you going to give me back my weapon, or are we going to have a problem?"

"You want your weapon back?" Gideon asked, still feeling the powerful effect of the spiritual blood. "Call off the hit you ordered on my wife."

"Don't you dare try and bargain with me, little man," Michael said. "For your information, Mr. Kane, Heaven is no longer interested in Maggie Black's demise. As far as I am concerned, I hope that she has a long, happy life. Now give me back my property before I lose my temper."

"Thank you, sir, for your weapon." Gideon gingerly handed it over to the Archangel. "It saved us."

"You saved yourself, Gideon Kane. A hammer and saw do not build a house. The man who wields them does."

"Thanks for the hammer."

"Thank you for taking care of a problem before things got out of hand." Michael smiled at the powerful weapon before depositing the mystic blade in his coat pocket. "Now that feels much better." He glanced at Aesir's fallen weapon lying in the grass. The device rose and hovered before Gideon. "For your trouble, Gideon Kane, Aesir's weapon is now yours. I think it might come in handy one day."

"Thank you," Gideon gasped as he snatched the incredible device from the air.

"Why are you being so nice?" Maggie asked. "I thought you Heaven guys wanted me dead?"

"Nothing personal, my dear. In fact, I find you to be a delight. It was the thought of your future offspring that caused me concern. You had the potential of mothering a tremendous threat to mankind's existence."

"So why the sudden about face?"

Michael signed. "Doll, I don't have the time or the inclination for a question and answer session." The mighty Archangel took a deep breath and snapped his fingers.

Larry appeared before them.

"Explain it to Miss Black," Michael ordered. "After all, she is your responsibility. Hold nothing back. When you are done, take them home. Do you understand?"

"Yes, sir," Larry said.

Michael took a moment and laid a hand on Larry's shoulder. "Well done, my friend," he whispered. With a tip of his fedora, he vanished.

"I suppose I have some explaining to do," Larry said with a sheepish smile.

"Yah think?" Maggie snapped. "For starters, why are you alive? I thought I killed you."

"You were supposed to think that, baby girl. It was a cracker-jack acting job, if I do say so myself."

"You're nothing, but a lying, lowdown snake! You threw me under the bus, so you could get back into Heaven. On second thought, I don't want to hear a word you have to say. Take us home now."

"Maggie, honey," Gideon said and slipped an arm about her shoulders. "Let the man talk."

"But—"

"You need answers."

"Okay," she said. "Let me hear your version of events."

"Baby girl, Michael came to me for help."

"Stop calling me baby girl!"

"Okay," Larry said. "I deserve that. You see Michael, 'The Big Cheese' himself, needed help to get out of a sticky situation. I still can't believe you called him that to his face. Even I don't have the nerve to do that." He shook his head. "Anyway, Aesir was created to be the ultimate Angelic War machine, more than able to take down anything in creation. The problem was he was a teensy bit psychotic. It was too much power for him to handle. So when Man fell, he was the perfect choice to guard the Tree."

Gideon nodded. "That's why he was chosen to guard a Tree that no one could get to in the first place."

"Precisely. To keep him from hurting anyone, Aesir was assigned to live in utter paradise. Unfortunately, over time, his version of paradise involved endless bloodshed. From Eden, he projected his mind and influenced the leader of the Black Circle, Simone Ravenwood, setting her on the path. Had nothing been done, Simone and her thugs would have breached the dimensional barrier and the Earth would now be a burned out cinder. Michael was about to take personal action against Aesir, but since technically Aesir was innocent, having never left his post, Michael would have been branded a rebel and condemned. I thought of a better way, so I redirected the path of the Black Circle by using you, Maggie, Mrs. Kerr, and *The Book of Xanadutha*."

"Do you know the hell I have been through? Why didn't you tell me?"

"I couldn't take the chance. As insane as Mrs. Kerr was, she would have seen through any deception. I needed you to utterly hate me to sell the story."

"And Gideon?"

"I arranged for you to read his wild adventures and used Spooky to get you two crazy kids together. You're welcome."

"Well, what about the story of you selling me out?"

"I could never do that to you. Michael did offer me a pardon if my plan worked and, yes, the stipulation was that you were to die. I turned him down."

"You turned him down?"

"I couldn't kill you, Maggie, but I knew that if I didn't, someone would be sent who would. I had to do something that would alleviate their fears while keeping you safe. I don't expect you to forgive me for what I did, so I will not ask, but it was the only way."

"What did you do?" she asked.

"The kiss you and Mei shared," Gideon said. "You were very ill afterward, remember?"

"Yes. But that was only a way to track me so he could be there when we found the Tree."

Larry shook his head. "Not exactly. He did it for a free ticket home."

"You mean he did your dirty work?" she asked.

"Exactly. The potion he gave you closed your womb and tainted your DNA. As you are now unable to conceive children or be a threat to humanity, Heaven no longer has a beef with you."

Maggie slapped him hard across the face. Larry never moved. Gideon gathered Maggie into his arms and held her tight. "Why did you do this to me?" she sobbed.

"Because I love you."

"Love me?" she snapped. "You mutilated me."

"Maggie," Gideon whispered. "Larry did it because he didn't have a choice. It was the only way to save the life of his baby girl—his daughter."

"*What*? It can't be."

Larry gave him a narrow-eyed gaze. "Gideon Kane, you are too smart for your own good."

"You're my father? But what about what you said back in Cades Cove?"

"The little scene in Cades Cove was to cover my swapping the pesky Phoenix for Michael's sword. The truth is, baby girl, I am Tarrazonne. I loved your human mother, but she died giving birth to you. I tried to hide you, conceal your abilities and heritage, but I knew that, eventually, Heaven would discover who you were. I made you my Paladin to keep you close and to show Heaven your good heart and noble intentions, but to no avail."

Maggie slipped away from Gideon and embraced Larry. Together father and daughter wept tears of joy. "When I thought you had abandoned me, I felt so utterly alone."

"You were never alone," Larry said. Stepping back from his daughter, his form changed into that of a smiling Megan Franks.

"*You* were Shortstack?"

"From the beginning, I have always had your back, baby girl. Before I took her place, I sent the real Megan back to her family and, after tweaking a few memories, her ordeal with Mrs. Kerr never happened."

"I should have never doubted you, Pappy."

The perpetual smile vanished from his face. "Let me tell you one thing, baby girl," he said, pointing his finger in her face. "You can call me Larry, Father, or a sorry SOB, but don't you *ever* call me Pappy again."

"*Pappy* it is," she said sweetly.

Gideon laughed.

"Listen to me, Gideon Kane," Larry said. "I may have to take crap off my baby girl, but you, I don't."

"Is that anyway to talk to your favorite son-in-law?" Maggie asked.

Larry snorted. "Come on, kids. I think your honeymoon is a little overdue."

CHAPTER 52

Maggie rolled over and snuggled close to Gideon in the huge, colorful hammock. "This is paradise," she said. "Even better than Eden, as long as you are with me."

"Amen."

The strip of sandy beach was immaculate white and the Pacific waters crystal clear. A few yards away lay a cozy, secluded bungalow next to a gleaming new seaplane.

"What are you thinking, Mrs. Kane?"

"I'm thinking I never want this honeymoon to end."

Gideon frowned as a harsh ringing reached his ears. Looking down he found an old-fashioned rotary-dial telephone phone sitting on the table next to the swaying hammock. He picked up the Bakelite receiver and placed it to his ear. "Hello?"

"I—um—is this um, Dr. Kane?"

"Yes," he said. "Who is this?"

"Umm—my name is Kim Stoddard and I need help real bad. I know this sounds crazy, but I had a dream about you and was given this number."

"Hold on a minute, darling." Gideon coved the receiver with his hand. "Maggie, sweetie, it looks like the honeymoon is over."

About the Author

Ken Newman has loved stories of the supernatural since listening to his grandmother's tales of witches, haints, boogers, and catawamps when he was a child. Author of urban fantasy novels, *The Paladin*, *The Ark*, *The Voice in My Ear*, and *Forsaken*, his fiction reflects his Tennessee roots and his love for all things-that-go-bump-in-the-night.

Mixing folklore with modern themes, Newman's novels create a twisted universe of supernatural creatures and larger-than-life heroes where nothing is as it seems.

When not writing, he enjoys sculpting, cheesy monster movies, and building the occasional trebuchet to keep the neighbors in line. A member of the Authors Guild of Tennessee, Newman lives in East Tennessee with his long suffering wife Christian and their three zany daughters.

Please feel free to contact him. He would love to hear from you.